Sacred River

A Himalayan Journey

Debu Majumdar

Bo-Tree House

Published by
Bo-Tree House, LLC
1749 Del Mar Drive, Idaho Falls, ID 83404 USA
www.Botreehouse.com.

First U.S. print edition 2016

Publisher's Cataloging-in-Publication Data

Names: Majumdar, D. (Debu)
Title: Sacred river : a Himalayan journey / Debu Majumdar.
Description: Idaho Falls, ID : Bo-Tree House, 2016.
Identifiers: LCCN 2016913572 | ISBN 978-0-9968516-3-3 (pbk.) | ISBN 978-0-9968516-4-0 (hardcover) | ISBN 978-0-9968516-2-6 (Kindle ebook)
Subjects: LCSH: Conduct of life--Fiction. | Mythology, Indic--Fiction. | Ganges River (India and Bangladesh)--Fiction. | Gangotri Glacier (India)--Fiction. | India--Fiction. | BISAC: FICTION / Literary. | FICTION / Thrillers / Suspense. | GSAFD: Allegories. | Suspense fiction.
Classification: LCC PS3613.A354 S23 2016 (print) | LCC PS3613.A354 (ebook) | DDC 813/.6--dc23.

This book is a work of fiction. The characters, names, and places are the product of the author's imagination; any resemblance to actual persons, living or dead, should be taken as purely coincidental.

Cover design, diagrams and maps by Sandy Rafferty Vivian, Creative Director, Evolution Design, Inc., Idaho Falls, ID 83402.

Sacred River: A Himalayan Journey

An intelligent and intricately woven tapestry of finely nuanced colours and characters, straddling diverse worlds between the West and India, providing rich historical, cultural and spiritual insights. The spiritual life of India is contrasted with Western interpretations and Native American beliefs, as well as the story of the immigrant to North America searching for something beyond needing to prove oneself. Set within a mystery tale of a hunt for temple treasures in India, Sacred River reveals a convoluted route of self-discovery where solutions are not always what they seem, and lives connect and intersect within a grander scale beyond the self. I enjoyed the rich detail and insight into India, and came to a deeper understanding of the worlds every immigrant traverses and battles with in order to establish a sense of identity and self-worth. Those seeking to learn more about India while questioning their own spiritual paths in life will enjoy the journey of this book.

- Jade Gibson, PhD, author of GLOWFLY DANCE (2015), Cape town, South Africa

Mystery, love and beautiful scenery wrapped into a terrific journey. This book has elements of both a murder/mystery and historical fiction. What is unexpected is the spiritual journey that the author took with his characters, which might also be a pilgrimage of sorts for the reader. There are some great life lessons shared in the book, intertwined with a love story, deception and intrigue and a wonderful travelogue on the trip to the head of the Ganges River. All of these different angles are woven together in a very enjoyable way. It is worth every minute!

- Jim Porell, IBM Distinguished Engineer, retired, Pine Plains, NY.

An absorbing story … One feels he or she is actually there. Majumdar wonderfully, and almost unexpectedly, reminds us of the contributions of the Indian past, often skirted by, even ignored, by our busy, modern life. A commendable work.

- Prof. Parimal K. Brahma, ex-deputy Comptroller and Auditor General of India (New Delhi), author of *On the corridors of power: The theatre of the absurd.*

Sacred River gives a fascinating insight into Hindu faith and practices, and also into Indian daily life. Marvelous local color. A very enjoyable read.

- Jean Datta, Retired English translator, United Nations Office at Vienna, Vienna, Austria

Dedication

To the memory of my mother, Amala Bala Majumdar. Amala is another name of Ganga, the sacred river, meaning always pure.

Through countless births in the cycle of existence
I have run, not finding
although seeking the builder of this house;
and again and again I faced the suffering of new birth.
Oh house builder! Now you are seen.

You shall not build a house again for me.
All your beams are broken,
the ridgepole is shattered.
The mind has become freed from conditioning:
the end of craving has been reached.

> \- The Buddha's first utterance after his Enlightenment
> Dhammapada 11.153 - 154
> The Discourse Summaries by S.N. Goenka

Contents

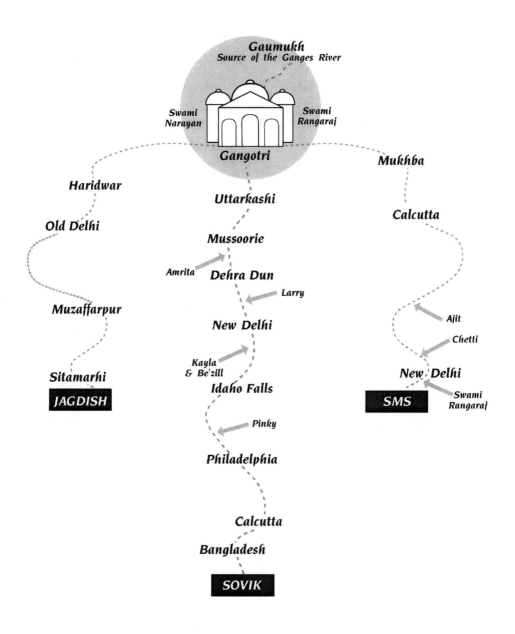

The progression of three narrative streams in this novel

Major Characters

Jagdish Lohar [Jawg-Dish]   Illiterate laborer/farmer

Gopal [Go-paal]   Childhood friend of Jagdish

Sukhi [Sue-khi]   Jagdish's wife

Sevanathan Chetti [Chet-Tee]   Fund-raiser for the SMS
                              organization

Swami Rangaraj [Wrong-go-Raaj]   Senior monk and priest at
                              the Gangotri temple

Ajit Boka [Aw-Jeet]   Assistant to Chetti

Sovik Bose [Sho-Vik]   Indian-American scientist

Pinky   Sovik's wife

Kayla   Travel companion of Sovik
                              and Pinky

Be'ziil [Beh-tsill]   Young Navajo man traveling
                              with Sovik and Pinky

Larry   An American traveler in
                              India.

Swami Narayan [Naa-Rye-awn]   Monk and head priest of the
                              Gangotri temple

Swami Anand [Aa-nand]   Monk and priest at the
                              Gangotri temple.

Mr. Sharma [Shar-Maa]   Driver of tour van

Brij Kumar [Bridge-Koomaar]   Assistant driver of tour van

Sabina   Tour guide for Sovik's group

Amrita [Awm-Rita]   Sabina's older sister.

Swami [So-Aah-Mi]   Title of all monks in India

Maharaj [MA-ha-RAJ]   Respectful form of address
                              for monks

Prologue

Ranipauwa, Nepal
August, 1909

Acharya Yogi meditated alone in front of the gold murti of Lord Vishnu in spite of the biting cold that crept in through the window shutters. When he opened his eyes, the snow-covered peaks of Dhaulagiri Mountain blushed with the rosy glow of dawn. He lit an incense stick and picked up the brass bell to start the worship service.

Abruptly and unexpectedly the door opened, bringing a gust of freezing wind. At 11,000 feet, few devotees came to this small temple at the foot of Thorong La Pass, a seven to eight-day trek from Pokhara through the Kali-Gandaki valley. Who would come at this hour?

The priest turned and saw a man wearing a yak cloak and a Sherpa hat. "Oh, you again."

"I want the book," the man said gruffly.

Acharya Yogi saw a curved, kukri knife in the man's hand. "You know the rule," he said calmly and turned back to face the deity. He rang the bell with devotion as his lips moved rapidly reciting mantras. The fragrance of incense drifted through the room and the sound of the bell reverberated throughout the temple.

The man stood behind the priest, impatiently listening to the chant—his feet solidly planted on the floor as if guarding the worship service. As soon as the ringing stopped and the priest put down the bell, he commanded, "Now let's go."

The priest walked up the long stone stairs of the pagoda-like temple, entering a room on the top floor. The man followed close behind. Manuscripts of various sizes, wrapped in cloth, were piled up on shelves lining the walls. The priest went to a corner and picked up a small book. He examined its pages. One page revealed a string of numbers:

01 35 18 02 25 27 03 15 04 59.

He looked at the numbers for a few seconds. "This will only bring trouble," he murmured. "No one has broken the code," he told the man. "You cannot achieve what you seek."

"We'll see." The man stepped forward and plunged the knife into the priest's back.

"Hare Raam," the priest moaned and collapsed to the floor.

"Here is another for your concealment." The man stabbed him again. Then he heard footsteps on the stairs. Seeing no other exit, he rushed down the stone steps, pushing through a cluster of oncoming priests. In the faint light of dawn, he missed a step and toppled to the edge. He tried to hold on to a stone slab, but couldn't and fell down to the floor below—his head smashing against the weathered granite. The thud broke the silence of the temple.

The priests gasped as they saw his Sherpa hat turn crimson.

They ran up the stairs and found Acharya Yogi's lifeless body hunched on the floor, a manuscript clutched in his hand.

The oldest priest picked up the manuscript. "This cursed book again! I thought so when Acharya rang the danger signal."

"We can't have any more deaths," another priest said. "We will get rid of the book."

Part I

The Beginning

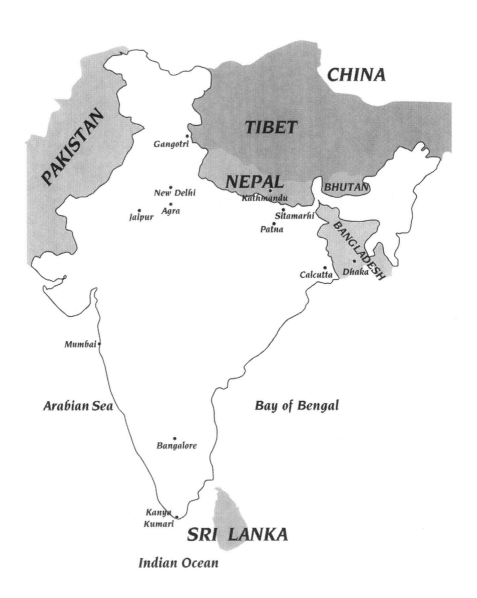

The Indian Subcontinent

1

In the Village of Sitamarhi

1.1

The moment Jagdish Lohar was born, the ground shook violently and two posts supporting the back of his family's hut collapsed. It was a little after 2 p.m. in Sitamarhi, a place five hundred miles east of New Delhi. His mother leaned over the baby and held him under her breasts. At that instant conch shells started to sound from distant places reminding his mother of Lord Krishna's birth in a jail during a tremendous hailstorm with lightning strikes falling all around mother and child. She gathered her courage and crawled out of the tumbled-down hut with some help from an aging midwife. Their only cow bellowed desperately at the top of her lungs. It wanted to run away but was tied to a post.

There was no one nearby to call for help. The village men were working in the fields or had gone to town. Mother and baby shivered in the cold. She held her newborn warm against her body, and the local midwife dragged heaps of straw across from the cow shed to shelter them.

That was 15 January 1934, the day of the deadliest earthquake in Indian history. Its epicenter was only seven miles south of Sitamarhi.

Jagdish's father, the local carpenter, dropped his hammer at the first tremor and dashed through the small town, only one thing on his mind—his pregnant wife back home. He could see the devastation as he ran. A fissure had opened right through the center of town, about eight feet wide and two hundred and fifty feet long. Many buildings had tilted and sunk. A third of the mud houses were destroyed. He hurried past the tumbled down cottages and fallen trees, ignoring desperate cries for help. When at last he arrived home, he rejoiced; not only was his wife alive but they also had a newborn son. It was a miracle they survived.

He named his son Jagdish, the Lord of the world, because as a defenseless baby, only the great Lord could survive such a calamity.

Holding his newborn son in his arms, his father went to the cow and patted her head with one hand, comforting the panicked animal. "See, we have a new baby." He lifted the baby and showed him to the cow. What dark hair the baby had! Then he looked at the small roof over the cowshed; it was fine, but turning, he saw that one side of their hut had collapsed. Jagdish's father gazed at the hut silently; it would be impossible to fix without a lot of money and he didn't have any cash. The sun was down, the sky cloudless. He felt a chill on his back. The night would be cold. He quickly handed the baby back to his wife, picked up his tools, and started to cobble together a shed next to the intact side of the hut. The baby needed a warm place to survive.

Jagdish had heard the story of his birth many times during his childhood. Today, standing in front of the Janaki temple with his ten-year old grandson, Vir, he wondered, had he lived a life worthy of his birth when 134 people died in Sitamarhi at the same instant he was born?

In ancient times, this was the land of Janak, the king who was also a rishi (revered monk) and a farmer. King Janak found baby Sita while tilling the soil of this very plain—Sita who later became Lord Rama's queen. That was how the place got its name, Sitamarhi—Sita's cottage—an auspicious land.

When Jagdish came into this world, Sitamarhi was a quiet little place. No passenger trains passed through town and bullock carts were the main form of transportation. Located on the Gangetic Plain, the land was fertile, and the elevation of the area nowhere exceeded 200 feet above sea level. The Bagmati River, a tributary of the Ganges River, ran through Sitamarhi; it was the creator and the destroyer of the place. It made Sitamarhi beautiful and serene—a flat green farm-country as far as the eye could see. Large trees grew all around, especially fruit trees—mango, jackfruit, and guava—and almost every house had a grove of banana plants. Only dirt roads, wide enough for bullock carts, and straw-roofed mud huts broke the green landscape. Nepal was seven miles north and beyond that were the Himalayas. One could not see the Himalayan peaks from Sitamarhi, but people knew the lofty mountains were there, where gods and goddesses lived.

When Jagdish was a little boy, a train station was built and later a bus station. The two stations and a bazaar constituted the main business center of Sitamarhi—all within a few minutes' walk of the river. The Bagmati River was a mile away to the east of his house and Jagdish had roamed along its banks all through his childhood.

In the Village of Sitamarhi

The oldest known site in Sitamarhi, the Janaki temple, was one and a half miles southwest of the town center. "About five hundred years back," Jagdish's father was fond of telling him, "an ascetic, Birbal Das, who lived far away in Ayodhya, saw a dream of Rama and Sita residing in this place. It was all jungle then. He came here, cleared the jungle, and discovered the images of Rama, Sita, and Rama's brother, Lakhsmana. Imagine this! God has his ways. Then Birbal Das built the temple."

"He could see God in his dream?"

"Yes, Beta. Such was his devotion. Birbal Das also knew the spot where Sita was born. That's Janaki pond now."

Jagdish had come to the Janaki temple with his father many times.

Jagdish, now an older man, walked the path of the temple with his grandson. "I wish I could tell you all the stories my father knew," he told Vir. His voice cracked a little at the memory of his father. He pulled his grandson off the path to make way for a gardener carrying a shovel, hoe, and a rake.

"Raam, Raam," the gardener said, lowering his head with respect for an elder, and went toward the old banyan tree.

"Raam, Raam," Jagdish returned his greetings but stared at the commercially made equipment he was carrying.

He remembered how his father worked to repair farming tools—yokes, hoes, and rakes—and did small carpentry jobs for rich landowners. His father also made tables and chairs, but he could only sell a few of those to the town folks. A job that his father loved most, and for which people admired him, was constructing small wooden altars where older women kept statues of gods and goddesses.

They often paid his father in grain instead of cash. He never earned much money, but he never complained. Jagdish knew that by saving a little at a time and by being very careful with his money, his father had acquired a small piece of land where he built their tiny hut, setting aside as much land as he could to grow vegetables.

"We have been in Sitamarhi for generations," his father told Jagdish. "I don't know where we came from before that. Our ancestors did what was needed in this community whether it was carpentry, farming or being laborers. My life is like theirs, and your life will be no different."

Jagdish's family belonged to the laboring class. That was the lot God had given them and only God could take them out of this state. Education had never been a concern of his class of people.

He held Vir's hand firmly at the entrance of the Janaki Temple and walked up the steps, ringing the temple bell that hung above their heads just inside the doorway. Several people stood in the worship room with folded hands, praying to the images of Lord Rama and Sita. Earthen oil lamps glowed near the altar and smoke rose from incense burners. Jagdish and Vir also prayed.

"Never think of going to work in the zari factory," Jagdish told Vir when they came out. "It'll be no good in the end."

"Subhas is going to Bombay," Vir told Jagdish excitedly when he released his hand. "He's only two years older than me. The company bought his train ticket and will give him money every month."

"Do you know what zari work is?"

Vir shook his head.

"Zari is a fine silver thread, sometimes gold. It is woven into silk material and brocades. The factories employ children because their small fingers can perform the delicate work. You see zari during weddings, on rich women's saris. They are very expensive. People like us don't have such things."

Unconvinced and undaunted, the young boy took a step toward his grandfather and pulled his hand. "Dadaji, tell me about the big cities. Have you been to Calcutta or Bombay?"

"I've never gone anywhere far away." Jagdish paused, looked at his grandson for a few moments and continued. "I'm afraid of the cities. People are different in big cities; they are modern. They wear Engraaji clothes and follow Engraaji customs."

"I want to go to big cities, see American movies, and have fun."

"You know what will happen if you go to Bombay? They will keep you in a tiny room with many boys and make you do zari work day and night. Then you will cry to come home."

"Dadaji, you come to this temple every week. Why don't you go on a pilgrimage to see the famous temples?"

"It's difficult for me. I don't know how to read and write."

"I can take you to places. You hold my hand and you'll be fine."

Jagdish contemplated his grandson's face. The world had changed. At Vir's age, he was working full time in the fields. Before that he had gone to the only one-room school in the village. He had learned a little of the alphabet and numbers, but that was all. Outside of the school there was nothing to read or any time for such things. He soon forgot the alphabet; he was never able to sign his name.

How foolish he had been to go to school! Jagdish winced at the memory. It was because he had wanted to go with his playmate Gopal. They had walked the mile and half together in the early morning to school. What fun it was! Gopal would often dart off the path and pick guavas or lichis from someone's trees; Jagdish could not do that. And Gopal never got caught. He was a little shorter and heavier than him, a round face, and never still. Even at that age Jagdish knew Gopal was smarter than him and knew much more about everything— the new railroad, people around town like Mr. Jha, the rich man, and many things beyond their village. He had fond memories of the walks, but he felt sad that he couldn't continue in school. He tried but he didn't belong there. He remembered the four posts that held up the entire one-room school with a straw roof and no walls. The teacher sat on a raised, solid lump of mud, which was also his table and where he kept two things—a worn out book and a light yellow cane. The boys sat on the smooth mud floor, and no girls went to school.

When he returned home the first day, he was excited and asked his father to buy a slate and chalk for him.

His father stared at him for a few seconds before responding. "What?"

"The teacher told me to bring one."

His father looked beyond him for some time. "Beta, what will you do with education in our family?" he asked him affectionately. "Neither my father nor I went to school. This is not for us."

"I want to go with Gopal."

"I'll think about it. Now go and play."

His father found a broken slate a week later. Jagdish was elated to have a slate and started to draw the letters he had seen in school. What he drew made no impression on his father or mother.

"The teacher said to ask you for help," Jagdish told him a few days later.

"How can I help, Beta? I don't know how to read and write."

"How can I learn, then?"

"You learn in the school."

Jagdish got an old book from the teacher, but he could not practice reading or writing at home. Every night when all his chores were done, the kerosene oil in the hurricane lamp ran out. The cup of kerosene they could afford barely lasted long enough to complete their necessary activities before going to bed.

Jagdish remembered the tiffin break at school when he quickly ate his lunch and then played with the other boys. There was no playground; they mostly ran around the four posts of the school and in the surrounding fields. Once he had glanced at Gopal's lunch and saw that he had a full meal—roti, dahl, vegetables, and pickles. Jagdish's lunch was the same as his morning meal—two pieces of roti with a tiny pickle and a little raw sugar that his mother had packed in a cloth. He knew that was the way their society stood: those who were better off also ate better. He hadn't seen the stark difference before; he simply went out to play with the other boys as soon as he finished his roti.

After a few days the teacher asked Jagdish what the fifth letter of the alphabet was. He didn't expect the question and couldn't recollect. He simply stared vacantly at the teacher.

"You don't come to school just to sit here," the teacher told him. "You must study." He called him to come forward and asked him to stretch out his hand. Then the cane came down sharply on his palm. A harsh red line burned through his skin and he cried out.

"Now go," the teacher told him. "You must memorize what I teach you."

From that day on Jagdish got caned every day. "How will you learn if you don't do your homework?" the teacher would ask. Then the cane would swish down on his hand. But there was nothing Jagdish could do. He told this to his father who finally asked him to forget school. "Stay with me, Beta. See what I do and learn the family business. One day you will do the same thing."

That was the extent of his school experience. He tagged along with his father from morning till night. Then he started earning a little money by doing chores on neighbor's farms and that helped his family. He never thought of going back to school.

Jagdish looked at the white dome of the temple and thought that fate had not allowed him to be independent like his father. "If you live a good, moral life," his father had often told him, "God will give you a better lot in your next birth." This belief in God had carried him and his father through life. Only, he lamented, his father's great wish for a pilgrimage hadn't come true. His father had told him stories about so many places! Yet his father could never afford to leave Sitamarhi. Would the same thing happen to him as well?

"I did go to Patna once," Jagdish turned and told his grandson. "But I didn't like it. Too many people there—everyone always rushing for something. It's not like our place." He glanced at Janaki pond. "Pilgrimage is a dream in our family."

"You will like the pilgrimage places, Dadaji. I'll take you there." Vir's face glowed in anticipation of a journey.

"You think of your education, otherwise you will remain indebted to someone for life, as I've been to Mr. Jha."

"No one likes him, Dadaji. Why do you work for him?"

Jagdish stared into the boy's face without saying anything.

1.2

Jagdish spent an uneventful youth. No epidemic or natural disaster had come to the area since the 1934 earthquake. Life was mundane, but he did not endure severe hardships. What his father earned met the necessities of the family; the one cow they had gave milk and the small vegetable garden produced potatoes, beans, eggplants, and okra, enough for their small family. Jagdish was fond of the cow; he fed her, milked her, and took care of her. His mother used the cow dung to make fuel patties for the chulha stove. Thus they carried on.

Then his father died unexpectedly when Jagdish was sixteen. Jagdish had depended on him, worked with him, and did what his father asked him to do. Now suddenly he became the man of the house, and he was not ready. He had learned a little bit of carpentry, but he was not good enough at the craft to step into his father's sandals. He could only find work as a farm laborer. He received wheat, rice, oilseeds, and a little cash as payment—just enough for him and his mother to live.

Soon he got used to being a landless farm laborer. He quickly learned farming and dreamed of owning a farm of his own.

One day, while Jagdish was working in the fields, a stranger came to their house. At first, the man simply stood in front of the house and stared at the extension to the side half-ruined by the earthquake; Jagdish's father had an affectionate memory of his son's birth and never demolished the old hut, even as he built up and repaired the other side.

The man introduced himself to Jagdish's mother, "My name is Jivan Ram, a marriage broker from Dumra, five miles east of Sitamarhi. I've arranged many marriages in this area. I wonder if it's time for your son's marriage."

She looked at him for a few seconds. Her eyes widened and she pulled her sari over her head, but she couldn't say anything.

"I know a girl from a good family," Jivan continued, "same caste, and they could offer a good dowry."

"I am alone," his mother said. "It'll be nice to have a bahu at home."

"Yes, this girl is quite adept. They are farmers."

"Jagdish is only eighteen. Please give me some time to think it over. I shall talk with my son."

"Certainly. I will be back after a month."

Jagdish didn't know what to say; he had not thought of marriage. Their house felt empty after his father's death and his mother did all the work alone—from the time she got up till she went to bed. Jagdish realized it would be nice to have another person to share work in the house and for company. Feeding another would not be a problem; they ate such simple food—no fish or meat.

His mother said, "Let's go to the temple and see what Hanumanji tells us." Jagdish agreed. "We'll go Tuesday."

Hanumanji, the monkey god, was a great devotee of Lord Rama. He helped Rama rescue his wife Sita from the evil demon, Ravana.

When Tuesday came, Jagdish's mother collected fragrant flowers from the neighborhood early in the morning and, when Jagdish left for work, she cooked a few laddus, round sweets made of chickpea flour, milk, coconut, and sugar. The widow usually offered a few batashas—small, round, light brown sweets made with sugar—at the temple, but this was a special event. She also fasted for the temple visit, as she had done on auspicious occasions. She remained a little nervous throughout the day, not knowing what the right answer was. She wished her husband had not died. In the late afternoon, she put on a clean sari and waited for her son to come home. In the evening, they walked to the temple. It took them half an hour; Jagdish talked about what he was learning at the farm, avoiding any talk about his marriage.

There was no one in the village temple; his mother put flowers on the statue of Hanumanji and offered the laddus in a small dish. She then prayed for a long time with folded palms and closed eyes. Jagdish stood a few feet behind her.

After some time, his mother looked up at Hanumanji's face. As she gazed at the stout figure, a flower petal fell down from Hanumanji's hand to the laddus. She was startled. It was a clear sign for her, a positive indication from Hanumanji. She stepped back to Jagdish, saying, "Did you see that? Hanumanji has given us his blessing. I'm so happy."

The thought that his mother was convinced of the rightness of his marriage lifted Jagdish's heart.

"God always looks after us," his mother said on their way home.

"Yes, mother."

When Jivan Ram showed up again, Jagdish's mother gave permission to proceed with the marriage.

"When do you wish to see the girl?" he asked.

"There is no need to see her," his mother quickly replied.

Jivan Ram was surprised and pleased at the same time. Most boys' families gave him such a hard time about the prospective brides—actually about everything from the details of the family, the dowry, the date of the marriage, to the little money he expected for a fee. Jagdish's mother did not ask for anything. She had received God's blessings; what more did she need?

"I shall negotiate the best dowry for your boy," Jivan Ram told her.

The girl's family agreed to pay 750 rupees cash, Jivan Ram reported to Jagdish's mother a few weeks later. They would have to sell a piece of their land, but that was fine with them. Jivan Ram said they were happy to do this for their girl.

A few days before the marriage, Jagdish's uncle, his father's brother, came from Muzaffarpur with several bags of homemade sweets. Jagdish touched his feet for his blessings, the custom when one met an elderly person, especially a relative.

"You are the only nephew I have," he said and hugged him.

The uncle, his wife, and their two children started to prepare for the wedding and the feast they would serve to friends and neighbors when the new bride came to the house. The neighbors also came together to help. They did it out of love for Jagdish's father, a man they all missed and remembered on this happy occasion.

On the wedding day, a palki—a palanquin—arrived at their house, surprising Jagdish.

His uncle laughed, saying, "You can't walk to your marriage!"

The palki was green outside with two small windows. It was painted with white and yellow flowers. The unpainted bamboo handles were discolored by the many hands and shoulders that had carried it. Strings of orange marigolds wrapped around the palki. In the afternoon, Jagdish was led to the palki and, once ensconced, he quickly pulled the cloth shades on the two windows. The ladies in the house sounded conch shells and the bearers lifted him up. His uncle, Gopal, and a few neighbors went to the bride's house in bullock carts behind the palki. Jagdish was in a daze; feelings of shyness, the memory of his father, the responsibility of a wife, and a pleasant feeling of having a girl for himself, all passed through his mind at the same time.

When they reached the bride's house, he was received with sounds of conch shells and ceremoniously led to the wedding room. The priest made an altar on the floor over a large, white alpana painting made with rice flour. He had placed mango leaves in a small brass pot marked with a vermillion Swastika symbol. A freshly cut banana plant leaned on the corner of the altar. Flowers decorated the place, and the fragrance of incense pervaded the area. Family members and their guests sat on the floor. The priest wore an ordinary white dhoti and no shirt, and a white, sacred thread hung from his left shoulder. He recited Sanskrit mantras and put flowers, dipped in sandal wood paste, on the altar. Jagdish did not understand what the priest did or said, but he followed the priest's instructions, occasionally putting a flower on the altar and folding his hands in prayer.

Finally, late in the night, the bride arrived, her face covered with a red veil. Jagdish's heart started to beat hard. He saw from the corner of his eye that she was a slight girl.

Family members and wedding guests crowded the area; everyone wanted to witness this important part of the marriage ceremony. The priest created a little fire and uttered more mantras. Jagdish could see that the bride wore a bright red sari and had several silver bangles on her wrists.

Then it was time for the first 'glance'—when the bride and the groom see each other for the first time. The priest took the bride and the bridegroom to one side of the altar and made them stand facing each other. He put a thin cloth over their heads. The bride's family members removed her veil and Jagdish raised his eyes. The bride continued looking down at the floor.

"Please raise your head so Jagdish can see you," Jagdish's uncle urged her.

She looked up and immediately put her head down in coyness. Jagdish got a glance of her small forehead and oval face, but something struck him. He was not sure what it was.

"Please lift your face again," his uncle requested the bride. "Don't you want to see whom you are marrying?"

She opened her eyes and Jagdish noticed it. Her eyes were askew. Lazy-eyed? No one in his family or in the neighborhood was cross-eyed!

Then he heard his uncle's voice. "We didn't know the bride was cockeyed. Stop the wedding! Where is Jivan Ram?" He became quite agitated.

A commotion started in the place. Jagdish's uncle and the few neighbors that came with them shouted loudly that this information had been withheld. Several from the bridegroom's side firmly held the arm of Jivan Ram and were ready to beat him. Jagdish heard Jivan Ram's feeble voice, "I wanted to tell his mother, but she didn't want to know anything or see the girl. She was happy that Hanumanji had given them blessings for the marriage."

"You have taken advantage of a simple woman," Jagdish's uncle said angrily.

"I got you a good dowry," Jivan Ram said.

The bride's family said they were not to be blamed; they didn't do anything wrong. In fact, they had sold a part of their land to give Jagdish a good dowry. What else could they do? In the midst of the uproar with the two parties shouting at each other, Jagdish suddenly spoke up.

"Please stop."

No one expected him to say anything. Bridegrooms never did. Both parties were astonished and quieted down.

"God has created us all, whatever we are," Jagdish said. "Please do not quarrel. It must be God's will that I marry her."

There was pin drop silence. The priest glanced at the stunned wedding guests, then silently took the right hand of the bride and put it atop the bridegroom's right hand. He wound a garland of small white flowers around their hands, chanting mantras. He sprinkled water on their joined hands; then he took the groom's hand, placed it on the chest of the bride, and asked the groom to repeat after him:

> Mama vrate te hridayam dadhaami,
> Mama chittam anuchittam tehastu.
> Mama vaacham ekamanah-jushasva
> Prajapanishtvaa niyunaktu mayam.
>
> – Hindu Samskaras

> Into my will I take your heart;
> Your mind shall dwell in my mind;
> My words will be in accord with yours;
> May Brahma join you to me.

The priest tied an end of the bride's sari to the bridegroom's clothes and asked them to walk seven steps together while he uttered prayers to Lord Vishnu, the preserver of the world. He sprinkled peace water on everyone present and declared the wedding complete.

Bride and bridegroom were ushered into another room and sat next to each other on a mat on the floor. The fragrance of flowers, which decorated the bridal bed, permeated the room. The women from the bride's family took over. They gathered around the couple and, one by one, gave the couple their blessings. They also brought many gifts of saris and silver jewelry into the room. Then they brought sweets and asked them to feed each other.

Jagdish looked at the bride's full face. She was a young girl, maybe fourteen. She would have probably been married off earlier if her eyes were normal. Their eyes met for a second and Jagdish saw how her eyes glistened with tears. What a beautiful face she had! A small nose, healthy cheeks, and thin, long eyebrows! He suddenly felt that her cross-eyes made her more beautiful. Love welled up in his heart.

The guests left them in the wee hours of the night, and the bride's mother, the last one to leave, told them, "Sleep a little; you have a long journey tomorrow." She shut the door, as she left.

The bride stood up. Jagdish also rose, not knowing what he was supposed to do. The bride bent down and touched his feet as younger people touch the feet of elders for blessings.

In his entire life, no one had touched his feet for his blessings. He was astonished and lifted her up.

"I shall make you happy," she murmured with her head down.

"What's your name?"

"Sukhi."

"What a beautiful name. I'm happy you are my wife," Jagdish could say no more. He was choked with love and held her hands tightly.

2

Sarva Mangal Society (SMS)

Sevanathan Chetti, the chief financial officer and fund-raiser of the Sarva Mangal Society (Society for the Wellbeing of All People), sat in his office in New Delhi, watching a young woman organize the filing cabinets in the next room. He had asked her to file a huge pile of letters for later action. A large, orange-yellow sign with the insignia of the SMS graced the front wall of his office. He stared at the sign.

He agreed with the goals of the SMS. More than four decades had passed since India's independence, but the lot of the people had not improved. In fact, it had worsened. Corruption was everywhere and the government was bogged down in bureaucracy. The SMS wanted to improve the lot of Indians through education, removal of social barriers, and by fighting against injustice—especially injustices done to the poor and the helpless.

He admired the vision of Suraj Thappa, the President of the SMS organization, who was once a renowned real estate and jute plantation magnate and owner of Thappa Jute Unlimited. Mr. Thappa was an ardent disciple of Mahatma Gandhi in his youth and had traveled all over India for almost a year, as Gandhi had done after returning to India from South Africa. He built up a thriving business empire and then resigned from everything in 1984 to found the SMS. He gathered together the beginnings of the organization that would serve as the foundation for a new society based on India's ancient ideals. Mr. Thappa had recruited him, or rather, he had inspired him to resign from Advanced Defense Systems and join the SMS. His job: to help the organization move beyond its initial successes—and on to sustainability. In three years he became an important man in the organization, not only for the vast connections he brought with him and the substantial funds he raised, but also for his ability to establish structure within the organization. While Mr. Thappa traveled around the country and continued to galvanize people into action, he stayed in New Delhi and worked diligently to put the organization and its finances in order.

But in spite of his many years of experience, he found it very difficult to keep up with the pace of the SMS; the demand for money to keep the organization expanding was huge and he could not raise funds fast enough. In the past he had always succeeded in all his endeavors. Could this be his first failure?

He reached into a desk drawer and took out an antique manuscript. A broad-brush, hand-painted, sacred swastika sign, symbol of Lord Vishnu, was on its cover. He untied the ribbons that held the pages together and opened to a particular page with a series of numbers. The pages, made from tree bark, were discolored with age. Chetti fixed his eyes on the numbers.

01 35 18 02 25 27 03 15 04 59

Mr. Thappa had received the manuscript as a gift from a priest in an obscure temple in the Himalayas. The priest was impressed with Mr. Thappa's desire to reestablish India on the principles of ancient Hindu ideals, and thought that Mr. Thappa might use the manuscript to raise money for the cause. He had warned Mr. Thappa that some believed the manuscript contained a secret code for hidden temple treasures. Over the ages, many had died in unusual and brutal ways trying to protect or steal the manuscript—guardian monks and wily thieves locked in a seemingly never ending battle. The priest earnestly cautioned him that this was a myth and not to spread the story or fall into the same trap. Mr. Thappa had passed it on to Chetti, saying offhandedly, "See what you can do with this."

Chetti had traced the history of the manuscript. Near the end of the nineteenth century it was in a small temple, 11,000 feet in the Himalayas, at the foot of Thorong La Pass in Nepal. No one knew how or when it came to be there, but because of several deaths related to the manuscript, the temple priests got rid of it.

Chetti observed a faint arrow below the numbers that pointed toward two vertical dots. On the opposite page there was a diagram that looked like a hiking path with several branches and many triangular and circular marks. The arrow, the two dots, and the symbols made no sense to Chetti. He had tried to decipher the numbers over the last two years, but all his attempts had failed. What could the numbers mean? He knew the priests had always hidden their secrets cleverly—they had even concealed sacred mantras from the public and passed them down orally to select disciples.

Chetti looked back at the young woman. Volunteers like her were the backbone of the SMS organization. But volunteers were not enough. His anxiety rose as he thought of the precariousness of his mission. If the great SMS revolution failed because of his inability to raise sufficient money, he would be ruined as well. He got up and moved to the window. "I have to do something different," he murmured.

The door opened. Mr. Thappa, returning from a meeting, plunked himself down on the rattan settee and glanced at the fan. The highest speed of the fan was not blowing enough cool air for him. Chetti noticed a few drops of sweat on the president's forehead.

"Anything new from the meeting?" Chetti sat down across from the President.

"The western section wants to host the Executive Committee meeting in March 1993."

"That's a year away. Anything else?"

"They asked for more money."

Chetti's face darkened as he looked at Mr. Thappa's fluttering white hair. He was well aware of the section's funding needs. After all, he was their chief financial officer and fund-raiser. It was easy to promote SMS ideals with words: India would be better served with ancient Hindu ideals, not secular Western ones that the old Congress Party had propagated. But implementing those ideas cost money.

Mr. Thappa ignored Chetti's grave expression and continued, "Boys and girls in remote villages can't go to school for lack of a few rupees. They said even a donation of fifty rupees could help."

"I know that." Chetti cut him off. "But, meantime, how do we sustain the organization?" He crossed his legs and shifted his glance toward the filing cabinets in the next room.

Mr. Thappa stared at the small scar on Chetti's cheekbone. Today the tiny patch looked redder than usual. "We've got to find a way," he said, redirecting his gaze to Chetti's well groomed, wavy black hair. "We've energized the country. We cannot let the people down. Just let me know how I can help you."

"As we've discussed before," Chetti turned to Mr. Thappa, "we have to make some drastic moves. Even asking for foreign help is not out of the question."

"Oh, that could bring unpredictable issues at this stage. Let's not discuss that."

"Then, we must find new resources within India."

"New resources?"

"Yes!" Chetti said with some irritation.

A silence fell over the two men. Sunlight shimmered outside the window, the heat of the sun burned the air. The finances of the SMS troubled Chetti very much. When he joined the organization four years before, the SMS had had an annual budget of 20 million Rupees. He had increased the revenue each year, but much more was needed. How to achieve this?

Chetti often thought of India's glorious past. What had happened to the prosperity of the golden age of India? When he was young, Chetti had visited the Raghunath temple in the city of Jammu. Three sides of its inner walls were covered with sheets of gold. That made an impression on him. In a little village, south-west of Bangalore, where he grew up, the Hoysala king had not only built a magnificent Kesava temple, but he had also sanctioned an annual gift of 3,000 gold coins for the temple's upkeep and maintenance. Where had all India's wealth gone?

Chetti turned back to Mr. Thappa and repeated his thought aloud. "Tell me, where has all the wealth of India gone?"

Mr. Thappa stared at his colleague, not knowing where Chetti was going with this question.

"Huen Tsang described India in the seventh century as peaceful and rich," Chetti elucidated. "Even the reports of Marco Polo in the thirteenth century depict a wonderful India. What has happened to the wealth from those days?"

"Good question." Mr. Thappa shrugged.

"You know, the invaders plundered the temples first. Mahmud Ghazni sacked Somenath temple in Gujarat seven times."

"So you think the Muslim invaders looted it all?"

"I don't know if the Muslim invaders or the British cleaned India's treasures out—probably both took what they could find." Chetti watched the stream of sunlight from the window for a few seconds. "I can't figure out where all of India's gold has gone. Priests are sly! They must have moved some of their treasures before the kingdoms fell and kept them somewhere safe and secret."

Chetti stood up and paced. His tall stature and ardent spirit crowded the small room. "Even now, I suspect, priests have a stockpile of gold in the temples."

Mr. Thappa scratched his head. "I know Maharaja Ranjit Singh donated one ton of gold for the Viswanath temple spire in Benaras."

Chetti nodded. "No outsider has an account of the temple gold. Not even the government. And they cannot collect any revenue."

"A tricky subject."

"And whose gold is this?" Chetti snapped. "Does the gold belong to the priests? Or the people?"

"I suppose the gift was offered to the deities, but really for the welfare of the community." Mr. Thappa ran a finger around his collar.

"Then it should belong to the people. Shouldn't it?"

Mr. Thappa listened quietly. Chetti sometimes talked about far-fetched ideas.

Chetti stopped pacing. He leaned against the back of his chair, his face calm. "The temples are simply holding this wealth for the people. You see, this could be a resource for our cause."

"The priests won't relinquish their treasure to anyone. You know that." Mr. Thappa raised his palm in emphasis.

"Damn the priests! Another corrupt, secretive group." Chetti sat down. He raked his hair with his fingers and stared at the wall. "It's time to put this gold to good use," he asserted. "You remember our great philosopher Chanakya?"

"The Indian Machiavelli who lived long before the Italian was born."

Chetti smiled. "Yes. We have to apply his dictum. We must draw on our monks to help us tap this resource."

"What do you mean?"

"Just leave it to me." Chetti suddenly grew quiet and shifted his attention to a running gecko on the wall. It caught a bug. Geckos stay still for a long time, he thought, before they spring into action. There was much to learn from the creature. His face relaxed further. He glanced at Mr. Thappa—a man still handsome, fair-complexioned with bright eyes and a large forehead. "Please keep this conversation between the two of us only." His eyes then fell on the old manuscript on his table. He quickly put it inside the drawer.

Mr. Thappa couldn't determine what Chetti intended. He knew Chetti was devoted to SMS ideals and he was a practical man. Chetti had done a superb job, but there was much about him he didn't understand.

Mr. Thappa dabbed his forehead with his handkerchief and observed that Chetti was calmly opening a file. His instinct told him not to probe further—let Chetti's idea, whatever it was, mature. Chetti had brought several new ideas to the organization. When he spoke now about using the gold secretly held in Indian temples, he must have another idea. He called the volunteer woman to bring two glasses of cool lemon-water for them.

3

Flood and Bondage

3.1

With the dowry money Jagdish bought a piece of land and worked hard to make a go at farming. It was not as easy as he anticipated. Many times the weather didn't cooperate; the intense tropical heat and the monsoon rains came at the wrong time or stayed longer than he needed. But somehow he pulled on, as his father had.

No child was born to Jagdish and Sukhi for six years. Then when he thought they would never have a child, a son was born. When he became nine months' old, an annaprashan ceremony was held for the boy, a ceremony where a child gets his first solid food, rice pudding. Jagdish invited Gopal to be the man to feed his son.

"Why me?" asked Gopal, "Shouldn't you ask Sukhi's brother?"

"I know you more than any one else. If anything happens to me, I know you will take care of him."

"Sure. He is like my son."

"What name should we give him?" Jagdish asked Gopal.

"Praan will be a good name."

"Praan?"

"Yes. He is your life, now."

Ten years passed by. Then one night in July 1969 Sukhi tugged Jagdish's shoulder several times and woke him up. Just then a bright light flashed through the window and a loud rumble and crash of thunder came. "I am scared," she said, clinging to him.

"A bad storm!" he said and sat up. "How is Praan?"

"Still asleep."

Jagdish opened the door but a gust of wind and heavy rain made him cautious about venturing out. The cow bellowed. He would look after her later; he went back to bed. His wife had brought their 10-year old son to their bed of straw and grass spread on the floor. The storm raged around their tiny hut. None of them could sleep.

Jagdish thought about the corn he had planted for the first time that year. He got the seed as a loan with a promise to pay back double the amount by September after harvest. If he took longer to repay the loan, the penalty would be severe. He was 35 years old; if he didn't take a risk now, he thought, when would he become self-sufficient? He took the opportunity when the corn seed man explained how easy it would be to grow corn in the fertile soil of Sitamarhi. These new seeds had been developed from American corn. They were wonderful, not like the hard kernels, suitable for fodder, farmers grew in the past. This variety of corn had created a great revolution in the state of Punjab and was in demand. He could easily sell the product in the grain market in Muzaffarpur and make good money.

"The plants are of good height now," he told Sukhi. "I hope the soil doesn't remain soggy for many days." He prayed that the rain would not last long.

But the rain continued for the next seven days. He and his wife had never seen so much rain. They remained confined in the house; Jagdish went out only to feed the cow and milk her, and at night he put an old jute bag over the cow's back to keep her warm.

On the eighth day the rain ceased, sun peeked through the clouds, and Gopal came over. "Have you heard the news?" he asked, agitated. "The Bagmati River is running high and has started to overflow its banks."

"How bad is it?"

"No problem for us on the west side. Water is already high on the east bank and Dumra is flooded."

"Chamunda village?"

"That too. People think it may flood this area also."

"Hai Raam!" Jagdish slapped his forehead with his right hand. "I planted corn this year." He sat down on the mud floor and put his chin on his raised knees.

"It will be ruined, I am afraid," Gopal murmured. "Officials are predicting bad news. It has been raining in the north for some time; they say the Lakhandei River is bringing too much water into the Bagmati River; more is pouring in by the hour. It cannot hold so much."

"What are we going to do?" Jagdish asked, knowing they could do nothing.

"Several villages in the north have been washed out. Water is rising every day and the current is very strong. The government has already called the military to rescue people."

The chop-chop-chop of a helicopter pierced the muggy air. The two men looked up.

"They are saving people in the north," Gopal said.

"I must go and visit my land."

"You can't do anything. You'll only endanger your life."

"No, no. I must see. I am ruined. We'll have no grain to eat next year. How can I pay for the seed?"

"Fodder has been ruined everywhere. Many animals have died. Save your cow." Gopal advised him somberly.

Jagdish looked at the cow shed. His crops were probably gone. If the cow also died, he'd be in unimaginable trouble.

They sat there silently for some time. After a while, Gopal added, "A stranger died in Sitamarhi Hotel yesterday."

Jagdish turned to listen.

"No one noticed that the man was missing until the hotel manager realized he had not seen the visitor for two days. The man was an accountant from Muzaffarpur. The Manager found his door locked. The windows of the tiny room were closed up tight. They had to break the door down. The man lay in bed on his stomach, a book in his hand—dead. The smell of kerosene smoke filled the room. An empty hurricane lamp lay on the floor. Everything else was intact."

"He died because of the fumes from the kerosene lamp?" Jagdish asked.

"Yes. The doctor said some gas from the lamp had killed the man. He called it carbon mono-something. You don't realize its effect until it's too late."

"But we use kerosene lamps everyday!"

"No problem when there is plenty of air," Gopal explained. "But in a small, closed room too much gets into your body and poisons your blood. A large amount can overcome you in minutes without warning and make you unconscious. You can suffocate to death."

"Don't tell me any more bad news," Jagdish pleaded.

Gopal went away. Jagdish remained on the floor, transfixed by the scene outside. When his wife brought a few rotis, jackfruit pickles, and gur—all she could gather up from their meager store—he didn't feel like eating.

Jagdish went out to evaluate the damage. He didn't have to go far. Within half a mile, the walls of several mud houses had slumped. Cows and buffalos stood up to their haunches in water, and in the fields, green stalks rose above a slate of water; a serene view, but Jagdish knew the crop was ruined. He approached the river and the town center. He gazed for a few seconds at a house collapsed on the ground. It was Mishra's house! His hands went up to his forehead and a cry came out from his mouth, "Hai Raam." He rushed toward a calf lying against the knotted roots of a mango tree. He put his hand on its ribs; it was still and cold. Several other straw roofs lay nearby on the ground. He could go no farther and went home.

As soon as he returned, he took out what lumber he had and started to build a platform where they could save the small store of provisions and clothes they had. He looked at the cow and decided that he might have to do something for her also.

The next day water slipped into their area like a thief. First it was only a little, then an inch or so. In three more days there were two feet of water in the fields. People piled their belongings on roofs to keep them from floating away. Water gushed in from the river. No one could stop it. He visited his cornfield— light green leaves touching the still water. It would rot and would not even make fodder for their cow.

"Hai Raam, what am I going to do?" Jagdish slapped his chest several times.

The flood waters receded a few weeks later, and the government rescue workers left the citizens of Sitamarhi to their own devices. The rich landowners could access government help, but there was no program for farmers like Jagdish.

Jagdish stood in front of his wilting cornfield. The soil was very soggy. There was no hope for the corn. All farm work had come to a dead stop. And there was no employment in the area. If he had learned carpentry work well, he could have some possibility of earning a little income.

What would he do now? He knew that the man who gave him the seeds would soon ask for his payment. There was no mercy here; the man would take his land if he could not give him the money. He had tried his luck, but God had a different plan for him. How was he going to feed his wife and son?

Jagdish stood in front of his failed cornfield, his hands clasped behind his head. He had heard talk about how the state government would help the farmers, but he couldn't read the newspapers or the pamphlets that the flood workers had given them. He didn't know anyone who could help him.

He saw a few people coming toward him. He squinted his eyes and saw it was Mr. Jha, the rich man in Sitamarhi. Why was he coming to him?

"Namaste, Jagdish," Mr. Jha said while still walking toward him.

"Namaste." Jagdish raised his palms together in front of his face in a gesture of respect. "I'd have come to your house, sir, if you called me."

"No. No. I am disheartened with the devastation. What a flood! Many lives have been ruined. I am going around seeing what I can do to help. Sitamarhi is our motherland and you are my people."

"I am ruined, Babu," Jagdish cried out. "I don't know what I can do."

"How will you pay the man who gave you seeds?" Mr. Jha asked.

Jagdish was startled. Mr. Jha knew of his problem. "Babu, I've no money to give him."

"Hmm. You know, he will take your land."

"I've no alternative."

"I can give you the money as a loan. Then you can keep your land."

Jagdish almost didn't believe his ears. Was this a Godsend? He wanted to prostrate and touch Mr. Jha's feet. Feeble words came out of his mouth, "How can I pay you back?"

"You work in my field and I'll deduct the loan money every month. If you want your son to work, we can arrange for that also."

"He is too young, Babu."

"If you agree now, he can start work two years later."

"No, Babu. My Praan is too little."

Mr. Jha looked at one of his people and said, "Give him the labor contract to sign."

"I can't sign."

"That's no problem. Just put your thumb print on the paper."

Mr. Jha's man took Jagdish's hand, smeared his thumb with black ink, and put an imprint on a paper.

"Baas. Saub thick hai," Mr. Jha said. "I will pay off the seed man. You start work in my house tomorrow." He quickly turned and walked away.

"You have saved my life," Jagdish murmured and thanked him, "Bahut Shukriyaa." He wanted to cry out loudly but no tears came. He walked slowly toward his house with a heavy heart. He knew Mr. Jha didn't do anything without some gain for himself. He had never put his foot in this area where the poor villagers lived. But what could Jagdish do? This was his fate and he accepted the fact: he was now a bonded laborer to Mr. Jha.

3.2

Jagdish sat on the ground at the edge of his small farm and ate the lunch of roti and eggplant sabji his wife had packed for him. He viewed the field contentedly. After he started working for Mr. Jha, 30 years before, he had barely been able to grow anything for lack of time. Six days a week he went to Mr. Jha's farm early in the morning and labored there, returning home late in the evening. He grew what little he could on his plot. Now his son did most of the work and Jagdish tended the field on Sundays. The field looked green and healthy. The barley was doing well. The potato plants at the other end of the field had small white flowers. Hopefully, he thought, this year he could pay off a good part of the money he owed to two people.

Then his thoughts veered to his life and what fate had brought him. He was fifty-eight years old now. His father had died at a much earlier age, but his life was nothing compared to that of his father. His father, whom he remembered as a wonderful man, had only missed one thing in life. He had wanted to go to the sacred places where the gods and goddesses appeared in ancient times— places like Haridwar in the foothills of the Himalayas, the place of Lord Shiva, and Gangotri, where Goddess Ganga had descended from heaven. If his loans were paid off, Jagdish thought, perhaps he could go on a pilgrimage. He would take Sukhi too. He must, of course, ask for Mr. Jha's permission; he hoped that after working for so many years without a day of leave, he would grant him the time off.

The sun glowed over his head. He drank water from his shiny brass pot and put it down on the ground, then turned as he heard Gopal's voice calling him.

"Have you heard the news?" Gopal asked, white hair fluttering around the edges of his bald pate. He had grown fatter, his muscles loose, and he walked slowly—he was an active boy no longer. "Your Mr. Jha is going to jail."

"Mr. Jha?"

"Yes." Gopal's face lit up. "I told you Mr. Jha is no good. He has exploited you. But you wouldn't listen."

"What are you saying? Mr. Jha has never done anything bad to me." Jagdish scratched his head. Each year Mr. Jha had told him his loan was decreasing, though it never ended.

"You're stupid. That's why you never questioned it. What can I say? This is your fate."

Jagdish looked up at Gopal. "What happened?"

"The High Court found that Mr. Jha cheated the government out of a large amount of money. He was awarded a school construction project in Muzaffarpur, but he embezzled the money and constructed a tiny building."

"He cheated the government?"

"Then the inspectors investigated his finances. They discovered he cheated on taxes on his farm for many years. They also found he had exploited many villagers, bonding them to work for him." Gopal looked at his childhood friend, trying to see if he understood it. "Many like you were deceived into continuing to work for him even when their bond was paid off."

"Truly?"

"The judge has sent him to jail for five years. Look, here is his picture on the front page of the newspaper."

"Such a bad news," Jagdish said, shaking his head. "I hope the Lord will help him."

"He is a crook!"

"Don't say bad things about him."

"You think I don't like him. Look, here is your name in the paper. He supposedly paid you 200 Rupees a month and then took most of it for loan repayment; he forced you to work for pittance for the last 24 years. The court has decreed you will get 10,000 Rupees from him."

"Ten thousand Rupees!"

"They said you deserve much more. Really, if he gave you only 200 Rs a month, he owes you over 50,000 Rs."

"Hare Raam. How is this possible?"

When Jagdish returned home, he found the news to be true. Several from his village would get money from Mr. Jha's estate. And they didn't need to go to Jha's farm to work anymore. Jagdish was a free man.

Sukhi cried with the news. Tears poured from her eyes; she felt a joy she never thought they could ever have. "Our youth is gone to struggles and struggles and sufferings and nothing else!" she slapped her forehead several times. "Let's go to the Janaki temple and offer a puja," she finally said.

Their grandson, Vir, was most elated. "Dadaji, now you can take me to Bombay," he said.

Jagdish was happy but didn't know what to tell his grandson. He simply gave him a warm hug. After a moment he said, "No. I want you to go to school."

"Then what about your pilgrimage?" Vir could not be stopped.

"We'll see what the Lord has in store for me."

Jagdish didn't count on receiving the money. He continued to work every day on his little farm. "If Lord Rama wants us to have the money," he told Sukhi, "it will come."

"It will be nice to repair the house," his wife said.

"We will have to pay back all our loans," Jagdish murmured and looked away to the cow shed. That also needed repair.

Eighteen months later the mailman brought a letter from the government. It contained a check for Rs. 10,000. Jagdish held the check and stared at it for a long time. The image of his father came to him. What would he have done? Jagdish pulled his winter shawl around him, sat down on the raised mud veranda, and stared into the distance. His father had never seen such a large amount of money. Jagdish thought he should use some of the money to fulfill his father's dream of going to the holy places: Haridwar, Banaras, and Gangotri. His father had talked about these places. Should he fulfill at least part of his father's dream, go to one holy place for him?

If he ever intended to go on a pilgrimage, he must go now. Didn't Sukhi deserve a trip out of the village? She had suffered so much all these years. But she had never complained, nor ever uttered a single word of reproach. He had not been able to do anything for her! Since the day she came to this house, she had only worked to keep him happy. The poor woman didn't have any of the comforts that would have made her life a little easier. Jagdish got up and went inside.

"We will go on a pilgrimage," he told his wife abruptly. "I got the money from the government."

Sukhi stared at him with apprehension.

"Our son can take care of the house and the farm," he told her. "It is now or never."

She looked away from him and put some wood on the chulha fire. After a few moments she said, "I cannot go."

"We'll go together."

But Sukhi didn't want to step out of their village. "Your good deeds will also work for me," she told him. "You go for both of us."

Jagdish's son and daughter-in-law insisted that he go on his dream trip. His daughter-in-law said, "Baba, we will take good care of mother."

After hesitating for some time, Jagdish finally decided to go to Haridwar. Haridwar—literally, the gateway to God—is located at the base of the Himalayas where the Ganges River enters the plains. The river is a goddess. Her water fell from heaven on to the Himalayas from the foot of Vishnu, the protector and preserver of the world. So it is a sacred river. A touch of the water will cleanse one's bad deeds and guarantee a place in heaven.

The trip was months away when Gopal showed up at his house. "I came over as soon as I heard the news," he told Jagdish with real warmth in his voice.

"I'm a little fearful of the trip, but I've made up my mind," Jagdish told him. "There may never be another time."

Gopal nodded. "My gurudev had asked me to visit him in Gangotri, but I've always been busy. I was initiated when he came to Muzaffarpur a long time back. I haven't seen him since. Very unfortunate because he is a great man."

"Why don't you come along?"

"I'm so busy, I can't. But I've come here with an idea. Could you take a little gift from me to my guru, Swami Narayan?"

"I am going to Haridwar, not Gangotri."

"I know that. I am asking you to visit him in Gangotri. The Gangotri temple is very special; the only temple where all the priests are monks."

"Gangotri is high in the Himalayas." Jagdish said, looking north toward Nepal.

"It will be nice weather there in June," Gopal said. "I've already inquired. There is a bus that goes from Haridwar to Gangotri. I will pay for your expenses.

"My father told me about the temple of Goddess Ganga." He sighed. "He said our land is fertile because of her."

"So please go to Gangotri and meet Swami Narayan. He is a devotee of Ma Ganga. Then you personally give him my gift— a gold necklace for the goddess."

"A gold necklace!"

"Yes. I promised it a long time back."

"You want me to take such a valuable thing?"

"There is no other man whom I trust as much as you. And I'll give you a letter for Swami Narayan. A true spiritual teacher. You'll like him. I'll bring the package later."

4

Bait and Switch

4.1

Chetti paced the drawing room in his house waiting for Swami Rangaraj, the senior monk of the Gangotri temple and the spiritual guide of the SMS organization.

The monk had joined Mr. Thappa before the SMS was founded. At the inauguration of the SMS in 1985, Swami Rangaraj had compared the goals of the SMS to those of King Rama who established an ideal kingdom in ancient times. "We could achieve that again," Swami Rangaraj had declared.

Chetti had read all of his speeches and knew that the monk would do anything for the success of the SMS. He wanted him to be an important ally for his new project.

He looked up at the clock on the wall; 9:30 already. He sat down and reread the headlines of the morning paper. Sitar music floated in from the radio in the kitchen, but the music sounded dissonant to Chetti.

The 1993 SMS Executive Committee meeting had been held only a month before in Gandhinagar. The memory of the meeting sent a shiver down his spine. Delegates from all over India had raised him to the stature of financial savior of the SMS. Mr. Thappa was the Founder and the President, but they considered Chetti the most valuable man. That also meant if the SMS failed, he would be blamed for it. He thought of Mr. Das. How sincerely the old man pleaded for more funds for the Eastern Zone.

Sweat started to form on his back. The April heat of New Delhi seemed too much at that moment.

He recollected Mr. Thappa telling the audience a story to highlight one of India's social problems: how the dowry system ruins poor families with daughters.

"Let me tell you a true story," Mr. Thappa had started quietly, "about a girl named Kamala who lived in a village 150 miles southeast of New Delhi. Her parents settled her marriage early, but were unable to pay the dowry installments for the final two years before the marriage date."

"Dowry is illegal," someone from the audience shouted.

"True but quite common in villages," another person said.

"In Kamala's case," Mr. Thappa continued, "her parents pleaded with the boy's family, promising to pay up after the marriage, but they refused the offer. They found another girl whose family paid them more money. Healthy and decent looking, Kamala was already fourteen years old—too old to find a suitable boy in her community, especially when the family didn't have money.

"What could Kamala's family do? They tried hard, but couldn't find anyone to marry her. The family began to blame her: it was because of her they were in such trouble, shamed before the whole village. Kamala couldn't say anything; humiliated, she kept her head down and did her chores silently and more diligently. The girl, who was once jolly, slowly became quiet and withdrawn. Her friends were married one by one and went away. Soon she was alone. Women in the village looked away from her, and young girls didn't talk with her at the well. No one offered the teenager any solace. Before the year was over, Kamala committed suicide by jumping into the well. She was wearing the sari her parents had bought for her marriage. Some in the village said, 'It is good that God has taken her.'"

Mr. Thappa stopped, but the entire audience gasped.

The delegate from Kamala's area stood up saying, "This is the kind of social injustice we must fight against."

Chetti knew of many such stories from letters the SMS received from all over the country.

"The suffering of low caste laborers is another issue," Mr. Thappa said at that meeting. "We must address this. Higher caste people hold land and exploit the landless laborers and poor artisans, all the while denigrating them for their inferior status."

"A perversion of the caste system," a woman called out from the floor.

"A recent incident happened 100 miles south of Benaras," Mr. Thappa told the audience. "A dalit musician and a Kurmi woman fell in love and were secretly married. When the marriage was discovered, the man was dragged out of his house, tortured, and publicly hanged and then burnt by agents of the girl's family—in the presence of some 500 villagers."

The delegates groaned quietly.

"No one had the courage to say anything," Mr. Thappa said. "The girl was stripped and branded for her transgression. She committed suicide in the local pond by tying a large, rock-filled brass pot to her neck." He paused and scanned the audience. "How can the SMS make progress without being able to help these down-trodden people and change the attitudes of those with wealth and power?"

Mr. Thappa's words rang in Chetti's ears.

When Mr. Thappa sat down after his speech, every eye in the room turned to Chetti, as if he had the solution.

He had nodded in acknowledgement of the concern. Chetti knew, along with everyone else in Gandhinagar, that the SMS must find a way to provide financial assistance to local offices so they could make progress. But their resources were limited. During the meeting Chetti's thoughts returned once more, forcefully, to the gold hidden in India's temples. He resolved that those assets should be used to uplift India. He whispered to Mr. Thappa, "I'm quietly working on a great idea. If it succeeds, our financial problems will be solved. All it takes is a strong will to carry it out."

Mr. Thappa gently slapped his back. "I've full confidence in you. Do what you have to do."

"Yes, It's time for bold action."

Chetti stood up and paced the drawing room again. The SMS troubles made the veins in his temples throb. He must not fail in this job as their chief fund raiser. The SMS challenge was one reason he had resigned from Advanced Defense Systems (ADS) and joined the SMS. He must live up to his promise.

He gazed at the picture of John F. Kennedy on the wall. He admired President Kennedy for his bold decision to go to the moon when so little was known about space travel. The picture always inspired him to strive for lofty goals. "Our SMS goal is like reaching for the moon," he mumbled to himself and sat down. "But India is different from the U.S.," he thought. "Here one cannot achieve anything easily."

Swami Rangaraj finally arrived. "I'm sorry," he apologized as he entered. "The traffic was bad."

"There's no rush in my own house." Chetti chuckled. "Please sit down. I've been thinking of an idea for some time; I wanted to discuss this with you privately." He studied the monk's lean, bearded face—eyes sharp and bright; there was a charismatic spark that conveyed an air of holiness, his ocher robes adding to the picture.

After they were comfortably seated, Chetti said, "There are many reputable scholars, philosophers, and monks in India. But many cannot give a public speech, some cannot speak English, and some will not come out of their lofty corners."

Swami Rangaraj nodded in agreement. The tips of his fingers touched on his lap, and he listened attentively. He was not sure where Chetti was going.

"Swami Vivekananda was a learned monk," Chetti continued, "but he did not shy away from public work. He even went to America in 1893 to tell the West about the Hindu religion. We need to send a similar man to America."

"That would be very good."

Chetti glanced at Swami Rangaraj's graying temples. "Among all the people I know, I think you fit the bill best."

"Me?" Swami Rangaraj's head jerked up. But within seconds his face relaxed and he understood the purpose of the meeting. He straightened himself up in his chair.

"Yes, Swamiji," Chetti said, "I've been thinking about this for some time. You clearly have all the qualities of our great monk Swami Vivekananda."

Swami Rangaraj remained silent for a few seconds. He had read all of Vivekananda's writings. If only he could follow in the famous teacher's footsteps! He would like to become a spiritual leader of India, but he had no idea how he could do that. So his desire remained dormant. Now he saw that with Chetti's help, he could go to America, be well known like Swami Vivekananda, and achieve his goal.

"I'm flattered, thank you. But I'm nowhere near him." His face, however, glowed.

"No, no. I mean it. But we'll have to promote you in this regard."

"What do you have in mind?" Swami Rangaraj's eyes focused on Chetti, his hands gripped the chair arms.

"We send you on speaking tours all over India. I've no doubt you will shine like Swami Vivekananda and create a spiritual revolution."

"I'd be pleased to talk to people."

"I'm sure, after a tour of the cities, you will be well known. We then sponsor you to America on behalf of the SMS. Vivekananda went there a hundred years ago. We will do much better this time. This venture will make us stand head and shoulders above other political parties." Chetti paused for a moment, observing Swami Rangaraj. "If you agree, I want to start working to make this happen."

"To go to America and spread the words of our religion would be a dream come true for me." Swami Rangaraj folded his palms and bent his head. "God willing, I'm ready. Please let me know how I can help you."

"It will take some time." Chetti said in a matter-of-fact voice, but he reassured him with a pleasant smile. "We should start your lecture tour this year. In the meantime, please work with me. We have much to plan." Chetti's small eyes shimmered in excitement.

"I will do what you ask of me." Swami Rangaraj knew Chetti had great abilities to make things happen. He felt proud; Chetti had chosen him. His face beamed.

"On a separate subject," Chetti suddenly asked him in a whispering, but serious tone, "could you explain to me what the priests do with all the gold they hold in the temples?"

"Gold?" Swami Rangaraj's face dimmed and an uncertainty came into his eyes. "I've never bothered to think about the gold in temples."

"Not even in the Gangotri temple where you are a senior priest?"

"I haven't seen any gold stored in the temple. Swami Narayan is the head priest. He'd know."

"You know, the Hindu kings gave plenty of gold and jewelry to the temples."

Swami Rangaraj nodded. "Yes, I believe so. The temples have received gifts over many centuries, and they must be somewhere. Our practice is that the head priest passes the secrets of a temple to the next head priest. It's an age-old tradition. That's how the sacred texts, the Vedas and Upanishads, were transmitted in ancient times. They were not written down. . . . Yes, I heard there is something hidden in the temple. It may be gold. I am a monk. I didn't care about those things and have never asked Swami Narayan."

"During the Muslim invasion," Chetti continued, "gold from temples in north India was moved away for safekeeping. It must have been taken to the temples in the mountains. I wonder if the Gangotri temple was one of the 'safe houses'."

"I could inquire about it." Swami Rangaraj was dubious.

"Would you please?" Chetti perked up. "But please do it discreetly. I'm only curious because India was so rich in the past. What happened to her wealth? Just a layman's curiosity. But if you determine there is plenty in Gangotri Temple, we could ask for some. You know how we're struggling."

Swami Rangaraj stared at him. His mind raced as to how he could carry out Chetti's request.

"Time is running short for us. Could you find this out as soon as possible?" Chetti continued, glancing at the monk's pensive face. "In the meantime let me schedule the lecture tour for you. Calcutta, Madras, and Bombay for the first round. What do you think?"

"That's good. We start with the big cities."

"We may also be able to raise some money if we advertise your lectures properly. That's my job, you know." He smiled teasingly and stood up, indicating the meeting was over.

As Swami Rangaraj crossed the threshold, Chetti said in a low voice, "Let me know as soon as you find out how much gold the temple has."

Swami Rangaraj nodded. "I'll look into it."

After the monk left, Chetti sat down, gazing at a large painting in the drawing room—a vivid and colorful picture of the Republic Day parade through India Gate. He had bought it at a charity auction for a local school in Jamshedpur, where his first job had been. His work was clearly defined at that place—Tata Iron and Steel Company—to expand the business in the railway sector, and he had the resources to carry out his ideas. The same was true with Advanced Defense Systems, his second job. Both companies had defined goals with money and authority to achieve their missions. The SMS business was so different, he thought, too many problems to overcome and a shortage of funds.

4.2

After persuading Swami Rangaraj to do his bidding, Chetti thought of Ajit Boka, one of his trusted men from Advanced Defense Systems. He liked Ajit, an expert in intelligence technologies, because he was a doer. Ajit was not religious and a loner; Chetti considered those useful assets for the job he had in mind. Ajit also had a quick mind and did not suffer fools gladly.

Chetti took out a small folder from the desk drawer in his office and looked up Ajit's telephone number. He knew that after he left ADS, the company had made several drastic changes. The new management directed the company toward production of big items for the military. The spirit of invention died, making people like Ajit rudderless and unhappy. He called Ajit. It was easy for Chetti to convince him to join SMS as a consultant. Ajit had earned an excellent salary at ADS, but at fifty-six, he could retire and live decently for the rest of his life. The idea of helping the country was enough to recruit him.

"The SMS is short of funds," Chetti told Ajit after he came on board in late April, "we're turning down good ideas that would help ordinary people because of lack of money. That's why I want you here."

"Can't make progress with a begging bowl," Ajit agreed.

"I have explored the usual methods to raise money. Those are bringing a decent amount, but nowhere near what the SMS needs. Other political parties are now following our techniques and cutting into the business. We must think of new ideas."

"What about manufacturing at the village level?"

"Good idea." Chetti remained silent for a few moments. "I was thinking of Shivaji. In 1659 he went to discuss a truce with Afzal Khan, a general of the Mughal Emperor Aurangajeb. Shivaji was forced to leave his swords before entering the tent to meet Afzal Khan. He handed over his sword smilingly, but he didn't trust the Muslims and hid tiger claws in his sleeves. When he met the general, he saw Afzal Khan had a small knife on his belt, and so, suspecting foul play, he attacked him immediately with his sharp tiger claws." Chetti paused and looked at Ajit. "You know the rest of the story. The tips of Shivaji's claws were dipped in poison. This was perhaps unfair, but Shivaji's cause was mighty. He wanted to establish a kingdom free of Muslim rule."

"I wasn't good in history, but I get the idea," Ajit said. "If you have to kill a few to save a thousand, wouldn't you do that?"

"What stops one from committing an unethical act if it's for a good cause?"

"Lack of courage!" Ajit proclaimed confidently.

"At ADS we took the challenge to enhance Indian military capabilities. I feel we have a similar challenge in front of us—this time to enhance the lives of civilians. Should we remain bound by ordinary rules? Or be bold?"

"Are you asking if the end justifies the means?" Ajit looked at Chetti. When Chetti remained silent, he finally said, "Why not?"

"We have to concentrate on the ultimate objective. Then we can free ourselves. I've been thinking hard about the SMS. If we keep going the way we are, we will end up being another party with lofty ideals, stagnated by mediocre means. Then the VHS and the BJP will dominate India with their old-fashioned, conservative beliefs."

"How drastic are your ideas?" Ajit asked, a look of reserve coming over him.

"I'm not thinking of robbing banks," Chetti said with a hearty laugh. "I was only wondering where there could be a substantial source of money to uplift the conditions of the people."

"I can think of only three ideas," Ajit said, "creating a new business enterprise, finding an ancient cache somewhere, or getting help from some foreign power."

"People have given generously to the temples for millennia," Chetti said. His eyes sparkled with anger. "But what have the priests done with that wealth? They ensnared people with rituals and hoarded the gold."

"You mean the gold in the temples?"

Chetti nodded.

"I see. Won't it be against the ideals of the SMS?"

"No one needs to know about this." Chetti walked over to the window of his office and stared out. He had thought about it for a long time. This was more than a Robin Hood act; this was stealing from God ... and stealing for God. He had not found any other alternative.

"And you know what?" Ajit smiled. "The priests can't talk about such a loss because they pretend they don't have the gold. What an idea! I wish I knew more about the situation in the temples."

"I've done some research." Chetti replied. "There are caches of gold hidden in the big temples."

"How could we penetrate this? We need to have our men infiltrate as priests in the temples, discover the secret locations, and find a way to take the cache out. It will take several years."

"We can't succeed that way. The priests must help us."

"Why would they give their gold away?

"Everybody has a weakness. Priests have their egos. We will use those to our advantage."

"I see you've been thinking about this for a while." Ajit was stunned by the audacity of the idea. His eyes grew bigger. "Which temple, and what do you want me to do?"

"The Gangotri temple will be our first case. I'm sure they are hoarding a large amount. Swami Rangaraj is our ally—unsuspecting at this time, so be careful. I'm reeling him in slowly. I want you to lead this effort. We need the Swami only to give us access to the gold."

"Understood."

"No one besides us needs to know anything about this venture. Go to Gangotri this summer and figure out the details—the layout of the temple, its chambers and passages, routines of the priests, especially of Swami Narayan, the head priest. Find out where the gold is. Then devise your plan."

"When we worked on the spy cameras," Ajit said in a low voice, "I kept a few of those with me. They will come in handy now."

"Don't tell me any more. I leave the operational details to you. I'll authorize 50,000 Rupees for this secret project."

4.3

Ajit mused over his conversation with Chetti as he drove his silver Maruti back home. He could not help but admire his boss's intellect and vision. What Chetti had asked him to do is unthinkable in India, especially if one was raised in a Hindu family. Stealing gold from a temple to give to the poor! Ajit thought himself small compared to Chetti, but felt an excitement and, at the same time, some hesitation. He had run many secret projects for the defense industry, but this one was a bolt from the blue.

He remembered an incident that had given him a similar jolt when he was only thirteen. His eyes were opened that day.

He was in front of the Mangaleswar Temple, not far from his parent's house in Agra, after following a kite through the narrow streets in the older section of Agra. The kite had been lost in a kite-fight and was falling freely. If he could catch the kite, it would be his! But before the kite could come down to street level, a man had reached out from a rooftop and grabbed the loose string. Disappointed, Ajit wandered around aimlessly and ended up near the temple. It was away from the Yamuna River that skirted the Taj Mahal. Only locals went there.

The sound of wooden sandals drew his attention. He saw a priest clumping along on his padukas, crossing the road, holding a large plate on his shoulder. The priest wore a white dhoti around his lower body but no shirt. A dirty beige sacred thread hung diagonally from his left shoulder. Then Ajit saw a man—dark complexion glistening from working outside in the sun—walking at a rapid pace. He carried a huge load of leather on his head; his shadow moved quickly on the road.

Suddenly Ajit heard the priest's angry voice, "Shala, Chamar, how dare you cross my path?" The priest had stopped in the middle of the road and glared at the man. The priest's face, which appeared peaceful a moment before, had an awful scowl. Ajit didn't expect such curse words from a priest.

The chamar took a few steps back and said humbly, "Panditji, I didn't come near you. See, I am walking by the edge of the road."

"Haramjada, you are a harijan by caste, an untouchable, you argue with what I said? Didn't you see your shadow touched my body and the food I am carrying for puja?"

"Forgive me, sir. I didn't see that."

"Didn't see that!" the priest imitated him. "Now I cannot offer this to God or ask any Brahmin to eat this." The skinny priest took a step toward the man with a raised hand as if to hit him.

Several people stopped to see what the matter was. One man, dressed in the dark slacks and white shirt of an office babu, asked the priest, "Panditji, what has he done to you?"

"What has he done? He has spoiled this food. Now I have to fast the whole day."

"The chamar has insulted the priest," one passer-by told another.

"The Dalits are becoming bolder every day," another man said.

The office babu moved to block the chamar's path.

"I didn't even come close to him," the low-caste man cried. "How could I disturb him?"

"Didn't you see me from where you were walking?" the priest shouted back.

"How could I with this load on me?" the low-caste man pleaded.

"It doesn't matter," the office babu said, "Panditji said you have spoiled his food. How dare you do that in this neighborhood?"

"Teach him a lesson," another man shouted.

Then someone grabbed the laborer and gave him a hard slap. The poor man stumbled. He barely steadied himself when a few other passersby joined to beat him up. His bundle fell on the street.

"Idiot!" the priest shouted. "God's forsaken people!"

By then the chamar was on the ground and moaning, as several men kicked him. Ajit saw blood trickling from the low caste man's nose. The chamar raised his two hands to protect his face and head as the blows continued.

One man went to the bundle and loosened the rope that tied the leather skins together. "Unfinished leather," he said and gave it a kick. The neat pile of leather fell apart. He picked up a piece and walked away. Then several others from the crowd grabbed a few more pieces. The low-caste man cried, "My goods, my goods. Beat me, but please don't take them. I will be ruined for life." No one listened to him. All boldly took their share. Only a few small pieces remained scattered on the road.

While cursing the man under his breath, the priest went inside the temple. The men who beat the poor fellow walked away. The scene was over in less than ten minutes. Ajit stood there gaping at the low-caste man who lay on the road groaning in front of the temple that was named after the "God" who bestowed bliss to people. The street soon reverted to its normal condition except for the low-caste man who now sat there in pain. "Hai Bhagavan, what have I done to displease you?"

An elderly man touched Ajit's shoulder, "What are you watching? Go home."

Ajit was about to ask him a question, but the stern face of the man intimidated him. He threw a last glance at the suffering man and turned away. He could not grasp why no one cared for the man.

Back home, Ajit quietly went to the room he shared with his older brother. He sat on the bed. His mother had already taken her shower and was putting flowers on the family altar where images of Radha and Krishna stood, smiling impassively. She would finish her worship in a few minutes, then serve lunch. Ajit felt sad in his heart. How could God create two sets of people so different that one man's shadow would spoil another man's food? Was this the same religion his family followed? Where was God for this man?

The screeching noise of a truck braking in front of him brought Ajit back to New Delhi. He turned off Tolstoy Road and on to Janpath, taking the short cut to his house. Before he reached home, his mind cleared and he agreed that doing something for the poor and the deprived is a good idea. He could certainly put in some effort, helping Chetti.

5

Sovik

5.1

When Sovik was born, the family called for the village astrologer, as they had done for all their infants. The astrologer, a heavy-set man with a protruding belly and large forehead, made horoscopes for Hindu babies in the village, and was highly revered. In his own life, the astrologer had predicted that his son would live no more than seventeen days. He didn't even go to see the baby. The boy died on the sixteenth day.

This astute man, now slightly bent with age, hurried to the rich man's house with old, rolled-up charts under his arm. His tiki—a lock of hair, two or three inches long, at the back of his shaved head—showed prominently as he walked in. At the sound of his sandals the house fell silent.

Sovik's father accompanied him, with tremulous heart, to the special room for the newborn. The astrologer took note of the exact time of the baby's birth, and found the locations of the planets and the stars in his charts. His eyes remained fixed on the papers, his face grimmer with the passing of each moment. He then examined the burgeoning lines on the baby's small palms and his face relaxed. He told the family that the boy would be healthy and that he would live a long life.

Sovik's father sighed with relief.

The astrologer's gaze then went to the baby's body; he held the baby's feet up. How pink the bottoms of his feet were! "This boy will be teji," he declared, "and he'll travel." His tiki bobbed in unison with his pronouncement.

"Teji?" his father asked.

"Yes, high spirited." The astrologer gazed at the boy for a few more seconds. "The constellations are in a conjunction I've not seen before. Quite unusual! He won't be an ordinary boy."

The predictions for his first son had been ordinary; so Sovik's father was pleased. This son would be exceptional and enhance the good name of the family.

Sovik's mother was delighted to hear the astrologer's verdict, as many babies died young. Still weak from the delivery, she sat straight up in the bed, face flushed and folded her hands in prayer.

Raipara, Sovik's birthplace, was a good-sized village—20 miles west of Dhaka, now the capital of Bangladesh. A tributary of the Ganges River flowed by Raipara and made the land prosperous. The place was not famous, but people lived there comfortably. Rice grew easily and the river and ponds swarmed with fish. No one went hungry.

Sovik's family owned lush, fertile lands that provided them with good income and a rich living. They had a large house, with a big orchard of fruit trees, and a fishpond of their own. This was the family's ancestral home for many generations. Like other wealthy families of Raipara, they hired laborers for farming, many of them Muslims, and managed them.

His great-grandfather had built a Shiva temple on their property. It had a white dome with a trident, Lord Shiva's weapon, on top. Each year a fair was held on their property to commemorate Shiva's Night. But Sovik didn't remember the fair and only knew about it from his mother. "Hundreds came from miles away," Sovik's mother often told him many years later. "What a festivity!"

When he was young, Sovik loved hearing the details of their life in Raipara; but his mother would become sad after talking a little and slap her forehead with her palm, saying, "Fate—all fate. Nothing your father could have done to change it." Then she would not talk about their past for some time.

She was right. No one could have checked the tide of history. The nineteen forties came with the rumblings of civil disruption. With encouragement from the British colonial rulers, Muslim leaders throughout India had been agitating for some time for a separate country of their own. Bengali Muslims also participated in this demand and started uprisings around the state. Turmoil spread to the villages of Bengal and relations between Hindus and Muslims deteriorated. Each week rumors of division of Bengal became more serious and more real; the Muslims would get east Bengal and the Hindus, west Bengal.

Some Hindus left for Calcutta in anticipation of the division. Almost every day the remaining local Hindus met in Sovik's father's house and discussed the situation. Sovik's father was an optimist. He didn't believe India would be divided.

"Have you heard the latest?" Rathin-babu asked Sovik's father one evening.

"More leaving the area?"

"The Chatterjees have sold their property and will leave next week."

"Chatterjees?" Sovik's father was surprised and stared at Rathin-babu. "Hmm. What'll they do if there's no partition of India?" he mumbled; but no one answered.

A crow cawed loudly from a nearby mango tree.

"People are scared," one man said.

"Muslims are gathering arms," said another.

"All fear-mongers," Sovik's father proclaimed. "What would they achieve by going to an unknown land?"

"I'm also thinking of leaving," Rathin-babu admitted. "I don't see any way out of this. If we leave now, we can take our money and settle somewhere in West Bengal."

"I'll stay here, this soil is part of me," Sovik's father asserted. "I'm sure this nonsense will soon stop."

He was reluctant to leave their ancestral house and prayed for things to change: first for no partition of the state of Bengal; then, for people of all religions to be able to live together as they had done in the past; and finally, for the riots to stop. But things only got worse. Well-to-do Hindus moved to Calcutta at the first sign of physical violence, but Sovik's father delayed and delayed. His wishes and hopes never materialized, and Bengal was divided. Their land became a part of East Pakistan. The intensity of Hindu-Muslim riots increased and civility lost its meaning.

Sovik was only five years old when the partition riots peaked in 1947. Bengali Hindus, with no government protection, found themselves in a disastrous position: Muslims pushed them off land they had lived on for generations. The Hindus had to decide quickly; to stay on the land to be dominated by the Muslims, or be homeless nobodies in a new place. Those who left earliest were the upper and upper-middle-class people: landowners, merchants, and professionals. Sovik's father belonged to this class, but couldn't bring himself to leave.

He changed his mind only when he saw houses burning in the distance, and men with torches coming toward their house. Ahmed, their loyal servant, rushed to him, saying, "Babu, please get away. Nothing I can do will save you."

There was no choice. His parents dressed their three children quickly, and left with what they could take with them. They boarded a train crowded with wailing, tearful women and silent, fearful men looking at each other, not knowing what lay in the future for them. They became a part of the mass migration from East Pakistan to Calcutta.

The division of Bengal into two countries essentially ruined West Bengal; the state could not handle the millions who poured in from East Bengal. Most, like Sovik's family, had simply fled, and couldn't bring much with them. Everyone scrambled for a place to settle in the unfamiliar land and for a job to survive. But there was nothing to build on. Both the state and the central governments had failed to foresee the massive refugee problem and couldn't manage the exodus. Chaos prevailed everywhere.

Sovik's father tried, but was not able to exchange or sell their property in East Bengal. They had no wealth; but being from the upper class, he had social capital and landed a job as a clerk in the West Bengal Government. Then, after two years of suffering in refugee camps, the family finally settled in a small town, Barrackpore, fifteen miles north of Calcutta on the Hoogly River, which the locals called the Ganges because it was a direct branch of the sacred river. Sovik, his older brother, and younger sister started a new life in a rented brick house in Barrackpore as children of a lower middle class family, no longer members of the rich landlord class of Raipara.

Sovik had very little memory of the ancestral property; all had been blotted out by the frantic flight to safety across the border. Sometimes Sovik's mother would tell them of their life in Raipara. "The day the fishermen came to collect fish from the pond," she said once, "the whole village would come to watch, and everyone got a fish. Not just a little fish—a big one." She would then look away in the distance and sigh. His parents rarely talked about their past life. Only when the older people from East Bengal got together would they express their laments and regrets.

Sovik's father often said the best thing was that they didn't have to borrow money to live. But the undercurrent of falling from their high position affected him deeply. He wanted to create a new world, where they returned to the position they had enjoyed for generations in Raipara as landed gentry. "We have no leverage here," his father told his children many times. "We have to create it ourselves." He figured earning professional degrees was the only way

46

to establish them in the new world, and single-mindedly guided his children to restore their glorious status through the only means he knew—education. It became his passion. There was only one goal for the children: to do well in their studies. Everything else besides schoolwork could wait. Except for Sovik's sister, there was no cultivation of arts such as painting and singing. "That will come later," he told them. When a political procession would pass by their house with its loud cries and slogans, especially by the Communist Party, he would close the windows on that side. "They have nothing else to do in life! Politics—the last resort of scoundrels!"

Sovik's first formal schooling came in the fourth grade. Sovik's father worked with his children every night, even though he was tired after the day's work and commute to Calcutta. Sovik came in first in sixth grade. It was then he saw his father's face relax, creating an expression that he had not seen before: he was beaming with joy. His father still scrutinized his report card, and suggested that he must do better in Geography. "These are the subjects in which you can score good marks. You can't guarantee good marks in literature."

Sovik nodded.

One day when Sovik was in eighth grade, the headmaster of the school declared the rest of the day off because one of their students had won a district scholarship in the state high school exam: a cause for great celebration for the school, which was a far cry from the best schools in Calcutta. The teachers went around to each class, telling the students that they too could become like this student if they studied hard, and then their future would be great. While walking home that day, Sovik wondered if he could also win a scholarship. Go to the best college in Calcutta. Be somebody. He knew his father would be most happy. Time passed and he went to Barrackpore High School. The excellent results he achieved each year ignited his ambitions further. Slowly he became a taciturn and serious student.

In the coming years, Sovik did very well, placing fourth in the statewide school final exam taken by over 100,000 students from all schools in west Bengal. That made his father's dream come true. The entire neighborhood was elated with Sovik's success.

"He has a great future," they all proclaimed.

Sovik touched the elder's feet for their blessings.

Four years later, he graduated in geology, top in his class, from the best college in Calcutta, Presidency College. Then on to Calcutta University and finally, the ultimate achievement, in his father's opinion, admission to a U.S. university—the University of Pennsylvania—for graduate studies with a scholarship.

The fate of his older brother, Manik, turned out differently. Their parents had named him Manik after man—jewel, but he did not become a jewel. Their father was frustrated. He expected him to be a grown-up man at age twelve. "I'm working hard to get us established," their father often told Manik, "and I only ask you to do well in school. You can't even do that?" Manik would remain silent. He tried, but couldn't live up to his father's expectations.

Manik was almost ten when their family fled East Bengal. He became a victim of the uprooting turmoil and could not cope well with life in the refugee camp or Barrackpore. Constantly rebuked by his father, and unable to do well in school, he felt ashamed and shied away from his father; then, as he became a teenager, he shied away from the family. He barely passed the high school exam and went to a local college.

"Do you want to be like your brother?" his father sometimes asked Sovik in a scolding tone. "Then go together and be nothing. Vagabonds." That was his favorite term of derision: Vagabond.

Sovik remembered the night his mother stayed up late because Manik didn't return home. She kept his dinner warm as long as she could; then she covered it, and waited for him.

"Don't worry. He'll show up when he's hungry," her husband told her, sarcasm in his voice.

"I wish you didn't scold him all the time," she said.

"What scolding? He deserves a beating every day."

But Manik didn't come home that night, or the next, or the night after.

Instead, they got a letter from him saying that he had found a job with the Gun and Shell factory in Cossipore, and would live there. He promised to visit them when he finished his apprenticeship. Sovik's mother cried quietly for several days, accusing her husband of driving the boy away.

"I tried my best to make him somebody, but no, he wouldn't listen." His father grumbled and walked back and forth in the corridor. He fumed in silent rage.

His father could not show any expression of love after they left Raipara. It was all duties, responsibilities, strategies, and plans to carry out goals. Everyone in the family tiptoed around him; no one wanted to disturb him. Everyone knew he was under great stress, working hard to make ends meet, and keeping as respectable a status for them as possible. But this continuous alertness and push to move ahead affected everyone. Moments of joy were overshadowed by future goals to be accomplished.

◆ ◆ ◆

When the day of Sovik's departure for the States came, the whole neighborhood crowded into their house to see him off. What a happy occasion it was!

His father waited somberly in front of their rented house. "Be successful in America," he told him, as Sovik bent down to touch his feet for blessings— the usual pranam. He looked for his mother so he could perform the same obeisance, but she wasn't there.

"Where is Ma?" he asked.

"She just went inside," his sister replied. "I don't know why she has to be away just now." A little irritation came through in her voice.

After a moment, his mother rushed out and Sovik went to her. She handed him a small piece of ocher cloth, a tiny handkerchief. "It is from our altar. My guru-ma gave it to me. Always keep it with you. It will help you in times of difficulty."

He put it carefully in his pocket, and then touched her feet.

His mother softly uttered, "Durga, Durga," for blessings from the goddess.

Sovik got into the taxi and sped away.

5.2

On a crisp day in August, 1965, Sovik landed in Philadelphia. Young men in India, even those attending a university, are guided and protected by their elders and the strong forces of society, but Sovik was alone in a foreign country and completely on his own. Fortunately, he had only one objective in mind, his studies. While his classmates relaxed on the weekends and went on dates, he spent time in the library, doing homework. He declined the invitation for Thanksgiving dinner with an American family and stayed in his efficiency apartment, studying for the exam to be held after the holidays. His devotion to succeed in the U.S. paid off. He earned the top honor among the first year graduate students in chemical engineering at Penn.

With the confidence that he could do well in America, he ventured out a little. He had no courses scheduled for the summer and he had received a research scholarship, so he felt no pressure. He participated in campus activities, especially those organized for international students. But he couldn't truly relax and take his mind off his goal, the reason he had come to the U.S. He devotedly went to his office every morning as he had done during the school year and carried on his research.

One day, before Spring Midterm, he dropped his routine to attend the Indian exhibit at the campus international fair. He had agreed to help Mrs. Nayar, whose husband was a professor at Penn. "Sovik," Mrs. Nayar told him, "you stay in the exhibit room and greet people, while we're busy frying samosas."

He nodded and went into the exhibit room. The exhibit had just opened and only a few students had come by so far.

He contemplated the large stone statue of Vishnu the university museum had loaned them. Vishnu, the preserver of the world, sat on his carrier, Garuda, who is half-man and half-bird. When the world becomes evil and chaotic, Vishnu is reborn on earth and restores order. The smooth, gray stone shone in the sunlight pouring through the window.

A girl had wandered in from the direction of the samosa fryers, nibbling on a samosa; she strolled around the exhibit looking at the handicrafts on display. Her curly, dark brown hair fell halfway down her back and shimmered as she stood in a beam of light from the window. She looked relaxed, as if she had just left her dormitory for a break. She was thin; but not skinny. She wore a denim skirt, an embroidered peasant blouse, and sandals. From his angle, he could see a small forehead, a small nose, and dark grey eyes.

She finished the samosa and moved toward a room across the hall. A sign on the door said, "Try an Indian Sari!" Several saris and an instruction booklet were on a table in the otherwise empty room.

Sovik followed her to the door, wondering whether he should get someone to help the girl. Several students came, chatting and laughing, and entered the exhibit room; but he stayed in the corridor.

The girl came out after some time, wrapped in a blue silk sari, and hesitantly stood near the door. Sovik was pleased that she had been able to put on the sari. "You are the most beautiful girl on campus!" he said jovially.

"Does it look right?" she asked him, blushing.

"Perfect. Come, I'll take you to the Indian ladies."

She followed him to the kitchen where three women were frying samosas. "See how nice she looks," Sovik told them. The women glanced at her from head to foot; their faces, cheerful a moment before, became expressionless. Mrs. Nayar, the oldest among the women, finally smiled, saying, "Come, I'll show you an easier way to wear a sari."

The two went back to the sari-trying room. Mrs. Nayar showed her how it was properly done: The girl had put on the sari mirror-reversed by following the instructions in the booklet; the end was over the wrong shoulder.

"You look nice," Mrs. Nayar told her when they were finished. "Light blue looks very good on you." Then she went back to the kitchen.

When the girl came out, Sovik was still in the hall. She ignored him, and started toward the exhibit room, clutching the sari. She glared at him when he took a step toward her, and was about to speak her mind, when Sovik said, "You look very pretty." There was no trace of sarcasm in his words or face.

She saw a round-faced Indian boy with dark, wavy hair, full lips and large expressive eyes. He was genuine—not what she expected. Their eyes met and she forgot her annoyance. "Thank you. I'm Marsha Mead, but everyone calls me Pinky." She extended her hand and he took it lightly.

"Pinky?" His eyes danced with curiosity.

"I guess I was a pink baby or that was what my father thought."

"My name is Sovik. Sovik Bose. I'm studying chemical engineering."

"I am a senior in English."

"Are you related to Margaret Mead?"

"I can't claim that." She adjusted the sari, which threatened to fall from her shoulder. "But shouldn't all Meads be related somewhere up the chain?"

"Why not?" Sovik said. "I'd like to claim all the famous Boses in my chain."

They looked at each other and smiled. Then they entered the room where the Indian displays were.

"Are you coming to the International Program tonight?" Sovik asked after a while. He felt quite at ease asking her.

"International Program?"

"The foreign students will perform various entertainments, and there will be a dance later."

"I don't know. I've got to study."

"I'll ask Mrs. Nayar to lend you the sari. You'll look stunning."

Her eyes lit up for a moment, but she said, "I don't think so. I'm not that bold."

"Come for a couple of hours. It'll be a very good program," he urged.

"I don't know."

"If you've never been to International Night, you should definitely come. I will take you there," Sovik said, surprised at his own boldness.

"You will?"

"I'd like to."

"Even if I'm not related to Margaret Mead?" She chuckled.

"Yes."

She gazed at him for a few seconds and saw innocence, like a boy in junior high.

"Then why not?"

"I'll tell Mrs. Nayar that you are borrowing the sari for the evening."

5.3

Pinky stood at the open door of Sovik's small graduate student office with a vase in her hands. Leaning on his desk, Sovik was writing intently on a yellow pad—a thick book open in front of him. Pinky saw the green lawn of the quadrangle through the window. She coughed a little to get his attention.

Sovik turned and his absorbed expression changed to rapture. He stood up hurriedly and banged a knee on the desk. "Come in, come in."

"I brought this for you," she handed him the vase. "I enjoyed the show last night very much."

"How beautiful!" Sovik put the vase on his desk and looked at it from the left and from the right. "The lily, the dry wheat and the leaf all at different heights. I like it very much—asymmetric but harmonious. Very Japanese."

"I learned this at the campus Ikebana club." Pinky looked around the room. There were no pictures or posters, only books on shelves and a pair of walking shoes in one corner.

"This will certainly brighten my office," Sovik said. "Please sit down."

"No, no. I have to go to a class now."

Sovik walked with her to the quadrangle. "Thank you for the gift. Now you know my office. Please come again."

"I'll try."

She hurried away toward the Arts Building. Sovik lingered in the quadrangle, gazing after her.

Pinky did not come over to Sovik's office, but one day Sovik saw her in the cafeteria during lunch time, eating alone. He went over to her.

"How are you doing?"

Pinky looked up, a little surprised. "Busy," she said, her face lighting up. "Come and sit with me." She was genuinely happy to see him.

They caught up with each other.

"I'm sorry, I didn't see you earlier," she said before leaving. "I eat here at this time. It'll be nice to eat lunch with you."

Sovik nodded.

After that they saw each other often during lunch. Pinky enjoyed listening to Sovik—his life in India, his aspirations and how his work was progressing. She loved it when he described his theoretical calculations. Even if she had no understanding of the thermodynamic terms and reaction rates he enthusiastically mentioned, she listened to him in a trance. And Sovik found someone very pleasant, to his liking, and easy to talk with. Soon they started to look forward to their meetings.

"How did you decide to study chemical engineering?" Pinky asked him one day during lunch. "I wonder what I should do after graduation."

"I didn't really aim for chemical engineering," Sovik said. "I studied geology and I liked geochemistry."

"Really, then you should have studied geology." She perked up.

"Perhaps, but Penn didn't have a suitable degree in geology for me. So I applied for chemical engineering. I was determined to come here."

"Interesting." She looked at him for a few seconds. "You changed your field in order to come here?"

"In a way that is correct. I got a chance to come here and that was a big deal from India."

"I graduate next month . . . and wonder . . ."

"Here you can study what you wish," Sovik mused.

"That makes it more difficult. I'll have a double major: English and Psychology. Which one to pursue now?"

"I decided on chemical engineering to come here but also because it has more opportunities than geochemistry. You should study subjects that have good potential for the future."

"I find it hard to decide," Pinky said.

"I'll finish my Master's degree this year," Sovik said almost to himself, "and then continue for a Ph.D."

"It's good when you know what you are doing," Pinky said and collected her plates on the tray. "See you next time." She sped away.

Pinky grew up in a well-to-do Protestant family in Swarthmore. She was a good student and involved in many activities from sports to high school band and led a busy, happy childhood. And in spite of the looming Vietnam crisis, she didn't show any interest in politics. Her mother thought Pinky would marry after her Bachelor's degree, find a nice boy in college, and live in a place not too distant from home. But when Pinky finished her BA at Penn, she found herself alone. She had broken up with the boy she dated in college and had no immediate desire to be married. When she met Sovik, she was definitely not looking to meet another boy, especially a foreign student.

Pinky was not sure whether to get a job or continue her studies. She had majored in English and psychology, but she wanted to do something different. Indirectly, Sovik helped her make up her mind. She decided to do a Master's degree in psychology with emphasis on therapy.

During the summer she took a temporary job at the Union Carbide office in downtown Philadelphia and stayed around campus. She often came to campus after work and met with Sovik. They ate together in the school cafeteria, went on long walks, saw foreign films shown on campus, and talked about themselves. It was not formal dating, but they started to see each other almost daily. She did not know whether it was rebellion against the boys she had known earlier, the exotic country Sovik came from, his Ph.D. candidate status, or what mysterious forces captured her interest. Perhaps circumstances brought them closer together—Sovik, a lonely foreign student who did not do anything but research for his thesis, and she having broken up with her boyfriend.

Soon Pinky felt an attraction toward Sovik; she loved watching him walk back to his lab after dropping her at her summer rental. The indent of his spine and the muscles of his back, which she could just see through his shirt, fascinated her. Such a nice shape! Like sculpture.

◆ ◆ ◆

The winter of nineteen sixty-seven was severe. Pinky had not seen or heard from Sovik for several days. She could not find him at his lab either. Saturday morning, she walked the ten blocks to his basement apartment on Walnut and 42nd street. She knocked on the door but no one answered. She stood there wondering what to do, then found the door to be unlocked. She went down the few steps to his apartment. In the dim light of the table lamp she saw Sovik huddled in bed, crying. She rushed to him. "What's the matter?"

He did not say a word, but covered his head with the blanket. After a few seconds, he controlled himself and mumbled, "I've been sick for several days."

"Why didn't you call me?" She knew many had caught the flu.

"I didn't want to give you my flu."

"How silly of you!" She walked to the refrigerator. It was empty.

"I've used up all I had." His lips quivered and tears slid down his cheeks.

She put her hand on his shoulder. "Why are you crying?"

He didn't say anything for a few seconds and then said in a small voice, "I was thinking of my mother." His voice choked and he stopped talking. He looked away from her.

Pinky patted his back, not knowing what to say. No other boy she knew had cried over his mother.

"My mother would bring barley soup and a wedge of lime when I was sick, but I'd push it aside. I knew I should drink it to get well. But it tastes awful. I'd keep my lips shut." Sovik's face relaxed a little and he raised his eyes to Pinky. "She would coax me to drink and stay with me. She would offer me lots of promises before I'd eat that awful soup. How much I demanded from her!"

Pinky felt embarrassed. He was a brilliant student, but how helpless he was now. He was crying because he was sick and forlorn, and homesick. She gazed at his miserable form, curled up in the blanket, and her heart filled with affection for him. No one she knew was like him—so sincere and so innocent. Some boys were fun to be with, but Sovik was a real person—no superficiality or bravado about him, and she was the only American friend he had.

"I'll get you some food and orange juice," she told him. "And then I'll take you to a doctor."

"You will?"

"I'll take care of you." She kissed his forehead.

She had found her true love.

5.4

Two months before the deadline for his thesis submission, Sovik was working furiously at his laboratory in the Chemical Engineering building when the department secretary brought a Western Union telegram. "An urgent message from India."

Sovik was punching computer cards in a heavy, gray machine. Without looking, he said, "Just a sec, let me finish the last card." The young girl stood there, watching him place the punched cards in a large deck on the table. He then took the telegram from her and opened it.

He read the four words over and over again: Father Passed Away Monday.

"Is it bad news?" she asked.

"My father has died," he told her and slumped down on the stool by the machine. His hand brushed the deck of computer cards and half of them fell on the floor; the telegram hung in his hand.

"I'm sorry to hear that," she said and started to pick up the cards, now all mixed up. "You want to go home?" she asked, replacing the cards on the table.

Sovik looked at her and couldn't say anything.

"Let me tell your professor." She walked out.

He stared out at the quadrangle through the windows. Boys and girls were rushing to classes on the brick paths through the lawn. Dark ivy leaves covered the walls of the buildings. He kept on watching, but he was not seeing anything.

"Make sure you don't leave out an item," he heard his father's words. His father was walking along the corridor and answering questions as Sovik sat at a table and filled out the application forms to U.S. universities.

"What do I write for the essay?"

"Why you want to go to America?"

Sovik nodded.

"You write, the U.S. is the frontier in science and engineering. And you want to take part in exploring the frontier."

Without his father's enthusiasm, determination, and support, Sovik could not have come to the U.S. Now his father was dead. He crumpled the telegram; he wanted to make it vanish. He put the ball of paper in his pocket. Voices of students walking in the corridor floated in. He shifted his eyes toward the door;

but no one was there. Instead his father came to his vision again.

His father was examining his report card from fourth grade. That was the first time he had gone to a formal school. When he received the card, he was surprised and ran straight home. "Look!" he told his father, breathing hard and thrusting the card in to his father's hand. "I've come in third in my class."

"How come you lost nine points in math?" his father asked him.

"I guess I must have done one problem wrong."

"See, if you got 100 in math, you'd have been first in your class."

Sovik stared at his father. It was too late to improve the score.

"Next year you must pay more attention to math. All good students get 100 in math." His father looked affectionately at his son for a few moments. "Do you know the story of the Eye of the Bird?"

Sovik shook his head. "Is it an old story?"

"Yes. Very old. It is in the Mahabharata. Let me tell you.

"In the time of the Mahabharata, a great archer lived in India. His name was Drona. One day he saw the young Pandava and Kaurava princes playing with a ball. The ball fell in a well and the princes couldn't think of a way to retrieve the ball. They stood around the well helplessly.

"Drona helped them retrieve the ball. He shot a sharp reed into the ball, and then shot a series of reeds, one after another, until he had a long string of reeds attached to the ball. The boys were jubilant when they saw how effortlessly Drona pulled the ball out of the well.

"Soon word of this feat reached the king, and he asked Drona to be the princes' archery teacher. Drona agreed. He was born in a Brahmin priest family, but he had single-mindedly devoted himself to mastering the martial arts. He knew what was necessary to obtain the skill of an expert archer.

"The princes practiced daily under his direction and learned all the archery techniques. Every day they rehearsed how to hold the bow steady, how to aim at a target, and then to shoot with a steady hand. In a few months they became good archers. The princes soon had the opinion that they had learned the skills, and they were ready to defeat any enemy.

"One morning Drona declared, 'Tomorrow, you will have a test.'

"The princes were elated; they would prove to their teacher that they had learned their lessons well.

"Duryadhan, the oldest Kaurava brother boasted, 'I shall be declared the best archer tomorrow.' Arjun, his Pandava cousin, had developed great skills but did not say anything. He went to one corner of the field to practice.

"For their first test, the youthful princes were dressed in colorful clothes by their mothers. When the princes had assembled on the practice field, Drona commanded all to fall in line. He explained to them what the test would be. He had hung a wooden bird in a tree, and they were to shoot the eye of the bird.

"The princes were excited and all clamored for the first shot at the bird. But Drona ignored them, and said, 'You shoot only when I tell you to.'

"He took a stick and drew a line on the field, about fifty feet from the tree where the bird was hanging. He first called for Yudhisthir, the oldest Pandava brother, and told him to stand on the line. 'Aim,' Drona commanded.

"Yudhisthir raised his bow and arrow, and aimed at the bird.

"Drona then questioned him, 'Tell me what you see.'

"'I see the sky and a tree. There is a bird hanging from a branch in the tree. I'm aiming at the bird.'

"'Stand on this side of me,' Drona told him gently pointing to another line, he had drawn earlier, away from the shooting line.

"Yudhisthir was surprised, 'Don't you want me to shoot at the bird?'

"'No, you are not ready yet.'

"Drona then called for Duryadhan, and asked him to stand on the shooting line. He gave him the same command, 'Aim.'

"When he had aimed steadily, Drona asked, 'Tell me what you see.'

"'I see a large tree and a bird hanging from a branch.'

"'Go and stand on the line next to Yudhisthir,' Drona told him.

"Drona called the other princes, one after another, and asked them the same question. Receiving a similar reply, he asked each one to stand aside, behind Yudhisthir. Drona was rather disappointed. Finally, he called Arjun. This was his last chance to see if any had understood the essence of his lessons. 'Aim,' he commanded.

"Arjun stood steady on the line with his eyes fixed on the bird. Drona then asked him, 'Tell me what you see.'

"Arjun said, 'I see a bird.'

"Drona enquired further, 'What do you see of the bird?'

"I see only the eye of the bird."

"'Shoot,' Drona ordered with great pride.

"The bird fell to the ground with an arrow piercing its eye. 'Ah,' said Drona, 'when you concentrate on one thing, the rest of the world vanishes from your sight.'"

"You like the story?" Sovik's father asked him.

"Duryadhan failed and Arjun won. The same thing happened at the end of the Mahabharata. I like that."

"Remember this story," Sovik's father told him, "then you will do well in all your efforts."

"See only the eye of the bird?"

"Yes."

Sovik stared at the computer cards on the table. He only needed to finish two more calculations, and revise the draft thesis. The date for his thesis defense was set and his professor had already promised him a job as a Postdoctoral Fellow. He had planned to go home after his degree. His father would have been so proud of his accomplishments. But his father was there no more! He could not tell him anything—ever! His heart swelled up and his vision blurred. He put his head down on the table and started to sob.

He wandered out of the lab half an hour later and walked around campus aimlessly. He did not know what to do. He could not call home because there was no phone at their house in Barrackpore. He tossed and turned in bed all night.

In the early morning, when the first sound of birds came, he decided to write a letter to his mother. He would not go home now, and would follow what his father would have liked him to do. His father's body had already been cremated, anyway, within 24 hours of death, according to Hindu customs. He would finish his degree, and work hard to become 'somebody' in the U.S., as his father would have wanted. His father's struggles and sacrifices for the family must not be for nothing. He promised his mother he would come home as soon as possible. He then hurriedly left the apartment for his lab. Dawn was just breaking in the distance and streetlights were still on. As he strode down Walnut Street, empty at this hour, a deep determination burned in his mind.

5.5

At the graduation ceremony, Sovik received a special award for the best Ph.D. thesis of the year. After a celebratory lunch at a German restaurant, arranged and paid for by his thesis advisor, Sovik and Pinky went back to the campus and lazily walked around the school buildings. They knew each building and the arrangements of ivy vines on the walls: where there were empty spots, where some leaves were darker than others, and where leaves had dried up. The day was magnificent—warm, with no breeze, under a blue canopy. Sovik told her he was going to devote his life to research. And Pinky talked about the need for therapists, especially in poorer areas, and her desire to help people. She would like that as her goal in life.

"You will be famous one day," she said. Then who knows where I'll be."

Sovik stopped, turned to her and took both her hands in his. He looked into her eyes and said, tenderly, "I think about you all the time." He had wanted to say this for a long, long time. His hands slipped around her, and he embraced her with intense ardor. She was soft, submissive, and surrendering, resting her head on his shoulder, her lips nuzzling his neck. As he held her tightly in his arms, an urge surged through his body. The primitive urge was so strong that Pinky felt it vibrate all through her body like the beginning rumblings of an avalanche. There was no mistaking Sovik's desire.

"Let's go to my apartment," she whispered.

Hand in hand they turned toward her apartment. No words were spoken. They simply walked on joyously.

As they entered her apartment, Sovik saw a large Ikebana flower arrangement on the coffee table. He was about to sit down on a chair, when she pulled him close, holding his face with her hands and kissing him tenderly. His lips were moist and like a ripe persimmon. She hungrily drank up the nectar. Sovik shivered in pleasure and reciprocated. He started to kiss the back of her neck, stroking her silky hair and held her in a crushing embrace—her breasts against his chest. It was the gentle pleasure of the gods. He felt no hurry in this pleasure, this was all he needed in life and wanted to continue forever. Time had stopped for him. His mouth moved to her ears. Pinky moaned softly as his tongue tickled her earlobe and darted inside. Sovik held her tight and caressed her breasts. He felt a strong stirring between his legs; he wanted to be closer to her—to be one with her—skin to skin. He caressed her back and started to unzip her dress. Pinky closed her eyes and enjoyed his hands stroking her skin. Like Sovik, she wanted this to continue on and on. Soon her excitement rose high. "Wait," she said and took her dress off. She unbuttoned his shirt and pulled his pants off as they climbed on to her bed.

Neither had realized they had such intense, hidden passion for each other.

They lived separately, but that made their new relationship mature steadily. They became passionate lovers, looking forward to their weekends together. Pinky introduced him to her friends, who accepted Sovik with open arms, inviting the couple to join their parties and activities. Their weekends became an enjoyable routine of going out to restaurants or movies or to parties and making love when they returned.

◆ ◆ ◆

After his time as a post-doctoral researcher, Sovik applied to several companies and received an excellent offer for a position as a research scientist from Exxon Research and Engineering (ER&E) Company in Annandale, New Jersey. Started in 1919, ER&E was the nation's first and topmost industrial research laboratory, and almost all of the petroleum processing technology used today in Exxon refineries and plants originated there. Sovik accepted the offer and moved to Annandale. That move also did another thing for him; he missed Pinky very much and realized he could not live without her.

It was the summer of 1971, a quite successful year for Sovik. But while Pinky went to a summer school in Germany for two months, her absence made him think of her more deeply: he appreciated all she had done for him—how she had sustained him through all his troubles and successes, and how much he depended on her. She was the only one dear to him outside of India. He realized in his heart how much she loved him. He went to receive her at Philadelphia Airport, surprising her.

She looked a little thinner when she came out of Customs, but her spirit was bubbly. "I have a small present for you," she said.

"I have something for you too," Sovik told her, his eyes sparkling as he put his arms around her.

"Really?" She gave him a kiss. "This is unexpected."

He pulled her to the tall glass window from which one could see planes landing. "Close your eyes," he commanded. He then held her left hand and put a ring on her finger. "You can open your eyes now."

Silently she examined the diamond ring for a few seconds and then looked at Sovik.

"Will you marry me?" Sovik said, holding her hand.

She embraced him and clung to him. "Yes." She had waited to hear this for some time.

"I don't have such a good present for you."

"You are my present," Sovik told her. "You don't know how much I love you. Let's get married as soon as possible."

"Don't you want to tell your family and ask them to come to the wedding?"

"No. My mother is a widow and she does not speak English. She wouldn't come."

"We could get married in India."

Sovik couldn't imagine that and stared at her. He was afraid to tell his mother. She would be unhappy and she might ask him not to marry Pinky. But he couldn't contemplate forsaking Pinky or living without her. This was why he had delayed proposing to Pinky for so long.

"Let's have a small ceremony," he told Pinky, "I'll write her a letter."

"You know your family, but I have to invite my family and some friends."

"Oh, certainly. We will do all that is appropriate here. We'll go home a few months after the wedding. When my mother meets you, she'll fall in love with you."

Pinky arranged for a small wedding at her church in Swarthmore, her hometown. Sovik liked the 75-year old Presbyterian Church, with its medieval-looking stone structure. Only a few of Sovik's friends and his professor attended the wedding, and of course no members of his family were there. Then Pinky gave up her job in Philadelphia and moved to New Jersey.

◆ ◆ ◆

The telegram arrived three months later. His mother had died. Sovik was shocked. He felt he had betrayed his mother. Affectionately and selflessly she had taken care of all of them—as if that was the only reason she existed—from the early morning till she went to bed. She should have been in his thoughts all these years, but she was not. He had also kept his marriage a secret from her. He had sent a wedding card to his sister, but told her not to tell mother. He'd break the news to her slowly.

Sovik was bereft at first. But as he had done when his father had died, he rationalized not going home for the funeral service. His mother's body had already been cremated. What was the use of going back now when both parents were dead? Wouldn't their memories be better preserved if he did well in the U.S.—the sole reason he had come to Philadelphia? He had had no correspondence with his older brother; he could not even remember if Manik had come to see him off when he left Calcutta. He received letters from his younger sister occasionally and that was all. He sent a good sum of money for her wedding expenses when she got married. She had two children now, but he had not kept up with them in any significant way.

His work had become his life; essentially, he had lost contact with his family.

Sovik

5.6

D r. Lattimer, the head of Exxon Research, who was known as the Big Boss to everyone in Annandale, called Sovik into his office one day. "You came to us with a great recommendation from your thesis advisor and we've been very happy with your work ever since," he said. "You've also won the title of 'Research Scientist of the Year.' Now that you are a Senior Research Scientist in this organization, I want to propose an idea to you."

Sovik had met the Big Boss several times, but had never had an intimate discussion with him about his work or his career. He was surprised, didn't know how to react, and stood quietly, his muscular body tense, not knowing what to expect.

"As you probably know, Exxon has expanded into the nuclear industry," the Big Boss said. "We think this will be the next big thing in the energy business. Exxon Nuclear won a contract in 1979 to run the nuclear fuel processing and uranium separation operation in Idaho. Our lab in Idaho needs someone to lead their research work." He paused for a moment and looked at Sovik's round face. "Would you consider going to Idaho to take the position?"

Taken aback, Sovik didn't know what to say; his light brown complexion hid the blush of excitement that came over him at the prospect of such a big promotion, but what came out of his mouth was, "Idaho?"

"Just for a few years. I am confident with your talent and enthusiasm, you can lead us to success."

"Thank you for thinking of me," Sovik said, barely looking at the big boss. "I came from India. Idaho or New Jersey, they are the same to me. But I should ask my wife."

"Yes, certainly. If I may speak to you man to man, I think this will be very good for you." He stood up, implying the meeting was over.

"Thank you."

Sovik walked back to his laboratory with slow steps. The big boss had considered him to lead a nuclear research laboratory. He had come to America to fulfill his father's dream. His father would have considered this a tremendous success and a restoration of his father's family pride—perhaps even put an end to his lamentations over the loss of their ancestral property in East Bengal.

65

By the time Sovik went home in the evening, the full import of the offer hit him and he was bubbling with excitement. The moment he saw his wife, the words came tumbling out, "Pinky, big surprise! Exxon has offered me an excellent opportunity, but it involves moving away from here, far away."

"How far away? To California?"

"No. Idaho."

"Idaho? Really?"

He told her about the meeting with the big boss and the new kind of work. "This is the future of research in chemical engineering. It deals with radioactivity. That's why they do this work in faraway, isolated places." His face flushed with excitement.

Pinky gazed into her husband's large eyes for a few moments. The first thing that came to her mind was the unexpected turn her life had taken and with it some reasons to leave the area she had always known.

The year before she had gone to her gynecologist and learned that she could not have children. She was disheartened. She couldn't talk to Sovik for a few days and moped around the house, brooding about the future, about their relationship. She became sad for Sovik because she knew Indian families desired a son to continue the family heritage. It would be a great blow to Sovik. How would he react to this news?

Then she told him.

Sovik remained quiet for a few seconds and said, "We've met by chance, and we must accept what life brings us. We'll make a good life together—come what may. You are the best thing that has happened to me. Don't worry. We will grow old together."

She put her arms around him and cried. She held on to him for some time and finally said, "I'm so relieved you feel this way."

"If this helps you in your career, and makes you happy, we will go to Idaho." Pinky said. "I'd like to get away from this place," she added with a sigh. "My friends are busy with their chidren; their lives are different. We don't have the same connection any more."

"Leave your work and all your family and friends on the East Coast?"

"I can find work in therapy anywhere. It will be an adventure." She took Sovik's hand in hers. "We will make new friends. Explore a new life together."

6

The Sacred River

6.1

Life went on smoothly for Pinky and Sovik for several years in quiet Idaho Falls. With the knowledge that they would not have children, they became more affectionate toward each other; each trying to console the other lest they be disappointed. They got involved with outdoor activity clubs—skiing in the winter and hiking and camping in the summer. They also focused on their careers, engaging more deeply in their work. She was happy not to have to prove her worth by being a mother and raising wonderful children. Sovik's zeal for work intensified. He was determined to make a worthy contribution in nuclear energy research. They became closer to each other each day. It was a happy time.

Nine years after he came to Idaho, the Department of Energy, which funded all government nuclear research, asked Sovik to organize a conference in Idaho Falls. Scientists from labs all over the country were invited; the Secretary of Energy came from Washington, DC and announced 20 million dollars in funding for advanced research projects in Idaho. Sovik had worked day and night to make the conference a success—both technically and politically. After all, this was his area of research. He was well-pleased and invited Pinky to the public meeting. At the end of the meeting, the General Manager slapped Sovik's back. "We are proud of you, Sovik. You have put us on the map."

It was a great day, and Sovik was still excited in the evening as he and Pinky walked to the parking lot. Then he stopped and said, "I feel out of breath. My jaw hurts."

Pinky held him for a few minutes, then brought the car over to take him home. Sitting in the car, Sovik felt better. But the next day their family physician sent him to a cardiologist, who sent him to the hospital right away. After looking at his angiogram, the cardiologist immediately decided to airlift him to Holy Cross Hospital in Salt Lake City for an angioplasty.

"I am in the midst of an experiment at the lab," Sovik told him. "It is very important and I have a deadline. Could we make this trip a week later?"

"You have a blocked coronary artery—the one we call the widow-maker," the cardiologist told him. "The artery is 95% blocked." He then turned to Pinky, saying, "The blockage could cause a sudden heart attack and death at any moment. I'd strongly suggest we do the angioplasty right away." Then he reassured Sovik and Pinky that once they were in the hospital in Salt Lake City, there would be nothing to worry about. "In only one in a thousand cases, is there a problem. I've already performed hundreds of these procedures, and no one has died."

"You can go back to your lab in about two weeks," the doctor told Sovik.

Sovik's angioplasty took place on Good Friday, April 17, 1987. The angioplasty balloon opened his artery, but then the artery collapsed unexpectedly and his heart went into fibrillation. His cardiologist, who had earlier said there was nothing to worry about, went to Pinky and thrust a paper at her: "We may have lost him, Mrs. Bose. But sometimes we can bring a patient back with bypass surgery. Please sign this."

The surgeon's hands quivered in the sudden emergency, but Sovik survived. The nurses said he had been in a lot of pain, but Sovik didn't remember. His recovery progressed slowly. Even after several days, his throat hurt constantly, raw from the intrusive respirator. One day a chest x-ray was taken. Then two doctors came and drained a great quantity of blood from his chest cavity. "He'll get better now," one doctor remarked to the other, speaking as if Sovik couldn't hear them.

Sovik lay in bed weak and unable to move sideways. He was half-awake; the room was dim and filled with muffled, dissonant hospital sounds. Dark images surrounded him. In a dream one night he saw himself lying in a darkened room, peeling his own body away layer by layer while a large rat quietly watched him from a corner.

He only felt at ease when Pinky held his hand and talked to him. Her voice was soothing. It was the same sustaining voice he had heard a long time back in a lonely basement apartment in Philadelphia when he was ill with flu.

After he was moved from the ICU to a 'Cardiac Care' room, the telephone rang one morning and Sovik felt a little excitement. He struggled to sit up in his hospital bed and picked up the phone. His boss was calling, and his mind raced back to work. A vision of the nuclear chemistry lab came to him: nitric acid dissolving uranium pellets in a small container behind the thick glass wall of the hot cell.

"I was in the middle of the test for line three," he told his boss lying flat on his back. "Please see that the work—"

"Don't worry about it now," the company Vice President interrupted him. "You get well first."

"No, no. It's a very important test." Sovik struggled to speak. Exxon Nuclear was his life. "Please make sure that the valve is calibrated so there is no criticality accident."

"Sovik, we'll handle it," the VP said in a firm voice. "You may not be back for a few months. I'll assign someone qualified to continue the work."

"We also need to try out hydrofluoric acid," Sovik said as if he hadn't heard his boss.

"Someone here will do that," his boss continued on the phone, "and perhaps some new ideas will come from others in your group. Don't worry about it, Sovik. We can figure out what to do."

The VP conveyed the best wishes of the entire company, and then hung up.

Sovik was stunned. Who would take over his work? He stared out the window and wondered about what his boss had said: they would continue the work without him.

A nurse bustled in. "You have to start walking today." She kept her gaze fixed on the brown-skinned man from India.

But Sovik had no spirit in him.

Two male nursing assistants, who were behind the nurse, lifted Sovik up, took him to the corridor, and escorted him on his first walk down the hall. The sight of other patients on the cardiac floor did not cheer him. He saw their pale faces and felt dejected as he limped along. The nurses brought him back to his bed and left him alone in the dimly lit room.

Sovik brooded about his life and about the future. An overwhelming sadness grew within him. He had followed his career obsessively, driven only by an immigrant's desire to succeed, but where was he going? He had no idea, and he couldn't find a deeper purpose in his life. He had achieved fame as a scientist, but he had paid little attention to anything beyond his research work. He felt that he had run his life like the one-eyed deer that cleverly went to the seaside and kept its good eye vigilantly fixed toward the forest while the hunter came from the sea.

He didn't feel like talking with the nurses or drinking and eating. Sometimes he held the fork for a long time without eating. When the nurse came to take the dish away, she had to coax him to eat a little. Most of the time he stared at the ceiling, trying to decipher patterns, or looked out the window.

Sovik stayed awake at night; he heard the rolling of a gurney on the corridor; hushed voices, and hurried movements of people; then silence. He mostly wondered what his next step in life would be. He liked listening to Pinky read to him, but he couldn't tell her what was going through his mind.

In these moments of despair, one day an image of his youth came to him. He was standing alone on the bank of the wide Ganges River in a town near Calcutta, where he grew up, admiring a ruffle of little waves. The pink disc of the morning sun was only a few feet above the horizon. Bare-chested men and sari-clad women bathed and offered individual prayers toward the sun with folded hands—a normal scene on the ghat, the wide stone steps leading down to the river, but it felt so peaceful. A little distance away two large boats stood still in the middle of the river. He continued to gaze in wonderment as the muddy water of the Ganges flowed by almost without a sound. He loved being in the serene scene and felt a sense of comfort.

This was a feeling different from the pleasure Sovik had experienced in scientific breakthroughs. It was a desire-less bliss. He could linger there forever. Then he heard thunder, looked out through the window of his hospital room, and the vision vanished. He longed for it to come back; the scene seemed to hold the secret to his happiness, but it was gone. Desolate, Sovik watched the rain splatter against the window pane.

6.2

When he returned home after twenty-one days in the hospital, Sovik experienced the most disturbing period of his life. Nothing appeared the same. Everything in the house felt empty; no pleasure in the pictures on the walls and the decorations. A sense of futility pervaded his thinking. Even his favorite place, his study, felt unwelcoming. On the physical plane, Sovik felt helpless—his life depended on factors over which he had no control. He wondered why there was no backup for the most vital part of the body, the heart. If the stitches of his newly grafted arteries came off, there would be no time to fly him back to Salt Lake City.

Fear of death pervaded Sovik's mind. Each night he wasn't sure if he would wake up in the morning. He was half-awake during the day and terrified of death at night. On a spiritual level, he searched through his life and found no consolation there.

Many colleagues and neighbors dropped by and expressed their surprise at Sovik's bypass surgery. "You're not even fat," George, his neighbor, said. "You will get well soon," each visitor said to comfort him. But they had no idea what was going through his mind and sounded so perfunctory, so monotonous.

Steve, Sovik's able lab assistant, came to visit him one day. After wishing him a speedy recovery, he said, "You remember our hard-working accountant, Willis? He had bypass surgery done three years ago. Just like yours, but he was back at the office in two months, and in better shape than before. You will also recover in a few weeks and be back soon." But Sovik didn't feel excited by the prospect of going back to work. Instead he kept on wondering what he had done with his life all those years.

All his adult life Sovik had been driven, trying to fulfill his father's dream; but his father died early and never knew of his greatest achievements. Now Sovik questioned his goals and the meaning of his success. Pinky had always supported him, but she never asked him to be 'somebody' to make her proud of him. If they had a child, the situation could have been different, Sovik thought, but that was not in the cards. Thus he continued to brood over his life.

Pinky was his only comfort. The second day after coming back home, he told her, "You are like Savitri of ancient India who brought her husband back from death."

"My job is to get you well," she said. "You still have many things to do. You've just faced the destroyer; the creator and the sustainer are waiting. So get well quick." The Hindu concept of God as creator-preserver-destroyer of the universe and its implications for human beings fascinated Pinky, but Sovik's mind was far away. He turned away from her and stared, unseeing, out the window.

Some days later he asked Pinky when she was putting folded laundry in the dresser, "Have you seen a small piece of ocher cloth anywhere?"

"Ocher cloth?" she asked absently.

"My mother gave it to me."

"You never told me about this."

"I used to keep it in the Chemical Engineering Handbook, but it's not there."

"I'll look. I've never seen it; it may have been lost in all our moves. Is it important?"

"My mother gave it to me," he told her again in a feeble voice. He thought of the altar in the corner of his mother's bedroom. She decorated it every day with fresh flowers. An ocher cloth draped the altar, and that made it very special, very sacred. He tried to remember where he could have kept his mother's last gift. He tried hard, but couldn't remember where it was. Had he lost it?

Days passed. He stayed weak in body and mind. Then one morning, while still in bed, the scene of the Ganges River that he dreamt of in the hospital came back to him. He saw the muddy-brown river; he watched it flowing and felt a sense of comfort. As he sat in bed, almost trance-like, he followed the murky water moving under the famous cantilevered Howrah Bridge in Calcutta with tram cars, old red double-decker buses, lorries, rickshaws, and masses of people crowding the only path over the river from the city to the main railway station in Howrah.

Then in his mind he followed the river upstream to the Himalayas and visualized he was next to it in the high mountains. He became transfixed by the river. He felt the river was alive, a maiden playing in the mountains. It was a most wonderful scene—tranquil and beautiful. She is a mighty river in Calcutta, where he grew up, 'but the Ganges is a Goddess, not just a river.' Then he saw a princely man meditating high up on a rock—a river flowing down from heaven, hundreds of souls rising to rapture, a lone monk in orange robes going down a green mountain trail. As these images faded and the bedroom around him reshaped itself, he felt enlivened, as though his heart had received a new, wonderful seed of hope and happiness.

The piercing blue sky of the late spring morning outside brought him a deep appreciation of nature—the beautiful sky, streaks of the sun's orange glow, and the light green leaves on branches outside the window. He could smell the fragrance of blossoming May trees. A feeling of joy swept through him, a very different sensation from the preceding weeks. He was happy to be alive, to enjoy the day. Who knew what might happen tomorrow, but 'I'm here today!' he said forcefully, and his recovery began that day.

He felt the river goddess was calling him to journey back from the West to visit her abode in the Himalayas.

He couldn't even walk around the block, let alone hike on rocky trails rising to 13,000 feet; but Sovik thought the secret to happiness could be understood on a journey to the river.

Several days later Pinky found Sovik looking at maps spread out on the bed. It was a bright sunny day but he still had the bedside lamps on. His finger was on a dot on the map at the bottom of the Himalayas.

"What are you doing?" she asked and noticed an old book on the bed.

"One can go up to the Gangotri temple by car," he told her abruptly.

"What are you talking about?"

"I was following the path to the source of the Ganges River."

"The Ganges River in India?"

"Yup, the one and only!" He showed her the book. It was written by an Indian four decades earlier—an account of a trip to the source of the Ganges River. "I found it at the end of the bookshelf," he told her.

"You bought it a long time back. But why are you reading it now?"

"I'm thinking of a journey."

"A journey to India? Now?"

"To the river."

"Are you thinking of India often?"

"Yes. I think I need to go there to get well."

She looked at him intently for several seconds and said, "If you want to follow the river, we will go together—after you get well."

He had been afraid that she would not understand what he was up to. He pulled her to him and held her in an embrace. He hadn't felt this good for a long, long time.

"I want to follow the river all the way," he whispered in her ear. "We have to hike to the glacier from the Gangotri temple. No car goes there."

"Then you have to become strong." She gave him a kiss on his nose.

Sovik felt very happy. After Pinky left, he put on his walking shoes. He must start exercising to regain his strength.

Part II

The Wheel Turns

7

Temple Gold

7.1

Ajit went to Gangotri to get a first-hand picture of the task Chetti had assigned him. In June, the pilgrimage season was in full swing; visitors crowded the temple during worship services. He quietly observed the worship ceremonies conducted by Swami Narayan and Swami Rangaraj in the mornings and evenings; he secretly entered the inside of the temple and studied the rooms and alcoves. He saw the meager habitations of the monks—no sign of any secret place, caves, or entrance to a tunnel. He observed the comings and goings of monks in the temple. There was nothing extra-ordinary; there was no indication that the temple was loaded with gold or money. Devotees brought some gifts, but they amounted to nothing on the order that Chetti imagined. As he explored, Ajit easily remained inconspicuous among the pilgrims, ocher-robed sadhus, mendicants, and the few hikers in Gangotri.

He talked with the locals and went around the area with his detectors, posing as a high-tech hiker. But he could not find any evidence of hidden gold. Finally, he went away from the temple and talked with the recluses meditating in their lonely caves. Some had been there for decades, but no one knew how the temple was run, how the priests supported themselves, or gave any hint of centuries-old hidden treasure somewhere nearby or under the temple.

After making his initial investigation, Ajit returned to New Delhi simmering in the hot July sun. While many took afternoon siestas at home to avoid the heat, Ajit searched through libraries and antique stores for books about temple history, looking for clues to hidden treasures. Finally, he went to Chetti's house and knocked at the door.

Chetti, who opened the door himself, looked at Ajit's concerned face, and, instead of inviting him in, said, "Let's go for a walk. I need the exercise." When they came to a big road, Chetti stopped an auto-rickshaw and they got in. "Chadni Chowk," he told the man.

Ajit sat quietly next to his boss. He knew Chetti always had a purpose in what he did. The auto-rickshaw merged with the traffic on Netaji Subhash Marg and went toward Old Delhi. The honks and beeps of buses, cars, and three-wheelers filled their ears. The traffic slowed after some time when they reached the centuries-old road to the Red Fort. As they went further, streams of people came in and out of stores on both sides of the road and walked in between the automobiles. Dense, black exhaust from a private bus gushed into their auto rickshaw, forcing Ajit and Chetti to cover their noses and mouths with handkerchiefs. Soon they could glimpse the majestic walls of the Red Fort. Chetti kept on looking at the red structure, as their rickshaw turned left to Chadni Chowk. He stopped the rickshaw and they got out.

"I came here for a reason," Chetti told Ajit. "We shouldn't talk about our activities in the office or in my house. They could be bugged." He turned toward the Jama Masjid.

"I haven't found any hint of a secret place for gold in Gangotri," Ajit told Chetti. "Several small caves exist in the area, but none where one could hide something valuable, because local people and hikers go all over the hills." After a pause he added, "I have made a detailed map of the temple—inside and outside."

"Did you use detectors?" Chetti asked him as they approached the mosque. His forehead furrowed deeply. "Visual exams won't reveal what we are after."

"My metal detectors didn't record any meaningful signal. Of course there are metals scattered in the area and in the rocks, but not a cache." Ajit paused and looked at his boss. "The detectors can't penetrate deep under the rocks. I made the acquaintance of local vendors and souvenir sellers. They are the people who go there, year after year, and know all the gossip. They couldn't tell me anything worthwhile."

"It must be inside the temple," Chetti asserted with conviction. "It has to be there!" He looked ahead for a moment and spoke softly, "The priests are not fools. They have kept it ingeniously hidden somewhere."

Ajit nodded his head slowly. "There could be a door that meshes so well with the surroundings that no one notices it. But the temple workers know nothing about a hidden room. . . . I've also sought out the few sadhus who stay in Gangotri all year round, even in harsh winters. No one could tell me anything about a treasure in the temple."

"Hmmm." Chetti's face became tense. "It has to be there," he murmured.

They took off their shoes, climbed the stairs, and entered the large, marbled courtyard where the Muslims gather for prayer.

"As you've told me before," Ajit said, "an insider would have to give us the information."

"Swami Rangaraj has not contacted me yet. But he is ambitious. He'll help us."

"I'm stuck for now." Ajit laid out his fears to his boss, as they strolled across the courtyard of the mosque.

"Soon they will close the temple for the season," Chetti said. "I guess there's no hope for this year."

"We need the time anyway," Ajit said, looking down at a box of apples for sale on the steps. "I must be certain of the whereabouts of every monk in Gangotri before I can put any plan into action."

"The monks follow a definite pattern," Chetti told Ajit. "They meditate at dawn, then bathe in the Ganges River and prepare for the worship service. They are absorbed during this time. The morning puja is complete by about ten."

"It fits with my observation," Ajit said. "How do you know all this?"

"Last year, I sent two boys with Swami Rangaraj to ease his journey to Gangotri. They prepared a map of the area and an account of the people."

"Excellent. I can compare my notes with theirs," Ajit said, but his brow creased. He studied Chetti's face. Why hadn't Chetti revealed this information before he left for Gangotri? This was not the same Chetti he had worked with at ADS. "What else do you know?"

"All the priests are monks in this temple and they participate in the worship service," Chetti said. "No exceptions. The head priest and Swami Rangaraj perform the morning puja and the evening Aarti ceremony. The younger monks help arrange the service and distribute prasad afterward. The monks are then free to do as they please."

"Did you ask for this surveillance?" Ajit asked.

"Yes."

"I need to talk with these two."

"I shall give you their report. Don't involve them. No one needs to wonder what we're doing. I have sent them away on another project."

"What did they say about Swami Narayan?"

"The head priest is an enigma. He doesn't talk much unless you have a question. He vanishes for some time during the day, and they do not know where he goes. They also noticed he visits a tall Shaligram stone next to the temple every day."

"A sacred stone?"

"I don't know. Supposedly King Bhagirath meditated near the stone. It is 30 feet tall."

"Maybe there is a secret door nearby." Ajit scratched his head. "So obvious that no one notices it—just like in Sherlock Holmes' stories."

"It's possible. Another thing: every evening Swami Narayan meets with his disciples and visitors. He tells them stories. They said he is a true spiritual man. People have great respect for him."

"What about Swami Rangaraj?"

"His actions are more known. He follows the same routine every day. He spends most of his time studying religious books and writing. He is a scholar, you know." Chetti chuckled.

Subdued sounds of traffic and hawkers touting their wares floated up to the open courtyard of the largest mosque in India. Ajit looked away from Chetti, realizing that Chetti was following multiple channels to collect information.

From the elevated esplanade, Chetti looked out at the expanse of old buildings between the Mosque and the Red Fort. This had been a Muslim area for several centuries. People had a different spirit here: everyone worked hard to make ends meet, and they had their networks and connections. They could bounce back quickly from adversity while the vast majority of the Hindus in villages were stuck in their circumstances and resigned to their fate.

Ajit also looked north toward the Red Fort. But his thoughts went to the people who had created the fort and the surrounding area. On Fridays this courtyard would be filled with thousands of Muslims, sitting row after row in a uniform pattern—all praying toward Mecca. The hatred between Hindus and Muslims was strong, almost irreconcilable, but those who did not go to Pakistan were all citizens of India. Many Muslims were as poor as their Hindu brothers, being similarly exploited by wealthy landlords and businessmen— actually by whoever had the power. If they succeeded, would the SMS use the gold from the temple to help only one group of people? Ajit wondered. If SMS followed the ancient principles, they must help all people irrespective of their birth or religion; otherwise, what was he doing in this scheme?

Chetti turned toward Ajit. "I've asked Swami Rangaraj twice to call me as soon as he has some information," he said, sighing.

"Perhaps your offer was not good enough for him?"

Chetti ignored Ajit's comment and continued, "We may have to look into his past. Perhaps we could dig up something."

"I've always wondered about the psychology of people who become monks." Ajit said. "It may be good to have some ammunition."

The two men stood together, each alone with his thoughts. Chetti broke their silence.

"He may be operating on Indian standard slow time. Let's give him a little longer."

"Next summer will be crucial for us," Ajit said.

"You develop the strategy and a plan of execution, and I'll find a way to get Swami Rangaraj to give us what we need." Chetti's eyes narrowed. "There's no alternative."

"I'll return to Gangotri in the spring, as soon as the snows melt and the roads are passable," Ajit said.

"Yes. Go as soon as possible." Chetti stopped and turned to face him. "I'll inform Swami Rangaraj that you will be coming. Work with him, but don't tell him any more than you have to."

7.2

The summer of 1993 was coming to an end. Chetti was eager to hear from Swami Rangaraj, but he didn't want to disturb the monk's duties at the temple. Instead, he organized Swami Rangaraj's lecture tour, which would take place when the hot summer temperatures diminished. He fretted, and anxiously waited for a call from the monk.

Meanwhile in Gangotri, life went on as usual; waves of pilgrims came to pray to Goddess Ganga, their numbers increasing steadily to a peak in August. As in years past, many gave heartfelt thanks to the Goddess for the good things that had happened to them, and many prayed for the Goddess to remove difficulties that had come upon them. They brought the best gifts they could afford for the Goddess. Everyone was happy that they were able to come to this holy place and complete their pilgrimage. The weather remained excellent, a little cool but not cold.

Every day Swami Narayan and Swami Rangaraj conducted the morning and evening puja ceremonies. They were an interesting combination: Swami Narayan, the older priest, with long white beard, Rangaraj with thick, wavy black hair and graying beard. One stooped a little; the other stood tall and erect. But it was clear that the younger Swami Rangaraj had great respect for the head priest and deferred all major issues to him.

In between his sacerdotal duties, Swami Rangaraj spent a large part of his time studying the Vedas and Upanishads and other Hindu scriptures. He didn't go out to mix with the locals and was happy to be left to his daily routine, including several hours of meditation. He wrote commentaries on the scriptures and hoped that one day, when he finished these writings, they would be published in the form of a book. The great rishis had done that in the past. His writings would be more appropriate for modern times.

When cold wind blew early that September and a few flakes of snow drifted down to the temple steps, Swami Narayan decided the puja season had come to its end. "The winter is early this year," he said and ordered preparations for the final service.

Most visitors had already left; only a few devotees and a handful of adventurers lingered in the town.

Swami Narayan and Swami Rangaraj performed the final worship service in the morning with sincere piety. Everyone in town came to the ceremony and made it a festive occasion. They brought milk sweets scented with cardamom and rosewater to offer to the Goddesses. Fresh flowers, brought up from lower elevations, decorated the deities and they looked gorgeous. Smoke from incense burners rose up to the ceiling and filled the room with fragrance. Tinkling brass bells and Sanskrit mantras reverberated in the temple. Worshipers sang devotional songs at the end of the ceremony. Swami Narayan personally gave them sweets from the altar. Then a feast began with the food the town people had brought. When the festivities were over, everyone felt a little sad. The temple was now closed for the season. Gangotri would soon become a quiet place. The sweet sounds of temple bells would be silenced until the next spring. The devotees bid farewell to each other and left the courtyard wistfully.

Once the worshipers had left, all the monks worked to take down the deities and dismantle the altar. They sorted items into different piles to be stored for the winter. Then they carried the garlands, flowers, and minor paper and tinsel altar decorations in a single file to the river at the bottom of the courtyard. This was the final ritual.

The monks stood silent, gazing at the waters running over smooth boulders, then laid the altar decorations gently on the water. They floated away, and all eyes followed their journey; the metallic pieces sparkled in the sun's rays; and the priests looked on as they rushed down the mountain. The snow-clad Bhagirath Mountain stood tall, a silent sentinel, overseeing the priests' activities. The ocher-robed priests thought the river looked lonely and beautiful at the same time. They were happy that another season of worship had been successfully completed; yet they too felt melancholy.

Swami Narayan bent down and put a little of the ice-cold water on his head. Cupping his hand, he lifted another handful and sprinkled it over the others, uttering, "Om Shanti! Om Shanti! Om Shanti!" Peace! Peace! Peace! Then all returned to the temple.

The monks and their disciples worked for a few hours to clean the temple and organize everything for the next spring when they would return for a new season. Swami Narayan thanked the younger monks and helpers and asked them to return to their winter monasteries or homes. "Swami Rangaraj and I will take care of the deities," he told them. "You go home."

The two Swamis packed the more valuable altar decorations and books in containers to be locked away until spring. The deities would be taken down to a temple in Mukhba for their winter abode. The place was fourteen miles downstream. Local people would go with them in a ceremonial procession.

Swami Rangaraj took down the statue of King Bhagirath and put it in a box lined with silk. He tucked soft cotton around the image to protect it. "Who pays for the musicians and the drummers that accompany the deities to Mukhba?" he asked Swami Narayan. "I've no idea how all this works."

"Oh, you don't know!" Swami Narayan glanced over at him while he worked. "When the Gurkha General, Amar Singh, built the temple, he also donated the stretch of land from Mukhba village to Gangotri. The revenue from the land pays for all temple expenses, including the storage and upkeep of the deities."

"I see. That's how the temple is run."

"Will you spend the winter in Rishikesh?" Swami Narayan asked Swami Rangaraj, as they wrapped the deities in silk.

"This year I've been invited to speak in several cities. The Sarva Mangal Society is organizing my tour."

"Excellent! Excellent!" Swami Narayan said, looking at him tenderly. "Who could do the job better than you? I'm very pleased."

"I'll be going on the lecture tour straight from here. Will you stay in Gangotri much longer?"

"I hope to stay longer, but my disciples will come in a month and insist I go down. They wouldn't allow me to stay here. They say I am too old." He chuckled and shook his head.

"I agree with them though," Swami Rangaraj said. "Please take care of your health."

"Your lecture tour is important. You don't need to be here for the procession to Mukhba. You can leave tomorrow." Swami Narayan put the image of Goddess Ganga in her beautifully carved wooden box.

"If that is good with you, I'd like that."

"Yes, go." Swami Narayan nodded. "This area becomes more serene and beautiful at this time—a wonderful place for meditation and contemplation. When you become the head priest, you will also want to stay here longer."

Swami Rangaraj stopped packing. "You think I'll be the head priest someday?"

"Who else?" Swami Narayan put the ornament that goes over Goddess Ganga's head in a box and looked at Swami Rangaraj. "You are the most learned among us."

"You are a true devotee; you don't need the book knowledge I try to acquire." Swami Rangaraj said it slowly and softly. He suddenly wished he could be simple and spiritual like Swami Narayan.

"You've been at this temple for seven years," Swami Narayan said. "You should know everything about the temple."

Swami Rangaraj stood erect, quietly taking in what Swami Narayan had said. Then Chetti's inquiry came to his mind. He needed Chetti's help. If he were to succeed in his larger goal, he must also help him. "Could I ask you a question?" He looked eagerly at Swami Narayan, not knowing how he would react.

"Yes, of course."

"I heard that gold was transported here over centuries and secretly kept in the temple. Is this true?"

"Oh yes! It's hidden in a cave."

"Inside the temple?"

"Yes and no." Swami Narayan raised his head. "It is in a chamber below the Shaligram Shila near the end of a tunnel." He paused for a moment. "You are truly devoted to this temple. I should tell you. A passage from the temple goes inside the mountain. It goes by a small, round area—the original cave where the earliest known image of Goddess Ganga was found. Many believe that King Bhagirath worshipped her there. I meditate in that space in the afternoons. It is a completely silent place."

"Have the head priests always used that inner chamber?"

"Yes, and you will do that too. You feel so peaceful when you go there."

"I've been to every room and passage, but I've not seen any separate chamber in the temple. How do you go there?"

"It's so obvious no one notices the passage." He stopped for a second and said, "The opening is in my room."

Swami Rangaraj's hand froze with the crown of Saraswati in his hand. He stared at the head priest in total amazement.

"At the end of the passage there is a large rock, which appears to be a part of the wall, but it can be moved. A small chamber is behind the rock."

"The gold is there?" Swami Rangaraj asked in wonder. This was exactly what Chetti wanted to know. He became a little excited. He didn't want to reveal his inner thoughts to Swami Narayan and restrained his excitement.

"The gold is behind the chamber. A huge pile!"

"Now that you have told me this, could I see it once?"

"No. Not until you become the head priest." Swami Narayan's voice was firm. "I have the only key that opens the door." He contemplated Swami Rangaraj; for a monk he seemed to be very interested in the temple's treasure. After a few moments he said, "The craftsman who built the treasure room and fashioned the key was not allowed to go outside the temple, and he died in the tunnel. So no outsiders know the location."

"If anything happens to you," Swami Rangaraj spoke in a faint voice, "then no one will know about this treasure."

"You don't worry about that. Through generations, monks have protected the key."

Swami Rangaraj felt a slight admonition. He looked away and started to put the altar materials in a container.

Swami Narayan watched Swami Rangaraj for a few moments. "I'll tell you what the head priest before me told me when I was in your position," he said in a more amiable voice, "ten pairs of numbers hold a clue for the secret chamber: 01 35 18 02 25 27 03 15 04 59."

"Thank you for your trust." Swami Rangaraj felt relieved.

"When you understand these numbers, the second and the third odd numbers give another clue."

"It was only my curiosity."

"I know. That's why I am telling you about these numbers." Swami Narayan bent down to pick up Goddess Ganga's ornamental necklace and added, "No one with evil motive has ever entered the secret chamber."

7.3

"Several wealthy families in Calcutta have asked to host you in their homes," Chetti told Swami Rangaraj on the plane to Calcutta. "The Birlas have made several requests, but I've arranged a small tent for you under the *banyan* tree in Dakhshineswar."

"Wonderful!" Swami Rangaraj exclaimed. "I always wanted to spend a night where Swami Ramakrishna meditated." Swami Rangaraj's face glowed with happiness. Was this the appropriate time to tell Chetti about his knowledge of the gold? He glanced around; the presence of other passengers stopped him.

"It'll be a little uncomfortable," Chetti said, "but I hope you understand why I've done that."

Swami Rangaraj nodded thoughtfully and stroked his beard.

"The *Statesman*, *Anandabazaar*, and other Calcutta newspapers have written great editorials about the lecture tour, especially that you're devoting time to rekindle a spiritual awakening in India. They've already compared your actions with those of Swami Vivekananda."

Swami Rangaraj felt elated. "Thank you." After a little pause he added, "You are the master in this area. I simply follow your guidance." Overwhelmed by how diligently Chetti had strategized the lecture plan, he became convinced again that he should help Chetti in achieving his goal, even though he hated spying on the inner workings of the temple.

"You are a master in spiritual matters," Chetti said with a bow of his head. "You'll also have a reception at the Kali temple." He looked intently at the Swami, hoping he would somehow give him a hint if he had found out where the gold was kept.

But the Swami simply listened and said nothing.

The living conditions of people a little distance away from the airport disturbed both Chetti and Swami Rangaraj. They put handkerchiefs on their noses to avoid the stench from garbage dumps. The headlights of the cars showed impoverished people living in palm-thatch hut slums along the path, their thin bodies meagerly covered with rags. As the car turned, they saw two dogs searching a dustbin for food while three small boys, wearing only worn-out shorts watched—ribcages showing on all five of them.

Looking outside at the abject poverty Swami Rangaraj said, "I understand why you are so determined to raise money."

"This is why I've asked for your help."

The Swami continued to gaze at the passing scene.

"Bengal was prosperous before Independence," Chetti told him. "People used to call this state Golden Bengal. They haven't recovered from Partition and the influx of refugees from East Bengal."

"I have an answer to your question," Swami Rangaraj suddenly said, turning to Chetti, "but we'll talk when we are alone." He shifted his glance to the outside.

Chetti nodded in agreement. His face did not reveal the pleasure he felt at this news.

In the faint light of street lamps, they saw placards on the walls with pictures of orange-robed Swami Rangaraj next to movie posters.

After Swami Rangaraj's lecture in the big central park in Calcutta, Chetti took him to Dakhshineswar. "So what do you think of the response by the people?" he inquired after they were settled in a tent near the famous banyan tree.

"I never dreamed it would be so enthusiastic. People are really crying for a spiritual basis for their lives."

"In Bengal they vote for the Communist Party, but they want the Hindu religion to be the foundation of their lives. What a paradox! But fascinating!" After a moment Chetti commanded, "Now tell me about the gold in Gangotri temple."

The expression of glory that was there a moment before suddenly dimmed on Swami Rangaraj's face. "I was going to tell you earlier," he quickly answered, "but preparations for these talks distracted me. The temple has gold in a secret room one can access only from the inside."

"Aha! Then, what I've heard is true?"

"Yes. I got this from a very reliable source."

"How much is there?"

"A huge amount, but I haven't seen it."

"Why not? Aren't you also a guardian of the temple?" The irritation in Chetti's voice came through clearly.

"I don't have the key to the secret chamber."

"Even the most renowned priest in the temple doesn't have access to its treasure! That's a shame. Why would one hide this from you?"

"The head priest has the only key; it is passed down to the next head priest."

Swami Rangaraj's face darkened; he felt uncomfortable with the interrogation.

"Don't you think it strange? Keeping this secret from you?"

"You have a point," Swami Rangaraj said slowly, and looked down at his feet.

"Swami Narayan is quite old," Chetti softened his tone and continued, "If he dies suddenly, then all the gold that had been donated through the ages could be lost."

Swami Rangaraj nodded in agreement. He had raised the same question with Swami Narayan, who had firmly refused him. Swami Narayan's terse words echoed in his ears: "You don't worry about that."

"And you know how desperate we are for a little money!" Chetti's voice admonished Swami Rangaraj.

"Oh! Swami Narayan told me another thing." Swami Rangaraj suddenly perked up and blurted out. "Ten pairs of digits have a clue to the secret chamber."

Chetti kept his gaze on him like a hypnotist.

"01 35 18." Swami Rangaraj stopped and looked blankly at Chetti. "I thought I had memorized the numbers well."

"Relax. It'll come to you."

"Swami Rangaraj closed his eyes for a few seconds and sat very still. "Oh yes," he murmured. "01 35 18 02 25 27 03 15 04 59. I got it." His face eased. "Swami Narayan said when one figures out these numbers, the second and the third odd numbers will give another clue. I guess it's a riddle."

Chetti's eyes glinted. Those were the same numbers in the old palm leaf manuscript. "This is difficult mathematics for us," he said. "You must find out more about the key."

The thought of asking Swami Narayan about the key put a damper on Swami Rangaraj's spirit. "When I return in May, I'll do that," he told Chetti.

"We may have no choice but to beg for some of that gold. See if you can estimate the amount. I think it is huge. A little of this could help us out greatly."

Swami Rangaraj's face turned grim.

"I'm not asking you to steal the gold." Chetti chuckled. "I only want your help in figuring out if this is an option for us. Then we can determine how to approach the temple for a donation."

"Oh, I see."

"Listen, when you find the key, please do not make a big deal about it." Chetti stared at him for a couple of seconds and then said, "You are a monk. You won't be able to estimate what is there. I'll send a man to you. His name is

Ajit Boka. Take him with you when you go to examine the treasure."

Swami Rangaraj got a little frightened, thinking of Swami Narayan. His face shrank, he looked down at the ground. How could he ask again to see the treasure? And if Swami Narayan agreed to show him the treasure in the cave, how could he take Ajit Boka with him? Finally, Swami Rangaraj said in a feeble voice, "I shall find a way. Mr. Boka must be a very trusted man."

"Absolutely. You must have faith in me." Chetti's tone had a tinge of rebuke.

"Please forgive me if I have said something wrong," Swami Rangaraj said. "I shall do what you ask of me. I know all your work is dedicated to the people of India, not for personal gain."

"Thank you. Mr. Boka will meet you when the temple opens. You will recognize him easily because he is a different sort of a man; you may call him an existentialist. Don't expect him to attend your pujas. He doesn't talk much, but if you get to know him, you will find him a genuine person. He is tall and thin, and often wears sunglasses. In the meantime, I shall make inquiries about your tour to America."

"Thank you. I'll find a way to learn more about the key."

"Please. Time is short for us."

Chetti left him for the night. He was happy. His plans were coming along slowly, but they were on the right track.

7.4

Winter came and passed and the snow started to melt in Gangotri. Soon it was time to open the temple again, and the deities would have to be brought up from their winter abode in Mukhba—a routine that has gone on for centuries.

The whole village of Mukhba was a swirl of noise and color for the annual festival celebrating Goddess Ganga's journey to Gangotri, which took place each year in the first week of May. Starting from early morning, drums had been beating, and several small processions with palanquins had come to Mukhba from nearby villages, carrying their deities and beating their separate drums. These deities would accompany Goddess Ganga to her summer abode in Gangotri. The village reverberated with drums, metal gongs, and conch shells. The villagers decked out in vivid clothes, looked gay in the chilly May weather.

The small procession, headed by Swami Narayan and Swami Rangaraj in a shiny black Maruti, labored up the steep winding road toward Gangotri. Those who didn't plan to follow them lined up on both sides of the road to watch the procession and their favorite monks in ocher robes: Swami Narayan with his thin, white hair and Swami Rangaraj with thick, black hair. Their car, moving in a slow, stately fashion, was decorated with flowers and draped in ocher and orange cloth. The deities of the Gangotri temple were carried on a grand palanquin by a procession of local priests who followed the car. Many walked behind the palanquin and the processions from lesser villages brought up the rear. All together they formed a joyous, multicolored snake that slithered its way up the hairpin turns of the mountain road.

As they reached higher elevations, white snow covered some of the road and all of the embankments. Sunlight glinted from the white crystal snowflakes that dusted the deodar cedars and other conifers. Swami Rangaraj gazed around in renewed awe and wonderment at the natural beauty of the place. The azure sky shone with happy blessings for the journey.

When the colorful procession reached the courtyard of the Gangotri temple, Swami Narayan ceremonially opened the temple door, saying a few mantras, and the local priests brought the palanquin to the courtyard in front of the temple. Swami Narayan and Swami Rangaraj sprinkled sacred water from the Ganges River on the steps and on the path leading to the altar. Then they carried the deities inside. They performed a small worship service and distributed a prasad of blessed sweets to the people.

Villagers from lower elevations had a huge picnic, sharing food they had brought with them. They sang devotional songs, filling the formerly silent mountain valley with life, and danced at the close of their time-honored ritual. The arduous climb didn't dampen anyone's spirit. Zealous devotees went to the ice-cold water of the Ganges River and took a dip.

On the second day Swami Rangaraj walked about a hundred yards uphill from the temple and stood near the confluence of the Kedar Ganga, a white water stream, and the Bhagirathi River that flowed below the temple. For almost seven months he had missed this place. He sat down on a rock and closed his eyes; the sound of the water surrounded him. The muddy waters of the wide river in Dakhshineswar came to his mind. So different from this ice melt water! He remembered how people in Calcutta had brought a mountain of flowers for him, filling their car. Finally, when Chetti had left him for the night, he sat on the bank of the Ganges River and floated flowers on the water for the goddess. He was elated because of the success of his talk, his acceptance by the people, and his joy at being able to meditate under the banyan tree, the place of the great sage Ramakrishna.

That night in Calcutta he also contemplated his life before taking on the ocher robes of a monk: how in his youth he had walked out of his family home in the darkness of night, leaving his parents and brothers and sisters. His parents were certainly dead by now and he didn't know how his siblings were. As a monk, he had no attachments and never cried to see them. His blood relatives were no different from all the other people in the world. He was a sanyasi.

He opened his eyes and observed the water going downstream. Now he would go to America and preach the essence of the Vedas to the whole world. Perhaps this was his calling in life. Chetti was a karma yogi—one who accumulated merit by good deeds—certainly, a man of action. People like him were needed all over the world. Chetti would help him. He should also help Chetti. He wanted to know how much gold was hidden in the temple. The monk's lips moved in a silent chuckle. What is gold? Only a metal! But very important to Chetti's cause. It seemed to him perhaps Chetti had a point. What good was the gold lying in the temple?

Swami Narayan's voice startled him. "The best time to be here!"

Swami Rangaraj hadn't realized Swami Narayan had been standing behind him for a while.

"Yes."

"Did you have a good summer?"

"My lectures went very well. I've met people all over the country. They are starving for spiritual knowledge."

"Were you only in the cities?"

"Yes."

"Go to the villages some day; the villagers love God with their hearts rather than their heads."

"I've seen so much poverty and suffering this year."

"Yes. Help them as much as you can. Now come, let us finish setting up the altar." Swami Narayan turned toward the temple.

The two swamis opened the baskets from Mukhba, found the decorations for the altar, and soon the deities stood looking down at them, gorgeously decorated. The statue of Goddess Ganga was at the center of several hand-carved statues. She emanated the exquisite qualities of feminine beauty; her crown was made of gold and shone brightly in the springtime light. Next to her were three other goddesses—Annapurna, Shiva's wife and mother Goddess of the world, and her daughters Lakshmi, the Goddess of Wealth, and Saraswati, the Goddess of Learning and Music, all dressed in colorful silk saris and gold necklaces. There was also a statue of King Bhagirath, who brought the Goddess Ganga down from heaven to earth.

Swami Narayan stepped back and examined the deities from a distance, especially Mother Ganga, and put another small garland around her neck. Swami Rangaraj observed him. Swami Narayan had such devotion! Swami Narayan examined the altar from different angles. When he was finally satisfied, he took out something from his shirt pocket and placed it under goddess Ganga's statue. He then put his palms together in prayer. Swami Rangaraj looked at Swami Narayan with great curiosity, wishing that he would explain what he put there, but Swami Narayan simply smiled and walked out, saying, "Mother is back in her place now. Please close the gate when you leave."

Swami Rangaraj stood in his place, gazing at the goddess. What had Swami Narayan put under the Goddess that completed the altar? He sat down in front of the deities to meditate. Half an hour passed by, but he could not calm his mind. He drifted back to the image of Swami Narayan's hand tilting the goddess and his other hand putting something under her. "Mother is back in her place now."

"Why didn't he tell me anything about it?"

Swami Rangaraj lifted the goddess. A good-sized key lay on the altar. Jolted, as if he had received an electric shock, he leaned back. This was the secret key! No one could suspect it there, and no one would have the courage to touch the deity on the sacred altar. He suddenly realized that if anything happened to Swami Narayan, the new head priest would find the key. The temple gold would not be lost.

8

Ajit's Plan

8.1

Ajit drove to Gangotri a week after the temple opened. He stepped out of his car and breathed the clean air. It was still cold in early May. The familiar sound of the river echoed from the gorge and reminded him of his time there last summer. He had searched hard to find the secret gold chamber but never found any evidence of it. Hopefully this time the work would be successful. He would contact Swami Rangaraj at an opportune time. He would also make accurate records of the monks' comings and goings and devise a plan to take the gold out. He locked the car and walked toward Subodh's house. He had befriended Subodh the previous summer, the owner and caretaker of the Koushik Dharmashala, and agreed to help him open the place in the spring. He had told Subodh this would force him to come early and enjoy the serenity of the place before the pilgrims and the hikers arrived.

Subodh—short, chubby, jolly—greeted Ajit warmly. "You are a man of your word," Subodh said.

The two started to clean the eight guest rooms in the dharmashala building and as they worked, Subodh told him how the dharmashala came into being.

His great-grandfather had a dream in which he went on a hike high up in the mountains. In this dream, he trudged through the snow toward the roof of a small structure. It took him a long time and, when he reached the place, the sun was on the horizon. The structure was tiny, not big enough for a man to stand up or even sit in comfortably, and there was a statue of Ganesh inside. As the sun was setting, Subodh's great-grandfather began to shiver. He realized it was too late to hike down the mountain, and he looked for a place to stay. He couldn't find shelter and thought he would surely die. Then a tall, thin, beggar-like man wearing torn clothes called to him. He followed the man to a hole under a huge, house-sized rock, which was covered with dry branches and brush. The man moved a log so they could enter the cavern-like room. Subodh's great-grandfather didn't understand a word the man said, but he was happy he had been given shelter and saved from freezing to death. He awoke from the dream, still overwhelmed by the man's generosity, and pondered its meaning.

"Many thoughts went through my great-grandfather's mind," Subodh said, "the important one being: what would have happened if the man hadn't given him shelter. The next year he went to Gangotri and built the dharmashala, a place where pilgrims can stay without paying."

"So you come here every year to serve the pilgrims," Ajit said, looking at Subodh's youthful face.

Subodh nodded. "We have done this for four generations. When I was young, I looked forward to the trip up here for play and fun; now it is my responsibility." He opened the windows of one room. Fresh cool air breezed in.

"You can't earn money during the summer months then. How do you survive?" There was genuine concern in Ajit's voice.

"Other family members look after our business when I come here. The dharmashala is run by donations from the guests and from our family members. That keeps us going."

"You know this area quite well then?"

"Yes," Subodh said, smiling broadly. "I've been coming here since childhood—I know every nook and cranny of this place."

"The pilgrims are ordinary people," Ajit said, starting to sweep the floor with a broom. "They cannot pay much to the temple. Doesn't it cost a lot to run?"

"You'll be surprised to know how generously the pilgrims donate. All the surrounding land also belongs to the temple."

"Is that enough?"

"I don't know," Subodh looked at Ajit, "but I've never heard of this temple having financial problems."

"They must have a secret source somewhere."

"People say the temple has gold hidden inside."

"Gold?" Ajit looked at him, pretending to be surprised. "Where would they keep it? The temple is so small."

"No one knows. My grandfather said there is a chamber under the black stone, the Shaligram Shila, but who knows? Nobody comes here to look for gold!"

Ajit glanced at Subodh. He was there for the gold, but he had to remain discreet. "The priests must know," he said.

"I've no idea." Subodh bent down and pulled the wooden platform bed to the middle of the room. Pilgrims brought their own bedrolls.

"People give money to the temple," Ajit said after finishing the floor, "but I want to have a feast for the pilgrims. Can that be done?"

"Certainly. One or two of the wealthier pilgrims do that each year. We can bring cooks from a nearby town. You decide the menu. How elaborate do you want it to be?"

"Very simple. Khichuri, fried vegetables, chutney, papad, and a sweet."

"We can handle that easily." Subodh was pleased with Ajit's intent.

"When I come back," Ajit said, "I'll bring rice, lentils, and cooking oil from Delhi."

"It'll be a pleasure to help you."

"Can we feed people from 10 in the morning?"

"Just after the morning Aarti? That's a good idea. I'm sure Swami Narayan would like that and will bless the food."

"You advise me about what to do." Ajit's mind raced with the thought that the feast would keep the attention of people away from his activities. "When do most people come here?" he asked.

"The crowds start in mid-June."

After the rooms were cleaned and made ready for guests, Subodh asked, "Why don't you stay here?"

"Sorry, I've already made arrangements." Ajit looked at Subodh's innocent face. He didn't want anyone in Gangotri to get to know him too well. He certainly didn't want this sweet-natured man to know that, unlike him, he had no belief in a supernatural being like God. "I'll see you later," he told Subodh and quickly left. He decided not to visit him again until he needed him for the feast.

8.2

A week passed in Gangotri. Ajit didn't participate in any temple activities. He had seen Swami Rangaraj on the steps leading down to the Ganges River, but didn't attempt to introduce himself. He didn't want to rush him.

The political problems of the country and the sufferings of the poor did not cross his mind during these days. His object was getting some gold for Chetti; the SMS could do the rest. He had time and, while he developed the details of his plan for the gold heist, he explored the trails above the temple.

Often, he spent time on the banks of the river, observing how the remnants of snow on top of the boulders slowly melted away. The free time also allowed him to think about his own life. His parents were dead; he had not visited Agra for quite some time and had not made much attempt to be acquainted with his nephews and nieces who lived there. They admired him for his accomplishments, but he didn't really know them. He was working to uplift the lives of ordinary people while making no effort to connect with his own larger family. He'd like to rectify that. He'd visit his family when this job was done.

Agra also brought memories of his early youth; how alone and freely he used to roam around the town. He remembered his days at St. John's College and his math professor, a Christian, who had helped Ajit develop his beliefs. The professor taught him that human beings have an absurd existence. Ajit was not alone; many suffer from unanswered questions. The universe does not care for anyone. A man is forgotten within a few years of his death. The only way to reconcile living is to accept the fact that we are here—nothing we have done made it happen. There is no higher authority and no one to guide him. So we have to make all our decisions in a conscious way and bear the consequences. At the same time, it is a wonderful challenge to make the right decisions. This was an un-Hindu line of logic (and also un-Christian), but Ajit liked it. Life is not predetermined and we do not beg a superpower for our destiny because, even if there was one, He or She does not seem to be listening; otherwise how could there be so much pain in this world? He became a free thinker and a devotee of the idea of karma. By the time Ajit graduated from college, he was no longer a believer of the religion he was born into, but he had not been converted to any other religion either. He became an existentialist and a karma yogi—someone who believes in good deeds without expecting something in return.

During this time, Ajit also thought of his wife and how little time he had spent with her in the last several years. He loved her but his work had always taken precedence. He couldn't remember anything he had done with her recently outside the house. He felt sorry that he had not gone to a movie with her for quite some time, something that she used to enjoy very much. After this job was finished, he decided, he would not take up any more serious assignments. He had done enough in his life! Hindu scriptures declare that a time comes for a man to give up the hankerings of the householder's life and go on Vanaprashta, to dwell in the forest. In ancient times, that was one way to distance oneself from the material world. Fifty was considered a good age for Vanaprashta. Good advice, even if he wasn't religious. Was this his time then?

Two weeks after he arrived in Gangotri, Ajit saw Swami Rangaraj dipping a brass pot into the river, the monk's ocher clothes glowing in the morning sun. This time he went to him.

"Namaste!" Ajit greeted the monk. "I wanted to introduce myself earlier, but I didn't get an opportunity. I am Ajit Boka. Mr. Chetti has asked me to get in touch with you."

"Namaste!" The monk's eyes took in Ajit nervously. "Mr. Chetti told me about you too. I'm glad to meet you," he said faintly.

"I'm here to help you in any way I can."

Swami Rangaraj's face became stiff and he stared at the flowing water for a few moments. "I know where the key is," he told Ajit in a feeble voice.

"Excellent!" Ajit exclaimed and immediately restrained himself.

"I cannot do anything now," Swami Rangaraj said. "I have to sort things out. I've also agreed to attend a meeting in New Delhi. Let us consider what to do after the meeting." He looked at Ajit for a moment. "Would mid-June be a good time for you?"

"Whatever you say Swamiji. I am at your service." Ajit paused for a second. "We both work for the same cause, the welfare of the people. I shall return then in mid-June."

"Yes. That would be a good time."

Swami Rangaraj quickly turned and walked toward the temple.

Ajit's heart lifted, as if a great weight had been thrown aside. He finally had hope that he could finish this job soon and go away to live his life differently.

Ajit immediately left Gangotri. Being a man of action, his brain raced over the details of what needed to be done. He forgot his earlier thoughts of Vanaprashta. Not many buses and cars were on the road, as the pilgrims had not started to arrive yet. Unconsciously, his foot pushed the accelerator to speed up. He wanted to reach home as soon as possible.

8.3

Lajjorani was happy to see her husband return early. Ajit was cheerful and told her he finally knew what was to be done for the Gangotri project. "One more trip, and then this job is over."

"You never tell me what you do on these special missions," she said. "You're not with the ADS anymore. Don't take any risks."

"I won't." He gazed at her for a few moments. She looked like the same young woman he had married years before. She had gained a little weight, but wasn't that normal for all women? "I missed life at home," he told her. "It's time I settle down." He went into his study and started to search through the boxes stored on the shelves.

"My school will close May 30th," she told him, standing near the door.

"Good." Ajit said without looking at her. His mind was suddenly preoccupied.

"You just returned!" Her voice expressed disappointment.

He turned back to his wife. "I'm sorry, dear. Let's have tea together." He came out of his study. "This job has kept my mind going. You'll be happy to know I had time on my hands in Gangotri and I thought about us."

"Really? What did you think?"

"We're getting old; we should spend more time together." He looked at her lovingly. "As soon as this project is over, we will take a vacation."

"That would be nice." She looked into her husband's eyes. Ajit had never proposed a vacation on his own. Perhaps the lofty Himalayas had an effect on him.

"I won't have to work like this anymore. In July, okay?"

"Wonderful. I'll go and make tea." He'll probably get involved in another project, she thought, but she liked that he was thinking about growing old together.

Ajit didn't go back to his study. When Lajjorani brought tea, he was paging through the family album in the drawing room.

"I put the pictures together last year," she told him, "when you were away. You like it?"

"Yes, very much. They bring back lots of memories."

She gave him a cup of tea and sat next to him. They sipped tea and looked through the pictures.

"It's nice just to sit together," Ajit said after a while.
"If you're around, we can have tea every afternoon."
"Soon. It'll happen soon." He squeezed her hand.

9

Jagdish on the Pilgrimage Trail

9.1

J agdish was happy and nervous at the same time. At dawn when birds still chirped in the trees, he walked to Hanumanji's temple. Today he would start his journey to Haridwar—a place far away from his little village of Sitamarhi. He thought of his father who had longed to go there, but couldn't. He entered the temple and stood before Hanumanji's image. He prayed for a long time. He prayed that his family would be safe while he was away, that no one would get sick and no calamity would come upon them. Then he prayed that his journey would be successful and he would return home safe. He walked around the temple three times with folded hands.

When Jagdish returned home, he gathered his luggage: two dhotis, two shirts, a chador to cover his upper body in cool weather, a sataranchi, which he could spread on the floor to sleep, his brass pot for drinking water, chewing tobacco, and a few other minor items.

Sukhi had prepared a good amount of food for his journey—roti, paratha, and dry vegetable curry; she had cooked his favorite sweet the day before— laddu. She quietly brought these to him, along with homemade mango and jackfruit pickles; she watched him pack without saying a word. Jagdish put everything on top of a folded cotton sheet and tied them up.

"Shall I give you some gur?" she asked, knowing how much he loved the brown, unrefined sugar.

"No. I can buy gur in Haridwar," he said without looking at her.

When the sun rose above the trees, Gopal showed up in an ox-cart.

"What is that for?" Jagdish asked him.

"How many have gone from our village to Gangotri?" Gopal replied. "You should start the pilgrimage properly."

Gopal gave him a gold necklace in a small bag, a letter for Swami Narayan, and some cash. "I'm so pleased you will meet my Guru."

Jagdish tied the necklace into the waistband of his dhoti to keep it safe.

"You have a long train ride," Gopal told him, "twenty-three hours. So get a seat as soon as you board. When you reach Delhi, ask someone for the bus to Haridwar."

Jagdish had heard all this advice before, but only as hearsay; no one they knew had gone so far. He wished he wasn't going alone on this trip.

His son, daughter-in-law, and two grandchildren touched his feet one at a time and embraced him.

"You all stay well and take care of everything," he said, but his voice choked and he took a step toward the ox-cart.

Tears came to Sukhi's eyes. "He has never gone so far from here!" she wailed. "Such a distance away!"

"Everyone will help you, Sukhi," he told his wife, "don't worry about me. I shall be back in a month."

Tears ran down Sukhi's cheeks. Their son and daughter-in-law supported her on two sides. "Everything will be fine, Ma," they assured her. But she would not be consoled. She covered her face with her sari to hide her tears. "Hanumanji, please protect my husband," she prayed over and over again.

Gopal whipped the two oxen. He was happy for Jagdish. Perhaps someday he would also go on such a pilgrimage.

The dirt road took Jagdish and Gopal through a mile and a half of bullock cart grooves and potholes to the town. There was a normal up-and-down rhythm to the journey. They passed farmland, banana groves and large mango and jackfruit trees. Straw and mud houses appeared here and there; women were out doing their daily chores—pounding spices, doing laundry, making cow dung patties. Men were working in the fields. Jagdish silently gazed at the familiar scenes. A melancholy feeling came over him. He remembered how he and Gopal had run around these fields playing hide and seek when they were children. Once he lay quietly under a large peepal tree to hide from other boys and a cobra passed by him. He stayed frozen until the snake slithered out of sight—then how he had screamed when the snake was gone!

"The bus will take you to Muzaffarpur in two hours," Gopal told him. "Then you go to the train station. It's right there. And wait for the express train."

Jagdish nodded.

He hadn't slept well for two nights, anticipating and dreading the journey. He had heard of cheats and crooks in railway stations, in the big cities, and even in holy towns. What if his things were stolen? What if he lost his money? How would he return home? What about diseases? A farmer from Riga and his wife had gone to Haridwar a decade before, but the wife came back alone; her husband had died of severe dysentery. Their story had frightened many. It would be very sad, he thought, to die far away from Sitamarhi. No one in his family—not his father, mother, or grandparents—had ever left the area. All had

Jagdish's pilgrimage trail

died in Sitamarhi. He did not wish to die in a strange land.

"Always keep the necklace and the cash with you," Gopal said, "tied in your dhoti at your waist."

"Yes. You have told me this before."

"Remember, my Guruji Swami Narayan meets with his disciples in the evening. Don't miss this. Ask him any question you have. He has all the answers."

"Sure," Jagdish said, but his eyes were glued to the old bridge on the narrowest part of the river. He had seen it being constructed; he had jumped into the water many times from the bridge. The bricks and mortar were falling apart now, and the steel girders could be seen in many places. Beginning in his tenth year, he had joined other young boys herding cows and buffalos to the river on warm days. They played in the river water, washing the cattle, chasing each other, splashing, laughing, swimming, and returning home in the evening. Would he be able to return to these familiar sights? He gazed at the fast flowing water.

When they reached the bus depot, Gopal bought a ticket for Jagdish and helped him put his bundle on top of the bus. The bus had seen better days, but fresh paint and colorful movie posters on both sides made it look up-to-date.

Gopal wished him a good journey and nudged him forward.

"Raam, Raam," Jagdish said under his breath, as he climbed in. He found a seat at the back of the bus. He fingered the chain of the silver locket that his son had given him. The sacred sign of Om was embossed on one side and his name on the other: Jagdish Lohar, Sitamarhi, Bihar.

"I've never given you anything, Bauji," Praan had said. "You sold all of mother's silver jewelry and anything else you had to buy land. Please wear this on the pilgrimage. We had it blessed in the Janaki temple."

He couldn't refuse.

9.2

Jagdish reached Muzaffarpur train station three hours before his train, the Guwahati-Delhi Express, was due.

"No reserved seats available," the man at the ticket counter told him. "But I got the cheapest fare for you."

Jagdish paid and asked the man, "Where will the train come?"

"Platform three; go over the bridge to the next platform."

Corrugated tin sheds covered four platforms. The heat of the tropical sun made the air shimmer above the rails between platforms.

Jagdish stared at the station clock for a few seconds. Sweat ran down his back. He wiped a few drops from his forehead and adjusted the cloth that was wrapped turban-like on his head. He lifted his bundle onto his head and walked to the bridge over the rails. He decided to stay on the platform until his train came.

Four trains came and left while he sat there. The station got very busy just before and after their arrivals. Then it was empty again; only the coolies and the few vendors remained there in the hot air. Soon the time for his train came and people started to gather on the platform.

A man with a small suitcase asked Jagdish, "Is the express train to Delhi coming?"

Jagdish nodded.

The man went away and came back after a minute. "Yes. This is the right place. It will come in ten minutes. How far are you going?"

"Delhi."

"That's the last station. I get off at Lucknow, early in the morning. You'll ride ten more hours." He looked at Jagdish's clothes for a few seconds. "Your first long journey?"   "Yes."

"The train journey will spoil your new clothes. Put on old clothes after you settle in the compartment."

"Thank you." Jagdish was uncomfortable in his new clothes, but how could he have started on the pilgrimage wearing old clothes?

"Don't worry now," the man told him, looking him over. Jagdish appeared to be a village laborer. "What's your name?"

"Jagdish, Jagdish Lohar."

"My name is Lakshmi Prasad. I've traveled many times on this train."

"I've never gone far before. Could you help me on the train?" Jagdish pleaded.

Lakshmi Prasad felt sympathy for Jagdish, a man going alone out of his village for the first time. "I will help you," he promised him.

"I'll appreciate that very much."

"Visiting a relative?"

"No. No." Jagdish shook his head. "I'm going to Haridwar."

"You're going on a pilgrimage?"

"Yes."

"The train is coming. Get ready and follow me."

The express train arrived with loud chuffing noises and people rushed to the doors even before it had stopped. Lakshmi Prasad guided Jagdish toward the end of the train, and while passengers were still exiting, they pushed themselves inside a compartment. It was fortunate that their luggage was small. But sadly, in spite of their speedy entrance, no seat was available.

The train had started from Assam, a long distance away, and picked up passengers along the way. The whole car was full. They stood in a small, cramped space between seats. "I didn't plan this trip earlier, so couldn't get a reserved seat," Lakshmi Prasad told Jagdish.

The commotion created by the new passengers subsided when the train started; everyone accepted their position and relaxed. A few squatted on the floor, which was filthy with dust and trash—food packages, cigarette buts, peanut shells, and spilled food and drinks. Those who had no seats, and that number was not small, stared at those who had seats, envied their happy situation, and occasionally looked outside at the scenery.

The compartment was hot. Air blowing in through the open windows cooled them a little.

A man coughed heavily and spat on the floor near where Lakshmi Prasad stood.

"Why did you spit on the floor?" Lakshmi Prasad scolded him, very irritated. "Don't you have any sense?"

The man looked at him sheepishly and then said apologetically, "What can I do, Babu Sahib? I am a poor man."

Lakshmi Prasad was disgusted at his logic. "I am a poor man so I can ignore hygiene and do whatever I wish!" he said in a mocking tone. Annoyed, he looked away through the window. Outside, the brown, dry land passed by.

"I need to go to the bathroom," Jagdish whispered to Lakshmi Prasad, "I haven't peed since I left Sitamarhi. Could you watch my bundle?"

"Certainly."

Jagdish pushed his way through people and luggage on the floor, and as he reached the toilet near the end of the car, he saw the space was almost blocked by a huge pile of luggage. Stepping over those, he rotated the handle and pushed himself in. Oh, someone had soiled the floor; the room stank. He wanted to leave but he had waited too long. He held his nose in one hand and put his feet on the two wet steps on each side of a hole on the floor. He could see dark stones through the hole between the rails. The motion of the train made him fearful that he would fall through the hole. He quickly finished and rushed out.

"It was awful," he told Lakshmi Prasad. "Worse than anything I've ever seen in my village."

"I know." Lakshmi Prasad looked at Jagdish and asked, "Can you go to Delhi like this—standing for twenty-three hours? I've an idea how to find some seats. I'm going to see to it. Can you afford a hundred rupees for a reserved seat?"

"So much money!" Jagdish muttered.

"Delhi is a long way, man. Tell me because I'm going now."

Jagdish felt Lakshmi Prasad was not trying to cheat him. "If you think I should spend that much money, please go ahead."

"Hold my suitcase and give me 100 rupees. I'll see if I can do something."

He took the money and went away along the narrow corridor.

Lakshmi Prasad returned after a long time. He whispered to Jagdish, "We have two seats in the next compartment, but they are occupied now. When the train reaches Sonpur in one more hour, we will get them." His eyes shone with pleasure.

"How did you do it?"

"I know how the system works." He winked with a happy smile. "Oh! Here, twenty-five rupees. I bargained the price down to seventy-five."

9.3

Before the train came to Sonpur, Lakshmi Prasad signaled Jagdish, and the two maneuvered their way to the reserved compartment. Jagdish couldn't believe his eyes: everyone had a place to sit, and all were decently dressed. Lakshmi Prasad went to the middle of the room and stood near a couple who were busily collecting their baggage. Lakshmi Prasad put his suitcase on the top rack and called Jagdish to do the same.

Jagdish got a seat near the window. Two passengers sat to his right and three in front of him. After the train picked up speed, Lakshmi Prasad introduced himself. A Bengali couple shared the seat with Jagdish and two men from Assam and Benaras sat across from him, next to Lakshmi Prasad.

"This is Jagdish," Lakshmi Prasad told them, pointing toward him. "He is going to Haridwar and then to Gangotri."

All the eyes shifted to Jagdish and looked at his leathery, weather-worn face. "I hope Lord Rama will allow me to see these places," Jagdish blurted out. "I've never gone this far before."

The older Bengali woman, Mrs. Mukherjee, said, "Very nice. How long will you stay?"

"I don't know. Perhaps a month." Jagdish folded his hands up in a prayer to God.

Mrs. Mukherjee turned her head and spoke to her husband, "Some day you should take me to Haridwar."

"Perhaps Bulu will take us in his car if you ask," Mr. Mukherjee told his wife, and opened the India Times. Pictures of the U.S. Secretaries of Commerce and Energy were on the cover; they would come to visit India. "Relations with the U.S. are improving," he mumbled to himself.

When darkness fell and nothing could be seen outside, passengers took out their food and started to eat. Jagdish opened his bundle and took out parathas and the vegetable sabji. He gave some to Lakshmi Prasad who at first said, "No, no," but eventually took one paratha. Jagdish offered some to the others, but they politely refused.

"Where do we get water to drink?" Jagdish asked Lakshmi Prasad.

"I forgot to get a bottle." Helplessly Lakshmi Prasad looked around.

Mr. Goswami, the man from Assam, offered a bottle of Bistlery water.

Both of them drank some in the Indian way—pouring into their mouths, lips not touching the bottle.

When everyone finished eating, Jagdish opened a bag and said, "Please have a laddu. My wife made these."

This time they couldn't refuse and somewhat reluctantly each took one of the golden-colored sweets. They held them in their hands and watched Jagdish eat one. Then they took a bite and were immediately pleased with the taste. "Excellent," Mr. Goswami said after the first bite. "They really know how to make these in the villages!"

"Excellent," everyone chimed in.

Jagdish shyly said, "Sukhi made these with homemade ghee. Please have another."

"No, no. Not any more now," Mr. Mukherjee said. "I have diabetes and must be careful. Perhaps tomorrow morning … if any are left."

The laddus helped to make the atmosphere congenial. The middle-aged man from Benaras, Mr. Gupta, who was graying at the temples, said, "I haven't had such good laddus for a long time. My mother used to make them, but that was a long time back."

"We have a cow," Jagdish said, "that gives us all the milk and ghee we need."

"Since you will follow the sacred river," Mr. Gupta asked Jagdish, "will you go beyond Gangotri?"

"I thought the river started in Gangotri."

"No," Mr. Gupta said, shaking his head. "The Ganges River starts from Gaumukh. You have to hike though. There's no road beyond Gangotri."

"You are lucky to live in Benaras," Mrs. Mukherjee told Mr. Gupta, "the holiest of all holy cities, you can take a bath in Mother Ganga's water every day. That makes up for everything."

"That's what the scriptures say," Mr. Gupta said, "but I'd like to go to the source of the Ganges River some day."

Jagdish was astonished. These well-to-do people have not gone to the sacred places! He was doing something that these people wished they could.

"Bengalis like Benaras," Mr. Mukherjee said. "Before they die they would like to take a bath in the Ganges water in Benaras."

"Benaras is a funny city," Mr. Gupta said, "controlled by the Brahmin priests and the Muslims."

"Muslims. Really?" Mrs. Mukherjee expressed surprise and pulled her sari around her shoulder like a shawl.

"Who weaves those Benarasi saris and does all the beautiful zari works?" Mr. Gupta asked. "The Muslims!"

"I see what you mean."

"And you know," Mr. Gupta went on, "the Mughal emperors always wanted to control Benaras, the Hindu center. They built a mosque right next to the Shiva temple."

"Emperor Aurangajeb also wanted to rename Benaras after Allah," Mr. Mukherjee interjected.

Lakshmi Prasad stood up, saying he would take one of the top bunks. "I'll get off very early in Lucknow, before 6 am."

Jagdish took out his sataranchi and climbed to the other top bunk. He had forgotten Sitamarhi for a while; now lying in the upper berth Sukhi's sad face came to him, and he wondered what they were doing: how she would handle everything—their family, the house, the cow, the small farm, and how much she would worry about him. Then he thought of the people he had met on the train; he had never been so close to well-to-do people who knew a lot about the world. Then he thought that in some ways they weren't very different. Their wishes were also like his. They had traveled so much, but had not thought of taking the time to visit sacred places. How strange! The rhythmic movement and the monotonous sound of the wheels finally sent him off to sleep.

9.4

Dawn was breaking when the train pulled into Lucknow station, a big junction. "Good luck on your pilgrimage," Lakshmi Prasad told Jagdish and hurried away.

Many stepped down from the train to stretch and see what was around. Several hawkers bustled into the compartment, selling newspapers, magazines, sweets, snacks, and tea. With the noise and commotion inside and outside the train, everyone got up. Mr. Mukherjee ordered tea from a vendor through the open window of the compartment. The vendor poured creamy, brown tea in a small earthen cup.

"Just one?" the man asked, after handing him the cup

"Another," Mr. Mukherjee said and then looked at Jagdish. "No. Make two more."

Mr. Mukherjee gave one to his wife and handed a cup to Jagdish.

"For me?" Jagdish was taken aback. "No. No."

"This will help you wake up," Mr. Mukherjee forced the cup onto his hand.

"Bahut Shukriya," Jagdish said.

The three of them sipped warm, cardamom flavored tea. Then a Sikh with a light yellow turban appeared before them. "I have a reserved seat here."

"You have Lakshmi Prasad's seat," Mr. Mukherjee said, "You sit here." He pointed to the end of the seat.

"Thank you." He put his small suitcase on the rack and sat down.

Mr. Goswami came back, holding a packet made of old newspaper and beaming with joy. "Freshly fried samosas. We got plenty for all of us,"

"I got the famous Lucknow paan, if any of you are interested," Mr. Gupta said.

Mr. Goswami gave one samosa each to the Muherjees and Jagdish. Jagdish accepted the samosas with a good deal of hesitancy; he was not used to this kind of treatment by Babusahibs.

"Ah! Sardarji, have a samosa with us," Mr. Goswami gave one to the Sikh.

"Very nice of you. Thank you."

The train started again. They munched on their snacks, sipped tea, and watched the station go by. Mr. Mukherjee opened the morning newspaper. Jagdish gazed outside and saw city buildings thinning out and giving way to farmland.

After finishing the last samosa and crunching the paper bag into a small ball and throwing it under the seat, Mr. Goswami asked Mr. Mukherjee, "Anything new in today's paper?"

"Same old news. Only interesting item is about the Sarva Mangal Society."

"The SMS?"

"Yes. They have expanded their chapters both in numbers and regions. They now claim they have offices and programs in all towns with 50,000 or more people. They are getting involved with women's education and court cases to seek justice for the poor. They also want to raise elementary and high school education so Indian students can compete with the West."

"A lot of work," Mr. Gupta said.

"They had a big conference in Gandhinagar last year," Mr. Mukherjee said, "and this article is a follow up—lot of discussion of their problems."

"What problems?" Mr. Goswami asked. "The SMS seems to be doing the right things."

"The article says their eyes are too big. They don't have the resources to carry out the programs. They have spread themselves too thin. They desperately need funds."

"That would be sad," Mr. Gupta admitted. "They have good goals."

"Goals just don't cut it," Mr. Singh asserted. "You need resources to make them happen. Otherwise the SMS will end up being like any other organization. All talk, no action."

"Farmers don't like handouts," Jagdish suddenly blurted, "we want to work for a living, but we have no one to support us when a calamity strikes."

"Then the rich landlord buys your land and you become a laborer for him," Mr. Goswami added. "Right?"

Jagdish nodded, wondering how he knew this.

"Yes, SMS would flourish in places like Sitamarhi," Mr. Gupta said.

"Any other news in the paper?" Mrs. Mukherjee asked to change the subject from politics, which she despised.

"Here is some news for Jagdish," Mr. Mukherjee said. "Because of better bus service, more and more people are visiting the sacred temples in the Himalayas. Buses run from Haridwar, Rishikesh, and Dehra Dun to Gangotri." Mr. Mukherjee looked at Jagdish and said, "There is your journey, but it will take many hours."

"That is my plan," Jagdish said.

"As I remember, " Mr. Gupta said, "the buses to Haridwar leave in the morning—before our train reaches New Delhi."

"You have to find out when we reach there," Mr. Mukherjee told Jagdish.

Mr. Goswami looked at his watch. "Still five more hours. Anyone for a game of cards?"

No one took him up. After a brief pause he asked Jagdish, "How long have you been farming?"

Jagdish said, "I've done farm work since I was eight."

"Since eight?" Mr. Mukherjee asked.

"Farm boys start work at that age?" Mr. Goswami said.

"Didn't you know?" Mr. Gupta joined in. "That's when they start work in villages."

"What about the girls?" Mr. Mukherjee asked.

"Don't even bring that subject up," Mr. Gupta said. "It is horrible."

Mr. Goswami looked at Jagdish.

"Sitamarhi grows a lot of rice," Jagdish said. "Women and girls help by transplanting the young rice plants and weeding."

"Is that hard work?"

When no one said anything, Mrs. Mukherjee asked Mr. Goswami, "Haven't you ever weeded your garden?"

Mr. Goswami's face brightened. "I grow roses in Shillong. So beautiful!" Then, a wry smile came over his face. "I don't do the actual work, you know. We have a mali."

"Farmer women spend the whole day in the field," Mrs. Mukherjee informed him, "working in muddy soil with their hands—under the hot sun. Then they come home and cook for the family."

Jagdish was listening to the conversation and finally said in a low voice, "Women start when they get up and work until they go to bed."

"What about the girls?" Mr. Goswami asked.

"They follow their mothers from childhood," Jagdish said. "Where else will they go?"

"Except for doing work at home and in the fields, girls are not an asset in a village," Mr. Singh commented. "Think about it. Education of girls brings no return to the family and doesn't add to their marriage ability. Still the father has to find a dowry. A big headache."

"It's bad for people like us," Jagdish said as if talking to himself. "Everyone must work just to survive. If there's sickness or disaster, we are doomed. Men become bonded laborers. What else can they do? They have no land, no money, no education, and no skills."

No one said anything after this. Only the sound of the train wheels—jig, jig, jig, jig, jig, jig—prevailed for a while. Then Mr. Goswami and Mr. Gupta went to the dining car for lunch. The train passed by dry barren lands. Hot wind blew outside and the temperature rose inside the compartment.

"The restaurant is the best thing on this long journey," Mr. Goswami announced when they returned a little jubilant. "The vegetable chops are great," he told Mrs. Mukherjee.

Jagdish ate roti and sabji from his sack. After lunch he offered his laddus again and each took one.

"I shall remember your laddus," Mr. Mukherjee told Jagdish.

9.5

In late afternoon the Guwahati-Delhi Express arrived at its final stop in Delhi. Passengers gathered their belongings and stepped out on to the platform. Mr. and Mrs. Mukherjee, Mr. Gupta, Mr. Goswami, and Mr. Singh wished Jagdish good luck on his pilgrimage, and hurried away through the crowd.

Jagdish lifted his bundle onto his head and paused, astounded by the overwhelming sense of urgency that swirled around him—streams of rushing passengers, butting-in coolies, hand-pulled wooden luggage carts piled with suitcases and bundles of all sorts, and the noise of hundreds of voices. Announcements over loudspeakers baffled him; he couldn't understand a word. He had to find a way to the bus terminus, but he was dazed by the sheer enormity of the situation and stood on the side.

When the crowd thinned, he asked a porter wearing a red shirt, where the bus stand was. "Just go outside," the man told him and hurried by.

Jagdish shuffled apprehensively toward the gate, but before he reached the exit, he saw a man struggling on the floor near the wall. He recognized the man; he had been sitting near where he stood with Lakshmi Prasad when they first boarded the train in Muzaffarpur. What was the man doing? He seemed to be in some trouble. Jagdish quickly put down his luggage and knelt down next to him. The man looked odd. His mouth was dry, his eyes seemed smaller—somewhat drawn in and clouded—and he was stammering as he weakly attempted to lift his hands. He tried to say something, but Jagdish could not understand him. Jagdish lifted him up into a sitting position, but the fellow had no strength and slumped over sideways. He heard the man mumble 'sugar.' Did the man want something to eat? He quickly opened his bundle and pulled out a laddu and put a portion of it in the man's mouth. While the man worked at swallowing the sweet, Jagdish stood up and looked around for help. He waived his hand at a coolie, but another train came at that very instant, and his calls for help were drowned out in the commotion of arriving and departing passengers.

"Amritsar Express. It's late today," another coolie shouted as he dashed by.

In the noisy ruckus, Jagdish didn't know whom to call or where to go for assistance. He looked back at the man, who sat upright now, looking at Jagdish with clearer eyes. "Are you feeling better?" Jagdish asked him.

The man nodded.

"Want some water to drink?"

He nodded.

Jagdish took out his brass drinking pot from his bundle, filled it at a nearby fountain, and brought him water.

Soon the man stretched his legs. "Come," Jagdish told him, "I'll help you out of this station."

"Do you have more sweets?" the man asked in a feeble voice.

Jagdish fed him the last broken laddu he had. The man seemed to regain his strength after a few minutes. "Can you get up now?" Jagdish asked him.

"Yes," he replied, although his voice was faint.

Jagdish lifted him up, held him with his right arm, and balanced his own bundle on his head. He picked up the man's suitcase with his left hand. They came out of the gate, but the man staggered and sat down on the steps.

"I am diabetic," he told Jagdish, who stared at him without understanding. "I haven't eaten anything for a long time, so my body went into shock. I missed my medicine. Thank you for saving my life."

"It's our duty to help others. Do you want to eat something more?"

"Could you bring me a bottle of juice or soda—any sweet drink?"

Jagdish opened his bundle and gave him a paratha and some raw sugar from his bag. Then he went to a vendor and brought him a sweet drink, Fanta.

The man sipped the fizzy drink and seemed to revive a little more. "My name is Joshi," he told Jagdish. "I am from the Chhapra district."

"Jagdish from Sitamarhi."

"You are practically my neighbor! Where do you live in Delhi?"

"This is the first time I've been outside of Bihar. I'm going to Haridwar."

"Really?" He looked at Jagdish intently.

"I want to go to the bus station and take a bus to Haridwar."

Joshi kept on gazing at Jagdish. "I think the last bus to Haridwar has already left."

"Hai Bhagavan! Now I have to find a place to spend the night. Could I sleep on the platform?"

"The guards will ask you to leave."

"Is that true?"

"Certainly." He looked at Jagdish for a moment. "You come to our house."

"Are you sure?"

"Yes. Then you can take me home. I still don't feel well."

Jagdish stretched his hand, and Joshi leaned on him to stand up.

They stopped an auto-rickshaw. "Sadar Bazaar," Joshi told the driver, after they piled in.

The rickshaw driver took them by Chadni Chowk to Sadar Bazaar Street, beeping his horn constantly and shouting at pedestrians to move aside. Nevertheless, people got in the way. Somehow the driver managed to slither in between the cars and people.

"Gupta Lane," Joshi told the driver.

They went through a narrower road and stopped in front of a three-story brick house with stores on the first floor. An elderly woman came hurriedly down the front steps to meet Joshi. "You came by auto-rickshaw?"

"I had to. I got sick. This is Jagdish. He has saved my life. I invited him to stay with us tonight."

"Namaste," said the woman, glancing at Jagdish. He had not changed out of his new dhoti and shirt, now crumpled by the train journey.

"Namaste," said Jagdish.

"Please come in. I'm Joshi's mother."

They went up a narrow stairway to the second floor, and Jagdish saw they had two bedrooms and a common sitting room. A door led to a narrow balcony over the street where a coal brazier oven and a few cooking pots and pans were lined up on the floor. A sari and two blouses hung on a string above the balcony.

Joshi sank down on a stool and asked Jagdish to sit on the chair. Joshi's mother stood next to her son. Jagdish saw a picture of a temple on the wall. The picture had sandalwood paste marks on the glass cover and a garland of dried-out flowers draped around it.

When she heard what had happened at the Railway Station, Joshi's mother was very happy that Jagdish had brought her son home. "You are a God-send," she told Jagdish. "Please consider this your home."

She brought two glasses of cool water for them. She went to the balcony, took the clothes down, and started the fire to cook dinner. Dark blue smoke covered the balcony and some drifted into the sitting room.

Joshi's father and his elder brother came late in the evening, just when dinner was almost ready. They all greeted Jagdish and thanked him. The evening meal was simple: chapatti, vegetable sabji, and dahl made with mung beans. Jagdish shared his jackfruit pickle and everyone loved it.

"This is not available in Delhi," they said with regret.

Jagdish told them about Sitamarhi and his family.

"Today," Joshi's father said after dinner, "the big boss showed up suddenly, and he caught a man coming late. He scolded the man, threatening to fire him if this happened again. 'Discipline, we must have discipline at the factory,' he told everybody.'"

"The landowners also abuse the laborers in Sitamarhi," Jagdish told him.

"In the village you have homegrown food to survive," Joshi's father said, "but here if you lose your job, you have nothing. It's much worse."

Jagdish didn't say any more, but he understood that the situation was similar for workers—whether it was in a city factory or on a village farm. These people thought life was smooth in villages. What do they know of floods or diseases? He looked at the men and said, "Only God can save us."

The night was hot; Joshi, his parents and Jagdish went up to the roof to sleep. They took cots and mats to spread on the floor. Jagdish could see silhouettes of people moving on many roofs; faint indistinguishable conversations floated on the night air. He asked Joshi's family if they had gone to Haridwar and if they knew of a place he could stay.

Joshi's mother said, "Oh! I wish." Then after a few seconds, suddenly remembering, she said, "Kishore is in Haridwar. He works at Sadhana Dharmashala. He could take care of Jagdish!"

"Ah! Why didn't I think of that?" Joshi exclaimed. He turned to Jagdish. "You saw the picture in our sitting room? That's a picture of the Shiva temple in Haridwar. Kishore gave us the picture. I shall write him a letter in the morning. You can stay there free."

"That would be very good of you," Jagdish said.

The cotton mill factory siren woke everyone up in the morning. Joshi's father and mother rushed downstairs to get ready. Jagdish didn't have an urgent need to be ready so early, and thought it best if he stayed out of everyone's way. He saw roof after roof, as far as his eyes could see—off into the hazy distance. Several minarets also poked up through the plane of roofs. It was an amazing scene, all concrete, very different from the flat green scenery of Sitamarhi. Downstairs the women were busy making tea and toast for breakfast and chapattis and a vegetable curry for the men to take for lunch. By seven in the morning the two men were gone.

Then, with instructions from Joshi, Jagdish walked out of their apartment toward the interstate bus terminus.

"It's quite easy to go to Kishore's place in Haridwar," Joshi told him. "Take the road in front of the train station and go toward the river. When you reach the river, his place is on the right side of the road."

10

Seekers from America

10.1

Warm air, honking cars, beeping three-wheelers, multitudes of vehicles, and diesel fumes all swirled around Sovik, reminding him he was finally in India. Their previous stop, Singapore, was too westernized and too comfortable. In Singapore Pinky said, "We will come back here for a vacation." She sat next to her husband in the van from New Delhi's Indira Gandhi International Airport and took in the ambience of India. Their other companions Kayla and Be'ziil sat in the back.

"I've taken many courses on India, you know that," Pinky whispered to her husband, "religion, philosophy, social life, but they don't amount to much. I feel I'm in a country I know very little about."

He squeezed her hand affectionately, but didn't say anything.

The shuttle van moved steadily through the traffic toward the capital. Sovik looked outside to assess how much India had changed. The city was faintly lit and seemed to have sprawled far out into the surrounding countryside. Skyscrapers hadn't dominated the city's upper space when he left thirty years before, and lights from several tall cranes loomed over the skyline—that was a rare sight in 1964.

He looked at Kayla. She was his lab assistant's niece and had come along for a "fun" excursion, but India was an adventure, never really a vacation. It had taken him seven years to plan this trip; still so many questions remained unanswered. Hundreds of people visit India from the States every year, but he had not heard of anyone like him who, after undergoing bypass surgery, had done what he planned to do: go to the highest temple of the goddess Ganga and then hike to the glacier where the Ganges River originates.

What would Kayla find in such a place? He remembered the day his assistant had approached him to take Kayla along.

"She has a boyfriend, but she seems reluctant to marry," he told Sovik. "I don't understand it. She is already twenty-four—too old for a Mormon girl."

"I thought you people could fix marriages quite easily." Sovik said in a bantering tone. He knew Steve was a Bishop in the Mormon Church.

"She is different," he said and paused for a few moments. "She grew up in Blackfoot, and the young man is from Teton County—a good match, really. His grandfather came to the Teton Valley and cleared a large portion of land. They grow potatoes and alfalfa—very good business. He is handsome, and I'm sure Kayla likes him, so I don't understand the delay. The fellow got a degree in business and didn't want to go any further. But she has continued studying."

"I see. Kayla wants intellectual stimulation and he wants to be a happy farmer."

"He wants to live in Driggs, a one-horse town on the Wyoming border, a long drive from Pocatello, and he doesn't want her to continue studying. 'What for?' he had asked her. She can read all she wants at home."

Sovik nodded silently.

"Kayla is a different sort of a girl," Steve laughed a little. "She's not the housewife type." After a pause he added, "The trip will be good for Kayla. She needs to sort things out."

Kayla sat quietly in the shuttle van, but she became suddenly alert, looking all around, when the van slowed down and stopped. Barricades were set up on the main road to New Delhi. Sovik saw several policemen with rifles hanging from their shoulders. The driver rolled down the window and talked in Hindi with one of the armed men.

The policeman peered through the windows. "All foreigners, eh?"

The driver nodded. "From the airport."

The policeman kept on looking inside as if trying to memorize their faces.

Kayla, Pinky, and Be'ziil looked at a little fire burning inside a short metal drum near the barricade. Two policemen stood there. Their rifles were clearly visible. In the faint light of the fire their military-style uniforms made their stance appear menacing. Sovik's eyes shifted to an ox-driven cart, loaded with large jute bags, going in the opposite direction. They still allowed these slow-moving vehicles on a major artery to the city!

"What?" Kayla looked at Sovik. "Has India become a police state?"

"I don't know what's going on," Sovik told her while nervously staring straight ahead.

"Cool," Be'ziil, the young Navajo man, said, and looked around. "Armed policemen guarding the roads."

"I've got only three weeks' vacation," Kayla said, "I don't want to waste my time."

"Perhaps something has happened on the road," Pinky said.

"In Mexico, they can keep you in jail without a reason." Kayla's voice was apprehensive.

The policeman waved his hand for them to proceed, and another pulled the barricades aside so their van could pass.

"This has started since the assassination of Mrs. Gandhi," the driver told them after they passed the barricade. "Police set up these road blocks at night to stop people from bringing weapons into the city."

"Is it safe here?" Kayla asked.

"You won't see anything like this in the city," the driver told them.

"Wouldn't it be fun if we are in the middle of a coup?" Be'ziil sat straight up.

"I wouldn't have come if I knew about this," Kayla grumbled.

The van sped up and moved quickly down the dimly lit road. Sovik saw old, tall trees lining both sides of the road. He glanced at Be'ziil. From his calm, stoic face, he couldn't say how Be'ziil was taking India, but his remarks comforted him. He was a full-blooded Navajo Indian and had grown up on the Reservation in Arizona. He seemed to be doing fine. Sovik and Pinky had met his mother, Anaba, and his stepfather, John, in the summer of 1990 at the Sho-Ban festival in Fort Hall. A friend introduced them in the dance arena.

The performers and many members of the audience were in full tribal costumes, but Anaba wore ordinary clothes, a dark blue skirt and a white blouse, nothing Native American, except for tiny turquoise earrings. There was no doubt though that she was a Navajo woman with rounded cheeks, high cheekbones, beautiful black eyes and dark hair flowing down her back.

"Could you teach me the steps?" Sovik asked her.

"I don't know how," she replied with a smile. "Looks easy, but it takes a lot of practice. I never had the time."

"But you are an Indian!"

"Yes," she said in her sweet Navajo accent, "But I've spent too many years away from home." Her expression did not reveal any of her inner feelings.

"Yeah, I understand that. I left Calcutta over twenty years ago."

"I go home as often as I can," she said, "but it's like I've a life here and a life there."

Sovik had not met Be'ziil until his parents asked if he would take the boy on this trip. "He is nineteen," Anaba said, "but has not graduated from high school yet. He needs some direction in life, but he won't listen to me."

"And you think a trip will give him direction? Well, perhaps, seeing conditions in India," Sovik said, "he will be inspired to pull his life together."

Sovik liked the quiet boy who looked like a young Nepali and agreed to take Be'ziil along. Later he told Pinky, "I grew up as a displaced person in India, like a refugee, I feel for the Native Americans. They seem so lost."

When they reached the hotel, it was quiet all around. The hotel staff helped them move their luggage to their rooms. Be'ziil was antsy to do something, but Sovik firmly told all three in his party, "We go to bed now. We'll have plenty of opportunity tomorrow." He quickly turned and went up the stairs.

"I thought you would be more cheerful." Pinky kissed him gently after they settled in their room.

"The police on the road and the aggravation at the airport have put a little damper on my spirits. I didn't expect hassles and roadblocks."

"Sleep now. We'll be tourists tomorrow and it will be fine."

"That's not it. It's all coming back to me. Everything is difficult in India." He glanced at Pinky. "I wonder if I'll find what I came for."

He had pushed away the memories of his life in India. New Delhi had brought the old days back to him with the immediacy of hitting a brick wall— the days filled with struggles, from morning till night. He had succeeded in blotting out those memories until now. Suddenly he realized that when he left for the U.S., somewhere in his subconscious mind, he knew he was not going to come back to live in his homeland.

Pinky had never seen her husband so tense. He had always been the solid pillar that she could lean against, at least until his heart operation. Here in India he seemed nervous and worried. Her professional training as a psychologist reminded her that this was normal. This trip was needed for his peace of mind, but it could go awry. What would happen to her husband then? She caressed his back and held him tight against her, spoon-fashion.

10.2

Early in the morning, Sovik went out alone for a walk around central New Delhi. The previous night's gloomy feelings were gone. He was excited to be back in India and longed to see the waters of the Ganges River. But river viewing would have to wait until he got away from the bustle of India's capital. He contented himself with the early morning scenes, sounds, and smells of New Delhi. The air felt warm even early in the morning. The smell of molten tar permeated the area. A road repair crew worked filling potholes before the heat of the day made the work too difficult.

He walked to a lovely park that surrounded the Jantar Mantar, an old Indian astronomical observatory. The sign said Maharaja Jai Singh of Jaipur had it built in 1725. He strolled among several large, slanted, red-brick structures. These were of gigantic proportions and looked as if they had been constructed by alien beings. Houses and apartment buildings had grown up around the park, giving him the impression of a jewel-like neighborhood park stocked with weird jungle gym equipment.

A young man in a magenta jogging suit ran past a line of imposing palm trees and disappeared behind the huge red-brick sundial. Only a few people were on the road, some out for daily food shopping. Sovik walked around lazily, soaking up the old atmosphere.

While he was absorbed in picture taking, a man spoke to him in terse Hindi, "You are not supposed to take pictures here."

"Why not?"

"That's the rule."

"I haven't seen any rules posted."

"See the small guard office there. The man will tell you."

No man was present in the office and there was no sign that anyone guarded the place. He couldn't find any notice regarding photography. Perhaps the rules were written somewhere, but no one followed them. This was India! He stood there, wondering why the man had taken it upon himself to ruin his moment, treating him as though he were stealing something. Then he heard a voice in English: "Are you from America?"

"Yes," Sovik replied, a little surprised. The speaker wore an ocher color, long shirt and dhoti—a Hindu monk.

"That man has disturbed you, hasn't he?"

"Yes. I've come back to India after many years. I don't understand why he stopped me from taking pictures."

"Different people have different motives. You can't waste your energy thinking about it. Just ignore him." He looked intently at Sovik with sharp eyes. "Are you visiting as a tourist?"

Sovik didn't know what to tell this stranger, a monk. "We are planning a trip to the source of the Ganges River," he told him.

"Ah! What a coincidence! I'm Swami Anand, a priest at the Gangotri temple. If you have any questions about your trip, you can contact me." He paused for a second, and before Sovik could respond, he added, "I also belong to the Sarva Mangal Society—SMS—a society for the wellbeing of all people. We have taken a pledge to work to uplift the people of India. We have our main office here. You should visit us sometime." He gave Sovik a card and turned to walk away, but then stopped and said, "You know, men like you can help India greatly. Why don't you come to our meeting today? A great philosopher monk, Swami Rangaraj, will speak this afternoon. He is a senior priest at the Gangotri temple."

"Both of you are from Gangotri temple? I'll try."

Swami Anand left.

"What a morning!" Sovik thought. One moment, someone had made him feel like a thief and spoiled his mood, and the next, a priest had popped up out of nowhere and opened a door to information about the Gangotri area that he had sought for the last four years. In a renewed, happy mood, he walked back to the hotel.

At the Yatrik Hotel, he found Pinky had ordered breakfast; her idea was to have a peaceful tea on the hotel balcony overlooking Jai Singh road. She told him Kayla and Be'ziil had gone downstairs to explore the restaurant. Sovik gazed at her for a few seconds. She wore a sari and looked pretty. He felt fortunate she had come into his life—she was the only one who understood him and had always supported him. He held her in an embrace without saying anything.

"I'm glad to see you upbeat," she said. "I presume you had a good morning walk."

"Yes." He sat down on one of the balcony chairs. "I met a monk from the Gangotri temple and I'm going to see him again this afternoon."

"How fortunate! He can tell you where to get food for the long hike." She poured him some tea.

Pigeons nesting in the eaves of the balcony cooed, and one or two bees buzzed around a vine covering the balcony. Muffled sounds of cars and three-wheelers drifted up on the soft morning air.

"Isn't it wonderful?" Pinky said and caressed her husband's hand.

"Yes. Very nice."

As they sipped tea and ate toast and scrambled eggs mixed with chopped onions and green chilies, crows cawed occasionally from the trees in the courtyard. The toast tasted different to Sovik; the slices were denser and smaller, and the butter was slightly rancid—but these were familiar tastes from the past, and he knew he would soon get used to them again.

"I want to visit the Old Fort," Sovik told Pinky. "Can we all go there this morning?"

"That's a good idea," she said and got up to gather Kayla and Be'ziil.

◆ ◆ ◆

The long road that ascended to the gate of the fort was nearly empty except for a few vendors selling cold drinks and snacks at the bottom of the hill. The Purana Qilla (Old Fort) was a dilapidated place, but the ornate architectural work of Mughal glory days was clearly evident on the gate.

Sovik's real reason for coming to this place stemmed from the Indian epic, Mahabharata. He had grown up knowing and loving the stories from this epic, and had determined earlier that he would visit places along the journey that had any connection to ancient India. This would be a journey of reminiscences of what he had read in the past, and perhaps find new meanings from them. "Thousands of years ago," Sovik told Kayla, "this was the capital of the five Pandava Brothers. Now it definitely has the imprint of the Mughal Empire." He could not feel the presence of the ancient Mahabharata kingdom that had once flourished here. He glanced at Kayla for a moment. Her curly brown hair, a mass of ringlets, stood out against her fair, almost pink face with strong cheekbones. She was not beautiful in the classical east-Indian sense, but looked pretty with her arched eyebrows and sweet smile.

"I've read a lot of American literature," she said, "but I know very little of Indian books. You'll have to tell me."

"There are two epics in India," Sovik told Kayla, "the Ramayana and the Mahabharata. They are very important to the Hindus. The first tells the story of Rama, an incarnation of Vishnu, and how he killed an evil king to save the world, and the second describes a long struggle between two groups of first cousins, the Pandavas and the Kauravas, for ownership of a kingdom in north India. Early in the story the Kauravas tried to kill the Pandavas by convincing them to go on a pilgrimage and then burning their house down. However, an uncle informed the Pandavas of their cousins' diabolical plan, and they were able to escape. When the father of the Kauravas realized what his sons had done, he felt remorse. He wanted peace and offered the Pandavas a kingdom where they could live separately. That was this region! At that time, Delhi was a parched desert land, but with the help of their advisor and friend, Lord Krishna, and his architects, the Pandavas built an enviable kingdom in a short time and named their capital Indraprastha—the place of Indra, the king of heaven."

Observing the stark grey walls of the fort, Pinky said, "I'm glad you brought us here. I'm sure places like this will bring back all the ancient stories you read while growing up in India."

"Indians believe in these stories?" Kayla said. Her voice was skeptical.

"These two epics are like the Bible to the Hindus," Sovik said. "They mold their lives, right from birth."

"Really?"

Sovik was pleased that he stood on the site of Indraprastha and did not answer her. Some say the octagonal room in the fort, called Sher Mandal, was the site of the original sacrificial altar used by the Pandavas to worship Surya, the Sun god.

"These stories give valuable lessons for life," Pinky told Kayla, "for all—Indians and non-Indians."

A paper kite flying across his field of vision brought Sovik back from his daydreams of the Pandava kingdom. "So many kingdoms have come and gone since the Pandavas," Sovik told Kayla. "There is no trace of ancient India remaining here."

"It's pretty ancient to me!" Kayla said.

"Visitors are sometimes disappointed in India. They don't find the India they read about."

"Tell me, was that the same Krishna, the Hindu God, we hear about?"

"Yes. He's an important character in the epic. On the battlefield of the final war between the Pandavas and the Kauravas, Krishna revealed the essence of the Hindu religion. That is known as the Gita."

Kayla glanced around from one side to the other. "Everything is so different here: the people, the sounds, the smells, the surroundings are so foreign from how we live." She looked at the boys playing soccer in the distance and sighed.

"Are you tired, Kayla?"

"Yes. Last night, when I went to bed, I saw a small crack in my ceiling. Then, late at night, when I went to the bathroom I saw the crack had moved and it wasn't a crack. It was a little beige lizard with black eyes. I couldn't sleep for a long time, thinking it might fall on me."

"When you go camping, are you afraid of small creatures?"

"Oh no. That's different." She laughed.

Sovik saw her weary face finally relaxed. "Well, geckos are harmless to humans," he told her. "They eat only insects. I hope you sleep well tonight. We have a long journey ahead of us."

"I am cautious," she said. "I have to watch out for myself. Don't worry." She focused her eyes on Sovik. "Self preservation!" Her eyes became stern.

"Let's go down to the street," Sovik said, not understanding her concerns.

They walked down the old fort hill to the street and ordered two green coconut drinks from a vendor.

"I was wondering what they were," Kayla said and watched curiously as the man lopped off the top of the green coconut with a short machete-like knife and made holes for straws.

10.3

With Swami Anand's card in hand, Sovik took a taxi and went to Chanakyapuri, an upscale section of New Delhi where the roads were wide and lined with trees. Near his destination, the police had set up a roadblock; cars couldn't go any further. He got out of the taxi and walked toward the address the monk had given him. People crowded the road, all walking in the same direction.

"What's happening?" he asked one man.

"Keshab Lal is coming to the SMS meeting."

Sovik looked at him blankly.

"When the Home Minister comes to a meeting, you expect something big to happen. Haven't you read today's paper?" The man said derisively, as he sped up and walked ahead.

Sovik soon saw a modern four-story structure, the SMS building, with a large gate and courtyard. Police guarded the building and no one was allowed inside. Sovik stood at the edge of the crowd and wondered what to do, when suddenly Swami Anand came out through a side door and spotted him. "I'm glad you could come to our meeting," he said by way of greeting.

"Thank you. It's so crowded."

"Don't worry, I'll take you inside."

He led Sovik to the front gate and people moved to make space for the monk. Sovik went in as if he were an honored guest. Behind him, a policeman barked at a few who were clinging to the gate in gruff Hindi, "Haat jao. Move. Haat, Haat."

"Today is very special," Swami Anand told him. "We don't have enough space in the auditorium, but microphones will carry the speeches outside."

Sovik saw several rooms with rosewood chairs and tables and white chalkboards.

"This is our headquarters," the monk told him. "You'll see everything modern here. We cannot uplift the people if we aren't up to the Western standard ourselves. The Sarva Mangal Society is an organization of selfless people devoting their lives for moral and economic improvement of all Indians."

"I haven't heard of the SMS in America," Sovik said, "Has this been going on for a long time?"

"Almost eight years. Articles have appeared in India Abroad and India Today, but you are right; we are relatively unknown in America. You'll see from today's meeting how we have put together a grassroots organization."

They reached the end of the hall and entered a large auditorium. Swami Anand took him to a seat near the front and gave him a program. "We'll meet again," he pressed his palms together. "Namaste."

Sovik folded his palms. "Thank you for inviting me."

The walls were richly paneled with wood and the seats were as comfortable as those in a modern theater in the States. The attendees, over a thousand, were well dressed. In one corner, a screen projected beautiful pictures from various parts of India as soft music played over the loudspeakers.

Soon the music stopped and four men came on to the stage and sat down. Sovik consulted the program and figured out that the man with white hair must be the SMS President, Mr. Thappa, and the monk—Swami Rangaraj.

Mr. Thappa stepped to the microphone at the center of the stage and stood in an elegant white robe before the audience. The hall fell silent and many observed him for the first time in a public forum—tall, well-muscled, strong, and resolute. "It is a great day for us; the Honorable Minister, Mr. Keshab Lal, is here. He is a strong supporter of our cause and will say a few words."

Mr. Lal spoke of the good things the government was doing for the people, but he stressed that the government could not do it alone, and that the country needed organizations like the SMS with their sincere goal of serving the people. The audience applauded at the conclusion of his speech. The minster left immediately.

Mr. Thappa went to the microphone. He pushed a lock of white hair from his forehead and proclaimed, "It's time the people of India wake up! Moral decay is all around us. Corruption has pervaded in all spheres of our lives and the youth seemed disillusioned and more disrespectful, day by day, with their western clothes, styles, and slang. Every day, newspapers abound with stories of exploitation of children, women, villagers, the poor, and the working class by landowners, factory owners, businessmen, and the government's own functionaries -- the police and the revenue officials. Where do we, the people of India, go from here? That is why people from every state have come together to create the Sarva Mangal Society. We will forge a new path for India. And it should be based on our ancient wisdom that has survived through all this time. As the SMS name says, we want to create a society for the good of all, irrespective of language, religion, and caste. Our motto is service to and betterment of people."

When he finished his speech, the people burst into thunderous applause.

Mr. Thappa then introduced Swami Rangaraj: "our guiding light—a pillar of the SMS."

As Swami Rangaraj stood on the dais and folded his palms with bowed head, the crowd hushed. He emanated a great presence and his visage brought immediate respect from the crowd. His tall, thin body showed the effects of years of yoga practice. He spoke of the importance of living a spiritual life which included caring for fellow citizens. "How could God be kind to you if you are not kind to others?"

He paused for a moment, looked at the audience, and said, "I'll tell you a little story today. Once a young man came to the great monk Vivekananda and said he wanted to achieve spiritual freedom. Vivekananda asked him what he had done so far. The man said he had tried to make his mind void according to the instructions for meditation; he had sat still, shutting the door of his room, and keeping his eyes closed, but nothing seemed to work, and he could not find peace of mind. 'My boy,' Vivekananda told him in a voice full of loving sympathy, 'you will have to open the door of your room and look around, instead of closing your eyes. There are hundreds of people in your neighborhood; they are poor and suffering, and crying for help. You cannot achieve spirituality by ignoring your surroundings. You have to serve those around you to gain freedom. You will have to feed those who have nothing to eat. You will have to nurse, as well as procure medicine for the sick. And you will have to teach the ignorant. If you want peace of mind, serve others to the best of your ability.'"

Swami Rangaraj scanned the audience and continued, "There is nothing new that needs to be invented to uplift India," he said in a serious voice. "The Vedas and the Upanishads have all the wisdom we need." His face glowed with this proclamation. "Swami Vivekananda has told us what we should be doing. It is futile to preach religion to people without first removing their poverty and suffering. So our first task is to eradicate poverty and ignorance. That is why we are working with the SMS."

He sat down and the fourth man on the stage went to the podium. He wore a black suit, was tall for an Indian, and had thick eyebrows. From his color and facial features Sovik knew he was a South Indian. The man gave a financial report of the SMS during the past six months. The SMS had raised a substantial amount of money, but the demand was growing at a higher rate. He asked everyone to contribute generously so the SMS could carry on the good work. Several other men and women followed him and talked about progress made in different regions of the country.

The speeches seemed very emotional to Sovik, as if their desire to establish a new India was driven by religious fervor. Their goals were praiseworthy, Sovik concluded, but India is a secular country.

When the meeting was over and Sovik was leaving the building, Swami Anand caught him at the gate and took him to one side. "I hope you liked what you heard today."

"Yes, fascinating. I've been out of touch with India."

"This movement is serious. Many influential people are involved, and we are committed." He hesitated for a moment and asked, "How long will you be in New Delhi?"

"We leave for Mussoorie in three days."

"Could you come here tomorrow afternoon for an hour? I want you to meet our President."

"That would be an honor for me."

10.4

The next day Sovik stood in front of the SMS building and took in the atmosphere. The air shimmered in the heat of the day and, in stark contrast to the day before, the area was quiet and empty. When he pushed the bell, a servant in a well-worn white coat answered the door and escorted him to a small conference room where ten people sat around a table. He recognized three of them: Mr. Thappa, the President, Swami Rangaraj, and Swami Anand. Mr. Thappa stood up and warmly greeted him, "Please come and sit here." He pointed to an empty chair near him. "We are very pleased that you could take a few minutes to attend our meeting. We will not keep you long."

"Thank you." Sovik sat down.

"I sincerely hope you agree with what we are doing," Mr. Thappa said. "We want to talk with people like you, who live in the West, and learn from your experience."

"I know very little in this regard," Sovik said politely. "I've spent all my life in technical work, but I'd be happy to tell you what I've seen in America."

"Men like you make us proud," Mr. Thappa said. "You could help us in many ways."

Mr. Thappa introduced the others. Sovik recognized the speaker from the day before, the South Indian man with heavy eyebrows. He was Chetti, their Chief Financial Officer. A lively discussion ensued about how Indians were doing so well in the West and could greatly help the SMS. Sovik found they were quite knowledgeable of Indians in the U.S. and familiar with how non-profit organizations work in America.

"They have too high an overhead," Mr. Thappa said, "our organization is supported by monks and volunteers so we can use almost all our money for the people."

"Still our real problem is financing," Chetti said. Today he wore a dark blue suit.

"Chetti is our driving force in the SMS," Mr. Thappa said, looking at Sovik. "He is finding ways to raise money for the organization. An invaluable man."

Sovik remembered listening to his financial report the day before, and began to wonder if they thought he was wealthy.

Chetti smiled, saying, "We must spread the news of the SMS outside India and look for help from expatriates." He then asked Sovik, "Any idea how we could send our emissaries to America?"

Sovik explained how the Indian population had increased in America. In the late fifties and sixties Indians went to America for graduate studies. They were respected in the universities and national laboratories, but now many were involved in businesses of all kinds. As a group, Indians now belonged to the top 5% in North America in terms of income and achievements. So Indians in the U.S. could be a great resource for the SMS. He suggested that Indians in big cities like New York and Los Angeles could host members of the SMS.

"We should do this soon," Chetti said.

Swami Rangaraj said, "I agree with you. The time is now."

Mr. Thappa scratched his head and looked toward Chetti.

Chetti said, "We need to send Swami Rangaraj to America as soon as possible. Mr. Bose, I'd like to explore this further with you. Could you help us?"

"I live in Idaho, a very remote place," Sovik said and chuckled a little. "But I might be able to find some who could help."

Mr. Thappa interrupted the conversation, saying; "We have discussed this before, Chetti. Unless we have raised sufficient funds, we agreed to table this idea."

"I know, I know," Chetti said, "but I strongly believe Swami Rangaraj's presence in America would add to our cause greatly,"

Swami Rangaraj's face brightened with the tribute. He looked at Sovik and said, "Swami Anand told me you are going to the source of the Ganges River. When you reach Gangotri, please visit us at the temple."

"That will be a great pleasure for us," Sovik said with sincere happiness.

"I've a request, Mr. Bose," Chetti said in a voice that was friendly and intimate. "I'm a direct man. You've only a few days in New Delhi, and I do not want to disturb your journey, but I feel I'd benefit from a discussion with you. Could I meet with you in the evening?"

Startled, Sovik stared at Chetti. He was an insignificant man in the scheme of their lofty goals. He didn't even know what he was doing in his own life. How could he help them? "I don't know what my wife has planned," Sovik responded, "but I could make time. She would understand."

"Perhaps we will go around New Delhi, showing your wife and your friends some spots they haven't seen. I shall pick you up at 6. Will that be fine?"

"Sure. You've already recruited me." Sovik gave a little laugh. Everyone else joined in.

"Chetti doesn't waste time," Mr. Thappa said and thanked Sovik for coming.

Swami Anand accompanied him to the door.

"Chetti is full of ideas," Swami Anand informed him. "He must have something on his mind. He is very busy, you know, being the second-in-command after Mr. Thappa."

10.5

Sovik could not imagine what Chetti might want to talk about with him.

"They probably think I'm an important person in the U.S.," Sovik confided to Pinky when he returned to the hotel. "I've told them who I am. I don't know why they still want me."

"Just listen to the man," Pinky said. "Perhaps you'll like doing something for the SMS."

"Their purpose seems to be noble."

"Explore the SMS. You may find a connection ... something worthwhile here. I can't come, though. Kayla and I have already made reservations for the sound and light show at the Red Fort. You go alone."

"Where is Be'ziil?"

"I haven't seen him since morning. The hotel manager said he went out with one of their employees—the gardener, I think. He said Be'ziil would be safe with him."

"I was worried," Sovik said, "but he seems to be doing well by himself."

Pinky nodded in agreement.

"I'll stay in the room for a while," Sovik said. "I need to think about all this."

"Just don't sign away the bank account," Pinky said, putting her hands on his shoulders. She gave him a gentle kiss on the lips. "Tell them you have a wife and a house to maintain in the U.S."

"I don't think they are after my money."

Chetti came right on time and expressed disappointment that Pinky had already left. "I'll have to meet her another time," he told Sovik, as the driver started the car.

They drove toward Kutub Minar.

"I've been to the U.S. only once," Chetti told Sovik, "a long time back, for company business. I would have loved to go to the States for graduate school, like you, but my grades were not good enough." His tone was friendly and he had an open and honest expression. "I admire people like you. Tell me more about yourself."

"It's an ordinary story. I applied to several universities for an assistantship, and Penn gave me the chance. I went to Philadelphia and stayed on after I finished my studies." He stopped for a few seconds. "My family came from Bangladesh—as refugees after partition. We had to do what we could to succeed."

"Don't feel sorry about that. People like you are our assets. You can contribute more from America than coming back to India."

Chetti's word, 'assets,' rang in Sovik's ears. He watched dusk descend on the busy city. How hard he had worked to be an asset! Yes, he strove with all his body and mind to be an 'asset.' His father would have been so proud of his accomplishments, especially hearing these words from Chetti, but what did this mean now?

Chetti's car stopped in front of a restaurant and they walked in. Several large Batik paintings of Rajasthani dancing girls decorated the walls. The orange and red batiks were echoed in the décor of the place, and classical Sarod music played in the background—clearly a posh restaurant. Very few tables were occupied—too early for Indians to have dinner and perhaps too expensive for the wandering hippie variety of tourists. As soon as they were seated, a waiter served them two tall glasses of cool lemonade.

New Delhi was hot; even the small walk from the car to the restaurant made Sovik feel thirsty. He drank slowly and, as he looked around, the colors of the paintings reminded him of the small, sacred cloth his mother had given him to take to America.

He heard Chetti saying, "I've a specific item to discuss with you. Let me give you some background first."

Sovik turned his attention back to Chetti.

"The goal of SMS is noble, but it is expanding too fast," Chetti said. "We cannot keep up with the pace. SMS looks to me to find the necessary funding for our programs, but this has become very difficult. Let me be frank with you. We've come to the make it or break it stage." He took a sip of lemonade. "I'm exploring all possible options, but there is a limit to what we can raise at home. I have to think seriously of raising money from America." He paused for a moment. "But that is not why I wanted to meet with you. You can relax." He smiled.

Before Chetti said any more, waiters in stiffly starched white turbans brought food and arranged the dishes on the table—dahl, two vegetable curries, a lamb dish, naan bread and rice pilaf. They also brought several bowls of condiments—pink, pickled onions, sliced beets, and mango pickles.

"Let us know if you need anything else," one of the waiters said. He left them and stood a little distance away.

From the window, Chetti viewed the Kutub Minar Pillar in the distance. He then turned to Sovik. "You have done technical work for many years. Isn't it time to do something different?"

Sovik couldn't say anything for a second. "I've been struggling with that subject for some time."

"You must be wondering what to do after retirement."

"Yes."

"From man to man, I'll tell you, don't think of coming back to India. If you want to do something good for India, do it from there."

"I thought you'd ask me to work for the SMS!"

Chetti laughed loudly. "You can certainly do that, although that's not why I brought you here." He looked at the wall fresco of Radha and Krishna surrounded by village girls in dancing costumes. "I want to get your opinion on another subject. This is confidential. Could you keep it secret for a while?"

"Yes, if it is that important."

"It is not something illegal; I just don't want the idea to be out."

"Tell me. Then we will see how to handle it."

"Before forming the SMS organization, Mr. Thappa went around India and visited monks and many temples. He received genuine support from the priests. They gave him what little they had—out of true sincerity. These 'souvenirs', or relics, are unique; some are museum material. But what good is it to hold them in a vault?" Chetti took a little rice pilaf. "In one temple in the eastern part of the Himalayas, a priest gave him some old manuscripts. If the priests can part with them and make them available for a good cause, we should be able to make them available to the world."

"You are thinking of selling these items?"

"Yes. We need money desperately. This afternoon your presence gave me the idea to offer the manuscripts to American museums. That's why I wanted to meet with you. Do you have any contact with the museums in America?"

"Not really, but what do you have in mind?"

"I want to sell one of these old manuscripts. This could generate a good sum."

"What's the manuscript about?"

"Temple construction. It has many details with hand drawn sketches."

"I'd be curious myself to know how old temples were built."

"It's written on the kind of leaves they used long ago. It's not an ancient, ancient manuscript, but certainly antique from an American point of view. It would be a fascinating book for scholars… and engineers."

"Have you read it?"

"I have browsed through it. I've brought photocopies of a few pages for you to see."

"I'm excited to see them."

"If you agree to help us, here is what I want you to do. I shall give you these pages and ask you to find out which museums would be interested in collecting such a manuscript, how we should go about selling the document. All this must be done discreetly."

"Certainly an immense task."

"Yes, it is. Can you help us?"

"It is way out of my area of expertise, but I'm intrigued."

"This will be your contribution to India."

"Okay, I'll try."

"Thank you. I'm hoping we can get a million dollars to part with such a rare document."

"The good thing is many will get a chance to research old construction ideas," Sovik said. "That's not bad. At the same time, the money will benefit India. I don't mind looking into this for you. I am honored, actually."

"I thought you could help us." Chetti took out a few pages from his coat pocket and handed them to Sovik. "A time comes when you have to engage in altruistic work."

Could he read his mind? Sovik wondered. Was his behavior that obvious or did all men go through this kind of searching at this age? Was this the normal midlife crisis?

10.6

It was almost ten o'clock when Chetti dropped Sovik off at the hotel. New Delhi seemed to have fallen asleep; the streets were quiet, almost deserted, and the streetlights dim. A lull had also fallen over the hotel, except for the lobby area, which was bright and where a few guests were chatting. Sovik ran up the stairs without waiting for the elevator.

Pinky was in bed, reading the *Lonely Planet* guide. "How did it go?" she asked eagerly as she put down the book.

"Unbelievable!" Sovik exclaimed. "He didn't ask for money. He wants me to help them sell an old manuscript."

"They gave you the manuscript?"

"He gave me a few pages of photocopies." He took them out of his pocket and held them up for her to see. "I can't wait to go through this." He put the papers on the table and started to undress, all the while glancing at the papers. He then lay down next to Pinky and looked at them more closely. He could read the title page because the script was in Sanskrit: Mandir Nirmaan Katha (Discourse on Temple Construction). No authorship given. The writing faint, difficult to decipher. It contained several diagrams of rooms, tunnels and domes.

Pinky nudged him. "We plan to get up early and go out before it gets hot."

"One more minute, please. It's about building temples, very interesting." He searched through the pages to figure out if there was a name he could decipher, but he couldn't. Since a priest in the Himalayas had given the manuscript, he thought it might describe a temple in the mountain areas. He would have to ask Chetti for more details. Could it be the temple where they were going, the highest temple in India? He searched for the letter G for Gangotri, but he couldn't find it.

"I can't make any sense," he finally said, "and I don't know which temple the manuscript is describing. Oh wait, I see some numbers, which I can read: 01 35 18 02 25 27 03 15 04 59. I wonder what it means."

"You're good at math. Sleep now. It will come to you in the morning."

"Ten sets of two digits. They can't be arbitrary. But what could it be?" He turned off the light. "You are right; I'm too excited to see it now."

He pulled Pinky closer.

10.7

In the morning Sovik walked with Pinky, Kayla, and Be'ziil to Baba Kharak Singh Marg, the street where many Indian State Emporiums had set up shop. Pinky and Kayla happily strode along in their newly bought salwar kameez—north Indian tunics with flowing scarves. Sovik cheerfully wore his new Indian kurta over dark pants. Be'ziil reflected the epitome of Navajo coolness with his new wrap-around sunglasses.

"When the salesmen in the emporiums offer you tea or a cold soda, be careful," Sovik told them. "You know what they are after."

"We're just going to look," Pinky told him, but her eyes danced.

"Don't let them sell you everything in the store," Sovik told her with a mock command.

Pinky was relieved to see Sovik his old self, full of enthusiasm and energy. He had perked up since he had gone to the SMS meeting and met with that fellow, Mr. Chetti, the night before. Perhaps the trip was working the magic she had hoped it would.

"I don't want to hinder your shopping by my presence," Sovik told them with a happy grin on his face. "I need to run an errand; I'll be back at the hotel around noon." He left them and hurried away. His mind was occupied with the numbers he had found in the manuscript.

He stopped a well-dressed Indian man on the street. "Excuse me, where can I find a library?"

"For tourist information?"

"I'm interested in ancient Hindu books."

"For that you go to the JNU library. It's too hard to explain how to get there. Please take a taxi. The driver will take you there."

"Thank you."

The taxi dropped him in front of a nine-story cardinal-red building, Jawaharlal Nehru University Library. Sovik took the steps two at a time and entered the main lobby. It was quiet and cool. He asked the man at the desk where the books on ancient India were kept.

"You can't go in without a card," the man said, looking him up and down.

"I only want to see if there is a book on a particular topic."

"Please fill up this form," the man handed him a paper, "and give me ten rupees for a temporary card."

After the formalities were completed, the man gave him directions to a room on the third floor. The library shelves were filled with old, leather bound books. Sovik browsed through books in the small Vedic Math section, but they dealt with computations, describing methods to add and multiply.

He went back to the front desk. "Is there any book on sacred Hindu numbers?" he asked the librarian.

"What are you looking for?"

"I want to see if anyone studied number sets in India."

"Then you'd be interested in Ramanujam's work."

"No. I'm looking for ancient texts."

"Ah, I understand. I'll take you to the section that has books by Bhaskar, Barahamitra, and others."

Sovik stayed in the library for more than an hour but couldn't find any Hindu writing that dealt with series of numbers.

As he passed by the librarian's desk, the librarian said, "I guess you didn't find what you were looking for. Would you like to see the Buddhist section?"

"Buddhist section?"

"Yes. The Buddhists paid a great deal of attention to the study of mathematics."

"I don't have the time now. Thank you though."

As he left the library, he saw a large bookstore across the street. He looked at his watch and strolled in to the bookstore. It pleased him to find many books in English. After quickly glancing through the titles of political books on India, he moved to the Religion and Philosophy section. The words of the librarian rang in his ears, and he stopped at a shelf of Buddhist books. He wished to find books that described Indian accomplishments during the Buddhist period, but his eyes stopped at one book. The title froze his attention: The Meaning of Life from a Buddhist Perspective by the Dalai Lama. Sovik picked up the book and read the back page: Each of us struggles with the existential question of meaning, purpose, and responsibility... all rooted in our misunderstanding of our true nature. The shop had many books by the Dalai Lama; one contained his 1989 Nobel Peace Prize acceptance speech. After glancing through them, he continued to thumb through the first book he had picked up.

The book fascinated Sovik. He lost himself in the Dalai Lama's writing about the meaning of life. The series of numbers that had occupied him so intensely a few moments before receded to the back of his mind. It hit him that he did not come to India to solve a riddle in an old manuscript. He would help the SMS find someone who could sell the manuscript. That was all he could do. Half an hour passed by; he wanted to read the book thoroughly, but he looked at his watch and realized that he was late. He bought the book and hurried out of the store.

◆ ◆ ◆

In late afternoon, Sovik pulled Be'ziil in to the hotel restaurant and ordered tea. He wanted to give him a little attention. The nineteen-year old boy had a pleasant personality, but Sovik had no idea if Be'ziil was bored or enjoying himself. He was big and strong, and looked like a Gurkha from Nepal; he might not get the courtesy afforded tourists from the locals. "I've been running around since we arrived," he told him apologetically, "I didn't get to talk with you much. Are you doing alright?"

"I'm having a ball." Be'ziil's face beamed.

Sovik studied him to gauge if he was sincere. "Great. You tell me if you need anything or want to do something together."

Be'ziil nodded. "I find it easy here."

Sovik's expression froze. "Don't do anything crazy that I cannot explain to your mother."

"Don't worry, man. I can take care of myself."

The waiter brought two cups of tea.

Sovik took a sip. "You find it interesting here?"

"Very. And stuff is cheap, man."

"You'll like it more when we are in the Himalayas."

"My mother said we're going to meet holy men in India. Are we?"

"I hope so."

"She also said we're going somewhere close to Nepal."

"You are interested in Nepal?"

"My friends told me all the hippies go there." His eyes widened as he said this.

"No." Sovik shook his head. "We're not going to Nepal."

Sovik took a sip and contemplated Be'ziil for a moment; Be'ziil was not intimidated a bit; he seemed to be quite at ease. But sitting at the restaurant in New Delhi, Sovik didn't know how to have a meaningful conversation with the young Navajo man. "How's your tea?" he asked him.

"I like it. It's thicker than what I've tasted before." Be'ziil lifted his cup.

"Tell me, when will you know your goal has been achieved?"

Astonished, Sovik stared at Be'ziil's broad face. After a moment he said, "Well, when we reach the source of the river."

"I thought you were here for a chant."

"Chant?" Sovik put the cup down on the table, almost dropping it.

"Like a Navajo ceremony to secure your well-being."

"No, no. I haven't come to perform a ceremony."

"My mother thought the trip would be like a chant for you."

Sovik considered his words for a few seconds, but didn't know the significance of the Navajo chant ceremony, and didn't know what to say. Had Anaba misunderstood the idea of his trip, and told her son something related to Navajo culture so he'd come along? "We have another day here," he finally told Be'ziil. "We could visit the white tiger at the zoo if you want."

"Maybe."

A group of Indian tourists entered the restaurant. Their animated conversation filled the room. Sovik looked around. The decorations appeared more Western than Indian, with white tablecloths over red ones, and slender vases of fresh flowers. He finished his cup and stood up.

"See you later. Remember we eat together tonight."

11

American Stranger

11.1

In the evening, just when Sovik's group planned to go out for dinner, Larry Sheldon showed up at the Yatrik Hotel.

"I'm so glad to find you," Larry rushed across the lobby and seized both of Sovik's hands. "I've spent most of my time visiting tourist spots in New Delhi."

"Are you enjoying your trip?"

"It's no fun without a friend to share the experience. I thought of you and came looking to find you. And you? Have you found anything new since you left India?"

"Well, I've met some people from a new organization called the SMS."

"I've seen their posters. Are they serious?"

"It seems so."

Four nights before, Sovik had met Larry at the Singapore Airlines counter in Los Angeles; Larry had been standing behind him and introduced himself. He had the kind of handsome features Indians admire in movie stars: tall, medium-build, brown-blonde hair, a strong square-jawed face, and fair skin.

"What places do you plan to visit in India?" Sovik asked to make polite conversation.

"I don't know yet. I'll spend a few days in New Delhi and then see."

What a contrast! Sovik gazed at Larry in wonderment. While Sovik had planned everything—down to which day everyone in his group would take their weekly malaria pills, Larry had no plans at all. This man was such a carefree person!

"I work for the International Investments Group in Denver," Larry said. "The last six months have been brutal. I needed a break from IIG. So here I am." After a pause he said, "I've always wanted to go to India and see the Himalayas."

Sovik had bought two mutual funds from IIG, so his interest was sparked. "Perhaps we could meet for coffee after we finish here," he suggested.

When they were all settled in the waiting lounge, Sovik found Larry, and they took themselves to what passed for a 'coffee shop' in the airport.

"So you are going to India on an impulse?" he asked Larry.

"You might say that." Larry took a sip of coffee. "If you plan too much, sometimes you miss out on the obvious."

"I like your attitude." Sovik lifted his cup. "I could never do that."

"It's no big deal, really."

Larry told him a little about himself. Born to a half-Jewish family in Queens, New York, he graduated from Bronx High School of Science, one of the top five in his class.

"What do you do at IIG?" Sovik asked.

"I'm an analyst. I was fascinated by numbers from childhood, so I studied math and economics at Cornell, and later got a master's degree in number theory from NYU. IIG recruiters thought I'd be a perfect fit!"

"I see. You do risk analysis."

"Yes, for a living. But my real interest is eastern religions. I've read a good part of the Vedas and the Upanishads."

"It's time for this trip then."

"All book knowledge," Larry said, smiling a little. "There was an Indian girl in my class at Cornell, very pretty, named Mala. I was infatuated with her; I guess I started learning about India then, but she would never go out with me. Her parents wouldn't allow it."

"Oh–ho, I see where it all started," Sovik said with a laugh. "So where is she now?"

"I don't know. I wish I had kept in touch with her."

"I see you have been charmed by the sweetness of an Indian woman."

"Who knows, I may find my Indian girl during this trip." Larry chuckled.

Sovik explained his plans to Larry. From New Delhi they would go to Mussoorie, after stopping in Dehra Dun to finalize their trip with the travel agent, and then on to Gangotri. 'We will hike from Gangotri to the glacier where the Ganges River originates."

"Is this your pilgrimage?" Larry's face lit up.

"I don't know about that."

Larry remained silent for a few moments. "I moved to Denver right after graduation," he said. "I've taken up new things that I didn't do in New York—mountain climbing, skiing, hiking. I love to go above the tree line and camp there, sometimes alone."

"What, are you trying to find yourself?"

"Yeah," Larry said absent-mindedly, and suddenly his face became serious.

Sovik sensed there was more to Larry than he had yet told him. The soft background music was interrupted by an announcement directing them to go to the gate—time to board.

Although they had chatted for less than half an hour, they had established the sort of instant bond that travelers often develop. "Larry, I'm really happy to have met you," Sovik told him. "When you get back to the States, please let me know how you liked India." He gave him his business card.

Instead of shaking hands, Larry folded his palms together. "I will. Namaste."

Sovik looked at his watch. "Why don't you join us for dinner?"

"That would be nice."

They took a taxi to a Tandoori restaurant, the Moti Mahal, in Old Delhi. It was located on a busy, poorly lit street near the Red Fort. In the gathering darkness they found a tiny courtyard filled with tables, dimly lit by electric lanterns suspended on strings. Indians crowded the restaurant's large room, but the romance of the dimly lit courtyard suited the foreigners best.

Sovik's plan for their journey to the source of the Ganges River

"Isn't old Delhi amazing?" Pinky said as she inspected the surrounding courtyard walls. "I can imagine traders from the old Silk Road coming down here with their goods."

"Yeah, except for all the three wheelers and exhaust spewing trucks, buses, and taxis!" Larry laughed.

"Well, the donkey and ox-carts fit in," Pinky replied. "This is what it must have been like for our ancestors in towns like ancient Rome or London."

They ordered Tandoori chicken, the specialty of the house. Sliced cucumbers, beets, and lemon wedges came with the dish. The chickens were somewhat lean compared to chickens in the U.S., but tasted delicious. They had also ordered koftas, ground mutton meatballs cooked in a rich, spicy sauce, too hot and spicy for Kayla.

Two waiters brought more Tandoori chicken and fresh naan bread.

It was a good feast and a good way to end an evening in New Delhi. Larry was generous and paid more than his share. All enjoyed his company because he had a way of accepting others without passing judgment; he also regaled them with humorous anecdotes from his own life. He described his first encounter with Indian food in New York. He had to drink seven glasses of cool, sweet Lassi before his mouth stopped burning!

"I don't know much about the Ganges River," Larry said, looking at Sovik as they got up, "but I admire the idea of your trip. How long will you be in the Himalayas?"

"About two weeks." Sovik told him. "None of us has done this before. So we are excited and at the same time I feel some wariness."

On the way back to the hotel, Larry asked many more questions about their "Himalayan expedition." What kind of gear would they carry? Then, he said somewhat shyly, "I've been thinking about your trip since you told me about it in LA. Is there a chance I could join you?"

"Are you serious, Larry?" Sovik asked him, quite surprised. "We're leaving the day after tomorrow."

"I'd be grateful if you take me along."

Sovik liked Larry, and he was knowledgeable about India. Pinky also felt at ease with him. But Kayla raised an eyebrow. "You came to India without planning where you'd be going?"

Larry smiled. "See, if I had planned—"

"But we don't know you at all," Kayla said.

Larry nodded. "You're right about that."

"Larry's experience in the Rocky Mountains would be valuable to us,"

Sovik said, "especially above 12,000 feet. One more person would also reduce our expenses."

"That's true," Kayla agreed.

"We've given our travel agent in Dehra Dun an approximate number of how many would be coming, so an extra person doesn't matter." Sovik turned to Larry and said, "Sure. Join our pilgrimage. You'll be an asset to the group."

He explained the details of their plan to Larry and the expenses he would have to share. Then he paused for a second: how was Larry going to meet them in Dehra Dun?

The previous day, when the manager in the hotel heard about their struggle to buy train tickets to Dehra Dun, he said, "Why don't you go by minibus?"

"Minibus?"

"India has progressed a bit in your absence!" The manager smiled pleasantly, lifted the telephone and dialed a number. He talked in Hindi for a minute or two. "It's all settled," he told Sovik. "They will pick you up in the morning, day after tomorrow."

One telephone call had done it while Sovik and Pinky had struggled to make train reservations before and after coming to New Delhi. They had similar problems finding suitable buses to Dehra Dun and reserving seats. Sovik was simply flabbergasted. This was India where things happen if you know whom to call. He could only say, "Thank you," and went to inform the others.

"You will also have to find transportation to Dehra Dun," Sovik told Larry, "our minibus is fully booked." He stared at Larry not knowing what to suggest to him.

"I'll be there," Larry told him confidently.

"If we don't see you in Dehra Dun," Sovik said, "I will assume you've changed your mind."

"I'll see you there. I should've planned a trip like yours—to go on a pilgrimage trail. I want to do it." Larry's enthusiasm came through clearly. It was apparent that the idea of the Himalayan trip had caught his imagination and he was elated at the chance to go with them.

11.2

Larry was bubbling with energy in the morning, elated that he would go to the source of the Ganges River with Sovik. He munched toast with marmalade in his room on the sixth floor of the Marriott hotel and read the India Times. The SMS, which Sovik had mentioned the previous evening, was front page news. The SMS would announce their programs for the coming year today in a public meeting at the Red Fort at 10 am—the same place where Indian Presidents and Prime Ministers delivered important messages to the nation. An editorial expressed the wish that this year's SMS program be commensurate with their resources. Larry read the editorial with interest since Sovik had told him the organization had merit.

He went down to the front desk and asked if they could arrange a trip to Dehra Dun the next morning. It was easily done when he was willing to pay western prices for eastern travel. "You certainly want an air-conditioned car," the concierge suggested.

"Yes."

The concierge booked a private car with chauffeur for him. An affable man, he added to Larry, "It's a little hot now, but I hope you are enjoying New Delhi."

"It's fine, but I really want to go to the Himalayas," Larry said. "I wonder about the SMS in today's paper. What's happening?"

"They are trying to improve the social conditions in India." He looked at Larry for a few moments. "Why don't you go to their meeting? It is open to all. This will be something new and you will certainly get a different exposure."

"That's an interesting idea."

"I strongly recommend it."

An organization based on ancient Hindu ideals in secular India? Larry had no plans and decided to check it out. By the time he reached the Red Fort, people were pouring in from all sides. He joined the crowd and moved toward the fort entrance. He seemed to be the only westerner in a sea of Indians. He heard only one comment in the crowd, "One of those tourists!" Larry inched his way to the SMS stage, set up against the wall of the Red Fort and decorated with ocher colored cloth, the color used by Hindu monks.

Arriving at a good vantage point, Larry looked around. The large crowd surprised him. People of all strata were present—from those wearing only loincloths to others in the ironed shirts and slacks of office workers. Many men had caps on—even ball caps and cricket hats. Women and old people held umbrellas for shade. Loudspeakers were tied to tall bamboo posts.

A man with a round pink and green 'SMS Volunteer' badge on his shirt looked at Larry and said, "I'm glad you have come to our meeting, but the talks will be in Hindi."

"Oh, that's unfortunate for me. I've learned only the numbers," Larry said.

"Hmm. I'll stay here. I could tell you the gist of their talks." He glanced at Larry's light-brown hair.

"That'd be great. Thanks. By the way, I'm Larry from the U.S."

"My name is Arvind."

They shook hands.

There were about a dozen people on the stage. Mr. Thappa spoke first. Arvind told Larry that Mr. Thappa was the President. White-haired Mr. Thappa reminded the audience that the SMS was for all Indians—from the beaches to the Himalayas. He said that this year their goal was to strengthen their basic units in the villages, the panchayets. He went on to describe some details of the program. Children's education and fighting social injustice would be their top priorities. The poor had been exploited too long, and if they were not helped, India could not progress. The SMS budget for this year would be the largest in their history, but still they were short of money to support all the programs they would like to carry out. The details would be published in the newspapers.

Next Chetti, the second man in the organization, Arvind told Larry, gave a short speech. Chetti appeared tall and confident. His dark, wavy hair shone in the bright sun light. He explained how they were raising money for the organization. This year the largest part had come from individual donors. He thanked all who had bought SMS mementos. He appealed for donations. A little from each would add up to a significant amount, Chetti reminded them, and he asked the audience to get involved and become SMS volunteers. If they joined with the SMS, they could fight together against the evil that had pervaded India for so long.

Several others spoke. Each one explained what good work they had accomplished in their part of the country and how much more they would have to do.

The crowd shouted in chorus, "Bharat Mata ki Jai—Glory to Mother India."

When the meeting was over, Larry thanked Arvind for being his translator.

"You really made it for me. I'll remember all their faces with your voice!"

The SMS volunteer laughed and they parted.

Larry spent a couple of hours arranging his luggage for the trip to Dehra Dun to meet with Sovik. Then, after lunch, he went to the Konkon Café, his favorite coffee shop in Connaught Place. He had started to enjoy the taste of Indian coffee at this place—a rich, slightly burnt flavor. The shop was dark and cool with a strong aroma of coffee, and not crowded at this time. He had lost interest in visiting the tourist places and sat there sipping coffee while reading about Gangotri in Fodor's travel guide.

While he was absorbed in reading, Chetti and his assistant, Ajit, entered the café. Larry didn't pay attention to who came and who left, and didn't immediately recognize Chetti, although he had seen him a short while before. He noticed them when he heard the numbers, 01 35 18 02 25 27 03 15 04 59. He looked up and was surprised to see Chetti. His darker complexion, compared to Mr. Thappa, had made an impression on him.

Ajit also saw Larry. He stopped repeating the numbers and said in a hushed voice, "There's a foreigner here."

Larry pretended not to pay attention, but his ears perked up.

Chetti glanced at Larry. "A tourist."

Ajit turned back to Chetti.

"Swami Rangaraj had mentioned these numbers to me," Chetti continued without any regard to Larry. "They have something to do with the gold. I should have told you about these numbers earlier, but didn't want to take your mind away from what you've been doing."

Ajit's eyes narrowed and his forehead creased. He raked his fingers through his hair. He mumbled the set of numbers in Hindi before speaking up in English again, "Ten pairs of numbers. Four pairs start with zero. Four fives and no six. A combination for a safe?"

"Swami Rangaraj didn't tell me any more than I've told you." Chetti took a sip of coffee. "I don't think he knows more."

"There are seven odd pairs," Ajit said, still trying to decipher the secret, "an auspicious number."

"It's a riddle that holds the secret of the temple," Chetti murmured. "Well, let me know if you find a clue."

"Zero appears four times, sequentially—01, 02, 03, and 04. Very interesting."

Larry took a sip from his cup. It was nice to see an important figure like

Chetti come to this ordinary café. Perhaps the SMS people practiced what they preached. He looked carefully at Ajit. This must be another important man in the SMS. He was thin with a sharp nose, unusual compared to other Indians; also, prominent cheekbones. They were speaking in English, as Larry had seen many Indians do; but he wondered why they were speaking in English here. So others would not understand them?

Ajit spoke the numbers in Hindi after he noticed Larry, so a foreigner wouldn't get them. But Larry had learned Hindi numbers for this trip because he was interested in exploring India, away from tourist places. Numbers would come in handy for bus numbers outside the cities. The series of numbers stuck with Larry, as the tone of the conversation sounded conspiratorial. Would an important man like Chetti be involved in something underhanded?

Larry had studied number theory at Cornell and his master's thesis at NYU was on Additive Number Theory. He took his time finishing his cup, waiting to hear if the two would say anything more about the numbers.

"You'll be back there soon then?" Chetti said.

"Yes, in mid-June" Ajit said. He paused for a moment. "I have advertised to hire two assistants."

"Do what you have to do."

Their conversation turned to other things and soon Chetti and Ajit left.

Larry jotted down the numbers in his guidebook.

Part III

Onward to Gangotri

12

Into the Hills

12.1

During the morning journey to Dehra Dun, Be'ziil sat near the back of the air-conditioned minibus, wearing his new sunglasses.

"How come you're wearing sunglasses in the morning?" Sovik asked him.

Be'ziil did not answer.

"Trying to see India through rose-colored glasses?" Sovik added and chuckled.

"I'll tell you later," Be'ziil said and looked away.

The other passengers on the bus were well-to-do Indians. A newly-wed couple sat across from Kayla; the young wife constantly fed her husband Indian delicacies. Another group of young men talked and argued incessantly. Pinky held Sovik's hand and looked out the window. She could not determine how her husband was doing. The trip was going fine for her; she was on a tour, but Sovik was searching for more. It was good that Sovik had taken time to visit the old historical sites and had met the SMS people. Perhaps these would lead to something for him. She would encourage him to venture out more. She turned and looked at his face. "I love you so much," she whispered and squeezed his hand.

The minibus dropped the four visitors in Dehra Dun around three in the afternoon. They had climbed only 2200 feet from New Delhi to this dusty little town in the Himalayan foothills.

Larry was already at the U.P. Government Tourist Office in the Drona Hotel when they arrived, and greeted them warmly.

"How did you get here before us?" Pinky asked, astonished.

"I hired a car at the hotel. It was easy. In fact, I had a great ride."

Mr. Tewari, the Tourist Office manager, greeted them cordially and assured them he would do his utmost to make their trip most enjoyable. He was quite puffed up and proud that they had come all the way from America to visit the area. His only concern was to arrange for their guide; the person he had in mind was not available. Mr. Tewari glanced at the door occasionally, but no one was there.

Then a well-dressed professional-looking man with a clean-shaven face and thick mustache entered the room. "This is Mr. Dixit, our famous astrologer," Mr. Tewari introduced him, "he has an office in this building." An official-looking metal nametag, pinned to his shirt pocket, read "Astrologer and Palm Reader." If not for the nameplate, they would have thought him a banker, with his starched white shirt and neatly pressed black pants.

"Anyone interested in knowing the future?" the astrologer asked, scanning their faces.

Larry stretched out his hand, "What do you see in my future?"

The astrologer looked at the handsome American man. "What exactly do you want to know?"

"Anything you can tell me."

After staring at Larry's hand for a few minutes, the astrologer spoke while still gazing at his palm, "Your fate line rises straight from the Moon. Ladies have a strong influence in your life. But the end of the line is diffuse. Very unclear." He then raised his head. "Your romantic life has not been terribly successful. Rather unfulfilling, I should say. Right?"

"I guess you are right." Larry said a little embarrassed, shrugging his shoulders.

"Your wish is for a Shakti, like Parvati, who understood Shiva and adored Him, but you may not find her easily. . . . Money will be no problem for you. . . . You will have good health and you will travel." The astrologer stopped and held both of Larry's palms. "Perhaps a solution is to find your Shakti or 'power' by looking outside your immediate circle. That may pull you out of your current predicament."

Larry did not respond to his words. "Will I be able to go to the source of the Ganges River?"

"Yes, you will succeed, but not without difficulties."

Larry gave him a fifty-rupee note, but no one else was interested in the astrologer.

Just then two young women, beautifully dressed in green and light pink saris, entered the office.

"Maaf ki jiye, haam thora der ho gaye," they said together to Mr. Tewari. "Sorry we are a little late."

"Mr. Bose, this is Sabina and Amrita," Mr. Tewari introduced them to Sovik. "I have asked them to come and talk with you. Perhaps they could solve our problem."

Sovik greeted them with folded hands. "Namaste."

They were slim, very pretty and their eyes twinkled with mischief. Sabina was about twenty-one years old and her older sister, Amrita, about twenty-six, Mr. Tewari explained to Sovik. They both looked slightly older and more mature because they wore saris. They spoke with the foreigners in polished English with a slight British accent and occasionally spoke with Mr. Tewari in Hindi.

Sabina, a student at a local college in Dehra Dun, was looking for a summer job. Amrita was taller, had already graduated from Delhi University, and worked in Bombay at the business office of Hindusthan Industries. She was home for a two-week visit and had come along to keep her sister company.

"I have been to Gangotri," Sabina told the group.

Larry asked, "Has either of you done any hiking or mountain climbing?"

Sabina was quick to say, "Amrita has climbed halfway up Nanda Devi, and she has hiked around the places you plan to go."

Larry and Amrita exchanged smiles. "That's impressive," said Larry.

Mr. Tewari asked Sovik, "So, what do you think?"

Sovik had no answer. Since his own knowledge of the area came only from books, he would welcome any guide with practical knowledge.

Before anyone could express their thoughts, Amrita asked Mr. Tewari in Hindi whether he could provide food and lodging for her if she wished to accompany the group. Mr. Tewari said that could be arranged. Amrita then spoke to Sovik in English, "Mr. Bose, I can come along with Sabina. You then have both of us for the price of one!"

Sabina exclaimed, "That would be great!"

Larry said, "Wonderful," and the group had to agree.

Sabina would be the official guide, and her sister would come along for the fun of it. Although Amrita had the experience, she had no official obligation.

Mr. Tewari had arranged a minivan for them, a new Toyota with plenty of storage space. The driver, Mr. Sharma, was a small, muscular, gravelly-voiced man. He was a little over fifty; his hair had started to thin, but he had oiled and combed it nicely as Indians do. He could speak enough English to get by. Mr. Sharma would drop the group off in Mussoorie and pick them up for the journey to Gangotri after two days. He loaded the luggage into the bus.

All set to go, but where was Larry?

Sovik went back to the office. Larry and Amrita seemed to be having a very amicable conversation. They spoke with the abandon of two free spirits. There was no inhibition in their laughter, as Sovik entered.

"If I were you," Amrita said to Larry, "I'd spend more time in little towns, not in New Delhi or Bombay."

"You're right, but I don't know which little towns to go to. Besides, what do I do when I go to an unknown town in India?"

"Larry, we have to go now," Sovik said.

"What's there to see in Dehra Dun?" Larry asked Amrita.

Amrita's eyes brightened, "It is the fairy land of India. If you were here for a day, I could show you how beautiful it is."

"Really! That would be wonderful."

"Sure. You'll enjoy it," Amrita was very enthusiastic. "You can stay at this place or perhaps at the Ajanta Continental."

Larry then turned to Sovik. "Would you mind if I spend a little time here?"

Sovik was shocked and a little angry. He looked at the two. How could they be so friendly in half an hour? And what about his commitment to travel with the group!

"That's fine," Sovik said in a resigned voice, and paused for a second. "Are you sure, Larry, you want to continue with the group? Perhaps you'd be happier traveling on your own."

"Don't worry; I want to go with you to the source of the Ganges. I'll meet you in Mussoorie on Sunday," Larry replied energetically.

This was a somewhat disturbing turn of events for Sovik, the planner. Did Larry find this girl so alluring that he could not resist her? Was he fishing for a romantic adventure? On his way back to the minivan, however, he changed his mind and thought how nice it would be to be as free as Larry, and wished he had the courage to be spontaneous like him. Perhaps Larry had already figured out what was important in life. If Sovik were like him, he would probably not have had the heart attack.

Sovik still had some reservations. Larry's conversation with Amrita seemed innocent enough, but this turn of events made him uneasy since Larry had agreed to come along; he had already begun to count on Larry's help during the hike. Larry seemed to be an honest, trustworthy person. Was he wrong in his assessment? Was Amrita being swept off her feet by the handsome American who was so interested in understanding India and discovering the ancient country's inner spirit?

12.2

In the morning, Amrita and Sabina came to meet Larry at the Ajanta Continental. Sabina greeted him cheerfully, "Your guide is here, sir. Now you can relax."

They shook hands and he took them to the hotel restaurant for tea. The Ajanta Continental had done a nice job of decorating the place. The walls were covered with fresco paintings copied from temples. The tables had fresh flowers. Amrita and Sabina wore colorful salwar-kameezes with matching scarves over their shoulders. Now they looked more like college students than they had the day before. Larry liked that.

Sabina talked eagerly, telling him all the things he could see in Dehra Dun. Amrita sipped tea and glanced at Larry occasionally. Then Sabina told him she couldn't accompany him; she had many preparations to make before she would be ready for the trip. "My sister will take care of you," she said and left.

Larry didn't want to see the usual scenic places. That was fine with Amrita. At first she was a little bashful and somewhat unsure of her role. After all, an Indian girl accompanying an American man was not a common sight in India, especially in a little town like Dehra Dun. But she quickly recovered from her initial nervousness and began talking as they strolled down the street. They went to the hub of the town, the Clock Tower, and ambled around the neighborhood and the local bazaar. It was quite a different experience from the crowds of New Delhi; Larry enjoyed seeing ordinary people going about their daily business.

When they returned to the Clock Tower, Amrita suddenly asked, "Have you ever had Paani Puri?"

"No. What's that?"

"You'll see." She took him to a stall on a side lane where a man was standing in front of a large basket containing heaps of different kinds of fried noodles, grains, and a large pile of round, fried breads, puffed up like golden balls, about the size of golf balls. "Those are miniature puris," she explained to Larry.

The man gave them each a dry leaf folded into a cone-shape, pierced with tiny sticks to hold it together. They held those in their hands and watched him prepare the food. The vendor took a small puri from the pile in his basket, made a hole in the middle with his thumb, put some spicy potato in the hole, and then dipped the whole thing into a watery sauce. He did this very quickly and placed them, one at a time, on the cone-plates.

"Put the whole thing in your mouth," Amrita instructed Larry.

It was crunchy, spicy and full of salty-sour tamarind water. The taste and the texture were foreign, but Larry soon got the hang of it. He observed how neatly Amrita ate, lifting each one to her mouth with only two fingers, and no liquid dropped on her clothes. The vendor served two other men at the same time. They all ate similarly. The vendor kept on serving, one after another, and soon Larry had eaten six. It was fun, although his face and shirt were drenched. Amrita watched him struggle; she tried to keep a straight face but her eyes sparkled with laughter.

Afterwards, as he strolled in his paani puri-spattered shirt, Amrita told him of the nearby places that tourists usually visit: Robber's cave, where there are no robbers, but the place generates fear because of its loneliness, and another place where streams suddenly go underground and reappear a little distance away. There were also sulfur springs and several nearby temples they could visit. She told him about the Boys Military Academy, and the fact that there was now a separate one for girls. He couldn't visit the academies because that required special permission. She also told him of the Forestry Research Institute.

"Let's just see the town," Larry said.

They went by bus through many neighborhoods. At one point she said, "I can't show you the Military Academy, but I can give you permission to see my high school."

By this time Larry was quite at ease with her and replied, "So, this must be the most modern school in India!"

"A very good guess," she said with a smile, but then admitted, "Not really, but it's my high school."

"Okay, I'll be honored to see your high school."

"Too late," she responded. "We are passing by it now. See the room at the corner on the second floor—that was my last classroom before I graduated."

"Ah ha! Bars on the windows like a jail," Larry teased her, "just right for you!"

Larry felt that what he was enjoying was not the tourist sights in the town, or the every-day Indian life that he got a glimpse of, but being with Amrita—she had made the day such a pleasant experience. She had so much vibrant energy. And he loved her spontaneity.

The green bindi mark on her forehead looked exquisitely beautiful against her light olive skin. Larry longed to know her better and wished the day would go on forever. But everything comes to an end, and she brought him back to his hotel. Before leaving, she took out a shiny brass bell, about an inch high, and said, "This is for you. Keep it in your pocket and, when it rings, it will remind you of your visit to Dehra Dun." Her eyes smiled into his.

She left and Larry stood transfixed, watching her go. The long braid that swung down her slim back seemed to reflect her spontaneous spirit. She vanished from sight, but Larry remained there, wondering how many there were like her in the whole world?

12.3

Larry arrived in Mussoorie after lunch and found the group on the Mall where they were window-shopping. "There you are!" he called in a jolly voice, and sauntered over to Sovik.

"How was Dehra Dun?" Sovik asked.

"Great! I'm glad I stayed over."

"So what do you think? Will the girls work out?"

"I don't know about Sabina. I spent the day with Amrita. She was wonderful. She has a charming sense of humor." His voice faded as if he were talking to himself.

"Now you'll be our liaison with the guides!" Sovik slyly said, and Larry smiled sheepishly.

They walked to a roadside tea-stall on the street and Sovik ordered tea for them. Larry watched the skinny, bare-chested young boy working as an attendant. Sovik watched Larry and remembered the last time they had tea together at the airport in Taipei.

At Taipei he had asked him, "Larry, can I ask you a personal question?"

"Go ahead."

"With your delightful personality, why are you going alone on this trip?"

"It's a long story," Larry said and paused for a few seconds, looking at the large fish tank in the middle of the corridor. "My girlfriend left me recently."

"I'm sorry."

"We were so dissimilar; it was inevitable that we would drift apart."

Larry told him he had met Angela on an outing to Pike's Peak with the Boulder Hiking Club. It had been his first hike on that trail. While lacing her shoes, Angela had proudly told him this would be her third time and that she loved the hike.

They had many interests in common, both enjoyed nature, and there was a physical attraction. That was how it started. They eventually decided to live together. Unfortunately, living together brought out the things they didn't have in common. Angela wanted to succeed, to go ever higher in everything whether in hiking or at work. Every event was an opportunity to get ahead.

"What was she looking for in life?" Sovik asked Larry.

"That's where we drifted apart. She wanted to be a winner—in everything—over everyone. And she was willing to fight to win. ... She never went with me to the Buddhist

temple. She was quite clear about it; looking inward was not for her. We started to clash over how I spent my time. She would ask, 'Why aren't you socializing with the people in your office? Wouldn't that be better than hanging around those Tibetan monks?' She just packed her stuff one day and moved out of our apartment. I don't even know where she is now."

Just then an airport official told them it was time to board the plane.

Pinky, who had been quietly sitting next to Sovik during this exchange, got up and said, "You just haven't met the right girl yet."

The two men followed her onto the plane.

Sovik heard the sound of the spoon stirring sugar into a large metal mug and watched the tea-maker pour tea into two cups for them. He took a sip from his cup and looked up at Larry. "Did Amrita tell you what she does in Bombay?"

"She is a business executive . . . She told me some stories about the Ganges River."

"Did you have a chance to visit her family?" Sovik was curious about how far this new relationship might have gone.

"Oh, no. But she told me she's a lot like her mother, a little impetuous; at the same time, she broods about the future—what life is all about." Larry looked at Sovik. "She is so different from Angela!"

"Larry," Sovik said, "our plans are complete. We start tomorrow morning."

"Hey, I'm here!" Larry laughed. "Ready to go on the journey!"

"That's great."

"I need to make sure I have everything I need for the hike. I'll see you later for dinner." Larry walked away.

Sovik stood there, watching people, wondering if Larry had been smitten by the Indian girl. Strange, how things develop. His own first meeting with Pinky had also been purely by chance.

Sovik returned to his group and found them near the Toyota van. Mr. Sharma, the driver, brought another man with him. The slender, tall man, Brij Kumar, in his mid-thirties, would be their second driver in case Sharma were to become incapacitated. Sovik noted the man was agitated. Was something amiss?

"Where is Amrita?" Sovik asked Sabina.

Before she could answer, Brij Kumar burst out, "She is here. I've seen her riding a rickshaw with that American fellow and they were singing a song in English. She is giving a very poor presentation of Indian women. Shameful!"

Sabina looked at Sovik. The expression on her face spoke for her: 'here we go again' mixed with 'can you believe how old-fashioned this one is.'

"Brij Kumar, she lives in Bombay," Sovik said. "They are the new generation!"

Sharma was the senior man and was addressed as Sharmaji by the younger Indians. He interrupted the argument, "Don't worry about her. I know she is a good girl."

Brij Kumar was still furious. "She may live in Bombay, but she shouldn't give such a bad impression of India to the foreigners," he grumbled.

Amrita had certainly struck a sensitive cord with Brij Kumar, Sovik thought. In Hindi movies young people could sing songs together in public, but real romance must be a subtle thing in India. He prayed that this would not create a problem during their journey to the source of the Ganges River.

12.4

Sovik, Pinky, Kayla, Be'ziil and Larry had their last dinner in Mussoorie at the old Grand Hotel. That was once the most elegant place in town, a hub for British dignitaries. But it had lost its old glory; the outside needed paint, the bushes and the trees needed trimming, and even the tennis courts looked shabby. The chandelier in the dining room was still gorgeous, sparkling with crystals. And the service had all the old charm and attentiveness one would have expected during the British Raj; the food was, thankfully, not British, and was superb.

"Tomorrow we'll be in the holy land and there will be no non-veg food," Sovik told them. "So remember this dinner for some time."

"The mutton was as good as we have on the Reservation," Be'ziil agreed.

As they strolled back after dinner, Sovik walked with Larry and asked, "I seem to remember you telling me you collect antique stuff for investment?"

"Well, I dabble in antiques," Larry said. "It's a diversion. I deal with mutual funds all day."

"No money in antiques?"

"Oh, there is, if you find something before others notice it." Larry winked. "No different than finding a good, undiscovered stock to buy."

"I had a private meeting with Chetti," Sovik confided to Larry.

"Really?" Larry said with a spark of interest. The memory of Chetti's intriguing meeting in the café came back to him.

"Yes. They want me to help them."

"Are you already involved with the SMS?"

"I went to a meeting at their headquarters, as I told you before. Chetti has shown great interest in me."

"He seems to be a sharp man."

"He's their man for fundraising and they are in great need of money."

"What do they want you to do? Are you a millionaire traveling incognito?"

"Oh no!" Sovik laughed. "They want me to help them sell an old manuscript."

"An antique manuscript?"

"Perhaps. Can you help?"

"I know a few dealers for libraries. Tell me more."

"He has given me photocopies of a few pages. It deals with construction of Hindu temples and seems genuine."

"Could you show me the pages?"

"I've made a Xerox copy of the pages for you. I want to help them."

"I'll be glad to help, if I can."

"Chetti thinks the manuscript is worth a million dollars."

Larry whistled.

"It's an authentic document. I tried to read it, but the language is mixed and I can only make out some numbers."

"Numbers?"

"The pages I have describe several chambers, tunnels, domes and a series of numbers. I don't know what they are all about. But I feel it could be a very valuable document."

"Do you remember the numbers?"

"There are ten pairs of numbers. I only remember the first few. 01 35 18. The second one is twice the third minus the first. So I remember these. There was an arrow next to the numbers, pointing toward a chamber."

Larry's interest was piqued. The numbers echoed in his memory from the cafe and he remembered Chetti telling the other man, *They have something to do with the gold.'* "Very interesting!" he said. "Did Chetti discuss these numbers with you?"

"No, not at all. I don't think he had time to study the manuscript."

"Hmm. He's smarter than that. Let me see the papers. After we return, I'll find out what we can get for it."

"That'd be of great help." Sovik stopped walking and put his arm around Larry's shoulder, feeling truly grateful. "You know, at first I was very interested in those numbers, but not anymore. They are a distraction from my goal. I cannot chase every new thing that comes along."

12.5

Sovik burned with resentment. The Indian travel organizers had delayed their schedule—first by starting late in the morning and then by arranging for an elaborate lunch stop. He stared out across the valley, unseeing. During the lunch Pinky had said, "Take it easy, Mr. Bose. This is India." But Sovik, an Indian by birth, was no longer in step with the Indian pace of life. "They want to impress us with fancy lunches," he remarked, "but I would be most impressed if they could just be on time!" The van proceeded through the hilly, terraced land. They rolled by small farming villages with only a few scattered buildings. Women were tilling the soil or doing chores, with hardly a man in sight. The little terraces, one above the other, made the Himalayan foothills look like giant stair steps. More hills rose in the distance. The high peaks were far away, but the hazy scenery heightened everyone's expectation of lofty mountains.

The Toyota van reached Tehri, a busy town at the crossroads of two important highways, one from Rishikesh and another from Rudraprayag. Traffic slowed down to a crawl as the van entered the center of town. A desolate shantytown had sprung up to serve the workers building a hydroelectric dam. This dusty, treeless area was a jumble of tin shacks, honking vehicles, and people on foot going about their daily chores. Sweaty heat and the enormous luncheon had made the entire group lethargic; they sat drowsily as the van carefully went over the rutted road. And on the dashboard, Brij Kumar's tape recorder kept on playing the same loud Hindi film songs over and over again.

A wide, fast-flowing river, hemmed in by huge boulders below dun-colored hills, came into view. After a little while, it dawned on Sovik that he was looking at the Ganges River. How quietly, how invisibly the river had made its appearance! He straightened up and sat erect. His sullen thoughts disappeared, and he was shocked by the ordinariness of the river. This was the moment Sovik had been waiting for, but nothing of any significance came to mind; he didn't feel anything special. He became a bit bewildered. It was a river, a big one, but there are many such rivers in the world. Was this the river he had thought about for the last few years and struggled to return to India to see?

The van moved out of Tehri, up into the highlands, and the gray-gold landscape gave way to beautiful green hillsides. He saw a thin man with shiny, dark skin, no shoes and almost no clothes, herding goats with a stick in his hand, watching the river. He looked up and for a moment they looked into each other's eyes.

"That's the Ganges River," Amrita announced from the back of the van, and all heads turned to the right. There was a murmur as everyone had a first look at the river.

After a few seconds, Pinky asked, "Why is the water milky-brown, not clear ice melt from the Himalayas?"

"The glaciers grind rocks to powder as they flow through the mountains," Amrita told her. "Geologists call this glacial milk."

Sovik looked back at the goat herder. The man had never heard of Pennsylvania, New Jersey, or Idaho, the places he had lived. He had probably never even traveled outside this area. Sovik imagined him bringing his goats home in the evening, milking them, doing chores around the hut, and while the women cooked, having a smoke among the village men. Sovik surveyed the river and thought admiringly of the man's simple life. He didn't have to strive to prove his worth to the world.

The day was hot and the journey long. Sharmaji stopped the van in a place near Dharasu. "This is the Silver Valley," he told the travelers. "Very famous." He opened the door and led them out of the van. The river flowed far below the road.

They paused at the embankment and watched while small boys, naked and glistening, played in the water. The sight of the cool water was too much for Be'ziil. He bounded down the rocky slope and was soon wading out into the stream. The rest quickly followed; all were eager to dip their feet in the water. Kayla walked a little down the stream and stood there taking in the view. Everyone felt wonderful. The tribulations of the long journey eased and, for a while, no one wanted to move on.

There were many huge boulders in and around the river. The water flowed quickly with a roar as it rushed over the rocks. On a hillside across the road, a small boy, attending a cow and her calf, looked at them in amazement. Sovik watched Larry and Amrita separate from the others. He remembered how they disappeared quickly after lunch and sat next to each other near the back in the van, causing Brij Kumar, the assistant driver, to take notice, giving Amrita angry looks.

Amrita stepped into the water and studied the huge rock in the middle of the river. Standing behind her, Larry said, "Isn't this place beautiful?"

Amrita looked back at Larry, whose muscular upper body was prominent under a thin T-shirt with DENVER printed in large blue letters against an outline of the Rocky Mountains. "I love to visit the Ganges River," she told him, picking up a handful of water. "She lets me forget the busy chores of life. Don't you have similar rivers in the U.S.?" She turned toward him, her long black braid swinging against her slender back. She looked very beautiful against the panoramic background of the river and the hills.

"An American and an Indian—what a vivacious young couple," thought Sovik.

"The rivers I know are different," Larry told her in a soft voice, "It's more peaceful here." He paused for a moment. "I'm glad you came along on this trip."

"Really?"

"Yes."

"You know, before meeting you, my impression of Americans was like the GI Joe dolls—all action, no thoughts or feelings."

"All Americans are not the same."

"I find you honest." Amrita's glance shifted from the river straight into Larry's eyes.

"In America," Larry winked, "now is the time I would hold your hand and invite you for a drink." They both had a hearty laugh.

Amrita's eyes sparkled and she countered, "And here I'm supposed to call my mother and tell her all about you!"

"Seriously, if you come to Denver, I'll take you hiking in the Rocky Mountains. Although they aren't the Himalayas, there are still a few great places where you can forget city life."

"I love mountains. Who knows? Everything is possible."

"Yes, who knew before today that I'd be standing on the banks of the Ganges River and talking to you?"

"Let me make your trip complete." Amrita took some water in her hands and splashed Larry. "This is holy water."

Larry hadn't expected a water fight, but when he returned fire, Amrita said, "You can't throw water at a girl in India!"

She quickly scurried over to the others and sat among them on the rocks. Larry followed and sat on a rock next to her. All dipped their feet in the water, letting it cool and soothe them. They had met their first goal; they had touched the water of the Ganges.

"Why is it called Silver Valley?" Sovik asked Sharmaji who was smoking a biri. "Are there silver mines here?"

Sharmaji raised his eyebrows. "You don't know the story of Yavakri?"

Sovik shook his head. "No."

"If you come here on a full moon night, you will see the river sparkle like molten silver flowing through the entire length of the valley. Goddess Ganga is most playful then and, like Yavakri, you will get spiritual inspiration for life."

"Please tell us the story," Sovik asked him. "I know there are many stories that took place along the banks of the Ganges River, but we know so few of them. Please, the stories will make our journey more interesting."

All gathered around Sharmaji. He stared at a distant mountain in the north for a little while and then spoke:

"In ancient times, the Vedas, the sacred scriptures of the Hindu religion, were learned by word of mouth only. Mastering them required many years of serious study and meditation under a guru. Sometimes it took a whole lifetime before one could obtain the wisdom. Yavakri, the son of a famous ascetic, thought that by embarking on a program of austerities and praying to Indra, the King of heaven, he would learn the Vedas quickly.

"He selected this quiet area to perform his ascetic ordeals. After a year, indeed, he drew the attention of Indra. Indra told him that self-mortification was not enough to acquire knowledge of God, but Yavakri did not like what he heard. In fact, this kindled a stronger determination in him, and he continued his austerities with more vigor.

"Yavakri's resolve was so strong that Indra concluded that words would not deter him from his course. He took the shape of an aged, feeble Brahmin and went to the Ganges River's bank where Yavakri came every morning for a sacred bath. Day after day Yavakri saw this old Brahmin taking sand in his hand and dropping it into the river.

"Finally, Yavakri went to the man and asked, 'Respected Brahmin, what are you accomplishing by dropping handfuls of sand in the river?'

"'I'm building a dam,' the Brahmin told him enthusiastically. Yavakri looked at him with astonishment.

"'If I keep on pouring a little sand at a time,' the Brahmin explained, 'I shall eventually succeed in creating a path, a bridge over the river. Then we can cross her stream easily.'

"'Foolish Brahmin,' said Yavakri, 'don't you see how strong the river's currents are? She will carry away your handfuls of sand. You'll never make a dam.'

"'If I keep doing this sincerely, someday I'll succeed. I'm determined to build a dam. Don't stop me.'

"'There is no way you can arrest the mighty rapids of the Ganges River, my friend. You are trying an impossible task.'

"The Brahmin appeared annoyed. He stared at Yavakri intently and asked, 'If you can learn the Vedas by fasting or standing on one leg, why shouldn't I be able to build a dam this way?'

"Yavakri was completely surprised. How did the Brahmin know what he was praying for? Yavakri realized that this man was not an ordinary old Brahmin. He was Indra himself. So he begged for Indra's advice.

"Indra told him, 'My son, you must have patience. The Vedas contain the supreme knowledge of life. This knowledge cannot be obtained without sincere work; one must be pure in one's actions and desires, and one must study. There is no easy route.' Saying this, Indra disappeared.

"Yavakri returned at night to the same place where he had met the Brahmin. It was a full moon night, and the ripples on the river glowed like a molten silver path through the valley. He was transfixed with the view—as if the goddess was showing him the path toward his spiritual goal. He understood Indra's message and changed course. He was able to gain the knowledge of the Vedas after many years of sincere study."

After Sharmaji finished the story, the travelers remained quiet for a while. Then Pinky turned to Sovik and said, "See, I told you, you can't rush on a pilgrimage."

Sovik stared at the river without replying. They had been in India for several days, but were only at the beginning of their journey. He didn't know why he was rushing. He glanced at Pinky. She was looking at him with a sweet half-smile on her lips. Her glance was comforting; he squeezed her hand.

"Don't worry, everything will be fine," she told him.

"I hope so." He turned back to the river.

But the fast-moving waters of the Ganges River, the same river he dreamed of in his hospital room, didn't bring any comfort to him. There must be a reason, he thought, still staring at the river, why this Yavakri story suddenly popped up. Was this a lesson for him? Had he lived too long in America, pursuing a driven life, forgetting its real purpose, a purpose that comes from one's heritage?

The van climbed higher into the hills and the river, still wide, flowed swiftly, noisily winding down through steep valleys. Pinky shifted her eyes from the river to her husband. They looked at each other and she felt he was that young man again who had shared long walks with her in Philadelphia. She took his hand and held it firmly. "The trip will be fine, you'll see," she told him.

The loud Hindi film songs from Brij Kumar's tape recorder didn't sound annoying anymore; Sovik started to hum the beginning, nonsense words a song that Brij Kumar played repeatedly:

> Boi boi bam badm boi,
> Boi boi bam badm boi.

12.6

The van reached Uttarkashi at about seven, their stop for the night.
The hotel, a large, apricot-pink, two-story government tourist house, was built around a grassy courtyard. Wide verandahs faced the interior garden on each floor.

After they were settled in their rooms, Be'ziil went out for a walk, alone.

Sovik wanted to buy a book about the Garhwal region, so he went to the town center. With no street lamps, only lights glowing from various houses showed the way. The town center was still busy with shoppers. Next to a grocery store, he found Be'ziil.

"What have you found so far, Be'ziil?" Sovik asked.

"I'm still looking."

"Have you eaten dinner yet?"

"Oh yeah. I went to a restaurant, but they had no meat. They explained to me, this is a holy land—you can't have meat, fish or even eggs. They told me killing another living being is a sin."

"You have to eat vegetarian food for a while."

"You know," Be'ziil told Sovik, "I haven't seen any holy men in this area."

"They are here; not on this busy street, but they are around."

Be'ziil pondered for a moment. "I see. They must be near the river." He walked away. "I'll see you later."

No bookstores were open. Sovik bought fruits for breakfast so they could bypass the cafeteria crowd in the morning, and returned to the hotel.

Back at the Guest House, an Indian family was having tea in the middle of the lawn. Sovik stood on the veranda and watched them. In the light that came from the windows, they looked relaxed and cheerful. Their laughter and happy faces reminded him he was not enjoying the trip. He felt the pressure of responsibility, and an apprehension that something might go wrong was eating at him. His purpose was to discover peace in the Himalayas, but was he too jittery to find it? Had he changed so much that he could not slow down from the Western pace of living and make a transition to an Eastern mindset? Would he have to carry on this "un-peaceful" state of mind for the rest of his life? He thought he had changed after his heart operation! But now he could see that peace was not to be found so easily. He had imagined a tranquil journey by the side of the Ganges River, visiting quiet temples on the riverbank, where they would have time to enjoy the surroundings. But right from New Delhi the trip had become a struggle, working continuously to make arrangements for the next day; he had to remain ever alert to avoid obstacles and troubles. Although he thought the government tourist office would arrange everything, they left many decisions for the last minute and up to him. Arranging things was not easy, and he was beginning to feel rather exhausted. Even in Mussoorie, where they were supposed to be relaxed, it did not turn out that way for him.

Standing on the veranda, Sovik continued to watch the joyful gathering of the happy family in the courtyard. "Will I be tense throughout the whole journey?" he lamented. "All the toils of preparing these last eight years—for nothing?"

He slowly walked up the stairs.

◆ ◆ ◆

After dinner, Amrita asked Larry if he was interested in seeing Aarti at a temple.

"Aarti?"

"A worship service with lamps. It's beautiful. You must see it."

"Sure. Let's check out the night-life here."

They were gone before anyone could think of joining them.

Larry and Amrita walked out of the hotel grounds and heard the sound of the flowing river. No street lights. Light from single and two-storied cement houses cast small illuminated patches on the road and made it possible for them to see their way. One or two men dressed in dhotis were rushing home or finishing the last business of the day. The town was quieting down for the night.

"We've a little time before Aarti," Amrita said, looking at Larry.

"Then let's go to the river," Larry replied.

A moment later they heard a shout: "Bahenchod, why are you so late?"

Larry and Amrita halted and saw a heavy-set man accusing an older, thin man who had just pulled a cart full of goods to the house.

"I expected you two hours earlier." He raised his hand to slap the cart-puller.

The man stepped back. "Babu, my son is sick." The cart-puller wiped sweat from his forehead with a piece of cloth.

"So you want me to lose money?"

The cart-puller remained silent.

"Now get lost and come back early in the morning."

"Babu, I need some money."

"No. Go home."

"I have to buy medicine, Babu."

"No money!" He closed the door with a bang.

The cart-puller stood there for a while and slowly dragged his feet away.

A dog howled in the distance. Larry and Amrita started walking again. When they came to the river, they could hear the flowing sound of water but could hardly see the ripples in the dusk. Larry looked up at the indistinct lights from houses scattered on the hills. Sounds of an ox-cart bell floated on the evening air—a farmer returning home late.

Amrita was buoyant. "Don't you love to stand at a place like this and forget the world?"

"Yes." He glanced at her. "It's nice." But his voice was cheerless. He kept on gazing at the hill.

"What's the matter?" She asked after a while.

"No, no, I'm fine," Larry said. He stared at the darkness of the river, but the incident he and Amrita had just seen forced him back in time to a family vacation in America's deep South, when his father and he, then a young boy, witnessed a lynching.

She came closer to him. "I'm a good listener. Sometimes it helps to talk things out."

Standing on the bank of the Ganges River, Larry continued watching the lights on the hill. "I was thinking about my father. My father couldn't stand the evil things people did in the name of religion or patriotism. He became sad about people's double standards—their hypocrisy and subversion of ethics. I understand my father now."

"Incidents like the treatment of the cart-puller happen in India all the time," Amrita said, but Larry didn't respond.

He remained quiet. "When I was a teenager," he finally said, "I used to walk to the East River and stand there until it was dark. I loved to watch the buildings light up in Manhattan. Then I used to wonder about the future. This evening reminds me of that period in my life."

"You're on vacation," Amrita told him. "No need to get melancholy."

"Manhattan really looks beautiful at night from across the river," he told her as if he hadn't heard her.

"Tell me more; I've never been outside India."

"America is a strange country. It's so rich and so poor at the same time."

"From here America seems wonderful."

"It is in many ways. Only I don't understand why people are cruel when they don't have to be."

Larry stayed silent for a while and Amrita didn't disturb him.

She heard temple bells and said, "It's time for the aarti."

They arrived at a nearby temple where a priest was standing, holding an earthen oil lamp in his right hand, out toward the deities. Larry and Amrita watched the priest. He moved the lamp in a circle before each of the deities. He did this many times while sounding a small brass bell with his left hand. A woman stoked a large clay incense burner. Smoke filled the room, spreading the scent of sandalwood. The rotating lamps, tinkling bell, and incense burning were a normal part of an aarti ceremony, but it all felt surreal to Larry, and he was quickly absorbed. He felt he had been transported to another world, and loved being there.

When the priest finished his worship, he handed the oil lamp to an old couple. The man and his wife held the lamp together and rotated it round the figures of Krishna and Radha. Other worshippers took their turns with the lamp. The priest encouraged Amrita by eye contact and nodding his head. Amrita picked up the lamp and asked Larry to hold it with her. Usually married couples do this together, but she didn't hesitate. Together, she and Larry did aarti.

At first Larry was bashful, but soon got over his reticence. They rotated the lamp around Radha and Krishna seven times. The priest kept on ringing his bell. In the sandalwood fragrance of the small room, Larry looked at Radha, the eternal lover of Krishna. So close to Amrita, his body touching hers, and performing the age-old Hindu ceremony together in the dimly lit temple, Larry shivered and the dark images of the evening vanished from his mind.

After the service, the priest sprinkled a little Ganges water over the heads of those present, and gave each a little prasad of sweets and fruits from the altar.

"I've never tasted this kind of sweet," Larry whispered to Amrita after a bite. "What are they?"

"Barfi sandesh made with sweet cheese. Aren't they delicious?"

Larry nodded and placed a few rupees on the plate in front of the deities.

"Thank you for bringing me to the Aarti," he told Amrita on their way out. "It was a beautiful ceremony."

She looked at him for a few moments. "Isn't this why you came to India?" she asked softly.

He nodded. "I'm also glad I met you." Larry stretched out his hand and took hold of hers. "Could we walk a little?"

"Sure."

Holding a man's hand in India is scandalous for a woman, but she grasped his hand firmly.

12.7

Temple bells were ringing when Sovik went out for a morning walk. The little town of Uttarkashi was waking up. The sun's crimson rays spiked through openings between buildings like colorful flags. Soon he heard the rushing sounds of the river and saw a small bridge at the end of the road. Across the bridge came a man bringing two ponies loaded with jute sacks; bells around their necks made a rhythmic, soothing sound. The scene was so serene and at the same time so ordinary. Sovik had wanted to see this type of everyday Indian life in the Himalayas; he imagined similar sounds ringing over all the mountain paths above this place.

Under the bridge, the Ganges River flowed mightily over giant cobbles. Uttarkashi is hemmed in by hills to the west, and the main road at the bottom of the hills ran directly through town; beyond the town are larger hills through which the river came dancing like a free but well-tempered maiden. To the north, there were many more boulders in her path, with hints of small rapids in the distance. A young boy led two small cows to graze along the river. The town sparkled in the morning sun, nestled in the green hills with the sylvan river flowing on a boulder-strewn path at its edge.

Sovik walked through the town. The neighborhood was quiet and peaceful. Young children in blue and white uniforms were making their way to school. He stopped in front of a small temple. Chanting mantras and ringing bells, an old priest—his body slightly bent forward with age—circled the courtyard of the temple. A stout monkey with a long tail and Ganesha with his prominent elephant's trunk were boldly carved on two sides of the entrance. Inside were statues of Krishna and his consort, Radha. Sovik visualized how the place could have been in ancient times—a little hermitage, a rishi living here with his disciples. He looked at the priest and the deities; the simplicity of the place impressed him. There was no place on earth like this.

On the way back to the hotel he remembered a discussion he had had with his friends when they were in high school. At that stage their main evening recreation was walking around the neighborhood or sitting in a park, with peanuts and spicy hot and sour chutney, while discussing 'life.' One of his friends, Ranju, had asked him, "Why don't you believe in God?"

"Because no one has seen Him."

"Do you believe in America?"

"Certainly."

"You have not seen America. Why do you believe it exists?"

"Now, come on. It is not the same thing."

"You believe in America because you read and hear about it."

"Yes. And I know people who have gone there."

"You know many monks have told us the same thing about God, but you don't believe them. Why do you believe only those who have seen America?"

"What do you mean?"

"I mean, say, Ramakrishna said he had seen God just as he saw people, and he knew the way to reach Him. It is a different path than taking a plane to America, but you won't believe him. And Ramakrishna was not alone; many before him have said the same thing. Monks have gone to the Himalayas and meditated for years. They came back and proclaimed a way to reach God, but you don't listen to them."

Sovik knew he was stumped. He believed in the triumph of science: if one repeats an experiment under the same conditions, one gets the same result. But this is not so with God, and therefore it is natural to become an agnostic; we don't have the full courage to deny His existence, we simply aren't sure.

Even today, as he walked along the river, he was not sure where he stood. He had not thought of God with any seriousness. Only in the last seven years, when he was examining the purpose of his life, he had started to feel a void. He knew that he didn't like the idea of a personal God judging his actions. God must be more than a judge and a punisher. Perhaps the Indian word Bhagavan was more acceptable—God is a personified form of Bhagavan. Bhagavan is an all-encompassing and more accepting entity, and Bhagavan can manifest itself in all forms, male and female, animate and inanimate. For example, he liked the forms used in the celebrations of the puja season—what a joy it was to be present near Mother Durga and ask for her blessings or to celebrate Viswakarma, the architect and engineer god, by flying kites in the sky. As he walked back to the hotel, he decided that he needed to figure out his spiritual standing. But was that possible? How? The Indian rishis had spent years meditating and performing serious austerities for this knowledge. He would be happy simply knowing what he should be doing for the rest of his life.

They boarded the mini-bus to continue their journey toward Gangotri. The van had barely reached the center of the town when Sabina asked Mr. Sharmaji to stop. "I have no backpack to carry my stuff for the hike. Please give me five minutes." She jumped down from the bus and hurried away.

At a restaurant next to the van fresh food was being cooked over coal-fired bucket-stoves, each one in its own well in a cement cooking 'counter.' Fresh chapatis, potato curry, and samosas were for sale. The restaurant had long communal-style wooden plank tables and benches for the diners. Sharmaji went in to chat with the cook. Pinky bought food for lunch and went on to browse other stores.

Sovik felt as if he would explode—everyone was drifting in different directions, and there was nothing he could do about it. So he went for a stroll, staying within view of the van.

Inside the bus, Kayla wrote a letter while Larry and Amrita talked.

"I know a pundit from Dehra Dun who spends summers in Gangotri," Amrita told Larry.

"Really?"

"Yes. He is a very learned man."

"Can we visit him?"

"We'll see. I am not exactly sure where he stays in Gangotri."

"Hey, look," Larry exclaimed, "that man is sprinkling water from a brass pot? Is he worshipping the steps of the store?"

"He is opening the store for business."

"I see. He is doing his puja before the customers are let in."

"Yes. Store owners sprinkle their place with Ganges water for good luck."

"Interesting!"

"This is not new. Ganga's water has been used for purification, even before Gautama Buddha's time. You know that." Amrita said with a playful grin.

Brij Kumar had been standing near the bus; he suddenly turned and barged into the restaurant saying, "Everyone is doing something or other, but no, not those two!"

Sharmaji looked up. "What's the matter?"

"Amrita and Larry are making a nuisance of themselves. I tell you, she will be ruined by that American."

"What has happened now?"

"These two are romancing in the bus. She has no shame."

"They are just talking, right?"

"Yes. But it doesn't look good. Would you allow your daughter to spend so much time alone with an American boy?"

"What can we do? They are adults and they are on vacation. Have a cup of tea, and don't worry about them."

"I wish they would go away. I can't stand it." Brij Kumar stared at the bus, wishing he had the power to control Amrita, and bring her to senses.

Sovik came to a little altar under a large banyan tree. Statues of Krishna and his consort were draped in orange clothes and flowers; someone had left small offerings on a plate. No one was there, but people folded their hands in prayer as they passed by. Sovik put a few rupees on the collection plate and stood there. He noticed the ocher cloth surrounding the altar—the same kind of cloth his mother had given him with Om written all over it.

Turning away from the little Krishna altar, Sovik walked back to the van.

At last, Sabina returned. She smiled guiltily, saying, "I needed to buy a pair of shoes also."

Today their destination was Gangotri, the end of this road, beyond which lies only the Himalayan wilderness. The van would climb to 10,500 feet. Everyone was eager to get a glimpse of snow-capped mountain peaks. The rainy season was due within the week, but the sky was blue and there was no sign of the impending monsoon. Occasionally the waters of the Ganges River flowed at the edge of a steep embankment below the road. In some places young rice plants grew next to the road in little terraced plots. Many such tiny fields, one below the other, were there, and mountain streams, sometimes overflowing the road, provided the water needed to grow the rice.

A ripple of excitement and dismay ran through the van when they saw smoke in the distance, ascending to the sky. Kayla whispered to Pinky, "Are they burning a dead body?"

"Oh my! I hope it's far away from the road," Pinky commented.

"You won't get a smell of flesh burning," Sovik told them. "The smoke covers it." Then a smile crossed his face. "Think how lucky the man is, being cremated on the banks of the sacred river."

Pinky and Kayla ignored his comment.

When the van came to a bend of the road, they found the smoke was coming from a crew heating tar to patch the road. This relieved Kayla. "I don't want to see a body burning," she said.

"If I die on this trip," Sovik said, "make sure to burn my body on the bank of the Ganges River and throw the ashes into it."

Kayla threw a disgusted glance at Sovik and would not allow further talk on the subject.

Into the Hills

Soon, beautiful mountain scenery opened up before them and everyone remained glued to the windows, but memories of the ocher cloth returned to Sovik. How could he have lost it?

The bus began a stiff climb with hairpin turns. As it labored up the hill, they caught a glimpse of a snow-covered mountain, which made them feel they were making progress toward their destination. Staring at the valley below them and experiencing the sharp switchbacks, Pinky and Kayla realized Sharmaji must be a very good driver with a lot of experience on these roads. No one felt queasy as the bus hugged the edge of the gorge on the turns.

13

Haridwar—the Lord's Place

Jagdish's bus trip to Haridwar was uneventful. He had a seat on the center aisle, but unlike the train journey, no one talked with strangers. Jagdish kept to himself, feeling a little nervous about reaching the holy city, one of the most sacred places on earth.

Two men talked incessantly in the seat behind Jagdish: about new technologies coming to India, about personal computers, satellites, the views of Bill Clinton, and whether the U.S. Secretary of Commerce would open new trade with India. Jagdish did not understand their discussions and wished they would be quiet. After talking about the Congress Party and their policies, one of the two men said, "The Sarva Mangal Society is a ray of hope for India. I've been to one of their meetings." That made Jagdish's ears perk up because he had heard of the SMS on the train.

"A bunch of religious zealots?" the other man questioned.

"No, no. And that's what I like about them—they are not religious zealots. They do not push Hindu rituals. They are led by a new breed of business executives."

"What are their views about other religions? The Muslims?"

"They are not interested in propagating religion, except for the good ideas from ancient India. But I don't know how they will reconcile with the Muslims."

"That might kill the SMS in the long run. No party based on religion can survive in India. Wait and see what happens with the BJP."

"The SMS is not a party of Hindu fanatics. They will do well."

"Hmm. No international organization will help them if they are based on Hindu religion."

"They will have to raise funds in India. Perhaps 'people power' will do it for them."

"Look," the other man said, "we are already in the outskirts of Haridwar."

Then they fell silent.

Jagdish gazed outside and saw flat lands and farms like in Sitamarhi, then a few buildings, scattered on the road like broken teeth, and finally many buildings. Those who live here are so lucky, he thought. They could go to the holy land as often as they wished.

When the bus stopped, fear came over him. He stood near the bus listlessly and saw the passengers scramble out. He was in a daze; he had finally reached the land of the great God Shiva.

"Where do you want to go?" the bus driver asked Jagdish.

"Is this Haridwar?" Jagdish asked him.

"Yes." He looked at Jagdish's bedazzled face. "Yes, Bhaisahib, you have reached the holy place. Now where do you want to go?"

"The road in front of the train station."

"There," he pointed his finger. "If you go right, you will reach the river," he added, knowing that was where everyone went.

Jagdish lifted his bundle up on to his head and ambled hesitantly toward the road. He felt a little disappointment; the place looked like an ordinary town. He came to the train station and saw a 20-ft tall, blue statue of Shiva at the entrance. Wide-eyed Lord Shiva was blessing the travelers as they hurried in and out. A snake coiled around his neck. A circular flower garden surrounded the statue and a sign, hung on the low metal fence, said "Northern Train Station," but he could not read it. The blue Shiva was so beautiful! Jagdish had never seen such a huge and gorgeous Shiva. Devotion welled up within him, and tears came to his eyes. "I'm in front of God in the holy land!" He sat down on the cement pavement and folded his hands in prayer.

Train passengers glanced at him and swiftly walked by on his left and right. One man told another, "A man from the village!"

The other man looked back with an approving smile. "A simple fellow."

After some time Jagdish wiped his eyes, got up and followed the road toward the river. The road was straight with buildings chock-a-block on both sides. It reminded him of crowded old Delhi, where he had been a few hours before. Saris and other clothes hung from balconies to dry. Signs, which he couldn't read, hung on ground floor stores, advertising 'clean and cheap' rooms above. Several restaurants had pictures of various food items—cooked in both north and south Indian styles. When he came to the river, which was not far, he saw the fast flowing water. He wanted to touch the water and put some on his head, but decided to look for the Sadhana Dharmashala first. Several buildings were on the right, but which one was his dharmashala? He asked a bored-looking man sitting on the front steps of one of the buildings, and the man told him that this was the dharmashala he was searching for.

Jagdish handed him the letter. "Joshi has sent this."

The man read the letter. His face softened. He came down from the top step and said, "Come, brother, you are my guest. You have saved Joshi; you are a member of my family. My name is Kishore. Come, come inside."

"Thank you." Jagdish was happy. He followed Kishore to a small room inside. A cot made of wooden planks stood in the otherwise barren, windowless room. Jagdish put his bundle down, saying, "The entire room for me?"

"Yes, but one can stay here only for a few days. You don't pay anything for the room, and the dharmashala charges a small fee for food. Here is the key."

Jagdish took the key from him.

"Now go and view Ma Ganga, attend the Maha Aarti ceremony in the evening. Come back for dinner and we'll talk."

Jagdish walked along the road by the river. Four and five story buildings, with stores on the ground floor, faced the water. Many stores on the alleys sold worship materials—flowers, leaves, and sweets. By looking at people's clothes, he could tell people came from all over India to visit this sacred city, but he noticed very few wore the rich silks of the wealthy. Somehow, all had become humble here. He walked to the broad cement bank of the river and looked across. The opposite bank was cemented as well and there were many people there. The stream was about 100 feet wide, but the current of the muddy-brown water was strong, so strong that a chain was fastened securely along the riverbank in case someone fell in. More chains lay across the river under the bridge from one bank to the other.

While he stood on the bank in wonderment, a thin man approached him. "Do you want to perform Ganga puja? You know, you must while you are here."

Jagdish simply stared at him, not knowing what to do or say.

"Are you from Bihar?" the man asked him.

"Yes."

"Ah! Great. I help all the Biharis. I am a priest."

"Namaste!" Jagdish put his palms together.

"You should do a puja at this place for your family and your forefathers. I do this for the pilgrims. I have all the material—leaf boat, flowers, and candles."

"Should I do it now?"

"This is the best time; it's not crowded."

"You are the priest. Whatever you say."

The man took Jagdish to the steps on the water, and asked him to sit down. He handed him a small basket made of a large green leaf containing red and magenta flowers. "Hold it with your two hands and repeat after me."

The priest said mantras in Sanskrit and Jagdish repeated as best as he could. Then the priest lit a little candle and put it in the middle of the flowers in the basket. The basket looked nice and mysterious to Jagdish. He had not seen this before. The priest asked him to float the leaf-boat on the water. "Place it gently so it goes a long distance."

Jagdish released the boat, and it swiftly sailed toward the chains under the bridge; but, as the current was strong, it overturned in a few seconds and flowed away upside down.

"All done," the priest said. "Now you must pay me."

"How much?"

"Fifty rupees."

"Fifty rupees!" Jagdish's eyes widened with surprise. "That's a lot of money!"

"You promised to pay me in the mantras when you offered the flowers to Ma Ganga. For rich people I make the mantra for one hundred rupees."

"I said that?" Jagdish stared at the man's sacred thread hanging from his left shoulder.

"Yes. Panchaas. That is what you pledged to Ma Ganga."

"Then I must pay." Jagdish opened a fold of his dhoti on his waist and gave him fifty rupees.

"If you come here tomorrow, we can perform the puja again. You will earn more blessings," the priest told him and went away.

Jagdish stared at the water and heard a splash. A boy jumped into the river from the other bank. He swam to the chains and held on to it. The boy moved along the chain, holding it firmly, and crossed the river. He was playing in the sacred river!

As Jagdish stood on the bridge over the river, the sun disappeared behind the buildings. Men and women crowded a small space under a white clock tower on the opposite bank. The time for Maha Aarti was near. More men and women came and lined up along the banks and on the bridge. Many sat on the bank and swung their feet in the water. Soon it became dark and Jagdish couldn't distinguish the faces under the tower. People started to release leaf boats on the water. The light of tiny candles and oil lamps on the boats glowed as they traveled down the river. Suddenly conch shells and bells started to sound from the surrounding temples and from the tower. Then small, lighted leaf boats flooded the river—all glittering in the dark, bobbing up and down and moving with the current. A lighted river flowing toward the sea! Jagdish loved the scene. He heard the Aarti song starting in the distance. Everyone joined in the chorus. Jagdish could not help but sing along and the devotional chorus roared up toward the heavens, lifting everyone's spirits together.

The ceremony was over in fifteen minutes. People left en masse while Jagdish remained transfixed, gazing at the tiny wavelets in the river. "May God bless my family and all in Sitamarhi," he repeated in his heart many times.

The next morning Jagdish walked around town, peeking inside the temples scattered along the river banks. In some places he sat down to watch the ceremony and received some prasad. Later in the day he returned to the Har ki Pauri area near the bridge and stayed there for a long time. The day before he hadn't examined the place thoroughly. Now he saw many beggars on the road, on the bridge, and particularly at the bottom of the bridge. In Sitamarhi there were few beggars. A boy with thin legs, arms, and a hugely bloated belly asked him for money to buy food. Jagdish saw many behind the boy, all begging. He felt sorry and moved away. He had become careful about money after being tricked by the priest. Kishore had told him not to give money to anyone without consulting him. Throwing a few coins in the temples was okay, but he should remain vigilant on all other occasions, including giving to beggars. Jagdish saw a woman sitting at the base of the bridge with two arms stretched out; she had no legs. It seemed to him that many beggars were deformed and some even sick. All begged for a few coins to buy food. An old, almost blind, man walked by him, beating a stick on the pavement. Very few people gave anything to the beggars. How did these people survive? How could they be suffering in God's most sacred land!

In the evening Jagdish asked Kishore, "Is it possible to buy a few rotis and sabji from here?"

"What do you want to do?" He looked at Jagdish's guileless face.

"I want to give a little food to the beggars."

Kishore gave him a long considering stare. "If you really want to do that, give me five rupees, I'll ask the cook to make some extra food for you."

"Thank you."

"No problem," Kishore said. There were very few like this man. "I shall give you as much as possible, but distribute the food very discreetly, otherwise they will swarm you."

Jagdish spent his days visiting various temples in the morning and distributed rotis to the beggars during the day in a quiet way. In the evenings he participated in the ceremony under the tower and sang the Aarti song along with the crowd. He was enjoying this routine very much. Finally, one evening Kishore told him, "Brother, guests can stay here only for seven days. You have already been here for six nights."

"So many days have passed by?" Jagdish said. "It seems I just came yesterday."

"No brother." Kishore looked at him for a moment. "Now, what is your plan?"

Jagdish had promised his friend Gopal to carry the gold necklace to his guru in Gangotri. "I have to go to Gangotri," he told him. "Then I'll return home."

"If you want to stay longer, I could find you another place."

Jagdish sat there silently for a few seconds. "You have been very kind and helpful, but I must go to Gangotri before it becomes cold."

"Then you take the morning bus, day after tomorrow."

"Yes, I'll do that." His head swayed in agreement and he stood up. "So high up in the Himalayas," he muttered, "I hope God will help me."

"I'll give you an address in Gangotri where you can stay," Kishore assured him.

"That will be wonderful. Thank you."

"Don't worry. God will always help you."

14

Red-eyed Monster

14.1

Ajit went out every morning in New Delhi and rummaged through electronic, computer, and hardware stores to find what he needed for Gangotri. In his mind he sketched various scenarios for the gold heist and evaluated equipment that might be of use to him and collected them. But he made sure he returned home before four to have tea with Lajjorani. His wife was always there, waiting for him.

Lajjorani spent her early afternoon correcting student papers, then prepared fried snacks with fresh vegetables dipped in besan (gram flour) batter, salt and spices for tea when Ajit returned. It became a pleasant routine for them, reminding them both of the times when they were first married. During his time at Advanced Defense Systems, Ajit worked late into the evening and they never had this luxury. Now both enjoyed their time together and looked forward to the afternoon every day.

"This is my last job with Chetti," Ajit told his wife one day after a sip of tea.

"Haven't I heard that before?" she said, teasingly.

"Maybe, but this time I'm sure." Ajit's tone was serious. "Haven't I done enough?"

"Won't that be nice?" she said. "I could retire from college in two years."

"What's happening with Runi?"

"Sunil thinks he'll get the position at JNU and then they want to get married."

Ajit munched a pakora and said in a low voice, "I've got to train myself to relax."

"I can help in that department," she nudged him gently.

"Do you want to go to a beach in South India in July?"

"The ocean area will be much cooler than New Delhi." She smiled, then looked at her husband—his face was pensive. "Are you all right, my dear?"

"I've been thinking. We have this house, a good Provident Fund, and our daughter is getting married soon. Why not take it easy and enjoy life?"

"Do you have another place in mind?" she asked.

"I just want to go somewhere far away from here."

"We could go to Kanya Kumari at the tip of South India."

"And we'll stay on the beach from morning till evening," he told her lovingly.

"Yes." She poured him more tea.

"We'll do it," Ajit pronounced, and took a sip from his cup.

Ajit had three weeks to get ready before his trip to Gangotri. He had prepared a list of items for the job, but revised the list almost every day, adding new items as they came to mind. The list included dish antennas, jackhammers, mountain climbing tools, survey equipment, cables, pulleys, cameras, etc. As he gathered some items, he kept them properly marked at one corner of his study. He did not have a single item that could be mistaken as a weapon. If he were to use force, he thought, the whole effort would be a failure. In fact, if he were truly successful, no one would ever know about the heist. It was the most harmless coup he could think of. But it must be executed perfectly. It must be done in a way that even the priests could not say anything was taken from the temple and would not call for an investigation. His face hardened; there was no tolerance for error.

◆ ◆ ◆

Lajjorani woke up one night to find her husband shaking. "Wake up, wake up." She pushed him several times. "Are you having a nightmare?"

Ajit stopped thrashing and opened his eyes. He was in his own bedroom, not on a lake. He straightened himself and lay on his back. "A strange dream," he muttered.

"What is it?" she asked.

"A monster chased me and got so close!"

He could still feel the monster's hot breath. He had been in a small boat, floating on a serene lake in a place that looked very much like Nainital, a popular hill station in the Kumaon foothills of the Himalayas. He was sailing alone toward the mountain, admiring a small temple on top of a hill, when something emerged from behind the temple and rose into the sky.

He observed it with great curiosity. "What an odd thing," he thought, "it is growing and taking shape!" Soon the figure became more defined: a gigantic creature with a large head. Does it have eight hands or ten? He was not afraid, and kept on watching, as one watches a game. The lake remained calm.

Then he noticed the monster's red eyes. He saw its matted hair spreading, corona-like, from its head. The monster's glowing red eyes stared at him. Strange! It had not been looking at him a moment before! Was he the target of this monster? He turned the boat around and rowed as fast as he could toward the nearest shore. The monster raced him. He could now hear the monster's growl; it sounded louder and stronger every second. The shore seemed to be far away. Should he leave the boat? Jump into the water and swim? He could feel warm air around him. Hot breath? His heart leaped to his throat. That was when Lajjorani woke him up.

His wife put her hand on his chest and rubbed it gently. "You've been very absorbed the last two weeks. Please take it easy."

Ajit did not say anything. What did his dream mean? Was it a warning of some sort or just a manifestation of his worries?

"It's too hot, that's all," he told his wife.

"Runi graduates this year, and Sunil got the teaching position at JNU. Why worry any more?"

"Right."

"Get some sleep now."

Ajit turned on his side, but could not sleep. The job must be affecting him. Was he afraid of failure? Was it because he was planning to steal something from a temple? But it was for a good cause, he told himself, and it would be done soon—one way or the other—and then he would definitely go on vacation. He and his wife would stay away as long as they liked. He was carried away by the lofty goals of the SMS. He wished he hadn't taken on this project, but he would do no more secretive jobs. He meant to help the unfortunate, but people could not avoid their fate. Their karma would guide them. He was unnecessarily involved in a futile attempt to save the world. Now he was committed and could not back out.

Ajit's mind shifted to the practical aspects of his assignment in Gangotri. He would rent a large van to take the equipment he was gathering. But, he thought, the van would be conspicuous in Gangotri, so he must invent a legitimate reason for the van to be there. He would invent something to distract people's attention. Ajit pondered and finally had an idea. He realized that those who go to Gangotri are simple pilgrims—not the inquisitive, calculating, and suspicious kind. Most of them were like Subodh, the owner of the Dharmashala. Subodh would never understand what Ajit was doing. His plans for diversion would work. Reassured, he dozed off to sleep.

14.2

Ajit's advertisement for two assistants for a geology project in the Himalayas said that they must be available on short notice and have some experience in mountain climbing. The job was to collect rock samples for a scientific exploration.

He received three hundred responses. The candidates varied from those with very little schooling to underemployed Master's degree holders. Ajit didn't want to select anyone with connection to the government, to political parties or influential people. He simply needed loyal, handymen. He hired Sanju, a young chemist, and Gujral, a student from Jammu, who was studying commerce. They appeared honest, straightforward and not too inquisitive about his project.

One application from a young woman remained lodged in his mind; she had a Bachelor's degree in physics and had been a captain in the National Cadet Corps in both high school and college. She also had hiking experience in the Himalayas. She stressed that she could do what was required; she hoped he would not discriminate against her because she was a female, "after all, this is modern India." Ajit thought of his daughter who was finishing a Master's degree in biology and looking for a job. "I know what you are saying," he told himself. "Yes, men and women should be treated equally, but this job is not what you think!"

Ajit fretted when mid-June neared and the new spy cameras had not been delivered; all other equipment had arrived. He collected what was readily available: prints he ordered, extra batteries, bottled water, and food for the feast in Gangotri. He ordered a large number of laddus from a sweets store. He'd pick these up just before leaving next week. He had already talked with Chetti the day of the SMS meeting at the Red Fort and informed him of his mid-June plan. He had also told him that two young fellows would help him on the project.

When he had told his wife about the scary dream, she had begged him not to work with Chetti on any more projects, however great the cause might be. He had promised Lajjorani this would be his last job with Chetti. How wonderfully her face had brightened up with the news. How many wives were there like her—so understanding and accommodating? Her young face came to him. He remembered when he first met her.

He was deeply engaged in work for defense technology at ADS and girls or marriage were not on his mind. For a diversion he went to a public lecture on education in Delhi University. There he saw her for the first time. She was intelligent and naively innocent at the same time. She wanted to know where young Indian women could make the most contribution to India's progress. Ajit was attracted by her sweet nature and progressive social outlook. She was logical and expressed her views in an amicable way, unlike him. When the lecture ended, Ajit sought her out and told her, "I like your line of thinking for modern Indian women. Are you working for the government?"

She was surprised that an unknown man would come to her and talk, but she liked what he said. Bashful, she replied, "No. I am only a Master's degree student."

"Ah. Excellent. Good thinking. What is your name?"

She glanced at the stranger and wondered for a second. He was older by several years and appeared respectable. "Lajjorani Panicker."

Ajit looked at her for a few seconds. "Are you related to Subhash Panicker by any chance?"

"He is my older brother."

"I know Subhash well. I am Ajit Boka. Please say hello to your brother. Here is my card. Hope you will come again for the next lecture."

She nodded shyly.

They met again at the next lecture and this time Lajjorani was at ease talking with Ajit. "My brother said you were the best student in his class."

"I was a nerd, not like Subhash."

That was how it started, and Ajit was married to Lajjorani three years later. They were from different states, different castes, and had different mother languages, but they enjoyed each other's company. Although Ajit was quite a bit older, Lajjorani fell in love with him. In a big, modern city like New Delhi there was no bar to their marriage. She had already finished her master's degree in social sciences and had a teaching job in Motilal Nehru College, a highly reputable school. Since then New Delhi had become their home.

When Ajit passed by Janpath in the afternoon, he saw many people crowding the street; a fair was being held to raise money for local charitable organizations. He had finished all he wanted to do that day and parked the car. Temporary stalls lined both sides of the street and vendors occupied every available space on the footpath, selling items from pottery to hand-woven saris. He walked aimlessly from one stall to another.

He saw a big stall displaying colorful hand-woven saris and it struck him that he had not bought anything for Lajjorani for many years. The last time he bought something for her was two years after their marriage!

"A sari for me?" she was amazed. "You went to a store and selected this one for me?" Her face glowed with joy.

"Yes. Do you like it?"

"I'll visit the tailor to make the blouse," she said, holding the sari up and admiring the pattern. "I'll wear it next time we go out together." She said, kissing him for punctuation.

"Sir, this is a special store," a man from the sari stall called out when he saw Ajit. "These saris are from Orissa. We have slashed our prices for this fair. Please come and have a look."

"I'm not sure what my wife would like," he told the man.

"We'll help you."

Ajit followed the man inside. The man shouted to his assistant, "Bring the special silk saris for this gentleman."

The man spread out five excellent saris in front of Ajit.

"Does your wife work?" the vendor asked.

"She teaches in a college."

"Hmm. You don't want a regular office-going sari. How about this one?" He held out a cream color sari with a beautiful blue and magenta border design. "Very good for special occasions. It comes with an extra piece for the blouse."

This would surprise Lajjorani; Ajit imagined her face and chuckled to himself. Why not? "How much?" he asked the man.

"Fifteen hundred rupees."

"That much?"

"We are a fixed price store, sir. This is a good price, special for the fair."

"Okay. Gift-wrap it please."

14.3

The spy cameras finally arrived. The next day, Ajit rented a large van from van from a company on Gokhale Marg and was pleased to find it had an extra tanks for gasoline. He filled up both tanks before driving home.

"Such a big van?" his wife asked from the door. "What are you up to?"

"The job in Gangotri is a difficult task and requires me to carry many instruments." He looked at her for a few seconds. "I promise this is my last involvement with Chetti."

Ajit lugged boxes out to the van from his study.

When the van was loaded, he went to his wife. "I will be back in about two weeks."

"You say two weeks and then it takes longer," she said, looking at him affectionately but pouting a little.

"No more than three weeks, surely by the end of June," he told her with a little smile. "I was thinking," he said shyly, "after this job, I will retire completely."

"Then we can have tea together every afternoon!"

"I'd like that very much."

"And on weekends we'll go to the movies."

"Yes, we will do all those things."

"I worry about you all the time. Please be safe."

"When I return," he said ignoring her worries, "we will go to Kanya Kumari, okay?"

"I'll get some tourist brochures. That will be so nice!"

He gave her a warm embrace and went out to the van.

"Come back soon," she said. "I'll get a blouse made from the sari-piece and take it on our holiday." She waived him as he drove away.

Ajit, happy at the thought of starting a new life, was determined to finish the job as soon as possible. He drove straight to Uttarkashi, spent the night at a small hotel, and resumed traveling early in the morning. When he reached Bhaironghati, about ten miles before Gangotri, he parked the van on a little grassy spot by the roadside. He took out two large signs that read, "Geological Survey of India" and pasted them on each side of the van. He also added a few small pictures of geological excavations. He then observed the van from a distance.

"Brilliant!" he told himself. "It looks official."

He took out a bottle of Fanta and drank it, admiring his work, then continued on his way. "My assistants arrive in two days," he calculated. "That gives me plenty of time to set things up and decide who will do what."

Deodar cedars covered the hillsides on this stretch of the road. The river, although narrower now, flowed swiftly. The road was not crowded. Ajit drove on, enjoying the beauty of the Himalayan terrain.

Sacred River : A Himalayan Journey

Part IV

Convergence

15

One by One

15.1

Ajit arrived in Gangotri well before the tourist buses, and parked his van as close to the temple and as near the base of the hill as possible. He took out two more signs in Hindi and posted them near the van: Official Government Business—Stay Away. Then he went to one of the many food stalls to eat lunch.

He worked the whole afternoon, attaching two dish antennas on top of the van, then put his sleeping bag on the floor of the van in the narrow space left by the boxes for the antennas. Next he went out to find accommodation for his two assistants. Their initial work would be in the mountains, far from his van. He wanted a hotel for them away from the tourist lodges. The boys would be happy living separately, and he would be free to do his monitoring work.

Ajit set up cameras inside the temple surreptitiously and tested his monitoring equipment. Everything worked well. He was happy and, as soon as the equipment tests were completed, he observed the comings and goings of the monks. He smiled to himself as he pulled out a large box of cables for a system to receive pouches from the roof of the temple.

A few days remained before Swami Rangaraj had agreed to take him to the secret temple treasure. It was unfortunate, Ajit thought, that he had not been able to locate the secret chamber on his own. Then he would not have to depend on the monk.

His assistants, Sanju and Gujral, arrived three days later. They had never been to the Himalayas. Their faces beamed with joy when Ajit met them at the bus stop. Sanju looked around with wide eyes and took in the grandeur of the surroundings.

"What a wonderful place!" Gujral said.

"Did you have a good journey?" Ajit asked.

"Oh, yes, we sat all the way," Sanju said, referring to the common Indian problem of overcrowded buses. "It was great."

"I've rooms reserved for you at the Deodar Hotel," Ajit told them. "It's away from the busy center, on top of a hill. You'll like the view." He started to walk. The two young men picked up their backpacks and followed him.

After they were settled, Ajit took them to a tea-stall and ordered tea. "You two rest today, perhaps explore the hills a little. We'll start work tomorrow." He did not want these two young men to spend too much time around the temple.

"Please tell us what we have to do," Gujral asked.

"We want to collect rock samples from the hills, and get those down to the van. I shall examine and arrange them in a particular order. But there's no rush. The trick is to get good samples."

"We could hike up the hill and collect samples from remote areas," Sanju said.

"We don't want the rocks from the surface," Ajit said. "We have to dig down one or two feet. I have drilling equipment. You will master it easily."

"I can do that," Gujral volunteered.

"That's good. Then we have to devise a pulley and cable system to bring sample rocks from the hill to the van. We'll have to experiment with the cable system to make it right."

"We'll brainstorm and solve any problem," Sanju said confidently.

"Yes." Ajit looked at Sanju. "When I was at ADS, we used to do that all the time."

"You worked for ADS?"

"I was in the new product development office. It was a lot of fun."

"I wish I could get a job with them," Sanju said.

"Were you behind all those secret gadgets we hear about?" Gujral asked.

"Some of them."

"Wow!" Sanju exclaimed. "That must have been very exciting."

"It was. But ADS management changed, and I thought I'd do something different. If we succeed in finding uranium or thorium in the rocks here, it will open up many new opportunities."

"Now I see the importance of your project," Gujral said.

"It will be very good for India," Sanju chimed in.

"See, no one has really investigated these rocks for the metals I am interested in. Uranium and thorium are worth more than gold to the energy sector. You know we will run out of the little oil India has, say, in thirty or forty years. At the same time, the need for energy and electricity will increase tremendously. If India is going to progress, we must find a way to make electricity. You can see why I'm interested in exploring for these metals."

"I am so glad you have given me the chance to work for you," Gujral said. "I shall do my best."

"I didn't realize how important the project is," Sanju said. "Count on me 100 percent. I'll work day and night to support you."

"Wonderful. I knew you two would be of great help." Ajit got up. "Come to the van tomorrow after nine in the morning. By the way, don't tell anyone what we are doing. This is proprietary information. Keep it secret."

Ajit walked out of the cafe and went toward the temple courtyard, wishing Swami Rangaraj would tell him the exact day and time of their rendezvous.

15.2

The bus arrived in Gangotri in late afternoon and Jagdish stepped down. His eyes swept the little valley from one side to the other and caught sight of the buildings beyond the gorge. Such a little town! In Sitamarhi green fields fanned out as far as the eye could see. He felt hemmed in by the steep valley walls, and the cool temperature made him shiver. He wanted to wrap his shawl around him, but it was in his bundle. Just then, the bus conductor threw his bundle down from the top of the bus.

When all the passengers left, Jagdish took out the paper that Kishore had given him. He showed the paper to three men sitting on a large rock at the edge of the gorge. "How do I go to this place?" he asked them.

One of them looked at the paper and said, "Cross the bridge, and go behind that big government guesthouse."

"Please pardon me; I have forgotten the name written on the paper—can you tell me the name?"

The man gave him a sneering look, as if Jagdish was questioning his integrity.

Subodh Kaushik, one of the fellows on the rock, had come to receive a guest, but the man had not shown up. "Can't you read it?" he asked Jagdish amicably. Subodh eyed the stranger from head to foot and realized, no, of course he couldn't read it. This was an unlettered villager on his pilgrimage.

"No," Jagdish admitted. "I'm a farm laborer from Bihar. I can't read or write." His innocent eyes looked pleadingly at Subodh.

"Are you looking for a place to stay?"

"Yes. But I can't afford an expensive hotel. A man in Haridwar gave me this address."

Subodh felt that his great grandfather had built the dharmashala for just this kind of person. He sprang up from the rock with a sudden rush of energy and said, "Come with me. I can find a place for you."

"Will it be expensive?" Jagdish didn't want to be taken in.

"It is free."

"Very nice of you." Jagdish said, swaying his head happily as he followed Subodh. "It's God's blessings that I found you."

Subodh led him to his family's dharmashala and opened one of the rooms for Jagdish. After putting his bundle down in the room, Jagdish asked, "Do you know of a priest named Swami Narayan?"

"Swami Narayan?" Subodh's eyes widened in surprise. How could this laborer know him?

"I have a letter for him."

"You know him?"

"No, no." Jagdish shook his head vigorously. "He is the guru of my friend. I only wanted to come to Haridwar, but Gopal insisted that I should also visit Gangotri. He has written the letter to Swami Narayan."

"Swami Narayan is the head priest of the Temple. He performs the puja every day and you will recognize him easily. He is the oldest monk."

"The head priest!" Jagdish bent forward as if he had not heard it right.

"Yes. I know him quite well," Subodh said. "I can take you to him."

"That'd be good. When can we do that?"

"You go and see the temple now, and I will take you to his talk in the evening."

"I don't want to disturb him."

"It's okay. These evening meetings are meant for everybody. He'd like you to come."

"Fine, then."

Jagdish stepped out of the dharmashala and, feeling a little more confident, walked toward the temple.

"Jagdish," Subodh called after him, "remember, we don't serve food at this dharmashala. You must buy your food at one of the stalls near the bus stand."

Jagdish raised his hand, acknowledging his words. Subodh stood there, watching him disappear and wondering about the guileless villager he had just met. There was something unusual about this illiterate man, but Subodh couldn't decide what it was. It felt good to help a simple man, and he wished that he could do more for him.

◆ ◆ ◆

In the darkness of evening Subodh took Jagdish to the temple. The temple appeared closed; only the black collapsible gate was partly open. Subodh went up the steps and walked inside through the narrow opening. Jagdish stayed behind. Subodh waved him in, but Jagdish hesitated. "I'll wait here until you get permission for me."

"It's okay," Subodh told him. Other visitors he had brought to the temple had followed him immediately; they didn't want to miss out on an opportunity to see the inside, but not this man.

"Are you sure?" Jagdish asked him shyly.

"Yes, come."

In the dim light of a 30-watt bulb Jagdish saw Swami Narayan's room. It was less than a third the size of his sleeping room in his house in Sitamarhi, and there were very few furnishings there—a small bed, a table, and a water jug at one corner. A thin towel and two ocher-colored, long shirts hung on a line on the wall. Swami Narayan sat on a wooden chair, reading a piece of paper. He was a thin, white-haired man with a long, unkempt white beard. His ears appeared unusually large.

"Maharaj," Subodh addressed him respectfully, "this is Jagdish from Sitamarhi. He has brought a letter for you."

When Swami Narayan looked up, Jagdish stepped forward and bent down, touching the Swami's feet. "I'm from Sitamarhi," Jagdish told him. "My friend, Gopal, has sent this to you." He gave him the letter.

Swami Narayan broke into a wide smile. "How is Gopal?"

Jagdish liked the monk's happy face that looked younger than the rest of him. He told the monk a little about Gopal. "One day he will come here to visit you," he added.

"Gopal is a good man," Swami Narayan said. "I remember meeting him in Muzaffarpur many years back—the land of litchis. I was the houseguest of a wealthy man. He invited many people to his home. Gopal was a young man at that time, but I could see he was genuinely interested in spiritual knowledge." He paused and looked thoughtfully at Jagdish. "Gopal took diksha from me. He came with his little daughter; she must be married off now." He started to read the letter.

"Gopal has given me another thing for you," Jagdish said, putting his hand inside his shirt. He took out a small bag hanging from his neck. "A necklace for Goddess Ganga."

"Why such an expensive item?" Swami Narayan murmured, as he examined the gold necklace. "He didn't have to do this."

"Gopal planned for this gift for many years," Jagdish said.

"Many people, like Gopal, send us gold jewelry. This makes them happy. Please give him my blessings." Swami Narayan put the necklace in a small bowl on the table. He raised his head and looked at Jagdish. "The temple has enough gold, what people need is devotion."

Jagdish listened quietly and love for God welled up in his heart. "Swamiji, how do I become more devoted?" he asked him very humbly.

"We'll talk another time. I meet with people at this hour. Why don't you come along?" Swami Narayan got up and moved toward the door, stooping a little as he walked. Jagdish and Subodh followed him down a passageway to another room. A few people, both men and women, had gathered there.

Swami Narayan strode to the front of the group and sat down on a small mat on the floor. Jagdish sat in a corner at the back of the room. There were no windows and, except for a sataranchi on the floor, there was no furniture. The white paint on the walls had a dusty, faded look. A mixture of sandalwood and rose incense hung in the air. Jagdish breathed in the scent and sat erect as if ready for a worship service.

"Namaste!" Swami Narayan greeted the people. "Today I have a special visitor from Sitamarhi." He waved towards Jagdish. "He has asked me how to increase our devotion to God, how to be more spiritual."

Swami Narayan paused for a few seconds. Jagdish glanced around the room. No one was dressed in fancy clothes.

"Let me tell you a folk story today," Swami Narayan said. He straightened himself a little and started: "Once there was a cobbler named Raidas. He belonged to a low caste, but he was a true devotee of Mother Ganga. One day, a Brahmin Pundit came to his shop and asked him to repair his shoes. 'I'm in a hurry to go to the Ganges River,' he told Raidas. 'Could you fix my shoes quickly?'

"Raidas had a lot of work to do that morning, so, he asked, 'Panditji, why are you in such a rush?'

"'You have no respect for the goddess. That's why you ask such a stupid question. I must take a bath in the Ganges water before the sun is high in the sky. If you were wise, you would also take a bath in her water once in a while.'

"Raidas had not read the scriptures and did not have the knowledge of the Pundit. He said, 'Panditji, Ganga is a mother to us. She is always with us.'

"'You are an ignorant chamar. What can I teach you? Just repair my shoes.'

"When the shoes were fixed, Raidas gave two betel nuts to the Brahmin, and said, 'I cannot offer much. Please give these two nuts to Ma Ganga.'

"The Brahmin took the two betel nuts, and went away.

Swami Narayan glanced around the room. "After he finished his bath in the river, and was about to get out," Swami Narayan continued, "the Pundit felt the betel nuts tucked in his dhoti. 'Oh I forgot!' he muttered. He took another dip in the water and said, 'Ma Ganga, Raidas gave me these two betel nuts for you.' He threw the nuts into the water. Then to his surprise a hand came out of the water—a beautiful golden hand with a gorgeous bangle on it. The hand then stretched toward the Brahmin and a gracious voice said, 'Give this bangle to my devotee, Raidas.' The Brahmin took the bangle and the hand vanished under water. He turned the bangle over and over in his hand. It was made of pure gold and was of exquisite workmanship.

"On his way back to Raidas's hut, greed overtook the Pundit. 'If I sell the bangle,' he thought, 'I can get a lot of money. I'll give a few rupees to the cobbler. That will do for him.' Then he thought, 'perhaps I can do better. If I take this to the King, he would surely reward me with much more than I can get in the market. Perhaps he will give me a large estate.'

"The more he thought about it, the more he liked the idea. So, instead of going back to Raidas, he went to the King and told him that while he was taking his daily bath in the river, Mother Ganga had given this bangle to him.

"The King was very pleased with the bangle. He praised the Brahmin for his spiritual power. No one he knew had received a gift like this from Mother Ganga."

Swami Narayan looked at Jagdish, who sat serenely in his corner, and continued. "The king turned the bangle over in his hand, examining it carefully. Then, he said, 'What an unusually exquisite bangle! But bangles always come in sets—two bangles for two hands. Why would she give you only one bangle? Mother Ganga is so happy with you, Panditji, please go back and ask her for another bangle.'

"The Pundit tried to get away by saying that it was a gift from the Goddess and he could not ask for more, but the King would not listen to his excuses. He told the Pundit, 'Mother Ganga will listen to her devotee. She always does. I shall go with you myself to observe this miracle.'

"The King and his court took the Brahmin to the bathing ghat on the bank of the Ganges River. The Brahmin had no choice but to go down to the water and ask for a second bangle from the Goddess. But no hand emerged from the river. In his fear of the King, the Brahmin cried to the Goddess, but still nothing happened.

"In the meantime the King's patience ran out. He shouted, 'Panditji, did you lie to me? Tell me how you got the bangle; otherwise, you will be executed.'

"The Brahmin came out of the water crying and told the King the truth. The King then took his party to Raidas where the cobbler was busy repairing shoes.

"The Brahmin confessed to Raidas what had happened and pleaded, 'Please save me from the King's wrath. Come to the river and ask Mother Ganga for another bangle! Otherwise, the King will chop my head off.'

"'There is no need to go to the river,' Raidas said. Mother Ganga is everywhere. If she wishes to give me a bangle, she will do that here.'

"Raidas went inside his house and brought a tray filled with ordinary water. He held a little water in his hand and said, 'Ma Ganga, would you please give me another bangle for the King?'

"To the amazement of all, a golden hand emerged from the shallow water in the tray, holding an identical bangle. Raidas took the bangle and thanked Ma Ganga. The hand disappeared under the water. He gave the bangle to the King.

"Seeing the miracle, everyone knelt down in front of the cobbler and asked for his blessings. But Raidas said, 'I'm a common man; please ask Ma Ganga for her blessings. She is around us.'"

Swami Narayan looked at Jagdish and said, "Like Raidas, you can be a spiritual man in your own place. Live your life with a pure heart. That will take you to God."

The monk stood up and left.

"What a great man," Jagdish told Subodh several times on their way back.

"Swami Narayan tells stories every night. You can go to all his talks while you're here."

"I will do that." After they went a little distance, Jagdish lamented, "I didn't bring anything for the temple. I don't have money to buy gold. What can I do here to help?"

"I wouldn't worry," Subodh said. He was getting fond of this illiterate villager. "God will find a way for you to serve when the time comes."

15.3

Sharmaji barreled around the last curve of the road to Gangotri just before 6 p.m. Sovik had wanted to arrive in Gangotri a few hours earlier, but he had begun to accept the vicissitudes of the journey. This is India after all—no sense complaining. He gazed outside at the scenery.

The river and the road flowed next to each other through a rocky gorge. Huge boulders lay in the river's path, their water-worn, smooth surfaces glistening in the fading sun. The water rushed over and around them, tumbling into a series of whitewater rapids. Deodar cedars blanketed the sides of the narrow valley. Between the river and the brown-red mountains there was barely space for the narrow road. When their small van finally strained up the last rise and Gangotri came into view, Sovik saw about twenty buses and cars jammed together in a small, flat place on the shoulder of the road, with only inches between them. Sharmaji expertly squeezed their vehicle into a narrow slot. A steep mountain wall rose in front of the van, and the river poured through the gorge next to the road.

Hotels and guesthouses, painted in shades of apricot, dotted the land on the other side of the river. Brij Kumar and Sharmaji helped Sovik, Pinky, Kayla, Be'ziil, and Larry carry their belongings across a short, sturdy bridge. Amrita and Sabina carried their own small suitcases and handbags. Sabina arranged for rooms on the second floor of the government guesthouse and helped everyone settle in before going to her own room. The rooms were large, but minimally furnished; there was no electricity and no heat, and only Indian style squat toilets.

All threw their bags down in their rooms and dashed out to see the temple before dusk. Sovik had expected a tall, grand temple standing out gloriously before the majestic backdrop of the Himalayas, but no such sight was anywhere to be seen. Two paths led from the bridge to the temple. One went by the stream and had stalls with trays of offerings and flowers, and souvenirs for devotees. The other path was a continuation of the road to Gangotri. They followed this path, which was more crowded. Crude flat-roofed, wooden stalls lined that road; not only souvenirs, but cooked and tinned food and hiking equipment were available. Both roads led to a courtyard, a flat cement compound hemmed in on one side by a steep hill and a small, stucco building on the other. An ordinary temple stood between these two.

The front and sides of the temple did not have the intricate ornamental workmanship of more famous Hindu temples; they were plainly plastered with cement, and painted pastel blue, above a four- or five-foot maroon base. Compared to temples on the plains, it was unpretentious. The white main building stood no higher than 25 feet and the top dome carried Mahadev's trishul, a large trident, on top. The four corners held smaller domes, each topped by a golden, decorative spire. From the courtyard, a few steps led up to two small, arched gates, one on each side of a slightly larger arched entrance to the temple foyer. Flexible steel gates, the kind one finds on closed storefronts in towns, covered the entrance. These, and the rickety electrical wires and fluorescent light fixtures, disappointed Sovik further.

Several pilgrims were singing devotional songs, sitting and standing in the courtyard, but the scene was casual. A loud chorus of "Bhaj man Raama charan" drew Sovik's attention; he remembered the song from his childhood. A man sat on the ground near the small stucco building and led the song while playing a harmonium. No tabla or other instruments accompanied them. One voice was definitely off key and a little behind the others, slightly ruining the tune of the beautiful bhajan. Sovik glanced over the faces and found the voice coming from a man with a serene face. He was certainly absorbed; his eyes were closed while his right hand moved up and down like waves. His dhoti, raised up to his knees, showed dark, rough legs. 'A farmer from the village,' Sovik finally decided, 'devotionally overwhelmed.' He turned his attention to the temple.

He hoped for some magic to happen, something to elevate him and give him an understanding of the place. What excited people's imagination? What enticed them to this high place—which could not even be visited during the winter—to build a temple and to write so gloriously about its greatness?

Larry watched the pilgrims. They fit perfectly with his expectations. Kayla and Be'ziil ambled around the courtyard, admiring the surrounding scenery, finally halting spellbound at the sight of the large, white peaks of Bhagirath Mountain, shining in the setting sun.

Amrita and Sabina climbed the temple steps and went inside. Larry followed them. The altar was near the entrance and one could view the deities from the steps outside. The electric lamp above the altar was dim and there were no oil lamps burning. It was not the deities, but the large, red swastika symbol behind the altar that caught Larry off-guard. He knew that it was an ancient and sacred symbol of the Hindu religion and that the Nazis had borrowed it for their own use, but this was the first time he had come face to face with a real swastika. He stared at the bright red sign for some time and observed that the Nazis had rotated it clockwise 45 degrees. He was surprised to see four dots symmetrically arranged around its four corners. It appeared to be freshly painted. Did the Indian priests draw it every day as part of worship service? He could not take his eyes away from it. The four dots on four corners of the Swastika were evenly marked, making the sign beautifully symmetric.

"Are those four dots normal?" Larry asked Amrita, pointing to the swastika sign.

"Yes, although some draw them and some don't. When my mother drew it, she always added the dots. It makes the symbol full. Pretty, I think."

"I haven't seen them in books."

"Then your books aren't complete!" she said with a smile, and turned to step down.

"Looks like a good place for meditation," Pinky told Sovik.

Sovik peered at her, as if from far away.

"Think of this place in ancient times—no temple, or houses, or people here—only the river and its natural sound." She turned toward the river. "It's beautiful. I'm glad we came here."

Sovik did not say anything. He took a few steps and looked at the far end of the courtyard where Be'ziil stood, staring at the snow on Bhagirath Mountain shimmering in the evening light. Then, as Sovik gazed at the Mountain, admiring the beautiful sunset glow that colored the large, white peak, his mind became calm. He observed the surrounding hills and trees. Standing at ten thousand feet Sovik suddenly appreciated the tremendous effort made by the many unknowns who, without the help of modern technology, brought materials and granite blocks up the mountain to build this modest temple. Their hard work was pure; they didn't do it for money or fame. In fact, he realized, their hard labor was not for glory at all. He started to value the unassuming simplicity of the temple. For centuries people had slogged through these mountains to come to this place. There hadn't even been a decent road until the 1960s as far as he knew. It had been their pilgrimage, and its importance was not in the outside beauty of the temple walls, but what they felt in their hearts once they completed the journey. The white domes of the Gangotri temple now looked very beautiful to him.

A monk crossed the courtyard, returning from the cement steps at the river's edge, bearing a brass vessel in his hands. He seemed familiar to Sovik, and in a moment he identified him: Swami Rangaraj, whom he had met in New

Delhi at the SMS office. Sovik quickly went to the monk and greeted him with folded hands.

"Oh! You have arrived!" Swami Rangaraj recognized him, shifting his gaze from the water-filled vessel to Sovik.

"We got here just half an hour ago."

"I'm carrying Ganges water for the evening puja. Could we meet tomorrow morning at eight?"

"That would be great."

Swami Rangaraj took two steps and stopped, looking back at Sovik. "Are you interested in mythology?"

"I've read some. My friends and I would certainly appreciate a little history of this place."

"Then bring them all. A little downstream from here there is a place, Gaurikund, where Goddess Ganga descended from heaven. We'll go there."

"That'd be wonderful."

"By the way, if you have time, attend Swami Narayan's talk this evening. He meets with visitors at 7:30 inside the temple."

"Swami Narayan?"

"Our head priest. He does not speak English, so your friends wouldn't benefit." He gave a wry smile and turned toward the temple.

16

In the Sacred Place

16.1

Sovik had selected Mussoorie to be the starting point for their Himalayan adventure because it was 6600 feet above sea level, almost 2000 feet higher than where they lived in Idaho. Now in Gangotri, at 10,000 feet, they would acclimatize for their hike to the glacier at 13,000 feet. They would stay at this quiet mountain place for four nights before hiking to the source of the river.

The group sat together at the Gangotri Guesthouse cafeteria for the evening meal, identical to the one they had eaten the night before in Uttarkashi: aloo-paratha and dahl. No one complained; they were simply happy to be in this temple town. Sovik quickly finished eating and said, "I'm going to attend a talk by the head priest."

"At the temple?" Pinky asked, a little surprised.

"Yes. Swami Narayan meets with pilgrims and tells them stories."

"That will be very good for you," Pinky said. "Can we also come?"

"Swami Narayan doesn't speak English," Sovik told the group, "so it will be meaningless for you."

"I like the idea," Pinky said, beaming. "You'll learn firsthand what they teach in temples—that is part of your pilgrimage. You tell us what he preached later."

"I'll be back in an hour," Sovik said and rushed out.

Pinky watched her husband's back as he hurried off. She felt his renewed enthusiasm and was happy for him. The last two days had been hard on Sovik. He wanted to make everything go right, but so many things proved to be beyond his control and upset him. "Well, now, this is good," she thought.

"Let's sit outside," Pinky suggested, after they finished eating.

Sovik found the temple courtyard dark and desolate. Only the fluorescent tubes near the door threw a dim light on the temple steps. He mounted the steps and saw Swami Anand, the priest he had first met in New Delhi, directing a man toward a room behind the deities.

"You made it!" Swami Anand greeted Sovik enthusiastically.

"Yes. How is everything here?"

"Great. The meeting is starting. Let's talk afterward."

They went into a small room where about ten people sat on mats on the cement floor. Sovik chose to sit at the back. He scanned the people. The same man who had sung off-key in the courtyard sat in the front row. That was Jagdish, sitting erect in a loose lotus position. There was something naïve about the man, totally lost, or blissfully spiritual? Sovik could not decide.

Swami Narayan, his back bent, came and sat down on a cushion on the floor. He appeared to be over seventy years old, of medium height and thin. A white beard flowed down to his chest. His eyebrows were also white. He had an unusually high forehead and only a little white hair remained at the back of his head. The monk fit Sovik's mental image of an ancient rishi, someone wise and peaceful.

Swami Narayan glanced at the audience. He pulled his ocher chador around him and said, "You know, Brahma has a plan for each of us; the thing is: we don't know the plan." He paused for a few seconds and continued, looking up at his audience, "If we do our duties well and live a righteous life, we will fit in Brahma's plan sooner; otherwise we will have to keep on struggling, sometimes through many births, to align with his plan."

He lowered his head and looked at those in the front row. "What shall we discuss today?" he asked.

One man from the middle of the room said, "Maharaj, I feel very happy here, but I'm afraid, when I return, I shall be back to the same rut and these feelings of bliss will go away. Please tell me how to overcome this?"

"The hardest thing for a man is to develop balance," Swami Narayan said, looking at the man. "Several years ago, I knew a man who did a lot of charitable work, but people asked him for more and more volunteer work. He liked that, but couldn't do enough, and he became frustrated. He asked me for something concrete that he could do to ease his frustration—like chanting a mantra. But I have no mantra."

He scanned the audience for a few moments. "We spend too much time thinking of ourselves. I advised him not to use the words 'I' and 'me' for one whole day each week. At first it was very difficult for him, but he succeeded in a short time. He then became calm and peaceful."

"Thank you, Maharaj," the man who asked the question replied. "I shall do the same."

Jagdish then spoke out, "Maharaj, I've no money and no education. What can I do?"

"Jagdish," Swami Narayan addressed him affectionately. "Everyone is equal in God's eyes. You carry out your duties with a pure heart. That will do for you."

Swami Narayan gazed at the floor for a few seconds. When he lifted his head, he said, "Let me tell you a story tonight from the Mahabharata. You know that after winning the war in Kurukshetra, the Pandavas got back their kingdom. It was a joyous occasion and they held a wonderful celebration. Yudhisthir, the eldest brother, performed the Horse Sacrifice ceremony. The Yagnya fire burnt high, and great offerings were made to the fire. People came from all over the land and were treated luxuriously. The most delicious foods were served. Generous gifts were given to every subject. Nothing was held back.

"Near the conclusion of the ceremonies, the cooks found a mongoose rolling on the earth where a little flour they had ground for the feast fell. It was not an ordinary mongoose. His head and half of his body was shining gold. The mongoose mumbled to himself, 'No, it's not good enough.'

"The priests came over to see the interesting creature. Surprised at his human voice, a priest asked, 'What is not good enough?'

"'The ceremony,' the mongoose said. 'This great sacrifice is not even equal to a handful of barley.'"

Sovik had read an abridged version of the Mahabharata when he was young but had not heard of this story. He was quickly drawn in. He saw that everyone's eyes were glued to the head priest, especially Jagdish, who was listening most devotedly and appeared to absorb each word. Although Swami Narayan was old, Sovik noticed that his face was smooth and placid and his voice was deep and calming.

"Those present were filled with wonder and asked the mongoose many questions: where he was from and why had he said that—because this was the most wonderful and greatest ceremony they had ever witnessed.

"'I heard about this ceremony,' the mongoose said, 'and came to make my body completely gold. I rolled in the best flour here but it didn't do anything.'

"'Please, we don't understand, tell us, why is your body half gold?' the priests pleaded.

"The mongoose then told them the story. He lived in a hole near the hut of a poor Brahmin family who followed the laws of dharma meticulously. The Brahmin sustained himself and his family by collecting grains and fruits left over in the field after the owner had taken his share. However, a drought came and bad weather prevailed for several years; this resulted in famine. The Brahmin could hardly find any food to eat. His family was starving, but they continued their religious practices.

"One day the Brahmin found a field which had a few barley kernels left. He collected a handful. The family was overjoyed and made a powder of the barley for dinner. It was divided equally among the Brahmin, his wife, their son, and daughter-in-law. Just as they were to sit down for dinner, there was a knock on the door and a guest arrived. They welcomed the guest and offered him a seat. After some conversation, the Brahmin saw that the guest was weak and hungry, and offered him freely his portion of the food. 'Atithi deva bhaba," he told himself—'a guest is like God.' The man was happy and ate it, but he was still hungry. The Brahmin's wife then offered him her portion of the dinner, and he ate that; but he was still hungry. The son and the daughter-in-law then gave him their portions, and he ate those too."

Swami Narayan paused for a moment and said, "The offerings were made without any regret or anger. They treated the guest with what they had without thinking of themselves. Then suddenly the guest transformed into a shining person. He revealed that he was the deity of righteousness. He was impressed with their pure hearts and granted them passage to heaven.

"The mongoose saw all this from a hole, and when they were gone, he came out and found a few particles of the barley powder on the floor. When he ate that, half of his body turned gold. 'Since then,' the mongoose said, 'I have been looking for another truly pious offering so I could turn the rest of my body to gold. But I have not been made gold yet.' Saying this, the mongoose went away."

Silence prevailed when the story ended. Swami Narayan stood up and folded his palms together, saying, "Sleep well. Namaste." He walked slowly out of the room.

All the eyes followed Swami Narayan's exit, but no one got up. Sovik turned to look at Jagdish. He had an ecstatic expression on his face. Somehow the devotional songs sung in Jagdish's untrained voice now sounded sweet to Sovik. There is beauty in simplicity, he thought, in deeds done with a pure heart. Then the face of a fellow worker in the U.S. came to his mind. Mike, who did a lot of volunteer work for the community, once came to Sovik's office, asking him if he could help out with the blood drive.

"What do I have to do?" Sovik had asked.

"You can do anything you like." He stopped for a second and then said, "You can serve orange juice to those who come to give blood."

"Just serve orange juice?"

"That'd be good," Mike said, but then, looking at Sovik's face, he quickly suggested, "Why don't you come and just give blood?"

"Yeah, I'll do that."

Sovik remembered his ego was hurt. If he was going to do charitable work, he wanted to do something substantial; serving orange juice was not important enough for him. He realized now that he had missed the whole point.

He saw Swami Anand looking at him. The two men were alone in the chamber. "Sorry," Sovik apologized, "I was still thinking of the story."

"That's the idea. Swami Narayan wants people to think for themselves."

16.2

Sovik and Swami Anand strolled back to the path next to the river. Sovik said, under his breath, "It is how you live your life—that's what I understood from Swami Narayan."

"I do not have the wisdom of Swami Narayan," Swami Anand said, "but I can tell you what I learned from the scriptures. Our major problem is ahamkara. Sometimes we translate it simply as pride, but it is more than that. This is a manifestation of maya, illusion, and we think of 'I,' and 'Me' all the time—what makes 'me' shine, what is good for 'me.'"

"This is what is called ego in the West." Sovik added, agreeing with him.

"In the Gita, Krishna talks about Nirmama, without proprietorship, and Nirahamkara, without pride—the way to attain peace."

"I guess Swami Narayan said the same thing through his story."

"The Indian sages have advocated reduction of ahamkara through selfless activities," Swami Anand continued. "One way to achieve this is to work to help the less fortunate. That way you really help yourself."

"Is that why you work for the SMS organization?"

"You may say that."

"If you have the time, would you please show me the path to my hotel?" Sovik asked. "It's so dark; I'm not sure in which direction to go."

"Surely."

They walked silently. Sovik thought of the story. The words of Swami Narayan haunted him. "All the royal gifts and sacrifices of horses didn't equal the good karma earned by a handful of barley," he repeated to himself. It is the sincerity and selfless act of charity, however small, that counts. Whether it is serving orange juice or stuffing envelopes for a charitable cause, it doesn't matter; ego-free giving is what counts. He must aspire to do this. Contrary to his first impression, Sovik felt this place was an isolated bubble of peace and joy in an oftentimes-joyless world—the perfect place for a pilgrimage.

"A few days back Swami Narayan told us a folk story about a low-caste cobbler, Raidas," Swami Anand said. "Do you know the story?"

"No."

"It has an uncanny similarity to today's story." Swami Anand said.

As they ambled along the path to the guesthouse, he told Sovik the story, finishing just as they arrived at the bridge. "When you do a pure act you can see the golden hand of the Goddess."

He walked to the middle of the bridge and stopped. "Your hotel is there," he pointed toward the lodges.

Sovik turned to Swami Anand. "Thank you for that beautiful story."

"Namaste." Swami Anand turned back.

As he walked the rest of the way, Sovik thought about the characters in the two stories: the truly sincere and generous Brahmin who followed his dharma in spite of the fact that he would starve and could die, the cobbler who had an earnest belief that God is loving and would listen to true devotees, and the pundit who was only after his own gain and glory. Sovik could barely see the water as he walked, but the sound of the river seemed to echo from all directions. Still he gazed at the river and couldn't rid his mind of the pundit and the cobbler. The pundit didn't understand the message of the low-caste cobbler, and he almost forgot the small thing the chamar had asked him to do. He had no cosmic understanding or connection. The bangle was the treasure of the spirit; the Pundit did not get it. Sovik started to wonder if he had behaved like the Pundit. Sovik Bose, the good student from India who went to the States and wanted to become somebody, a famous scientist or an engineer, or acquire a high position or become rich! Ambition for power, admiration, and self-satisfaction! He had forgotten the message of his heritage and uncoupled himself from the spiritual world. Like the pundit under the wrath of the king, he was on the verge of dying. The more he thought, the more he became convinced that he would have to look deeper. This journey was not to touch the water flowing in the river, or to walk on the boulders on the river's banks, or to hike to the glacier from where the river started. It was to find the river flowing within him. He must reach the source of his own river.

"Sovik," Larry called from the guesthouse courtyard as Sovik walked toward the front door, "we're here. Join us."

Larry and Amrita sat on chairs under a large tree.

"I thought I was late."

"Pinky went to bed sometime back," Larry told Sovik. "Stay with us." He pointed to an empty chair for Sovik.

"Did you have a good visit with Swami Narayan?" Amrita asked.

"Yes. It was wonderful. He made my whole trip worthwhile."

"Swami Narayan is the most respected monk in Gangotri," Amrita said. "Everyone loves him."

"I saw that tonight. He talks to people simply and they understand him."

"We're enjoying the quiet atmosphere here," Larry said. "I can't imagine a better place to be."

The place was under the spell of the stars; no light from the kerosene lamps of the restaurant fell on this spot. The bright Milky Way shone overhead. Sovik had rarely seen such a glorious night sky. The sound of the river reverberated from all corners. They sat silently for a while, each enveloped in his own thoughts.

In the faint starlight, the dome of the temple reminded Sovik about what Swami Narayan had said. Ahamkara, ego or pride, was the problem. He sought glory through his technical work, but that was selfish and impermanent. On the way back, Swami Anand said that our soul is enveloped in ignorance by lack of true knowledge, and this lack of knowledge has led us to Maya, illusion, instead of the truth. Could he ever achieve pridelessness and be without desire?

After some time, Amrita got up. "I'm tired. I'll see you tomorrow." She went to her room.

"I'm starting to see the value of the Indian teachings," Sovik told Larry after a while.

"Aah!"

"Although they always talk in the context of God, what they really teach is that good actions are the path to happiness."

"Good karma leads to heaven," Larry said, "and bad karma to hell."

"Yes."

Larry spoke after a brief silence. "I want to talk with you about the temple manuscript Chetti is trying to sell. I've thought of a person in New York who deals with old manuscripts. He could give us the information we need. He could even sell that manuscript for a commission."

"Great."

"But that set of numbers in the manuscript, I believe they mean something."

"I see your knowledge of number theory has you intrigued. But we can figure that out when we return to the States."

"I know, but I've got a hunch Chetti knows of its importance and hasn't figured out what it means. That's why he gave you the pages. He has a purpose. I wonder if he is suspicious, as I am, that these numbers might contain clues to secret chambers in temples."

Sovik stared at Larry for a few moments. "Yes, that's possible." He nodded. "I was also very interested in those numbers when I first read them."

"Priests all over the world have secret places to keep their treasures."

"Larry, please don't get involved in a treasure hunt," Sovik said. "That's not why we're here."

"Amrita and I will see a monk in Gangotri. Is it okay if I show him these pages? Perhaps he can shed some light on their content."

"That's a great idea." Sovik nodded and sat erect. "He might be able to tell you more about these kinds of manuscripts, and if this one refers to a particular place or temple."

"Perhaps," Larry muttered, then fell silent. He shifted his eyes toward the river. The numbers ran through his mind like an obsession. Chetti and the other SMS man he had seen in the café were talking about the same set of numbers; that haunted him.

16.3

In the morning, Pinky, Kayla, Be'ziil, Larry, Amrita and Sabina followed Sovik to the temple where he introduced them to Swami Rangaraj. For the first time, the four Americans met an Indian monk face to face. He looked young and slim, for a senior monk, with a handsome salt and pepper beard. They followed the monk out of the temple, passed by the shopping stalls and continued for two kilometers downstream, finally stopping at the edge of a place strewn with rocks.

"This is Gaurikund—the most sacred place here," Swami Rangaraj told the group. "Please go and have a look." He pointed toward the river, which creased a small valley studded with glistening cobbles.

Everyone advanced cautiously, as the river flowed through a meter-wide opening in the rock and dropped down pounding the narrow gorge below. The thundering sound of the falling water and the sight of the drop scared them. Isolated patches of small trees and shrubs grew above the gorge; its sides were very steep—the strong current had polished the rocks smooth. A small oblong stone stood upright at the bottom of the gorge, defying the strength of the stream.

"This stone is submerged Shiva," Swami Rangaraj told them. "In winter, when the flow is low, one can see the stone in the form of a Shiva Lingam. According to Indian mythology, Lord Shiva sat at this spot to receive Goddess Ganga in his hair."

"Do Indians really believe this?" Kayla asked, her eyebrows rising slightly.

Swami Rangaraj glanced at Kayla. This was his first conversation with an American woman. "Mythologies cannot be proven," he answered. "They mold us and help us assess things. The stone in the middle of the stream could very well be the starting point for an imaginative person to create the story of Goddess Ganga's descent." He glanced at Kayla. "Think of its effect on the devotees. By coming to this place, they feel they have come as close to God as they could. They go home inspired."

"On our way here, Sharmaji told us the story of the river's origin from Vishnu's foot," Larry added.

"That makes the water sacred, I understand that," Kayla said, "but why do the Hindus burn their dead on the banks of the river?"

Mildly amused, Swami Rangaraj said, "Let me tell you the legend of Goddess Ganga's descent; it will answer your questions." He scanned their faces for a second.

"There was once a great king named Sagar who wanted to perform the Horse Sacrifice. In this ceremony a horse is colorfully decorated and allowed to roam freely. If another king stopped the horse from entering his kingdom, a war would ensue. When there was no king left who challenged King Sagar's supremacy—by restricting the movement of the horse—a great Yagnya would be performed and the horse sacrificed. King Sagar's horse roamed over the earth protected by his sons and a huge army."

Swami Rangaraj paused for a few moments. Larry, Pinky, Be'ziil and Kayla stood still, their eyes intently on him. The sky was blue; there was no breeze— an ideal day for a mythological story tour, Pinky thought.

"Indra, the Lord of heaven," the Swami continued, "became worried that the Horse Sacrifice would give King Sagar great power, and he might challenge Indra himself one day. He stole the horse and let the horse browse near a powerful sage, Kapila Muni, in the underworld.

"It took a long time for King Sagar's sons to find the horse. When they found it, they rushed to capture it. Kapila Muni's meditation was broken by the noise. They didn't show him courtesy or respect. In his anger, fire came out of his eyes and King Sagar's sons were burnt into ashes.

"Then King Sagar's grandson went to Kapila Muni's place under the ocean, and prostrated in front of him. Pleased with his manners, the Muni told the grandson that he could take the horse, but his uncles would go to heaven only if the sacred waters of Goddess Ganga could be brought over their ashes. Ganga's water would purify their souls.

"The grandson returned with the horse and King Sagar completed the ceremony, but the royal family didn't know how to bring the waters of Ganga from heaven to earth. Their forefathers' remains lay in ashes.

"A long time passed. Finally, King Sagar's great-great-grandson, Bhagirath, succeeded in bringing Goddess Ganga down to earth. He achieved this by first praying to the Goddess for many years, and then to Shiva to receive her so her impact did not destroy the earth. The souls of his ancestors were finally released with the touch of her water."

"Is that why Indians cremate the dead on the banks of the Ganges and throw the ashes into the river?" Larry asked.

"Yes," Swami Rangaraj nodded. "Otherwise they will carry the ashes to the river. This is the stream that King Bhagirath led to his ancestors—the

Bhagirathi River—daughter of Bhagirath."

Everyone's eyes shifted to the river and the surrounding rocks. They tried to imagine a man beckoning the river from the distant mountains and leading the stream to his ancestors for their salvation.

Pinky asked Swami Rangaraj, "How old do you think the story is?"

"Folklore says there was a temple for Goddess Ganga in a cave in this area two thousand years back." Swami Rangaraj paused. "Indians were never interested in time, so our history is rarely recorded well."

Larry said, "It seems to me Gaurikund should have been the spot to build the temple."

"The temple is where King Bhagirath prayed to Goddess Ganga," Swami Rangaraj said.

"I thought," Be'ziil said, "the source of the river is in Gaumukh."

"It is now," Swami Rangaraj replied. "This place, Gaurikund, was originally the location where the river started. The front of the glacier has receded 18 kilometers to Gaumukh." He looked at Be'ziil affectionately. An American Indian. They had suffered so much in this world and were still trying to preserve their ancestors' way of life. He wished he could spend some time with Be'ziil to understand their religion. He then wondered, when he went to America, if he would meet many Native Americans.

"We are hiking to Gaumukh in two days," Sovik told Swami Rangaraj on the walk back to town. "How is the SMS doing?"

"Fine." Swami Rangaraj's face and voice became serious. "Their main problem is lack of funding. Otherwise they are doing excellent work."

Sovik nodded his head. "That's a problem everywhere."

"Mr. Chetti is determined to send me to America," Swami Rangaraj said. "They want to build good relations with the Americans and the expatriates there. When you return from Gaumukh, let us meet again. I'd like to talk with you and your friends. I want to understand Americans."

Their walk back through scented deodar cedar trees was tranquil. An introspective silence fell over the group. Sovik remained absorbed with the legend—a story of determination, perseverance, hard work, and eventual success. No great deed could be achieved easily, whether it is spiritual, material, or simply understanding oneself. There was perhaps another message here: noble work satisfies not only individual needs, but it also goes beyond. Contrary to what some may think, Einstein's theory of relativity was not achieved over a cup of coffee; it required serious toil, mental anguish, and a bold move. Sovik wondered if his journey would require suffering to gain wisdom. Today, people wanted everything quickly and easily, contrary to age-old Indian mythology. Interestingly, he thought, Hindus grow up with this story, as he did, but most have, quite possibly, missed the real message—that there is a King Bhagirath within everyone, and one can carry out heroic actions like him. One only needs to activate the King. Then it occurred to Sovik that Kapila Muni is like the wisdom of the past, and when one ignores that wisdom, one gets mortally burnt. It would take the effort of generations to relearn the past and rectify the mistakes made. He would have to struggle the same way to unblock his heart.

16.4

Sovik and Sharmaji strolled through the town. They noticed Ajit's large van, parked near the base of the mountain. It had two dish antennas on top and a large sign on the side: "Geological Survey of India."

"Are they exploring the geology of this area?" Sovik asked Sharmaji.

"I heard the van showed up three or four days back," Sharmaji told him. "No one knows much about it."

"This must be a mobile research unit," Sovik said. The sight of the van excited him. When he studied geology at Calcutta University he had gone on geologic expeditions to the mining areas of Bihar and on oil explorations in northeastern parts of Assam. He had wanted to explore the Himalayan geology. Instead, he went to America and never had the opportunity to continue. They saw Ajit on top of the van adjusting one of the dish antennae, his thin body bent at an angle to reach some wire. Sovik stood there, watching him.

When Ajit came down, Sovik asked him, "Are you doing a geology project in this area?"

"We're exploring the mineral contents of rocks," Ajit told him.

Sovik could not contain his curiosity. "Will you examine many hills around here?"

"We'll do as much field work as possible. We're interested in thorium. We have very little data from this area. The government cannot make a decision from only a few samples, you know." He looked at Sovik and Mr. Sharma for a few seconds. "We will be a little noisy, but only for a few days."

"That's very smart," Sovik told him. "If you find uranium and thorium in the Himalayan Mountains, you will solve India's energy problem."

"That's the idea," Ajit replied and made a move to enter the van.

"You'll also be sitting on gold," Sovik said.

Ajit turned back to Sovik. His face stiffened, but he said nothing.

"You are so close to the temple," Sharmaji said.

Ajit's gaze shifted from Sovik to Sharmaji. "I've taken permission from Swami Rangaraj. We won't disturb the affairs of the temple. We may go on top once or twice to put cable lines. That's all. No one will even notice us."

"A very nice project for the summer," Sovik commented.

"No. No. We will be done in a week or two." Saying this, Ajit went inside the van. It was clear he didn't want to chat with strangers.

"When we return from our hike, they will be in full swing," Sovik murmured. "I'd like to learn what they find. You know, India is developing a thorium fuel cycle for nuclear power."

A blank expression crossed Sharmaji's face. "The man quietly does his work," Sharmaji commented. "Like an invisible man. No one talks about him."

Ajit fumed inside the van. The onlookers were getting more curious every day. And, more frustratingly, the day before he had come across Swami Rangaraj bringing Ganges water for the evening Aarti; Rangaraj had seen him but he looked the other way. He had rushed back to the temple before Ajit could reach him.

16.5

In the morning, while Sovik arranged for their hike with Sharmaji, Kayla and Be'ziil followed a trail that started from where the Kedar Ganga joined the Bhagirath River. It went to Kedar Tal. Larry, Amrita, and Sabina also went with them. Pinky stayed at the hotel, resting and writing cards.

After lunch Sovik and Pinky decided to examine the trail to Gaumukh, the steep path that started near the bus stand. Soon conifer-clad green slopes surrounded them, and they could no longer see the river. Those who had gone to Gaumukh that day had left earlier. The trail was empty except for two young men 30 feet or so above them, with no climbing gear and no climbing shoes.

"Are you trying to reach the top of the hill?" Sovik shouted at them.

"No," one of them replied. "We're figuring out how hard it would be to excavate here."

"Excavate? Are you with the Geological Survey van?"

"Yes," one man replied and started to come down.

Pinky pulled Sovik's hand to move on, but Sovik was intrigued with the idea of geological exploration and stood there until the two men came down. "My name is Sovik Bose," he introduced himself. "I am from the States. This is my wife, Pinky."

"I am Sanju and he is Gujral," the thinner one said. They shook hands.

"You live in America?" Gujral asked Sovik.

"Yes. We're here to hike to the source of the Ganges River."

"We will do that too after we finish our job," Sanju said.

"What job is that?" Pinky asked.

"We'll collect rocks," Gujral said.

"So what's the Geological Survey's big plan for this area?" Sovik asked them.

Sanju and Gujral looked at each other.

"That's way above us," Sanju said with a chuckle. "I'm only a chemist."

"And I am studying commerce," Gujral said.

"But you came with the Geological Survey's van, right?" Sovik asked.

"We have been hired for only a few weeks," Gujral said. "We will help Mr. Boka in his project; whatever he needs us to do."

"I see. Is Mr. Boka the geologist from the Government?"

"I guess so," Gujral said. "We have no appointment from the government—we really don't know about these matters."

"At least you must have read about the Gangotri glacier and how this valley was created? It will help you find the right kind of rocks."

Sanju shook his head. "I haven't read about it. Good suggestion, though."

"What company are you working for?"

"I forget the name, something like Himalayan Exploration," Gujral said, and grinned. "We don't really care. Mr. Boka is paying for our travel, daily expenses, and a good sum of money. We are happy."

"Well, good luck with your job," Sovik said as he turned away from the cliff face and moved on with Pinky.

"Look!" Pinky pointed across the path. The valley floor dropped away revealing the river gorge. "The river is down there."

Sovik looked briefly at the river and kept on walking. When they had gone a little further, he said, "I'm puzzled. There are so many geology students in the universities. I know they would have given anything to go on an expedition like this one. What an opportunity! Why didn't they hire geology students?"

"Perhaps they are saving money," Pinky replied. "So many peculiar things go on in India! These two young men could be Mr. Boka's relatives!" She glanced affably at her husband.

"No. They are not related," Sovik said. "They come from different parts of India."

"Oh. Right. They sounded different."

"There is a definite disconnect here. It doesn't jibe."

"Look," Pinky pointed back down the trail, "the temple."

The main dome of the temple and two smaller front domes seemed to float serenely in the midst of the green forest. They stood admiring the wonderful view. "Let's attend the worship service this evening," Pinky suggested, and Sovik agreed.

The sun was near the horizon when Sovik and Pinky returned from their walk. They browsed through the souvenir shops until bells rang, then went to the temple. A small crowd of devotees stood in the foyer.

Sovik got a good look at the deities. The main image was a statue of the Goddess Ganga. The other images were: Lakshmi, the goddess of wealth; Saraswati, the goddess of learning; Annapurna, the mother goddess; and the river goddess, Yamuna. There was also an image of King Bhagirath who brought Ganga down from heaven.

Pinky inhaled deeply, breathing in the fragrance of incense as it rose in smoky clouds. "I love the 'ominess' of this place," she whispered in Sovik's ear. "It's so . . . ancient."

"Ominess?" Sovik repeated under his breath. He smiled and shook his head.

Swami Narayan and Swami Rangaraj stood in front of the deities, practically smothered in fresh flower garlands. A large brass lamp, with five wicks, glowed on the floor. The fragrance of sandalwood pervaded the space. Devotees stood with a flower or two in their folded hands. One young monk gave Sovik and Pinky flowers from a bowl. Swami Narayan adored the deities with a small oil lamp, raising the light up and moving it in a circular motion around each deity, while Swami Rangaraj rang a small bell. Then Swami Rangaraj repeated the same act with the larger brass lamp, chanting mantras in Sanskrit. In the semi-darkness of the room, Sovik was transported to his childhood when he had participated in pujas with his mother.

When the Aarti was over, Sovik and Pinky followed the devotees and threw the flowers from their hands at the feet of the deities, then prayed with heads bowed and palms together.

They returned by the river path; Sovik held Pinky's hand. He felt no rush and had no thoughts of his life in America. The cool temperature was pleasing, and, as they walked, they observed the flowing water. Rocks were piled upon rocks in splendid confusion; he found their haphazard appearance beautiful.

17

Distress

17.1

After their hike along the Kedar Ganga, Kayla and Be'ziil sat in the cafeteria, sipping tea and eating fried onion pakoras. Kayla loved the quietness of the surroundings and the deodar cedar and birch trees that lined the trail. They saw beautiful green valleys thousands of feet below the path and later two white peaks, one to the southeast and the other, much sharper, due south. Then Kayla felt she had gone far enough; the trail was a steep uphill path and poorly maintained. Larry, Amrita, and Sabina had continued farther and had not yet returned.

"I am tired of this trip," Kayla told Be'ziil and looked outside into the dusk. "It isn't turning out the way I thought it would." She turned to Be'ziil. "So much time wasted in arranging for things to be done. Remember, how we wasted time in Mussoorie cashing traveler's checks in the bank?"

"I hate the driving," Be'ziil said, stretching back in his chair.

"We're always on the go," Kayla added. "I wish we stayed in one place."

"It would be nice to explore India alone," Be'ziil said, "but we can't do that."

"The hike will be another hassle," Kayla grumbled. "Who knows what surprises are waiting there? Too many things to plan for, and then the plans get messed up anyway."

"Hey, look at the baby near the cashier," Be'ziil exclaimed. "He has such thick, black eyeliner! Looks cool—I suppose that's to ward off evil."

"I wonder if I should go on the hike." Kayla looked at Be'ziil with questioning eyes, teacup raised in her hand.

"That's the only reason we came on this trip. Why don't you want to go?"

"To be honest, I have no time to myself. I can't take it any more."

"Not even for two weeks?"

Just then Sovik and Pinky returned, Pinky holding a small bag of souvenirs and beaming. Kayla waved, calling her to sit with them and have tea.

"We got a few little brass deities and copper plates with pictures of gods and goddesses," Pinky told them. "It was fun."

"I'll go to the market." Be'ziil got up. "See you later." He waved to the group and walked toward the shops.

"First let me put these in the room," Pinky said and left with her shopping bag.

Sovik brought a cup of tea from the counter. "Was your hike good?" he asked Kayla.

"I'm missing Pocatello."

Surprised, Sovik studied Kayla's stiff and impassive face for a few seconds. She did not blink, but rather stared at him with some hostility.

He took a sip of tea. "You are not enjoying the trip? Sorry, I guess I didn't plan this trip as a fun vacation. I was so wrapped up about reaching the source of the river!" He paused to stare at the baby with broad black marks under his eyes. The mother picked up her child and scooped him under the covering of her sari to nurse.

"Really, this trip has been one hassle after another," Kayla said.

"Oh, I think we are over the hurdles of arrangements."

She pursed her lips. "You solve a problem and a new one shows up every time."

"You are a little homesick," he told her affectionately. "Trust me. You'll be very happy when we reach the source."

"I'm not so sure anymore."

"Sometimes we have to go through struggles," Sovik ruminated, "before we appreciate things."

"I do not enjoy unnecessary difficulties."

"We don't get anything easily. Steve must have told you that."

"Steve? My uncle?"

"Yes."

"He told you about me?"

"Yes. About your situation. Otherwise how do you think you came to be with us?"

Kayla jerked back. Her face turned red and her eyes flashed.

"Look, your uncle is a bishop, a respected man in your community. I told him that the trip wouldn't be a regular sightseeing tour. He said you needed this kind of a trip to get a better focus on your life."

Kayla glared. "Before we started, you said honesty and openness were important to you. I see both my uncle and you are not trustworthy. I came on this trip trusting you, but you have kept things from me."

"What are you talking about?"

"I feel betrayed. You knew everything about me, and pretended to know nothing. I hate you. I hate my uncle." She put her elbows on the table and held her face with both hands.

Sovik was perplexed. Why was Kayla so upset?

Then Kayla moved her hands from her face and confronted Sovik. "So my uncle talked about me at the office?"

"Steve and I have worked together for several years. We are close."

"Why didn't you tell me this before?" Kayla almost screamed.

"The important thing is to move forward. Go beyond the past."

"Go beyond the past. Is that it?"

"I don't know what to tell you. I myself am trying to develop a sense of purpose in my life."

"So you gossip about other people's secrets, and you expect all of us to be happy about it?" She could no longer hold her tears. "Who else have you discussed my life with?"

Sovik did not know what she was referring to and simply stared at her.

"Betraying trust will get you nowhere," she cried and stood up.

"Betraying? I don't understand what you're talking about." He paused for a second, and then said in a strong voice, "Listen to me. I come from an old culture, but I didn't listen to the wisdom of the Rishis and the Munis. I ran after modern goals. I've paid a price for that. Now I'm trying to find myself and rectify the past. You ought to calm down and search for the next step in your life."

"Listen to the words of the bishop in my ward? To restore my place in the celestial kingdom?" She turned to go.

Just then Pinky entered the room. "No, no. Don't go now."

"Will it be a big problem if I don't go on the hike to Gaumukh?" Kayla asked Sovik.

Pinky looked at both of them. "What's the matter?"

"Don't you want to go to the source of the river?" Sovik asked Kayla, ignoring Pinky.

"I better not." She looked away from him. "I want to go back to New Delhi," she told Pinky.

"Kayla is tired of the trip," Sovik said.

Kayla gave him an angry look, and told Pinky she preferred to return to New Delhi. Her time in India was limited to a mere two weeks. It would be a shame to travel so far and not see the Taj Mahal.

"Well, you probably would have more fun sightseeing," Pinky agreed.

Sovik went to the counter to get dinner. He remembered Kayla at the bank in Mussoorie and then when they gave cash to Sharmaji. Although he had sent a check from the U.S., the travel agent didn't cash it and requested cash in Rupees. The group wasted a whole afternoon cashing traveler's checks in a bank and then watching Sharmaji count each note twice. Sovik had insisted that all should be present during the transfer of the cash. He remembered Kayla's face. She was beside herself with annoyance—almost distraught—and didn't talk with him for some time.

Kayla was gone when he returned with food.

"Why was she so upset?" Pinky asked Sovik.

"I really don't know." He sat down. "Her uncle told me she needed a new perspective on life. She thinks that was a great betrayal—that we had been gossiping about her in the office and I know all about her secrets."

"She grew up a Mormon in Blackfoot, Idaho," Pinky said. "How deep and dark a secret could she have?"

Sovik wondered about Kayla; how little he knew her. It was because of her that they changed hotels in Mussoorie. Their hotel had booked a big party and forgot all about them. They couldn't eat in the dining room and they couldn't even get room service. In the morning, Kayla was firm with the hotel manager—she wanted out and she wouldn't listen to any excuses. Even though she had been born and brought up in Idaho, she had a lot of hidden spunk. What else didn't he know about her?

♦ ♦ ♦

Seven years before, Kayla had been the most popular girl in their Ward in Blackfoot, and she admired and loved her uncle, who became the bishop when she was a junior in high school. She was a true believing Mormon. She did not smoke, drink or use any swear words, and dressed conservatively. She was the leader of the Young Women and had led two young girls' camps in Utah. She regularly gave 10% of her earnings from baby-sitting to the church. She had been dating boys since she turned sixteen—but mostly in groups—to movies or dances. She did not do anything to tempt a boy, as she was taught in church.

The day after she graduated from high school, her uncle said, "Kayla, you know you are a young lady now."

"What do you mean, Uncle Steve?"

"Marriage, motherhood, and church are the three most important things in a woman's life."

"Marry now?" She giggled at the thought.

"You know women are given to multiply and replenish the earth. Your mother had three babies by the time she was your age. Your grandmother had twelve children and your mother eight. They all became good members of our community."

"Uncle Steve, no one should marry before finishing college!"

"You have always been respectful of elders and authority. You don't want to disappoint them. Think of our community. You need to marry to enter the celestial kingdom."

"I don't know," she said and walked away, laughing to herself. "Let me enjoy the summer."

A month later a boy from Shelley came to their ward for Sunday service. He was invited by her uncle to tell the Young Men's group about a wonderful project that had been done by Boy Scouts in his Ward. Later, her uncle introduced her to the boy. "She is our Young Women's leader," her uncle told the boy. "You two have lots in common and should know each other."

He was a tall, muscular, good-looking boy. They went to the sacrament meeting together and chatted for the rest of the time he was visiting. A few days later he called and asked for a date and she agreed.

After two dates, her uncle asked, "So how is it going with the boy from Shelley?"

"He is nice," she said and gave an approving smile.

"He is from a good farming family. They have large potato and sod farms in Shelley. I know his parents."

On the night of her third date, however, she returned early, her car screeching to a stop in front of her uncle's house. She came out in an unsteady state and banged repeatedly on the door.

"Why knock so hard?" her uncle said as he let her in.

She put her head down on the dining table and started to sob. Her hair was a mess and dress disheveled, not the way she usually presented herself.

"What's the matter?" her uncle put his hand on her shoulder.

"He did this to me," she cried out loudly.

"What?"

"He forced it. I could not stop him." She showed him her torn clothes. Tears running down her cheeks. "Please call the police."

"Calm down, Kayla. Has the boy molested you?"

"Yes."

"Oh my Gosh! How could a good Mormon boy do that?"

"He took me away to the end of their farm, and no one was there." She looked down on the floor. "Please call the police. We must report this."

"Wait, wait. First tell me, does it hurt anywhere?"

"Yes, it hurts. I feel torn up inside." She started to sob again. "I think we should go to a hospital."

"No, no. No hospital. That's too public. Everyone will know what happened. Let me take you to our local doctor first."

"What about the police?"

"We'll think of that later. Come with me."

"Is auntie home?"

"Just come with me," he commanded and held her arm firmly, lifting her up from the chair. "The fewer people know about this, the better."

The doctor examined her and gave her an injection, saying, "This will bring on your period. You rest for a few days. Everything will be fine."

"No one tells about this incident to anyone," her uncle told the doctor.

"Certainly," the doctor agreed. Then he gave her a tablet. "This will help you sleep tonight."

The next day she woke up late and saw her family and many relatives there. All were happily arranging for a trip. Her younger brothers and sisters were elated at the prospect of going away for the summer. They surrounded her with excitement and, before she could think of the horrors of the previous night, they were out of the house. Her family drove them to a relative in Vernal, Utah—a rather secluded area near where scientists and students were working to restore dinosaur fossils and create a museum. There were several lakes in the quiet, wooded vacation town and many Mormons from nearby areas went there in the summer. Kayla had often pleaded to go to this area, but now she felt numb and viewed everything as one asleep—looking at it all through a hazy lens. The family in Vernal had several boys and girls her age who were happy to have distant cousins visit from Idaho. They did their best to pull her into the many summer activities available in the area.

Two months later when Kayla returned to Blackfoot, no one mentioned the incident, as if the rape had not happened. It haunted her, but she could not talk about the rape to anyone, not even to her mother. What surprised her most was that her mother did not say a word about the episode. This made her wonder if her uncle had ever told her mother about it. Could her mother be pretending that the rape never happened? Who really knew about it? Did her uncle make up a story to send her away to Vernal? These thoughts tore her apart, but there was no one she could talk to and life in her family went on as usual.

Then she started college in Pocatello. The incident remained lodged in her heart as a dark secret. It was like a lump in her throat that would not go away. She bore it alone and silently. Until the moment Sovik mentioned her uncle.

17.2

After dinner, Sovik went to the temple to hear Swami Narayan's talk. Swami Anand was standing with Jagdish in the foyer when he came in. He welcomed Sovik with folded hands.

The monk's happy face lifted Sovik's spirits. He returned the greeting. The irritation and consternation he felt earlier in the evening was forgotten. He beamed at Jagdish. "I've seen you singing bhajans in the courtyard. You must be spending all your time in the temple."

"Babuji, I'm so fortunate to be here," Jagdish said. "What else would I do?"

The three men went to the meeting room together. Today there were a few more people; Jagdish went to the front, while Sovik sat at the back.

After a brief inquiry into everyone's welfare, Swami Narayan said, "Most of you have come from far away. What do you wish to take back from here?"

Silence prevailed for a few seconds. Then one man said, "I'm happy I was able to come here. That's enough for me."

Another man said, "I wish I could take back the peace I feel here."

A woman with gray hair, dressed in the white sari of a widow, said, "I wish for more bhakti—devotion."

"I often search for answers in our epics," Swami Narayan said. "Tonight let me tell you a story from the Mahabharata—the Pandavas' last journey."

He scanned the audience for a moment and started. "After the five Pandava Brothers defeated the Kauravas in the Great War, they established a peaceful empire and ruled the country for thirty-six years. Then they handed over the kingdom to their grandson, and went on a journey through the Himalayas. Their religion told them that if a person has lived a flawless life on earth, he or she could reach heaven in the flesh. That was their goal.

"Six of them hiked up the mountain toward heaven. This included the Pandava brothers: Yudhisthir, Bhim, Arjun, the younger twins Nakul and Sahadev; and Queen Draupadi, their wife. Sometime during their journey, a dog joined them. No one noticed the dog."

Sovik looked around the room. Jagdish was fully focused on Swami Narayan's words.

"The hike was hard and exhausting," Swami Narayan continued. "Suddenly Draupadi sat down on the path and died instantly. They all cried, and, in their grief, the four younger ones asked Yudhisthir, their eldest brother and the most righteous man on earth, why the queen could not go to heaven in the flesh? Had she not been without sin?

"'Draupadi did everything right in her life except for one thing,' Yudhisthir replied. 'She was married to five of us, but she loved Arjun more dearly than others. Because of her favoritism, she couldn't go to heaven in her earthly body.'"

The devotees had read the Mahabharata, but, like Sovik, they all listened intently. Jagdish thought of his wife. Sukhi would never have Draupadi's problem as she had only him as her husband. She loved him totally, had never asked for anything for herself, and cared for their family all through their troubles. He felt fortunate to have her.

"They continued their journey," Swami Narayan said, "but soon Sahadev, the youngest brother, was struck with a severe headache. He stopped walking and also died. Those that remained mourned again. Yudhisthir said, 'Sahadev thought no one was his equal in wisdom. That's the reason he fell.'

"Nakul died next," Swami Narayan said. "Nakul thought no one was equal to him in how handsome his appearance was. It is because of his vanity that he died.

"They moved further up the trail through the snows. Now Arjun could not go any further. Arjun was too proud of his ability as an archer. This is why he couldn't go to heaven in person.

"Bhim soon became powerless to climb. He surmised it was his time to die and asked Yudhisthir what his fault was.

"Yudhisthir consoled Bhim and explained, 'You were extremely proud of your strength. Pride makes one ignorant, and makes one forget limitations. You were also a gluttonous eater and ate more than your share.' Bhim breathed his last as he listened to his brother."

Sovik read a shorter version of the legend in his childhood. But Swami Narayan's telling of the story affected him deeply. He thought of the legend in terms of his own life. Sometimes the qualities we are proud of turn out to be faults. He glanced at others in the room. Had he forgotten the lessons of the Mahabharata and followed a path that leads only to hell, to frustrations and ultimate failure?

Swami Narayan said, "Yudhisthir was alone now, except for the dog, who continued walking with him. He climbed higher and higher in the mountains. Finally, there were only snowy peaks above.

"A golden chariot appeared suddenly before Yudhisthir. Indra, the king of the Heaven, came out of the chariot and said, 'I've come to take you to heaven. Please board my chariot.'

"'Tell me first, please, what has happened to my brothers and Draupadi?' Yudhisthir asked.

"'They're already in heaven.' Indra replied.

"Yudhisthir was relieved and about to enter the chariot, when he felt something soft touch his feet. He looked down and saw the dog, wagging his tail. He looked at the dog, then at the chariot. 'This dog has accompanied me all this way. I'll take him with me.'

"Indra laughed loudly. 'A dog is an inauspicious animal. He cannot go in my chariot.'

"Yudhisthir pondered and said, 'Then, I'm not coming with you.'

"'You have left behind your brothers and your wife. Why do you care so much for this stray dog?'

"'This dog has come all the way to the gate of heaven with me, whereas my brothers and wife could not. I cannot forsake him at this stage!'

"Yudhisthir looked once again at the dog. But there was no dog. Instead, Yama, the Preserver of Dharma, stood before him. He had accompanied Yudhisthir in the guise of a dog. Yama gave him his blessings, Yudhisthir boarded Indra's chariot and rose to Heaven in human flesh."

Swami Narayan sat silent for a few seconds, then rose and walked out of the room. The meeting was over.

On his way back Sovik was amazed that he hadn't thought about the story since he left India. The story clearly said: one should not be blindly proud of any quality God has given one, nor should one take more than one's share. Yudhisthir followed his dharma without any hesitation. He could have forsaken the dog, as the King of Heaven asked him to do, but he didn't. Sovik wondered if he was too selfish and cared only for his own accomplishments. Had he taken the wrong path in pursuing his goals?

17.3

A t breakfast, on their last full day in Gangotri, Sovik told Pinky he would meet with Sharmaji and Brij Kumar to ensure everything was in order for tomorrow's hike.

"Don't forget the porter," Pinky reminded him. She took a bite of aloo paratha with a touch of spicy, hot and sour mango chutney. "Kayla was so upset last night. Today, I'll spend time with her. The next time we see her will be in the U.S. If we see her again."

"Fine, if you want to. She seemed so irritable—erratic last night. Rude, even. . . . I don't understand her behavior." Sovik took a sip of tea and looked away toward the crowded breakfast room. "I really thought the trip would be good for Be'ziil and Kayla. ... Be'ziil is wandering like a vagabond . . . and Kayla wants to return. Maybe I am all wrong . . . even with the best of intentions." After a few seconds, he put his hand on Pinky's. "Perhaps, as a therapist, you can figure it out."

"She grew up in a society where men are in charge—afraid to express her feelings. Perhaps she will open up to me."

"I wish I knew what is bothering her. She spoke to me as if she blamed me for her unhappiness."

"I don't know what we'll do," Pinky interrupted. "Don't wait for us for dinner."

"What's Be'ziil doing today?"

"He finished breakfast earlier and went out. He told me not to worry about him."

Sovik shook his head, sighed and left.

Kayla and Pinky sat on the hotel porch. Mellow sunlight shimmered through the Deodar pines making long shadows on the rocky ground, and mist rose from the thrashing waters in the gorge. Voices in various Indian languages floated out of the cafeteria behind them.

"Have you bought any souvenirs from here?" Pinky asked.

Kayla shook her head. "I can't decide what to buy."

"Well then, let's browse through the market. It'll be fun."

They walked over the wooden bridge and entered the narrow lane with stores on both sides. The shop owners called them eagerly, but they ignored them and strolled through the market. Kayla peeked into the stalls that sold all the 'pots and pans,' as Pinky called them, needed for worship services, but found nothing to interest her. Finally, they halted at a store that sold statues. Kayla found a sandal-wood statue of Saraswati, goddess of learning and music. She loved the intricate work—a swan and a lotus flower on which the goddess stood holding a musical instrument—and bought it.

"She is one of the deities in the temple," Pinky told her.

At the end of the market lane they discovered a store selling paintings. The seller brought out some paintings for them from inside. "These are my best," he told the women. "Please have a look." He did not act like the other shop owners, pressuring them to buy. Pleased, Pinky and Kayla settled in and inspected his wares.

Kayla liked a water color painting of the area: white water on the rocks, the surrounding greenery, and Bhagirath mountain in the distance. "This will remind me of Gangotri," she told Pinky and bought it. The painting cost $15.

"I need some rest," Pinky said, "Let's sit down somewhere."

"I like the ghat," Kayla said, referring to the steps down to the river.

They went to the far end of the ghat where there were no pilgrims, and sat down. The sun warmed their backs and it felt good. Morning worship service had concluded some time before, but there were still people in the courtyard. Murmurs of the pilgrims' gentle voices could be heard in the fresh morning air. Pinky and Kayla quietly watched the pilgrims' activities—the everyday life in this place. No one was in a rush.

A middle-aged man lay prone on the pavement near the river for a few seconds. He rose, took three steps forward, and stretched out again face down. He continued the prostration toward the temple. This was probably his penance, Kayla thought. He would feel happy after completing his task.

Several people gathered in the middle of the courtyard. One man played a harmonium while he sang a devotional song and others joined him in the chorus. Jagdish was one of these men, but Kayla didn't know him.

None of the pilgrims wore fancy silk clothes—colorful cotton saris and blouses for women and cotton dhotis and shirts for men—a contrast to well-dressed churchgoers at home! No Sunday best here. But who knew, Kayla thought, maybe these were their best clothes.

Bhagirath Mountain loomed majestically at the far end of the narrow valley. How wonderful the scenery must be along the hike to Gaumukh! But

Kayla reassured herself that she had made the right decision not to go on the hike. The trip had become a burden; she didn't want to deal with the hassles of group travel any longer. And last night's discovery that her uncle had talked about her to others disgusted her. She felt good about standing up to Sovik and deciding to return.

Kayla watched the muddy-brown swirls and currents rushing by the boulders. Blackbirds flew from tree to tree, calling each other. Not a single cloud in the sky. Just like the halcyon days of her childhood. The same sky she had seen above the lake in American Falls. The water of the lake was blue, reflecting the sky. She remembered running around the shore with her brothers and sister. How wonderful those summer days were! High school . . . graduation . . . violation . . . her face tightened. She closed her eyes.

When she opened her eyes, Pinky was there with her. It took Kayla a moment to focus on her. "On a nice day like this," Pinky said, "you must have gone on picnics by the Snake River."

Kayla stared at Pinky for a few seconds and came out of her daydream. "I was remembering my childhood in Pocatello."

"Tell me more."

"Nothing special, really. Just running around in the summer. So free."

"It's very normal. We all do this . . . remember the carefree days of our youth."

They sat together silently.

After some time, Pinky asked Kayla, "Have you visited the deities in the Gangotri temple?"

"No, I haven't. I didn't feel comfortable going there alone."

"Then I should take you there."

"All right."

"We'll go to the Aarti service in the evening. It is beautiful."

They watched a woman filling up a brass pot with river water and sprinkling the water from the pot as she proceeded toward the temple.

"I've asked for hot water to take a good shower before we go on the hike tomorrow," Pinky said. "Let's go back now. We will return for the aarti service in the evening."

17.4

After his talk with Sharmaji, Sovik approached the place where cars were parked. He saw Ajit's van and his interest in geology welled up again. He walked up to the van and knocked at the door, but no one answered. As he turned to go, he saw Ajit coming up the road, a cup of tea in his hand.

"Hello!" Sovik greeted him. "I stopped by to see how you're progressing."

"Hello," Ajit said blandly, glancing at him once, clearly displeased to see this man from America. "I'm setting up procedures. We're making progress."

"I admire what you are doing. India should explore all its resources."

"That's the idea." Ajit skirted by Sovik to enter the van.

"We leave tomorrow morning," Sovik said, "I was wondering if you would tell me about this area so during our hike I could recognize the signs of glacial movements."

"That's not really my expertise." He glanced at his cup and took a sip.

"Before coming here, I read up a little on the Gangotri Glacier," Sovik told him with enthusiasm. "It's fascinating."

"There are many glaciers in the Himalayas."

"Yes," Sovik nodded. "The last Ice Age created these glaciers so we now have rivers full of water all year round."

"You seem well informed. How long ago did this happen?"

"A million and a half years," Sovik said. "Glaciers in this region are receding fast though." How odd that a geologist didn't know much about the last Ice Age.

"I'm only interested in rocks," Ajit said. "Tell me: do you really believe the glacier has receded that far—from here to Gaumukh?"

Sovik's mouth fell open. How could this fellow with the Geological Survey of India ask such a question? This is taught in any geology class. Keeping that thought to himself, he said, "There is lots of evidence and it is well documented in British travel accounts from the last two centuries. In some areas you can still see accumulation of moraine debris in the hills and in mountains of the Lesser Himalaya, even though the glaciers themselves are gone."

"So! You have studied this," Ajit said with a tinge of sarcasm.

"The present glaciations are small compared to what they were during the last Ice Age," Sovik told him confidently.

"Are all Americans like you?" Ajit teased. "Brush up on the geology where they're going for vacation?"

"You're giving too much credit to Americans!"

"You are probably videotaping your trip too!" Ajit gave a small laugh. "When will you be back in Gangotri?"

"We'd like to spend some time in Bhojbasa, I heard it is beautiful. We will return on Thursday afternoon. I hope you will have samples by then; I'd like to see what you find. Any obsidian in the Himalayan rocks?"

"I've not started any examination yet. What I'm doing is proprietary. I can't tell you about our findings."

"It'd be interesting to know what percentage is porphyritic."

Ajit's face stiffened. "That will take time." He glanced at the van.

"Granite rocks would have a good potential for thorium. Are you prospecting and analyzing placer deposits?"

"No. That is too slow." Ajit took a step toward the van. "I'm really busy now," he told Sovik.

"If you're looking for a particular metal, surely it would be easier first to look for it in the streams."

"In the streams?"

"Granite and metamorphic rocks will contain uranium and thorium. You examine the grains in the streams with placer deposits. The sediments will help you determine which hill has the mineral you want. Won't it?"

Ajit simply looked at Sovik without answering.

"You put sediments from a stream in oil," Sovik kept on talking, "and see where they stay. Lighter ones float to the top, denser ones sink. So, by choosing various densities of oil, you can figure out if the hills have the mineral you're looking for."

"I didn't bring that equipment."

"What about binocular microscopes and magnetometers?"

"We'll take our samples to Delhi. The lab will do the tests."

"Could I see what instruments you have? I can then tell you if they use different instruments in the U.S."

"No, no. Everything is scattered in the van. I wish you a good hike." Ajit stepped into his van and closed the door with a thud. Sovik was asking too many questions. What an irritation! He wished Swami Rangaraj would hurry up and take him to the treasure. Then he could take some gold and get out of this place. 'I've four days to complete this job,' Ajit concluded. 'I'm going to corner Swami Rangaraj today.'

Sovik strolled back to the bazaar. The Geological Survey project baffled him. Ajit was unfamiliar with the most basic methods and tools of prospecting. GSI had been a credible organization when he left India. Why would the government send people who were not geologists? Had corruption and nepotism spread that far?

One stall owner was playing loud rock music, a new American song. The sound pulled Sovik to the stall. "Hello, Hello, Hello, How low?"

There sat Be'ziil, ensconced with a few of the locals. He had his sunglasses on.

"They're playing my song. They dig it!"

"They like Nirvana? Even I don't understand what they sing!"

"The beat is good. They like the sound."

"Have you been sitting here all morning?"

"Oh, no. I was at a tea stall before. They're cool. I told them I was from America. They were very friendly. I bought tea for everyone. It cost me only a dollar."

"Wonderful!" Sovik put his hand on Be'ziil's shoulder, giving him an affectionate squeeze. "I'm glad I don't have to worry about you."

"Don't worry, man. I'm doing fine. I like that I'm not tied to the group."

Be'ziil, pleased with himself, smiled, saying, "These people told me all about this place. It's cool, man." Collecting his cassette, he walked out with Sovik. "I really like India. People are nice here. I can jive with them. After a few steps he stopped and faced Sovik. "You know, Sovik, I want to come back and live here."

Sovik didn't expect this. Anaba sent Be'ziil on this trip hoping that by seeing the conditions here her son would straighten his life around when he returned. "Be'ziil, India is good to visit," he told him, "but very hard to live. Don't think of coming here to live."

"I know how to make Navajo jewelry, and I'm good in hand work. Maybe I can learn Indian jewelry and combine the two forms."

"It is possible, perhaps. But Be'ziil, I was born here. I know life is not as easy as it seems to you now."

Be'ziil's face changed and he looked at Sovik calmly, saying nothing. However, Sovik read his mind: "What do you know of a Native American's life in the States?"

"See you later," Be'ziil said and drifted away toward the cement steps below the temple.

Sovik stood there silently for a few minutes and looked over a stall's offerings—mostly temple worship items. His eyes noted a piece of ocher cloth with religious writings on it. He gazed at the cloth. It was just like the small cloth his mother had given him when he left India; he had lost it somewhere. He would buy one when they returned from Gaumukh.

17.5

After lunch, Sovik saw Kayla sitting alone on the steps of the river below the temple. She watched the water intensely, as if she were counting the waves and was afraid one would sneak by. Her hands were clasped over her knees.

He came down and stood next to her. "Hi, Kayla!"

She jerked around and looked at Sovik. "Hi."

"Did Pinky take you around the stalls?"

She nodded.

"Can I talk with you for a few minutes?"

"If you wish."

"Last night was very upsetting to you."

She eyed him from head to foot. "I guess you'll never get it."

"I'm sorry." Sovik glanced at her face for a few seconds. "I know I've lost your trust somehow."

She turned back to the water. A crow cawed and flew over their heads to a large deodar tree. The afternoon sun's gentle rays hovered over the area and the sound of the river continued in the background.

Sovik stood there, not knowing how to comfort her or what to say. Something had traumatized her. There was some similarity between their situations, he thought: her distress that prevented her from trusting people and his own futile ambition that separated him from others and kept him from seeing life in its full perspective. He had realized his mistake, but only after almost dying, and he still struggled to find the right course. He was so anguished in the hospital and for a long time thereafter. It is hard to get out of such predicament, once one is hooked as deeply as it seemed she was. Did she need some drastic event to intervene—to come to terms with life? Perhaps that is why her uncle had sent her on this trip. Sovik felt sympathy for her.

"Would you like to go for a walk?" he asked her.

Kayla did not answer.

"The walk by the river is quite nice."

"Please leave me alone."

"Okay. I'll go. But if you want to talk anytime, please let me know. I had hoped we would all benefit from each other."

Kayla turned her head toward him. "Do you understand what it means for one to lose her dignity, her soul?"

"No. My problems have been different. But I believe you. You seem to have been dealt a bad hand. I can only tell you what I have learned in the last few years."

"What can you tell me?"

Sovik moved a little closer. "There is something inside each individual that is sacred—that is inside you, inside me. Your body can be tortured, but no one can hurt your inner sacredness unless you allow it. I allowed social circumstances to control me. I have since learned I have to evolve on my own and figure out what I ought to be doing—what my fulfillment in life is. Allow your situation to help your life become more centered."

"That easy, huh?"

"Listen to the music of the river; see the beauty of the place. Perhaps they will help you figure out where you want to go from here. What you want—not what people want you to do. That's what pilgrimages are all about."

She remained quiet.

"I'll leave you alone. Remember: in one way or other we are all working for restoration, redemption, whatever you want to call it, for growth."

Sovik ambled away along the river. He wished Kayla would call him back, but she didn't. He hoped Kayla was looking toward him and wanted him to return, but he didn't want to be further disappointed and could not look back.

17.6

When evening came, Kayla wanted to dress up as if she were going to her own church, and laid out the salwar kameez she had bought in New Delhi. She wanted to shampoo her hair, but a glance in the mirror showed it was beyond redemption at this time. She then knocked on Pinky's door. Pinky also wore a salwar kameez. "Two girls on a night out," Pinky said touching Kayla's elbow, "let's go."

They walked to the courtyard where monks were arranging materials for the service. Yellow-orange light on the peaks of icy white Bhagirath mountain glowed in the distance. Soon devotees gathered in front of the steps to the temple, and Pinky and Kayla followed them.

Swami Anand spotted the two women and greeted them. "Namaste. You came with Sovik, right?"

"Yes." Pinky said. "We want to participate in the Aarti."

"That's wonderful. Please stand here." He showed them a place on the side of the room providing a clear view of the service.

Swami Narayan and Swami Rangaraj lit the incense burners and the oil lamps. Soon the fragrance of sandalwood, typical of all Hindu temples, filled the air. Kayla liked the fragrance and took a deep breath. Swami Anand distributed flowers to the worshippers. Pinky and Kayla took flowers from him and held them in prayer-clasped hands like the other people. Smoke from large incense burners filled the temple. In the lamplight, the deities, partially veiled in smoke, appeared magical to Kayla. The priests offered flowers dipped in sandalwood paste to the deities as they prayed in Sanskrit.

The priests rang bells and rotated small earthen lamps around the deities. This went on for some time. The ceremony seemed to hypnotize Kayla. She felt herself transported to a special place, free from unhappy memories and worries for the future. Along with the others, she threw her flower to the deities. The pilgrims sang the aarti song. The chorus echoed from all corners of the temple.

Pinky and Kayla came out along with the rest of the crowd; but they lingered on as worshipers drifted away.

Pinky said, "This is our last night together. Let's sit on the river steps for a little while."

"I'd like that." Kayla moved toward the river.

There was a pleasant, cool breeze and it felt good to sit on the bank again as night gathered. They could not see the flowing water clearly, but they could hear the continuous rush of the river. A peaceful calm pervaded the place.

The ceremony had moved Kayla, and filled her mind with images of the worship service. But Pinky's words, 'This is our last night together,' rang in her ears. Tomorrow Sovik, Pinky, and Be'ziil would be gone. Fear, sadness, and also relief flooded her. But mostly, she felt lonely—she would be truly alone in this curious little town. She heard Pinky speak. "Aren't we lucky to be here, to experience this ancient place."

Kayla was startled; her face shrunk a little. "Lucky?" she raised her chin.

"Think of it this way: how many Americans have come here?"

Kayla couldn't say anything. Indeed, how many people did she know, who had ever heard of this place? If they had, would they ever even consider coming here? 'Lucky?' The word ripped through her mind. The dark shame that she harbored welled up in her heart. She believed she was the unluckiest girl in the world.

'Never talk about this to anyone,' her uncle had told her that night, and she had not. She had not said a word, even to her mother. She wanted to, but there was no one to listen to her secret. There was never an opportunity to talk about the incident of her rape to anyone.

This was the seventh year she had borne the event in her heart. Sometimes late at night she woke up, feeling as if she were being forced again, but it was only a nightmare. The month of June, when she was raped, had always been the worst time of all.

"What will you do when you go back?" Pinky asked.

Kayla stared at Pinky blankly, not knowing immediately how to reply, searching for something to say, but the only thing that came to mind was the farmland in Shelley where her rape had occurred. She had been blowing in the wind with a shameful secret locked in her heart. How could she explain this to a stranger? She stared at her speechless, and her mind struggled. A few words finally came out of her mouth, "I don't know."

Pinky looked at Kayla tenderly and held her hand in hers. "You're too young to be burdened with such sad expressions."

"I'd like to start over again." Kayla said as if talking to herself.

Pinky looked at her. Lots of regrets seem to be bothering Kayla, but she only said, "We'd all like to do that, start over again, but we can't."

Kayla didn't respond.

"We have to move forward," Pinky told her, "no matter how hurtful the past was, and build our future."

Still, Kayla could say nothing. The mountains had vanished; she could only see silhouettes of trees in the darkness. The rippling sounds of the stream surrounded her.

Pinky massaged Kayla's palm. "You seemed far away last night. I didn't say anything to you. But I thought, behind your anger and frustrations, you were sad."

Kayla didn't respond and so Pinky continued. "Last night you thought Sovik knew something about you from your uncle. He doesn't know any secret of your life. I'd know because he shares everything with me. Are there any secrets, Kayla?"

One tear fell from Kayla's eye, and she began to sob.

Pinky put her hand on Kayla's shoulder and pulled her close, embracing her. "There seems to be a lot of pain hidden there. Your tears are allowing it to come out." She stroked her back, as Kayla wept.

"I've been raped," Kayla said, looking into Pinky's eyes cautiously.

"Oh! I'm sorry. Did this happen recently?"

"No, no. Seven years back." She cried out loudly and clutched Pinky's body, as if to hide there.

"You were just a teenager . . ."

"I tried to be a really good girl." She sobbed, her body shaking heavily, tears streaming down her cheeks as Pinky rocked her.

The day before yesterday was the anniversary of the rape. Every year as the day approached, she had become more anxious and agitated.

She had been a different person before that day. Everything had changed in those few minutes. It was not just the loss of innocence; it was the knowledge of the cruel world, her shame, the knowledge of her trouble with the celestial heaven as taught by her church; and most profoundly no one—not even her uncle, whom she had trusted and revered, or her mother—paid any attention to her situation. She thought her uncle regarded it only as an unfortunate incident; the quicker she forgot it and moved on, the better for her. But she couldn't.

Pinky held her and swayed her body gently and rhythmically as if she was comforting a small child.

"I'm not the same person any more. I want to go back to who I was before that time . . . but I can't." She sobbed again. "My family has hushed it up. I haven't talked about it to anyone until now."

"I'm so sorry you had to bear this burden all alone. It took a lot of courage to share this with me today," Pinky whispered to her. She held her in a strong, encircling embrace.

"I feel relieved that I could tell you."

"Sharing secrets can be very freeing. What would you like to happen now?"

"I don't know what to do."

"I understand your confusion. This happens to many young girls."

"What do they do?"

"Very few have a choice in this matter; they go on living in spite of their pain. Just the same as you. I hope you're not blaming yourself."

"Sometimes I've wondered if I was stupid not to see it coming and shouldn't have walked to such a lonely place with that boy."

"Most people tend to blame themselves when something bad happens. You were an innocent girl. ... Looking back now, what would you change?"

"I think I would get to know a boy before going out with him."

Pinky nodded in agreement. "You have been through one of the most humiliating, painful experiences a person can have and kept that a secret for seven years. Consider this trip your pilgrimage—to be free. You have come here all the way from America. Let this Indian sacred place be where you start a new life. How does that sound to you?"

"That is exactly what I've wanted. I realize I'm not bad. A bad thing has happened to me; that's all. I feel better just talking with you. What hurts me most is that I have had to bear it alone," Kayla continued. "My community views life through rose colored glasses, where evil things do not happen."

"And please remember all men are not bad."

"I'm sorry I blamed Sovik."

"Don't worry about Sovik."

"I know a boy who is very nice to me. I'm the one who has held up our relationship—all because I can not tell him about the rape."

"If you want to continue with him, tell him what you told me tonight. And then, if he loves you, he will help you to work through your pain. He must understand why you react as you do." Pinky stopped for a few moments. "And if he cannot deal with it, then he isn't the boy for you. There will be someone else."

They heard footsteps. Kayla straightened herself up, wiping her face with a hanky.

Two men went away along the bank of the river.

Kayla said, "I've almost finished my Master's degree; I wonder what I should do next."

"Keep thinking and working at it. You will find your direction."

"You are so confident! I don't know."

"It will come to you. Perhaps this trip will give you ideas. It's like climbing a mountain. You first climb a hill; then you see more of the vista, wider horizons. Then you can decide which hill to climb next or which direction to go."

"I like that."

"You know our purpose in life develops from our experiences and our aspirations. Yours will also come through your own experience."

Pinky and Kayla remained together by the river—each with her own thoughts.

All her life, Kayla mused, she had followed rules; her Mormon Church upbringing had drilled obedience into her from childhood. What Pinky suggested was to find herself on her own, the way Sovik was doing. Although she had no illusions about the church any more, could she suddenly become brave and follow her own impulses? Would she ever be able to let go and do what she wished to do? She argued with herself. 'Whose permission do I need?'

Indian men and women worship the goddess with such devotion—she couldn't understand it. The Goddess Ganga is a mother to them, Ma-Ganga. If they were Catholic, it would be like saying prayers to the Virgin Mary. Kayla didn't pray to Mary. She prayed to God—a powerful man who has jurisdiction over her. She was reverent toward Him. She was not sure if she had love for Him; it was more awe than love. In some sense she was fearful of Him. But here, everyone loves the goddesses as affectionate mother figures and worships them as God.

Kayla thought about her observations of India. She had run into many different experiences—the whole trip had been a struggle, and, at the same time, she had moments that were precious. She remembered she had seen disgusting things—from people spitting in the streets, leaving red trails of betel-nut juice on the sidewalks, to very sad beggars with gross deformities. She had also faced situations where the Indians were quick to say, "This can't be done," or, "This is not the time," instead of making the small effort necessary to give the visitor a positive experience of India. "No," they would answer, as if their minds were already made up. Then, bang! You would meet someone who would solve your problem and be nice to you for no reason! That they were so kind was surprising and touching.

Last night she had seen people lying down on the ground to sleep. It was so bare! So much struggle to just get through a day, but they got on with their lives. She had come on this trip thinking her situation was miserable and unsolvable. Her sadness and her depression sometimes crippled her and made it impossible to get out of bed. She had thought that she would never be able to overcome her depression, that the only way to get out of it was to do away with herself. That thought had occurred to her several times.

Kayla stared at the ripples on the dark water for some time. Her condition was not that disastrous. She might not be at peace with herself, but she had room and space and freedom. She had options. She was blessed with good health, a pretty good intellect, and many life choices lay ahead of her. India had made her grateful for all the small blessings she had. The people she had seen in India had more basic problems of survival, but they also appeared to be more contented. How did they do that?

She thought about her apartment in Pocatello and the posters on her walls. Then she remembered how scared she was in New Delhi when she first saw a gecko above her bed. She was not afraid any more. She thought of the incident at the Shiva Continental Hotel in Mussoorie, where the manager wouldn't let them leave the hotel. It had taken her only a few minutes to realize that he was bullying them. "If we didn't want to stay in the hotel, who was there to stop us?" She felt right again about standing up to the manager; she knew she had surprised the group, because they had not seen her like that before.

Suddenly Kayla felt determined: she could turn over a new leaf, she would embark on a new journey. Before she had taken up her present job, she had an assistantship offer from the University of California at Irvine. But she hadn't acted on it; she was hesitant, afraid. She made up her mind that she would move to Irvine for her Ph.D. Her journey was over. She would leave Gangotri after the group left for the hike. She did not have to go by the crowded bus or wait for someone to take her; she would hire a car. She had dollars! She could do everything by herself.

"Thank you," she told Pinky abruptly and hugged her. "I know what to do now."

Sacred River : A Himalayan Journey

Part V

Hike to Bhojbasa

18

Above the Tree Line

18.1

After a breakfast of aloo paratha and hot tea, Sovik, Pinky, Be'ziil and Sabina assembled in the courtyard, ready to go on the hike to Gaumukh. The morning was excellent, with a clear sky and no breeze. This was the journey Sovik had been waiting for, to go to the source of the sacred river—the culmination of many years of planning—his pilgrimage to find peace and, perhaps, some meaning to his life.

Be'ziil was muscular and strong and had recently hiked sixty-three miles in the craggy mountains of central Idaho. He carried a backpack stuffed with some of their sweaters, ponchos, food, and water. Pinky was also a pretty good hiker and had a small pack on her back as well. Sovik was the only one with a heart condition, which prevented him from carrying a load. So he hired one porter. Pinky said that was why God made porters.

Sovik did his stretching exercises.

Kayla watched them from the steps that led to the river.

They were all set to go. It was long past departure time, but Larry and Amrita had not shown up. Brij Kumar was furious. He found the hotel manager and learned they had paid their bills the night before and checked out. After quickly scouting the temple area, he returned to the group saying, "They are nowhere. I knew from the beginning those two were a problem."

Pinky turned to Sovik and asked, "Now what?"

Sovik was hesitant, pursed his lips and frowned.

"Look, they are not a part of our group," Pinky told him. "Larry has been flaky before. Remember? He left us in Dehra Dun. We can't let them spoil our plans."

"I have to agree with you," Sovik said, reluctantly.

"We should get going," she told him firmly. Pinky felt the whole purpose of the trip would be foiled if they didn't reach the source of the river, and she couldn't let that happen. Turning toward the path, she muttered "the hell with 'em" under her breath.

After waiting a few more minutes, Sabina said, "Mr. Bose, my sister knows this area very well. She has gone to Gaumukh twice. Let's not wait for them. If they are not on the trail already, they will catch up with us."

Everyone agreed with Sabina. Brij Kumar said, "If I see them, I'll tell them what a sticky problem they created for you."

Sovik was surprised and annoyed. Larry and Amrita didn't seem to be the type of people simply to go away without telling them. Sure, they were spending time together, but this morning's situation was very unusual.

Somewhat uneasily, they began their hike near the small market where the buses were parked.

"Have a good time at the Taj-Mahal," Pinky called to Kayla.

"Don't miss your bus," Sovik shouted back from the trail.

The beginning of the trail was a fairly steep climb, but soon the grade became gentle. The sandy path, about two to three feet wide, took them along the top of a narrow valley covered with deodar cedar and birch trees. The muddy Bhagirathi River tumbled 800 feet below them, and from this distance the sound of rushing water could not be heard. Only the occasional cry of a bird broke the quietness of the clear, cool morning. The five of them marched along in a line, the young porter going ahead, Sabina and Be'ziil at the rear.

After a while Sabina caught up with Sovik. She wore a blue salwar-kameez and, despite her hiking shoes, she looked fashionable. "Mr. Bose," she told Sovik, "I didn't tell you when we started the hike, but Amrita told me late last night that she might go her own way. She wasn't certain at the time."

How could she not tell him this earlier, when everyone was running around looking for them, he thought as he looked her, stone-faced.

"If she gets an idea into her head," Sabina continued, "she'll do it, even if others tell her not to."

"Do you think Larry has gone with her?"

"I think so."

Sabina was only a young college student with her first summer job. Sovik was irritated, but the look of apology in her innocent eyes caused him to restrain his anger.

"Are you worried, Sabina?" he asked her sympathetically.

"No. Amrita always knows what she is doing." She glanced at Sovik and then cast her large, dark eyes downward.

"Thanks," Sovik said, but he didn't understand why Sabina hadn't told him earlier and wasn't apprehensive about her sister's behavior. "I hope they are okay." He went ahead to walk with Pinky.

Pinky hiked in a cheerful mood, looking around and admiring the rugged mountains and the muddy stream of the river below.

"Are we really, truly here, hiking in the Himalayas?" Pinky exclaimed when Sovik joined her.

"Yes, my dear," Sovik said in obedient-husband manner. "We are truly here." He turned back and saw the temple nestled like a tiny white gem on a green velvet cloth. It looked like a distant fort in the middle of vast, unspoiled nature, guarding the frontier, a symbol of man's salutation to God.

"Our first impressions are often wrong," he admitted to Pinky. "I was let down when I first saw the temple. Now, how grand it looks! Beautiful."

"I hope you won't be disappointed when we reach the source," Pinky said.

"I hope not. But I don't expect anything special, really. And I have learned something in the last few days."

Pinky turned her head, waiting to hear more.

"This journey is not really to see the physical source of the river."

"You figured that out in Gangotri?" she said, tilting her head.

"Yes. It dawned on me while I was listening to Swami Narayan's talk."

"I thought you always knew that."

"It was in my subconscious mind. Now it's clear to me. That's how, I guess, we grasp the meanings in legends. Although one vaguely understands, the deeper meanings come later and suddenly."

"I'm glad you are getting something out of this journey. I worried this trip would be too strenuous with your heart condition, but you are up to it. It was worth the risk."

"Why worry?" Sovik shrugged.

"I still need you." She squeezed his hand affectionately.

Around them, mica-impregnated granite rocks glowed in the morning sun—incandescent, red and brown.

They hiked above a gorge carved by the Gangotri Glacier, from which the river originates. Over the last two centuries the glacier had receded to Gaumukh, leaving behind a rough, rock-strewn valley floor. Sovik quickly recognized the trail left behind by the glacier, but to most others it was only a broad uneven gorge with rocks of different shapes and sizes scattered haphazardly across the valley floor. Basalt cliffs rose high above the wide floor and formed a U-shaped valley.

Several small, tumbling streams fell almost vertically from tiny ravines and hanging valleys in the basalt cliffs, joining with the river below.

Sovik was admiring a steep, precipitous slope formed by an old watershed, when Be'ziil said from behind, "You didn't expect Larry and Amrita to quit, did you?"

"No, it's quite disturbing." Sovik turned; Be'ziil had always been very respectful to him, but for the first time a mischievous smile appeared on his countenance.

"And Kayla didn't join our hike. Guess Coyote's playing tricks with you."

"What are you talking about?" Sovik asked, irritated. "Coyote, the trickster in your legend?"

"Coyote always tests you." Be'ziil was serious again. "He is unpredictable—he does both good and evil."

"So he is creating problems for me purposely?"

"Yes. He interferes. Starts trouble."

"And what do you recommend?"

"He pushes you and demonstrates your limitations. He is testing you about something. I don't know what. In the end he usually turns out to be helpful."

"You mean it may be good that Larry left?"

"Maybe. He guides us in strange ways."

"I can't sit and wait, Be'ziil. I must follow my goal."

Be'ziil grinned again. "Perhaps that's what Coyote wants to see."

Sovik tried to understand what Be'ziil was conveying to him. None of the Hindu gods and goddesses play the role of a trickster to teach a lesson or misdirect people until they find the right direction, but Navajo wisdom might be saying something to him. Maybe it was no accident that Be'ziil was on this trip. Perhaps all that he had pursued in his life was really the Coyote spirit luring him to eventually find the right path. He could not grasp the concept fully and resumed his place ahead of the young man.

The group kept their steady pace through the Himalayan terrain, appreciating its beauty, when, in startling contrast to nature trails in the U.S., they came upon a tea stall. An entrepreneur had piled up flat rocks into a broad U-shaped platform. Over this, a canvas tent top had been raised on supporting poles. Travelers sat on the stone platform and the "cha-walla" served nourishing

Indian tea made with sugar and whole milk in steel tumblers. Biscuits, snacks, cigarettes, soft drinks and bottled water were also available. Sovik, Pinky, and the porter sat on the platform and filled up on tea and sweet biscuits. Soon Sabina and Be'ziil joined them. Their happy expressions indicated that they were getting along pretty well. Be'ziil had his sunglasses on.

When tea was served, Be'ziil lifted his cup and said, "Here is a toast to Sabina. May you remain as pretty by the end of the hike!"

Sabina glanced at him and said, "Humph! We'll see how you do at the end of the trail."

"And may we all still remain friendly by the time we reach Gaumukh," Be'ziil said, smilingly.

While they were sipping tea, the Cha-Walla's gaze shifted between Sovik and Pinky several times. He spoke with the porter very fast in local dialect and handed him a small envelope. The porter turned to Sovik and said, "An Indian lady traveling with a Sahib left this envelope here for an Indian man with memsahib wife. That must be you."

Sovik saw his name on the envelope. He put down his cup and almost snatched it from the boy. "When did she give you this?" he asked the cha-walla in Hindi.

"Oh! Very early in the morning. They were my first customers."

He tore the envelope and found a hastily written letter:

Dear Sovik,

I am sorry to have to write you this note. By now, you know that Amrita and I are not going with the group. I apologize for this and hope you will understand.

Last night Amrita arranged a special visit for me with a monk for whom she has great respect. But, when we came back, a nasty scene occurred at the hotel.

Sharmaji and Brij Kumar were waiting for us and confronted Amrita. Brij Kumar was very rude and demanded to know where she had been. He said they'd searched the temple area for her.

Amrita was deeply offended. She tried to pass by without giving an answer, but Brij Kumar blocked the door, shouting—you can't just do these things here. This is not America!

I told him we went to visit a monk, wanting to smooth the situation out, but it was of no use; I was an American, and Amrita's accomplice, and therefore had no credibility with them.

Amrita pulled me away, saying we were not accountable to these fellows, she didn't need to explain her life to them.

A few other Indians came over to see what was going on. It became an uncomfortable scene for Amrita and me. This inquisition in front of strangers was extremely embarrassing.

I believe Sharmaji is levelheaded, and realized Brij Kumar was wrongly accusing Amrita. Brij Kumar is overly protective of his country's reputation and thought it his duty to teach her a lesson. There are many like him in every society. Sharmaji took Brij Kumar away, trying to hush his partner, but the damage was done.

I felt deeply wounded for Amrita. She said Brij Kumar would spread gossip in the morning. She doesn't trust him—who knows what he'll make up about our visit to the monk? So we decided it was better for us to leave the group and go on our own. Amrita wanted to help the group out, but she was not officially hired. Sabina is the guide; Amrita is only a volunteer.

We're really sorry to take off like this—but it can't be helped.

We'll continue on the trek, but we'll start early—at daybreak.

It's too bad we had to separate! I'll write to you again.

With sincere regards,

Larry

Sabina watched anxiously as Sovik read the letter. He looked up at her and nodded. "You're right. They have gone on their own."

"Are they going to Gaumukh?"

"They are ahead of us," Sovik said, in a matter of fact manner. He stood up and picked up his small load. He didn't want to finish the rest of his tea. Who knew what other complications lay ahead?

They hiked ten kilometers uphill at a gentle pace. The sun glared as they walked along a broad stony slope. All felt the tropical heat, even at this altitude. Suddenly, as they turned a corner, they came upon a grove of pine trees nestled among big boulders. They had reached the halfway point, Chirbasa, where they had planned to eat lunch. The cool shade was a welcome relief. The trail curved around cottage-sized boulders and a merry little stream flowed below those.

Food stalls were set up under large, makeshift, tarpaulin 'roofs' among the boulders, some with benches for travelers to sit on, some with big cooking fires where sabji and savory parathas were being made. Sovik and his group passed the makeshift restaurants and munching pilgrims. They found an isolated place a little farther on to savor their picnic lunch brought from Gangotri.

Sabina sat near Sovik. "I wonder what Amrita is doing," she said after a few bites of her aloo paratha.

Sovik glanced in her direction without saying anything.

"She's my sister! I'm entitled to worry about her."

Sovik paused in his munching and considered her.

"She's a capable girl," Sovik finally said. "She'll do fine."

"I know that, but I wish they didn't have to separate from us."

"Yes. It's unfortunate." He nodded. "In India, it's hard for a woman to have her own identity, isn't it?"

"You know India." She took a bite of her paratha and added. "Amrita got more of our mother."

Sovik looked at her questioningly.

"My mother was an Anglo-Indian; she was more outgoing and more independent than most Indian women. She was the head nurse at the army hospital in Dehra Dun."

"What is she doing now?"

"She died when I was nine."

"I'm sorry to hear that. Did your father raise you two alone?"

"Yes. That's why we're such daredevil girls! Aren't we?" Her eyes sparkled.

"Yeah, now it fits!"

"Amrita was close to our mother."

"Now I see. Amrita has more of the genes from your mother."

"And I have the fun-loving parts of my father."

Sovik observed a man in ocher robes, a sadhu, sitting near them and looking him over. The sadhu was thin and quite dark and had a childlike expression on his face. He had no sandalwood paste marks on his forehead or arms, so he did not belong to a specific Hindu sect. The sadhu said, "Hello," with a pleasant smile.

"Going to Gaumukh?" Sovik asked him in Hindi.

"Yes. You too?"

"Yes."

The sadhu began to talk. This was unexpected; sadhus usually kept to themselves. He told Sovik he had been to Gaumukh many times; it was a very nice place. He offered to show Sovik around.

"Me?" Sovik was surprised at his spontaneous offer.

"Yes. You will like it."

Sovik did not know what to make of this offer. He had worn-out sandals on his feet and only two items with him: a thin rolled-up bundle and a brass water pot—all his possessions. Not much protection in a mountain region where the nights were quite chilly even in summer. Yet, there was such calmness on the sadhu's face.

"Perhaps we will meet at the source in the morning," Sovik told him.

"I'll see you there."

After lunch, Sovik broke a Hershey bar in two and offered half to the sadhu. He was not sure if it was appropriate to offer a portion of his food to a sadhu—a holy man—but he took it without any reservation.

"Very nice taste," he said.

"My grandfather was a sadhu," Be'ziil said off-handedly.

"What do you mean?" Sabina inquired. "A sadhu in America?"

"He was a medicine man. That's like being a sadhu here."

18.2

The hike started again.

A short time after leaving Chirbasa, all the remaining shade on the trail vanished; there were few bushes and no overhanging rocks or protruding walls to hide under. The five in Sovik's group toiled up the narrow trail between a wall of sun-heated solid rock, and a steep drop-off covered in loose rock rubble. It promised a quick slide down to the river and death. The air shimmered with heat and the sky was a white dusty haze. The path rose steadily; Pinky and Sabina fell in behind Sovik and Be'ziil. Only occasional bird calls broke the silence of this Himalayan furnace. They had come a little over halfway to their destination. The hike became a struggle.

However, Be'ziil was in great shape and hiked cheerfully. The face of the thin sadhu in Chirbasa circled in his mind. Both his grandfather and this sadhu had calm demeanors and something peaceful about them. He was sure, after meeting several sadhus along the way, that Navajo medicine men were like sadhus. He remembered the chanting ceremony his mother arranged for him at his grandmother's place when he was twelve. He had seen chants and heard many stories of the Navajo ceremony, but this time the chant was just for him. And his grandfather, whom he loved very much, performed the ceremony. Be'ziil remembered it so well. It began at sunset and continued for almost two hours. He sat on the floor inside the hogan. His grandfather sat in front of him and fixed his gaze and attention on him. Then he sang a chant in a low voice. It was hypnotizing. Be'ziil participated in the ceremony with a full heart.

Then there was a family feast.

"Grandpa, would you teach me chants?" Be'ziil asked his grandfather when he found him alone.

"You're too young."

"No, Grandpa. I want to learn now. I'm ready."

"Okay, my son. I'll teach you a little at a time." He stopped for a moment and caressed Be'ziil's back. "But first you have to learn to be quiet inside. Remember that Mother Earth cares for us because we are a part of nature. When you understand this, you'll be ready to learn the chants."

"Have you herded sheep in Arizona like other Navajo boys and girls?"

Sovik asked. Be'ziil heard Sovik talking to him but for a second he wasn't sure where he was.

"I had to do that when I was young," Be'ziil finally replied, turning his thoughts away from the chant in his grandmother's hogan. "When I visited my grandparents, I helped them with sheep herding."

"But did you get a chance to go to school in Arizona?"

"I went to the public school like other boys. I didn't like school."

"Why not?"

"It's difficult for a Navajo boy. My father never forced me to go to school. My stepfather was nice to me, but he had no time. Then, when I needed him most, he went away to Idaho. It's all very complicated." He paused for a few seconds and picked up a rock. He threw it toward the river. "My first school was in Kaibito, a short distance from our home," Be'ziil continued. "I remember my father took me to my first day at school. He parked the car in front of the school and let me get down. 'There,' he pointed to the door, 'you walk in there. Just go.' I stopped near the door and saw many children with their parents. Then the bell rang. They went to classes; I went to a tree in the playground and started to cry."

"Oh my, how scary for a little boy."

"The principal saw me and came out to see what the matter was. 'My father brought me here and went away,' I told her, while crying. She asked my name and patted my shoulder. 'We have been waiting for you,' she said. She seemed kind. I went with her when she offered to take me inside to my class." Be'ziil looked toward the barren landscape, which was hazy and desert-like. He turned to Sovik, saying, "I didn't really get to know my father."

Sovik remained silent. This was such a different experience.

"When I was very young," Be'ziil continued, "I was with my parents, but they fought all the time. When they split up, I went with my Mom. But my father never looked me up."

"Have you lost touch with your father?"

"Yes. I never spoke with him after I left Arizona."

"So he lives alone there?"

"My father died last year."

"Oh! I'm sorry. A sudden heart attack?"

"He was way into drugs and alcohol for a long time."

This was a surprise and Sovik did not know what to say. Finally, he asked, "I'm curious, Be'ziil. Did you go to his funeral? What kind of service did he have?"

"We had a regular ceremony, like the white people. A Mormon burial. I found out a surprising thing from my father's girlfriend. She told me my father was proud of me because I had a job in Idaho Falls. He thought I'd do well in life." He looked at Sovik with hooded eyes, "My father called me the day before he committed suicide. I didn't know. I wasn't home."

Sovik glanced at his stolid face and felt the sadness there, but Be'ziil looked away. Sovik was now truly lost for words. Soon Be'ziil went ahead of him.

As the afternoon wore on, the trek became unbearable with the heat and relentless sunlight. They could see a very long, narrow stretch of trail in front of them, a similar long trail behind. The six-kilometer afternoon hike, from 12,000 to 13,000 feet, through a barren landscape felt like being in the middle of a desert, and they started to feel there was less oxygen as they went up. No resting-place along the trail. No tea stalls—only one way to go—forward. There were no hikers ahead of them or behind. They walked silently on the desolate path.

Glacial debris, all sizes of rocks and boulders, were strewn on the valley floor. It looked as though a tornado had devastated the region—but it was the result of a glacier squeezing through the hills. Several places showed signs of snow runs and streams that no longer existed. The topography varied. Sometimes, a steep slope of scree bordered the narrow hiking path and a rippling stream came down from above. Occasionally taller mountains would raise their heads above the horizon, with streaks of white snow on their black and brown rocky surfaces. The gorgeous scenery broke the monotony of the hike. Except for the crunching of their boots, silence prevailed.

At almost 13,000 feet, great effort was needed to keep going. During their 'training hikes' in the cool green forest of Wyoming's Teton Mountains, they had approached 10,000 feet. No cool forest here—they were above the tree line, and the path went on and on. Everyone wished someone would tell them the end was near, but no one came down the trail to give them encouraging words. Finally, in the late afternoon, from the top of a small rise, they saw the river gorge open to a wide flood plain. A tiny settlement nestled on the valley floor below them, and their hearts were lifted. They were finally near Bhojbasa, or birch grove, the last human settlement on the way to the source of the river.

They expected a grove of trees, but they could see none. Their legs were heavy; they moved down the hill impelled by inertia and sheer determination.

Soon they saw the top of a temple. They increased their speed. Finally, they scrambled down a rock and rubble-strewn hill toward the few buildings in the middle of a wide flat valley.

The Guesthouse was surrounded by small, bright flags—yellow, pink, red, green and blue —dancing merrily in the wind. An effervescent feeling of happiness bubbled through the hearts of the weary hikers.

As Sovik, Pinky, Be'ziil, and Sabina walked toward the guesthouse, they were immediately absorbed in the serenity of the site. In the enormous and quiet beauty of the valley, the group stood stock-still, gazing at the view above them. Silent, sharp-edged, snow-white mountains stood tall in the deep blue sky like eternal sentries. Time had no meaning in this place. They had to force themselves to break away from the panorama and enter the guesthouse.

Inside they found rooms set up dormitory style, wooden platform beds covered with thick mattresses, hard pillows, and several quilts. At the end of their room were two large windows with magnificent views of the lofty Himalayas. They had an austere tea. Legs and heads aching, Pinky and Sabina lay down on the beds.

Sovik went out to survey the area. The majestic Bhagirath Mountain was directly upstream from the Guesthouse, rising to meet the cloudless evening sky, shimmering pink, purple, and gold, guarding the quiet solitude of the place. All vibrations stopped here. Beyond these tall, silent sentries was an expanse of crystal blue sky. Sovik distinctly felt their long journey had been worth the effort. This serene corner was indeed the place described in the stories of ancient India, a place for meditation and realization of one's unity with God. Looking at nature's own temples he felt suspended between the earth and the sky.

18.3

Sovik had hoped they could go to the temple in Laal Baba's ashram, a good-sized dwelling near the guesthouse, for the evening Aarti. Unfortunately, the Aarti would be at 7 p.m., the same time as dinner, and everyone in his group was famished. He had some free time before dinner and found himself on the path to Laal Baba's.

To his surprise and relief, he found Larry and Amrita inside the ashram sitting on the floor with a large quilt around them, having tea from metal tumblers. No one else was in the room.

As he entered, Larry rose and greeted Sovik. "I'm glad you found us," he said and gave Sovik a warm hug.

Amrita also joined him. "Has everyone arrived?"

"Except Kayla," Sovik told her. "She decided to return to New Delhi on her own and be a tourist."

Sovik thanked Larry for sending him the letter explaining their situation.

"What did Sabina say?" Amrita asked.

"Oh, she has great confidence in you."

"I can't stand the gossiping, meddling nature of Indians," Amrita said. "It is unfortunate we had to separate from the group, but there was no other way."

"I understand," Sovik told them. "You did what you felt was right and it is fine with me."

"Do you want some tea?" Larry asked.

"No, thanks."

"You know, Sovik," Larry said as they both sat down with Amrita, "I'm happy about what happened. This has given Amrita and me a chance to know each other."

"I hope you two understand the gravity of Amrita's situation," Sovik said.

Larry looked up, surprised.

"There are unwritten rules in Indian society, especially for girls; they can't just do what they like."

"I see your point. This isn't the U.S."

"What are your plans now?" Sovik asked them.

Amrita explained they were considering a stay in Bhojbasa for a few days, and then go back to Uttarkashi before returning home. Sovik went over their plans so they could avoid other members of the group if they wished to. Sovik got up to leave for dinner.

Larry rose to accompany him. "I'll write to you at the address you've given me."

"I'd like that very much."

Larry intended to tell Sovik that on his way to Bhojbasa, he had identified the man in Gangotri with the Geological Survey. He was positive that he had seen him with Chetti at the café on Connaught Circle in New Delhi. He could not forget the conspiratorial tone of their conversation in the cafe. But Larry thought Sovik didn't know the man and he might shrug it off as inconsequential. Chetti talked with many people and his methods might be unusual. Besides, what was he hinting at? He was not sure himself. He looked intently at Sovik as these thoughts ran through his mind, but all he could say was, "One thing has been bothering me for some time. Perhaps you can explain. It's about that old manuscript. I wonder why a patriotic organization would want to give away an important, ancient document to a museum outside India."

Sovik looked at Larry's face for a few moments. "I've wondered about that myself. It feels like an underhanded deal, something they shouldn't be doing. The truth is SMS is in deep financial trouble. They have built up great expectations but cannot deliver. They need money desperately."

"I've read articles where Indians complained the British stole their treasures, and now they have to go to London to see them."

"And how many can go abroad?" Sovik said in a resigned tone.

"So the SMS is desperate. Might they take other drastic steps as well to raise money?"

"I don't know. It's possible. Chetti told me they are in a make-it or break-it situation."

"The end justifies the means, huh?"

"Larry, I haven't got any answer. I hadn't heard of the SMS before landing in India. What we've come across is purely a coincidence. I'm sure they have their plans, and they are not depending on us."

"I know. Chetti is smart and clever. I just wanted to find out what you had heard." Larry's voice was subdued. He felt frustrated and a little guilty that he somehow couldn't express what was bothering him.

19

Gaumukh

19.1

Sovik returned from Laal Baba's ashram and found Pinky lying down; she had a bad headache and was nauseated. His mood quickly changed from satisfaction to concern. After about ten minutes, the loud noise of vomiting came from outside. Sabina came in and lay down under the blankets with a bucket next to her. Her face was an interesting shade of green. Sovik became worried. The two women tossed on their beds, unable to find a position that relieved the terrible aching in their heads. The room now looked like a makeshift army hospital and the darkness outside reminded Sovik of his group's isolation, alone to themselves. Who knew what fate had in store for them? Altitude sickness can cause swelling of the brain and even death. There was only one cure—to return to a lower elevation.

Be'ziil and Sovik quickly ate dinner without much appetite. Sovik's mind spiraled with worry about the two sick women. He had not expected altitude sickness to be a problem, hence had no plan for this emergency. They were at 13,000 feet. Returning to Gangotri seemed to be the only answer. But it would be impossible to follow such a difficult trail in the dark, even with flashlights.

Sabina and Pinky took "super aspirin" and finally lay quiet. Sovik, tired from the long hike, dozed off; then awoke again and thought about returning to Gangotri as soon as day broke. He could not take a chance of anyone developing brain damage. Planning the emergency descent, he drifted in and out of sleep.

The two women slept soundly, but Sovik remained alarmed for them, disappointed for himself. He felt sad; they had come so far, but he would never reach the source of the river. He thought of the letdown of mountain climbers when they had to retreat without reaching the summit. Would it be the same for him?

Gaumukh

Sovik woke again with his mind racing between two thoughts. He could not take any chances with others' lives, but he also wanted to go to the source of the river. He had planned for this for seven years. This was his last chance—he wouldn't be able to come on such a trip ever again. He had never failed in anything in his life. Could this be his first failure even though he had planned so carefully?

Then a new thought struck him. Even if he wanted to start their return hike early in the morning, they must eat something. This was India. They could not get organized before 8 a.m.; perhaps there was time for a quick trip to the glacier in the early hours of dawn. If he started before 5 a.m., he could return by eight. Pinky and Sabina were sleeping. Perhaps they were not in such bad shape as he imagined. He decided he would take Be'ziil with him.

Sovik turned to look at Pinky and found she was not sleeping; her headache had returned. He told her his idea, and she agreed.

"Be careful, and don't do anything crazy. I love you and want you back in one piece."

19.2

Bundled into down jackets, Sovik and Be'ziil left the relative warmth of the guesthouse for the icy chill of the pre-dawn Himalayas. The beginning of the trail was steep; it was still dark, but Sovik was driven; having come this far, nothing was going to stop him. He was almost running, and although Be'ziil kept up a good pace, he barely stayed even with Sovik. Sovik's heart beat fast; despite the knowledge of his damaged heart, a powerful determination overtook him.

Half an hour later, the climb became easier. After one more hour passed, they saw scattered tents and knew they were close to the source. Boulders were strewn everywhere and the path disappeared into the rubble. Fortunately, the dawn light allowed them to see the obstacles before them. Several small lakes of glacial melt blocked their passage. They crossed these by walking on boulders that formed "stepping stone" bridges, and came very close to a place where water gushed out of the bottom of the glacier, a surprise for Sovik. He had expected a trickle of melting ice—not a roaring gush of water.

Snow-white and majestic, Bhagirath Mountain rose before them to 22,500 feet just behind the glacier. Bathed in the early morning light, Shivling Mountain, the Matterhorn of Asia, hemmed them in on the right with its sharp triangular peak. From where they stood, the glacier filled a wide ravine with tons of dirty, soil-filled ice. At the bottom of the front "wall" of the glacier water poured out from a low, arched opening. Dark and cave-like, this was "Gaumukh," or Cow's Mouth—the source of the Bhagirathi River and, hence, the source of the mighty Ganga, the holy Ganges River. Sovik saw how a Hindu devotee could see the source of the sacred river to be like the mouth of a cow, a very holy symbol to all Hindus.

The glacier region reminded him of coal mining areas he had visited: in the faint morning light, it appeared black, with rocks and water scattered all around—breathtaking when combined with the white, towering peaks above them. The iridescent colors of early morning danced off the sunlit peaks. Sovik was overwhelmed: he had arrived at the source of the Ganges River. He had planned this journey for so many years, been discouraged so often by many well-wishers, but he had made it! His heart leapt with joy; an echo sang within him, "I am here. I am here! I've made it."

A deep tranquility came over him. The still rocks and the rolling sounds of the flowing river slowly took him to a transcendental state. Ancient sages found the insight of human existence in such places. It is the inner self that awakens and one sees life in the bigger context of nature, of the universe. He had been searching for meaning in his life these last several years. It would have been easier if he could surrender to the will of an omnipotent, omnipresent God, but he had never understood or accepted the existence of such an entity. Now he realized that was beside the point. He was a part of the universe, as were these mountains and the streams. The river changes every moment. So does everything else, including the mountains and himself. He had to start from this state and proceed to his next state. It was a journey like the river. Acceptance of this reality is the essence. No point lamenting what could have happened. Like the river, each moment one is born into a new state, he told himself, and the next state depends on his actions. There was no turning from this idea and there was no other way to live. He was a part of the world surrounding him, just like the river. We are all connected. We are all a part of the network of animate and inanimate objects. He had made himself separate by thinking only about himself.

A scene flashed through Sovik's mind.

He was putting files in his briefcase.
"Make sure you take Friday off," Pinky told him from the door. "We are going to Yellowstone Park. I've reserved a hotel."
"Friday?" Sovik looked at her with irritation. "I have a big report due at the end of the month."
"My nephews are all excited about going with you."
"Can't we postpone it?"
"No. You agreed to this trip weeks ago."
"You don't understand my position." He frowned and looked intently at Pinky, thinking for a moment that she would give in, but she remained silent. "Fine, then we'll go." He slammed the briefcase shut.
How grudgingly he had consented to her little request; he had taken papers from work with him and all he thought about was how he was going to present his report when he got back. He had chased the goal of higher positions, titles and responsibilities, and hence more status, money, and respect. He had no other goals, and he had thus separated himself from his family, from other human beings, and essentially from everything else in life. It was pride in his success and ambition that separated him, confined him to a narrow, sterile world. Standing at the source of the sacred river, Sovik saw a different world. Egos dissolve in this place and one could enjoy the aspirations and achievement

of others and feel sadness at their failures. He stared at the river and visualized a golden hand rising in the misty stream—a gold bangle shining brightly in her hand in the light of dawn.

He could not have understood this before; no words can express this knowledge; no one can explain this to another person—it can only be experienced. Perhaps one could grasp this realization only when one came to a place like this.

A little distance away, Be'ziil stood still, looking at the Cow's Mouth and glancing at Sovik occasionally. After some time, he went to Sovik. "Are you happy that you've reached your goal?"

Sovik broke out of his trance. "Yes. I'm very happy." He took a step toward Be'ziil and put his arm around his shoulder and pulled him closer. "Be'ziil, is this place what you thought it would be?"

"Physically no, but mentally yes. I feel an echo of the spirit."

"Wise men have tried to tell us what they found," Sovik said, "but only when we come here, can we understand."

"The Navajos say we are all part of The One; we will continue to seek until we obtain awareness of this—unite with the spirits. It is a state of being." Be'ziil's eyes focused on the Cow's Mouth. "I see all these busloads of pilgrims going up the mountains like salmon going back to their spawning area. Going back to their beginning. These mountains, touched by the Sun. All these come together here and the pilgrims feel close to the source of their being." After a moment, Be'ziil turned toward Sovik. "You know you are in your sand-painting."

"You're telling me something Navajo, right?"

"Yes. It's the most important part of a healing ceremony. It happens on the last day. A medicine man creates the painting inside the hogan during the day to summon the spirits, the good forces. Then he leads the patient to sit in its center, facing east so he will see the sun when it rises. The chant summons the Holy People. They arrive and fill the painting with their healing power, with all their blessings. The medicine man puts sand from the painting on the patient. This way the patient is made one with the spirits and shares their power. Then the patient comes out to breathe the dawn. He faces the sun and the rays bathe him. He is healed." Be'ziil looked toward the east at the pink color in the sky.

"How does this fit with me here?"

"Don't you see? During a chant ceremony the chanter prepares the patient and chants for the spirits to come. The patient goes through strict rituals, some suffering. It takes several days. All your preparations and struggles for the trip were just those. Now you have come to the center of your sand-painting, the source of the Holy Spirit. Look around you. The mountains, the sky, the river, they are all Holy Beings. They are immersing you in their spirits, curing you."

"I see." Sovik nodded. "This whole area is my sand-painting." He spoke in a very low voice, almost whispering, "Yes. I'm inside the sand-painting, immersed and being enveloped by its power."

Be'ziil started to recite in Navajo:

> Shikee' shá'áádíídlííl
> Shigáál shá'áádíídlííl
> Shijáád shá'áádíídlííl
> Shits'íís shá'áádíídlííl
> Shigaan shá'áádíídlííl
> Shijéí shá'áádíídlííl
> Shiinéé' shá'áádíídlííl
> Shíni' shá'áádíídlííl

> Restore my feet for me.
> Restore my health for me.
> Restore my legs for me.
> Restore my body for me.
> Restore my arms for me.
> Restore my heart for me.
> Restore my voice for me.
> Restore my mind for me.

> Shitsiji' hózhóó doo
> Shikéé'déé hózhóó doo
> Shiyaagi hózhóó doo
> Shik'igi hózhóó doo
> Shinaa hózhóó doo

> May it be beautiful before me.
> May it be beautiful behind me.
> May it be beautiful below me.
> May it be beautiful above me.

May it be beautiful all around me.

Yaadídah shitsiji' hózhóó doo
Yaadídah shik'éédéé hózhóó doo
Yaadídah shikáá'déé hózhóó doo
Yaadídah shiyaa hózhóó doo
Yaadídah shinaa hózhóógo naasháá doo

May it be happy before me.
May it be happy behind me.
May it be happy above me.
May it be happy below me.
With it happy all around me, may I walk.

Be'ziil took a few steps closer to Sovik, still reciting:

Bee nitsiji' hózhóó dooleel'
Bee nikéédéé hózhóó dooleel'
Bee niyaagi hózhóó dooleel'
Bee nik'idéé hózhóó dooleel'
Bee sa'ah naaghai bik'eh hózhóó nílíí dooleel'
hózhóó dooleel'

Go with blessing before you,
Go with blessing behind you,
Go with blessing below you,
Go with blessing above you,
Go with happiness and long life,

Be'ziil then turned to the east. They both stood there and saw the orange disc of the sun rise over the mountains. "The sand-painting has covered you completely," Be'ziil told Sovik, "now the painting will be gone, but you will have the blessings."

Sovik faced the east for some time, taking in the sunshine rising over the mountains and all around him. "I appreciate what you did for me," he told Be'ziil. In traditional Hindu fashion, Sovik then put some water from the newly emerged Ganges on his own head and sprinkled a little on Be'ziil.

They trudged out of a jumble of boulders to the more defined trail and walked quickly down to the guesthouse. Sovik's worries about Pinky and Sabina came back to him. Could he find ponies to rent? And if no ponies were available and the two women were weak, how were they going to make the long trek down the mountain to Gangotri? He'd consult the guesthouse manager.

They passed by the few isolated tents where sadhus and yogis lived, and Sovik spotted the sadhu he had seen in Chirbasa, holding a water jug—out for his morning wash. He smiled at them broadly.

"Aap Aa Gaye!"

"Yes," Sovik nodded. "I've already seen it."

"I was planning to show you Gaumukh." The sadhu stared at Sovik, hesitating. He smiled shyly. Finally, he blurted out, "I've had this water jug for a long time. It is broken. I wanted to ask you for money to buy a new one."

This monk, who wandered the holy mountains, praying and meditating, had only sandals on his feet, an orange cloth on his body and a water jug in his hand. His entire possessions! Sovik took out his wallet without hesitation. "How much would it cost?"

The sadhu did not know.

Sovik put ten rupees on his hand, then another note to make twenty, then thirty. The Sadhu stopped him, saying, "Thirty will do."

Thirty rupees—one dollar—for a brass water jug, fulfilling his needs. Sovik looked at his smiling face, and yesterday's happy scene of sharing a candy bar with this sadhu came to him vividly.

The sadhu said, "Thank you for your kindness. God will fulfill your wishes. Namaste."

"Namaste." Sovik returned his gesture and continued downhill.

When they returned to the Guesthouse they were surprised to find Pinky and Sabina dressed and exuberant. There was no trace of the previous night's problems; they had adjusted to the altitude. Sabina and Pinky felt well enough to go to Gaumukh. A tremendous joy came to Sovik's heart and, once again, Bhojbasa became a peaceful hermitage surrounded by lofty mountains, all shining in the morning light. There could be no place on earth more serene and beautiful.

Pinky and Sabina marched toward the source of the river with Be'ziil as their escort and guide.

"Take your time and don't rush," Sovik told them. "We'll be here two more days."

20

Quandary

20.1

Amrita was not sure if she was dreaming or awake. Eyes still closed, she pulled the woolen blanket over her head and curled up to drift back into sleep, but the song floated in. She could hear a guitar. How could the voice be so similar to Larry's? Her eyes popped open.

> These are the lovely mañanitas
> That King David sang
> Today we sing them to you
> Because we want you to be happy
> Wake up my dear, wake up
> And you will see the beautiful dawn
> The birds are already singing
> And the moon is leaving

Amrita jumped out of bed and cracked the shutter open. Larry was singing, and a man with a clean-shaved head and pastel orange clothes played the guitar. Freezing cold air came in through the glassless window; she wrapped the blanket tight around her and watched the two men in wonderment.

> How beautiful is the morning
> I have come to share with you.
> The day is dawning
> Pink is on the horizon
> Awaken early, my dear, and see that
> The light of day is upon us.

A smile spread across her face. She opened the window and asked, "What are you doing?"

Looking at her sleepy-eyed face, strands of disheveled hair trailing around her shoulders, Larry kept on singing.

These are the lovely mañanitas
That King David sang
Today we sing them to you
Because we want you to be happy

"Okay, okay, I got it," Amrita told them, fully awake now and a little embarrassed. "Don't wake up all the guests in the ashram."

Larry stopped singing and gave her an affectionate, silly smile.

"I didn't know you could sing," Amrita said.

"Did you like the song?"

"Yes." She paused for a moment. "What is mañanitas?"

"You come out; then I'll tell you."

She couldn't take her eyes off Larry—if only she could jump out of the window and hold him tight! But one does not do that in India. "I will be out soon." She closed the window gently.

Larry shook hands with the Hare Krishna man, Govinda Das (formerly known as Tennessee Jack), both of them laughing wildly. "We did it!" Larry said. "Thank you."

Amrita came out wearing jeans and a white shirt. "You know, you are crazy," she smiled flirtatiously at Larry. "And where did you get the Hare Krishna fellow?"

"Let's eat some breakfast first; I have a suggestion for today."

They moved inside. "When did you get this idea of singing?"

"After you went to bed last night, a group of Hare Krishna people came in, carrying their instruments and chanting—they had dholak drums and cymbals and Govinda Das had the guitar. They were a lively group."

"And you felt at ease with your fellow crazies!"

"Well, you can say we had a good time together." Larry's voice was cheerful.

They went to the kitchen and received hot tea in metal tumblers. "I'm starting to like this place," Larry said, and sat down at the nearest table.

The morning's breakfast was upma, savory cream of wheat with vegetables, that they took large helpings of, with yogurt and mango pickles.

"I think Sovik and Pinky will go to Gaumukh today," Larry said. "Could we explore the Bhrigupanth Peak to the south?"

"There is no trail to that peak," Amrita said.

"Well, we can walk toward the Bhrigupanth Glacier and see how far we get, or we can walk along the river."

"Walking along the river would be nice." She took a sip of tea. "Then you can tell me about mañanitas."

Larry and Amrita spent the day lazily. First they sat on the bank of the river and watched the rising sun creep over the mountains. The snow-covered peaks glowed and the sound of water cascading over rocks soothed them.

Though he felt guilty leaving the group in Gangotri, Larry was now quite pleased that they had. Things work out in mysterious ways, he thought. Amrita looked vivacious with her long, black hair spread over her back. Larry remembered her youthful face in the Silver Valley when she playfully splashed Ganges water on him. Now she looked more mature. Had the events of the past few days changed her so much?

"Isn't it wonderful," he said, turning toward her and taking her hand, "that we don't have to rush anywhere and have time to ourselves?"

"A truly gorgeous place," she said, looking at Shivling Mountain.

"Let's walk along the river."

Next day they hiked steadily, without hurry, toward Gaumukh when the sun rose a few feet above Bhagirath Mountain. At the source of the Ganges River, Amrita took a handful of water from the stream and sprinkled a few drops on Larry's head. This time, instead of splashing water back on her, he simply gazed at her and affection welled up in his heart. Standing in front of Bhagirath Mountain, he felt she was not just playing with water—she sincerely wanted Goddess Ganga to bless him. Amrita looked beautiful—not a young executive from Bombay but the embodiment of the Goddess herself. Larry took a little water from the river and sprinkled a few drops on her head. He felt fortunate to have found her—an intelligent and sensitive woman—someone beyond nationality, someone he had been searching for. He remembered the astrologer's words in Dehra Dun: 'Your wish is for a Shakti, like Parvati, but you may not find her easily . . . Perhaps a solution is to find your Shakti from outside your circle.' He glanced at her, but couldn't say anything. He was afraid.

Perhaps Amrita felt his fear too. She took his hand and held it. She asked Larry, "When you go back to Denver, will you keep in touch with me?"

"Of course," he replied. He wanted to say more, something that was in his heart, but fear of rejection froze him. He only held on to her hand. Finally, he asked her if she would have the courage, if he asked her something—something that might sound foolhardy.

"I'll always have courage for you."

Their eyes met and both felt an unspoken communion.

"This is enough for me," he told her. And if she misunderstood him, he didn't want to know. They walked together quietly, at peace.

In the evening they returned to Bhojbasa and Larry pondered. Was this fate? Or merely coincidence? There he was, standing behind Sovik at the Singapore Airline counter in LA; he got involved with the group going to the Himalayas. Meanwhile Amrita came from Bombay to the Tourist Office in Dehra Dun. They met. A peculiar Indian situation had separated them from the group. And now he was alone with Amrita and very happy.

Were these all parts of some bigger scheme that he could never comprehend?

20.2

Larry and Amrita sat in the altar room, waiting for the evening Aarti service. He could hear Laal Baba singing in the distance. The words were not clear, but he had heard him croon the tune before. It had a simple, homey nature to it.

"He's coming," Amrita said.

Laal Baba entered the room and started the song afresh. Larry observed his red (laal) robe, loosely flowing over his heavy-set body. His eyes were half-closed; he was oblivious to how many came to the service. His hands moved in the air with the tune. Larry whispered to Amrita, "Is this a common song?"

"I haven't heard it before."

"He must love the song—he has sung it several times. What is it about?"

"The words are simple. I'll translate as he sings:

Mad man, let go
Of your ego.
Wake up from your slumber
Meditate on the numbers.

What a shine
Each adds up to nine.
What it means?
Secret of life, it seems.

Mad man, let go
Of your ego.
Listen to the song of the epic
Heroine cries, vying for her right.

Centuries later Krishna sings in delight
Certainly she in his mind
Reveals the secret
Hiding it in an epithet.

Numbers shine like letters
Take the lower odd numbers
Add the auspicious digit to one
What a joy-giver it becomes.
The other add the 15th prime
Not a cube, not a square,
You have your answer.

With one change of a letter
She becomes the center.
Strange is the mode of life
How Krishna restores the loyal wife.

Mad man, let go
Of your ego."

Laal Baba opened his eyes and looked around the hall with a happy expression on his face. "You're back," he said, looking at Amrita.

"Yes, Maharaj," she said in Hindi, "my friend enjoyed your song very much."

"I love this song," he said, looking at Larry. "When the mood comes, I sing it for several days."

Amrita translated his answer to Larry.

"Is there a deeper meaning to the song?" Larry asked and Amrita translated back to the monk.

"Meaning? Whatever you want to make of it. It reminds me of Gangotri, of the wonderful man there, Swami Narayan. It is his song. He used to sing it often when he became the head priest."

Laal Baba went to the altar and lit the earthen lamps.

Several men and women walked in and sat down on the floor. Soon the fragrance of sandalwood incense and the sound of Sanskrit mantras filled the air.

Larry's eyes moved to the large Swastika sign on the altar. Smoke from the incense burner made the red Swastika sign mysterious. He kept on looking at the sign through the smoke.

The darkness of the room, faint lights and shadows of the earthen lamps suddenly took him back to the recess of the Konkon Café in New Delhi. He remembered the conspiratorial voices of Chetti and Ajit. Then the set of numbers came to him: 01 35 18 02 25 27 03 15 04 59. He was certain the numbers contained a secret, a secret to find gold in a temple! But how to decipher them? He repeated the numbers in his mind 01351802252703150459. Twenty digits. They could be grouped by 2, 4 or 5 sets of numbers, but he found no clue in these sets. He had tried earlier to put the numbers in different orders; that did not help either.

He stared at the four dots on the Swastika. They formed a circle around the center of the Swastika symbol. He never saw these dots in the usual pictures of swastikas. He remembered a sadhu on the bank of the river who taught him that 'life is not linear.' The sadhu had a law degree from Allahabad University, but later gave up his practice and became a monk. The sadhu told him that everything is non-linear in nature. So why was he thinking of the numbers in a linear way? Perhaps he should put the numbers in a circle.

He arranged the numbers around the Swastika sign, with the zero on top, but it did not reveal a clue. He rotated the numbers on the circle, placing the next number 1 on top—13518022527031504590, but he could find no hint. He rotated the numbers further, bringing each number systematically on top of the Swastika sign, trying to see if they divulged any clue. Then when the fourth zero came on top—04590135180225270315, suddenly a picture came to him. It was so simple: the numbers formed the geometrical angles of a circle around the Swastika symbol—like the hands of a clock: 3 o'clock is 90 degrees and 6 o'clock is 180 degrees. The code numbers broke into eight places on a circle around the Swastika: 0, 45, 90, 135, 180, 225, 270, and 315. The four dots of the Swastika symbol fell on the odd numbers. His eyes widened with this sudden realization.

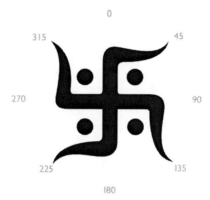

Then Laal Baba's song came to him:

What a shine
Each adds up to nine.

The digits in each of these numbers add up to nine as the song said. What a coincidence! Could Lal Baba's song refer to the riddle?

The room filled with the chorus: "Om, Jaya Jagadisha Hare," and Larry stood up along with everyone for the Aarti song, but his eyes remained fixed on the Swastika. The numbers of the riddle refer to the Swastika! He repeated that several times in his mind.

It dawned on him the lower numbers were 135 and 225—both odd numbers. But what does that mean? Why did Chetti say it might have something to do with gold?

He stared at the four dots of the Swastika sign and saw that if he formed a circle around the four dots and connected the two top dots with the center, it formed an M inside O of the circle. "Wow! I see the sacred word OM in English inside the Swastika symbol," he muttered. "Fascinating!"

"What?" Amrita leaned against him. "What is fascinating?"

"I just saw OM written inside the Swastika sign."

"Really? I never knew that."

"I'll show you later."

Larry started to think of 135 and 225 again. What did the song say?

> Numbers shine like letters
> Take the lower odd numbers
> Add the auspicious digit to one
> What a joy-giver it becomes
> The other add the 15th prime
> Not a cube, not a square,
> You have your answer

From his mathematics classes at Cornell, Larry knew the number system originated in India as early as 3000 BC and 9 was considered the perfect number as it completed the number system. It was also an auspicious number in Hindu sacred mantras. The digits in the code also add up to 9, making it a common thread among these numbers. He added 9 to 135, getting 144. He knew Harshad numbers, first discovered in India, are called joy-giver numbers, because, in Sanskrit, 'Harshad' is harsa (joy) + da (give), meaning joy-giver. Indeed, 144 was a Harshad number! 1+ 4+4 is 9 and 144 is divisible by 9, hence a Harshad number.

Then he counted the prime numbers and determined that 47 was the 15th. He added 47 to 225. That made 272. He found, to his astonishment, that 272 is neither a square nor a cube. He got these numbers—144 and 272—following the song, but he couldn't make any more sense of the numbers and couldn't proceed any further.

The Aarti chorus reached a crescendo.

> "Bhakta Jano Ke Sankata,
> Dash Jano Ke Sankata,
> Kshana Me Dur Kare.
> Om, Jaya Jagadisha Hare."

The Aarti finished and everyone sat down. Laal Baba gave prasad to the worshippers. When he came to Larry, he said in Hindi, "My son, there are many ways to reach God. One can express the same truth in many languages. Keep searching—any way you want to."

Amrita translated what he said to Larry. "I think he likes you," she told him, and was pleased.

The devotees went away one by one. As they opened the outside door, a cold wind swept in and made them shiver, reminding them they were high in the Himalayas.

"I think Laal Baba's song has a secret hidden in it," Larry told Amrita when everyone left the room. "Do you make any sense of the song?"

"All folk songs make you think of something deep." She held his hand and looked into his eyes.

"I wonder because the song talks about numbers that adds up to nine." Larry's mind was absorbed with the riddle.

"You are thinking too hard." A smile spread across her face and her eyes sparkled. "Nine is the largest digit, an auspicious number!" she exclaimed. "Nabagraha—nine planets—are mentioned in mantras often."

"I'm really puzzled."

"We don't analyze a song the way you're doing," she said. "Everything has more than one meaning in India."

"I thought of two numbers that add up to nine: 135 and 225."

"You are crazy to analyze a spiritual song this way." She put her hand on his arm, gently caressing him.

Larry's focus was on sorting out the mystery. "You remember the old manuscript we showed to the monk in Gangotri the night before we left? I got these numbers from that manuscript."

"Yes, I remember. The monk didn't know anything about the manuscript or the numbers."

"When I asked if he could read a name or identify a temple, he searched through the pages and the only thing he could come up with was the letter G. I wonder if it could be Gangotri."

"G could also stand for Ganga," Amrita said, "the river or the goddess. And there are many temples on the Ganges River. Or perhaps G could mean Gaumukh."

"That's the thing. There are so many possibilities." Frustration came through his voice. "I've a hunch that there's a hidden message in Laal Baba's song. Could you please think about the numbers 144 and 272? What could they mean? The song says they have the answer."

"You said 135 and 225 before, now these two numbers?"

"Oh! I followed the song and came up with these two new numbers."

"I'll think about it, but don't get crazy with numbers. Let's go to the dining room. I'm famished from our hike."

Larry continued to stare intently at the Swastika sign. "I am puzzled, Amrita. What does gold have to do with temples?"

"Gold?" She stared at Larry for a few seconds. "Temples always have gold. Haven't you seen the jewelry on the deities?"

"So the Hindu temples are not poor."

"Only village temples are poor. Well-known temples have wealth. During the first India-Pakistan war, Hindu priests gave a substantial amount of gold to the government."

"They have such a cache of gold?"

"They have collected gold from ancient times. Think about it—for thousands of years."

"Where do they keep it?"

"No one knows."

"Then if one steals some gold from a temple, no one would know."

"I guess not, but why do you ask?"

"I thought of something, but never mind." He stood up.

"Tell me."

"It's so ridiculous, if I tell you, you'll think I'm crazy."

Amrita didn't say anything, and waited.

"I think the Swastika sign holds a clue to finding the gold."

"From the Gangotri Temple or this place?"

"I don't know."

"Are you thinking there is gold hidden in the Gangotri temple?"

Larry nodded. "I'm afraid someone could be planning to steal that gold."

Amrita looked away from him. "I thought you came here so we could spend time together." She turned to walk away.

Her voice brought Larry back from his excitement about the numbers. He had broken from Sovik and the others for this woman and now he was losing her because of his obsession with numbers. She must think he was a gold-hunting opportunist.

"Please wait."

She had already walked a few steps toward the door. "We're only nimittas in this world," Amrita told him gently.

"What are you saying?" He went to her. "Please don't be angry."

"Nothing goes on without God's blessing. He knows everything, even if someone is planning to steal gold from a temple. And if He does not want the gold to be stolen, He will see to that. If He allows that gold to be stolen, there must be a reason for that."

"You mean I don't have to act."

"If God wants you to act, you will. You will be inspired to do so. We are only his vehicles. We don't know and cannot see the plan that God has."

"How did you learn all this?" He was surprised to find her so thoughtful.

"It is all in the Gita."

"But then, no one would do anything."

"It seems fatalistic, but it's not. Rather it is submissive to God's will. You have to act, as Arjun finally acted. You know that God does not need our prayers. Prayer is really for our own well-being, and it energizes us. You will know when the time comes for you to act. Then you'll rush down from the mountain."

"I see your point."

Amrita didn't say any more, and stepped away from him.

"I was so absorbed. I'm sorry," Larry said, but she didn't come back.

He didn't expect her to react this way. In his heart he was truly concerned someone was planning to steal gold from a temple. If he knew that, should he sit still? Shouldn't he figure out the plan to stop it? He dragged himself to the dining room, but Amrita was not there.

20.3

The manager of the guesthouse told Sovik the hike downhill to Gangotri would be easy. They could even start at 1 p.m. and reach Gangotri before dark. The place was so soothing, idyllic, and quiet that no one could willingly leave Bhojbasa. So they lingered on.

Be'ziil stood on the porch of the Guesthouse taking in the view.

He looked different, and Sovik realized what it was. "Be'ziil, how come you aren't wearing your sunglasses. Are you okay?"

"When I was in Gaumukh, I thought about what I've seen here. I made some decisions."

"You decided not to wear sunglasses?"

Be'ziil looked straight at Sovik and said, "Didn't you realize I was high all through the trip?"

"What?"

"I was high on marijuana and hashish."

"Really?" Sovik hadn't caught on at all.

"What do you think the sadhus do when they sit and gaze at nothing?" Be'ziil looked at Sovik. "They're high on ganja!"

Sovik knew that drugs were a problem on the Indian Reservations, and Be'ziil had had some encounters with it, but he had no idea Be'ziil was smoking all through the trip.

"How did you find marijuana here?" Sovik asked.

"At the hotel in New Delhi."

"New Delhi?"

Be'ziil explained to him how on the first morning in New Delhi he shared an American cigarette with one of the guards at the hotel. The guard gave him a local biri to try out. Be'ziil asked if it was possible to get some real stuff to smoke. Sure, everything was available for a price. When he agreed to pay $10, the guard sent a man to get some marijuana. Within a half hour he had a large bag of marijuana, an enormous amount for the money. The stuff was very good. He had been "floating" since then.

"Be'ziil, you are mingling with the locals so well. How do you do it?"

"It's easy. You just go and talk to them. When I was in New Delhi, a man who drives a three-wheeler took me all over the town at night. I've seen where they live and how they live. I can mix with them. They're good people."

"It must have cost you a lot of money to go all over town?"

"Oh no. I told him I had no money. The driver said he'd show me anyway. I paid him only twenty rupees for gas."

What a discovery! Sovik worried about Be'ziil all this time, while he had made himself at ease with the Indian people. He had gone out alone and had shared their experiences. Sovik, Pinky and Kayla were seeing India from the outside, and Be'ziil was observing India from the inside. He also felt better here because he was not judged by a set standard, as he was judged in the States. Be'ziil was really happy.

Sovik remained silent for a few minutes. His own self was so important, so all-encompassing that he didn't notice what was going on in his own group. First Kayla, now Be'ziil. It occurred to him that Be'ziil had also spent his time among the holy men and mendicants along the river and on the hills.

Be'ziil was calmly gazing at the white peaks outside.

"Tell me, Be'ziil," Sovik said, "how did you get along with the sadhus who wander along the river? . . . When I was young, I wanted to know what they did and what they learned from their meditations, but I didn't have the courage to talk to them. How did you do it?"

"I just walk over to an ash-covered, matted-haired sadhu and start a conversation with signs and gestures. The sadhus didn't mind. Sometimes I offered some marijuana. They are not that different from some people I know on the Reservation. Some shared their clay chillum pipes with me. Wow! What they smoke is powerful. Holding the pipe with both hands, they take a long breath until a puff of fire spouted out of the top of the pipe. 'Bohm,' they would say, and be still for a long time. We sat together. Sometimes they talk with me."

"You understand them?'

"Well, they tell me with signs and some words. After a good ganja session, we understand each other. The sadhus accepted me." Be'ziil looked up at the clear, blue sky for a second. "They think I am like them. I sit with them, smoke and just float."

"Did they tell you what they find?"

"To the sadhus, chillum smoke is their connection with God. Sometimes they feel they are with God and feel his presence all around them."

No wonder Be'ziil stayed alone all this time!

"I have learned something else," Be'ziil continued. "The sadhus accepted me in the same way we accept other tribes when we go to ceremonies. They accepted me even though I have a different way of seeing things. They have learned this over many generations, but these sadhus have kept their way of searching for God."

Sovik listened to Be'ziil without saying anything.

"I've learned a lot about myself," Be'ziil concluded. "You may not believe it, but I've thrown my pack of hashish into the river."

"Really!"

"I enjoyed being high, but I often searched through my life when I was alone. The sadhus know what they are doing. For me it is not the same thing. The poor beggars are smoking to forget the day. What is my goal? Where am I going? I don't know. I am simply floating." Be'ziil stopped for a second. "I know my mother sent me here to get a hold of my life. My father was happy that I was holding on to a job that he couldn't. Drugs killed him. I'm not even twenty! Coyote is playing with me through the drugs. I must try something else."

"So you don't need the sunglasses now?"

"No more drugs, no more sunglasses." Be'ziil gazed at the snow-white peaks around them and murmured, "I wish I could stay here longer."

20.4

In the morning Amrita hurried to the porch where Larry was sipping tea from a metal tumbler. She wore a sari and a matching blouse, but had no makeup on and had barely combed her hair. She went to him, almost running.

"You're up early!" Larry said, obviously pleased that Amrita had a joyful expression on her face. "I'm sorry for last night."

"I've found a meaning for the two numbers," she told him, ignoring his apology. "It's thrilling."

"Shall we go outside so you can tell me in private?"

"There's nothing secret in what I've found." Her eyes widened. "Remember what I told you? The monks talk in riddles. The numbers turn out to mean G-I-T-A." She smiled and sat down on the chair next to him.

"Really?"

"Yes. I thought about your numbers and what the song was saying. When I was in bed, I remembered the song, 'Numbers shine like letters,' and thought of the coded messages we used to send each other in high school. So I tried to substitute letters for the numbers."

"It referred to the sacred book?" Larry asked, still puzzled.

"In our alphabet vowels come first. The first vowel A will be one, the second vowel sounds like Aah and will be two, etc. So I is 4, G is 14, soft or dental T is 27. The numbers become Gita."

"Then what about the rest of the song, about the epic and the heroine?"

"It all fits in," she said. "In the epic Ramayana, the wife of Lord Rama, Sita, is a sad character. She was abducted by the evil king Ravana. Lord Rama rescued her, but in the end he sent her away to exile because she had been imprisoned in the evil king's palace. It wasn't her fault, but her purity was questioned. A heart-breaking story! If you replace one letter as the song said, Gita becomes Sita. That's how 'Krishna brings back the loyal wife.' Krishna transforms the sad story of Sita to the song of Gita; he makes her name the most important word. Laal Baba's song weaves both our two epic mythologies together and refers to the essence of the Hindu religion."

Larry looked at her transfixed.

"So what do you think?" she asked.

"I am proud of you." Larry held her hand for a few seconds, grateful to feel its softness once more. "You are brilliant."

"I guess I've earned my tea this morning."

Larry saw that Amrita was bubbly again. The riddle had helped her. Amazing, how things work out in mysterious ways in India. "Let's go for a short hike," he told her. "I need to clear my mind."

"First, my tea."

"Of course."

It was a beautiful day with a cloudless sky. Larry and Amrita strolled along the bank of the river. The morning bathed their surroundings with a pearly pink light, and the sound of the river calmed them.

Amrita cheerfully talked about her earlier hiking experiences in this area.

Larry listened half-heartedly; his mind was occupied with the numbers, the Swastika symbol, the word Gita, and what all these could mean. Perhaps they have no connection with each other. India is difficult to understand. Now he finds monks talk in riddles. Nothing is straightforward. Nothing is linear. When the monks and the priests talk, they do not give a direct answer; one has to find out for oneself. He had allowed himself to become so preoccupied by this. It was probably nothing, but he didn't know how to stop mulling it over.

He stopped and pulled Amrita by her hand. "Tell me how the temples survive in India? Who supports them?"

Amrita stared at him for a moment. "Something is eating you. Tell me. Then I can help you with what I know."

"I'm sorry. I cannot take my mind off the puzzle. I feel I'm close to something, but I don't even know what I'm looking for."

"I'm listening."

"I've a gut feeling that somewhere, something bad is in the making. If only I could solve the puzzle, I could stop it."

"What puzzle? The numbers?"

Larry could not say anything for a minute. "Let's sit down. I'll tell you from the beginning."

Larry explained to Amrita the little he knew about the SMS and how Sovik got the old manuscript from Chetti, who was the SMS fund-raiser. Larry told her of his encounter with Chetti and his assistant at the Konkon café in New Delhi. The SMS was desperate for money and he felt that Chetti was the kind of man for whom success was very important. He thought Chetti could engage in under-handed activities; selling the ancient manuscript was, perhaps, only one example among many. Then when he saw Ajit in Gangotri and knew Swami Rangaraj was helping the SMS, he became very concerned. He was not sure what Ajit was doing there, but he knew whatever Ajit was doing would be completed soon.

"Are you worried they could steal gold from the Gangotri temple?"

"Yes. I'd be happy to be wrong, but suppose I am not wrong? Then wouldn't you blame yourself if we did nothing?"

Amrita looked at him for a few seconds without blinking. "You forgot to add another clue—G for Gangotri."

Larry's head moved in a jerk toward Amrita. "Then we must go back to Gangotri immediately. I want to talk with Swami Narayan."

"Does Sovik have any more information?" Amrita asked. "He is right here. Shouldn't you see him first?"

Larry agreed. "Let's walk further. I want to think this through. I'm afraid it could all be my imagination."

Larry went to the Guesthouse in the afternoon to talk with Sovik, only to find Sovik and his friends had already left two or three hours earlier. Larry might not be able to catch Sovik because he knew Sovik would leave Gangotri the next day. Who could Larry consult then?

Larry's mind was in a whirl. He didn't know what to do. He felt strongly that what he had figured out so far meant something, but he had no way to be sure. Only one man could clear this up: Swami Narayan, the head priest of the Gangotri temple. If he could talk to him, all his suspicions would go away, and he could stop obsessing. As he walked back to Laal Baba's ashram, he tried to find alternatives, but could find none but to hurry back to Gangotri.

"Sovik has already left," he told Amrita almost out of breath, "and he'll leave Gangotri tomorrow." After a moment he said, "If I could reach as far as Chirbasa tonight I could be in Gangotri in the morning."

"Are you crazy?"

"I'll camp on the trail."

"If you are hoping to find treasure under a Swastika sign," Amrita said, "there are many, many Swastika signs inside the temple. You know it is a holy symbol."

Larry's face fell at the thought of the futility of his effort. "I could at least talk with the head priest and clear my mind," he told Amrita.

"If you must go, let us start right away," Amrita said. "We need to collect two blankets so we won't freeze at night."

Surprised, Larry looked at her for a few seconds. "You want to come down with me?"

"I know the path better than you."

"It's very risky."

"So, would I stay here and let you go?"

Amrita went to her room and returned with a small bag. "We take only the absolute minimum," she told Larry.

"Yeah. The ashram can have the rest of our stuff."

Within half an hour they started their descent. "I'm glad you didn't wear a sari," Larry told Amrita.

"Salwar-kameez is much easier."

The beginning of the trek was enjoyable. The sun was lower in the sky, the temperature pleasant, the path long but straight. Only when it became dark did the hike become difficult, but by then they were close to Chirbasa. They took out their flashlights and walked carefully, one step at a time.

When they reached Chirbasa, the place was very quiet and the restaurant workers and porters had gone inside their tents. One man came out to inquire about them and found them space inside a large tent.

Larry could not sleep well. As soon as he saw a tinge of light on the eastern sky, he woke up Amrita. They started down immediately. The moment Larry saw the spire of the Gangotri temple, the rush of the previous afternoon came back to him, he hurried on hoping what he had figured was worthwhile. It held a clue to something important. Then, as the spire of the Gangotri temple became more distinct, a feeling of apprehension descended on him and grew stronger by the minute. What if he was wrong? And even if he was right, what was he expected to do?

Part VI

Remembering Sitamarhi

21

A Locket

Every morning upon arising, Jagdish went to the river and took a quick dip in the sacred water. The rivers in Sitamarhi were only tributaries of the Ganges River, but this was Mother Ganga's water. After his chilling dip, he went to the market for a cup of tea, then back to the temple for the morning puja. If he arrived early, he sat on the steps until Swami Anand opened the door.

During the puja he observed each movement, each word of the monks. Swami Narayan often gave him a flower from the head of the Goddess Ganga statue. He took it reverentially and raised his palms to his forehead. Everyone at the temple knew Jagdish by now, and he received a good portion of the prasad from Swami Anand. The prasad was enough for his breakfast. When the morning Aarti was over, he sat near the Shaligram Shila stone, gazing at Bhagirath Mountain. This was his way of worshipping the Himalayas, the home of the gods and goddesses.

If there was no event in the courtyard, he walked along the bank of the river, had lunch in the market place and went back to his room in Subodh's dharmashala. He returned to the courtyard for afternoon devotional singing, then the evening Aarti puja, a simple supper in the market, and finally to Swami Narayan's talk. He loved this routine and forgot how many days he had been in Gangotri.

One day it occurred to him that he was able to come to this holy place because of the good deeds of his father and his grandfather. "We are not isolated human beings," he surmised. "Nothing comes out of nothing. It takes several generations to achieve something great. King Bhagirath brought the Goddess down to earth, but his ancestors began that task. It was perhaps the same with me." That he had come on this wonderful pilgrimage was the result of his ancestors' good deeds, and he felt choked with gratitude. He decided to perform a special puja to provide for the souls of his ancestors. Subodh had asked him to help with the feast for Ajit Boka. That could also be a fine day to perform the worship service for his ancestors. He would ask Swami Narayan about it.

In the evening he often thought of his family and his village. "What a long journey I've made," he said to himself one day. "I'd love to stay here forever, but my family, my people are in Sitamarhi." He felt melancholy. He thought lovingly of his home and everyone in Sitamarhi. He hoped Sukhi was able to manage all she had to do. He remembered the old jackfruit tree that his father had planted at the back of their house. It always produced a lot of fruit, more than they ever needed. He remembered the cow and hoped that she was fine. Then memories of the fields and trees in the village came to him. He longed for his life at home.

Suddenly the image of a red flag atop a bamboo pole came to his mind. He put that up in front of the house each year to honor the god Hanuman during Diwali. On Diwali night young men from nearby villages carry such decorated poles, Hanumanji ka Jhandas, in procession to the Hanuman temple and plant them in front of the temple. Then a festival begins with drumbeats of dholaks and trumpets. The youth display their strength in mock fights, wrestling, and dancing. Sounds of "Jai Ho"—be victorious—reverberate from all sides. Finally, all greet one another with "Jai ho, jai ho," and return to their homes while the Hanumanji ka Jhandas are left standing in front of the temple until the next year's festival.

He remembered he had promised Vir he would help him make a wonderful Hanumanji ka Jhanda this year.

Jagdish had carried Vir on his shoulder to these festivals and returned home late at night. By then earthen lamps had been lit, decorating all the houses. Little oil lamps glowed from the corners of each house and in rows along the roof. They looked so wonderful.

"Next year," Vir had demanded from Jagdish during the last festival, "You help me and my friends make a great Hanumanji ka Jhanda. We are old enough. We can take it to the temple."

Jagdish saw the excitement and the enthusiasm on Vir's face and could not refuse. "Yes, we will make one."

"It must be the best in this area."
"Surely. We will collect materials during the year."
"You promise?"
"I promise. But you must practice wrestling."
"Oh what fun we will have," Vir had said as he ran in circles around his grandfather.

There were still several months left before Diwali, but Jagdish remembered he had not collected any material for the pole. Vir's happy face danced in his thoughts. Then he murmured to himself, "Yes, it's time I return." He decided to leave as soon as he had performed the service for his ancestors.

What should he take back for his family? He knew his family and neighbors would keep reverently whatever he brought from the holy place. One day, he browsed through the souvenir stores. In one upscale stall, he saw a small stone locket with the picture of the goddess Ganga embossed on it. The stone was emerald green and the goddess a glowing pastel pink. He loved the locket. It would be a wonderful gift for Sukhi. "How much?" he asked the vendor with some trepidation.

"I see you pass by everyday," the man said in a kind voice, "you are a true devotee. You spend all your time at the temple. Most people spend more time here, shopping. But you know what? It is too expensive for you."

Jagdish knew that in his heart. But he thought he had never given his wife anything. "You have told me the right thing," he admitted to the vendor. He turned the locket round and round in his hand. He then stretched his hand to give it back, but still asked, "Please tell me anyway."

The vendor looked at him silently for a few moments.

"You see," Jagdish told him. "I've never given anything expensive to my wife. She is a good woman. That's why I ask."

"It's really expensive," the vendor said, "but for you, 225 rupees."

"Two hundred and twenty-five rupees!" Jagdish almost jumped back.

"It has a sterling silver chain," the man told him.

"Thank you," Jagdish handed it back and turned to walk away.

"Come back when you have made up your mind. I could reduce the price a little more for you, but don't tell others about this price."

Jagdish nodded and went to another stall; he examined small copper plates with different pictures of the temple and gods and goddesses. They were only five or ten rupees each. He decided he would buy a few for his neighbors. He also found brass statues of gods and goddesses. He liked the statue of Ganesh with an elephant trunk and that of goddess Saraswati standing on a lotus flower.

They were twenty to thirty rupees each. He could buy many inexpensive items, but as he walked back to the dharmashala, the locket kept coming back to his thoughts.

Two days after Sovik left for the source of the river, Jagdish was in the market when he heard a commotion from the river bank. The courtyard was usually quiet in the early afternoon, with no activities in the temple and few visitors. He walked toward the noise.

The uproar was loud enough to be heard inside the temple. Swami Narayan came out of his room and stood in the foyer. A few had gathered near the river's bank, surrounding a man. The priest could hear their conversation.

The middle-aged man was slapping his chest and forehead, crying out loudly. "Now I do not know what to do. How am I to go back home?"

"You should have been more careful with your money," one man said.

"Didn't you see the current was very strong here?" another man said.

Everyone was talking with one another and to the man at the same time. The man wore a dhoti raised up to his knees in the South Indian style. He sat down. He was ruined.

Swami Narayan saw Jagdish coming to the courtyard.

Jagdish went to the crowd. He asked the man in distress what had happened.

"I went to get a little water to put on my head," the man told him in broken Hindi, "and my wallet fell off in the stream. Before I could pick it up, the current swept it away. All my money is gone." The man started to lament again.

"Hai Raam," Jagdish said. "This is what I am always afraid of! If I lose my money, how am I going to survive?"

"What's going to happen to me?" the man cried. His dark, sad face was creased with anxiety as he looked at Jagdish.

"Are you alone here?" Jagdish asked him.

"I've come alone from Madurai. It took me several days to come here."

"Could someone send you money from home?" one man in the crowd asked.

"I'm a laborer in a cinnamon factory. Who will send me money?"

"How much money do you need to go back home?" Jagdish asked him. He knew how difficult, almost impossible, it would have been for him to write a letter home to ask for money. And who would give him the money?

"A lot: 120 Rupees. I have no money to eat. I'll die here."

"You're in God's place," Jagdish said. "God will help you." He looked at the man kindly; he was a laborer like him from a far-away place. And his situation was probably no different than his own. Jagdish had been able to come here because of God's grace. He had received money unexpectedly. Perhaps a similar thing had happened to this man or perhaps he had saved each penny to come here. Sympathy welled up in his heart. Jagdish took out a small cloth bag that hung against his chest, inside his shirt, and counted some money. "Here is 150 Rupees. I was going to buy a gift for my wife, but your need is much more." He thrust the money into the man's hand.

The South Indian man stared at Jagdish for a few moments, not believing what had just happened. "It's God's grace! Thank you," he finally said, accepting the money. "You are a Godsend." He prostrated on the stone floor toward the temple. When he got up, he told Jagdish, "Your gesture will not be forgotten. God will bless you. I shall mail you the money when I go home. It will take some time, but please give me your address."

"You've come here like me. I'm happy that I could help you. If you want to know, my name is Jagdish Lohar from Sitamarhi, Bihar."

All eyes were on Jagdish because no one expected what he had just done. That made him feel uneasy. He went toward the temple where Swami Narayan was.

The crowd stared at Jagdish as he walked quietly away from them.

The next day Jagdish went to the market again. The South Indian man had reinforced in him the idea that he should go home now. Yesterday Swami Narayan had conducted the service for his ancestors; he had offered balls of cooked rice and Ganges water to the souls of his ancestors. He had also performed pujas for his family, for his friends and for the entire village of Sitamarhi. Now he must go back.

He bought small items from the souvenir stores—copper plates with pictures of gods and goddesses, statues of gods and goddesses that weren't expensive, small bells and metal oil lamps for family altars. His jute shopping bag became full. Then he came to the store where he had seen the gorgeous locket. There were a few customers buying and he stood behind them. When they were gone, he told the shop owner, "I came to tell you, I'm going home, but I cannot buy the locket. I don't have the money."

The man looked at Jagdish for a moment. "When are you leaving?"

"I shall start in two or three days—Friday or Saturday." He paused for a second, looking at the beautiful items in the store. "I have a long journey home."

"How much money do you have?" the store owner asked him in a soft voice.

"Only three hundred rupees. You know I need money to buy bus and train tickets. If I buy the locket, I wouldn't have money left to go home." He looked at the man's face. "Sukhi would like to see me return more than she'd want to have the locket. So thank you and God bless you."

The store owner had seen many buyers in his life. They would lie to him and tell him fancy stories to get a lower price, but he knew this man was telling the truth. "I've heard about you," he told Jagdish. "You gave away your money to help the South Indian man." He gazed at the poor farmer benevolently.

There was no change of expression on Jagdish's face. "How do you know that?"

"This is a small town." He smiled wryly. "People talk."

"I had to give him the money," Jagdish shook his head and whispered. "Otherwise, how was he going to go home?"

The store owner looked at him for a few more seconds. He finally asked, "Can you manage to go home with two hundred rupees?"

"I think so. The extra hundred is for emergency."

"Then give me a hundred and take the locket for your wife. I lose some money, but I want you to have it." He went inside and brought out the locket with the picture of Goddess Ganga on it.

Jagdish held the locket and admired its beauty. "Sukhi will love this," he told the man in a choked voice. "Bahut Shukriya—many thanks."

Part VII

Pilgrim's Feast

22

Final Arrangements

22.1

Ajit was surprised to hear a knock on the door. The two signs he had posted kept the locals away, and the pilgrims didn't care about the van. Sovik was the only person inquisitive about the geology project and bold enough to come to his door, but Ajit knew Sovik had left for Gaumukh. "Good riddance," Ajit had mumbled when he saw Sovik leave. He turned away from watching Swami Anand's movements on the monitor and opened the door. His mouth fell open: Chetti stood in the doorway.

"I'm on my way to Tapovan," Chetti said.

"What a surprise! Please come in."

"I've wanted to come here for a long time. Two days back I thought, 'Why not do it now and also visit you?'" He looked around. Two monitors displayed the inside of the temple. Small equipment lay on a table— a camera, pliers, various electronic gadgets, and flashlights; on the floor coiled black wires lay next to a rolled-up sleeping bag and a plastic pillow. The windows on one side were blocked by the wall of a mountain and the other side showed the road and the market. The smell of coffee permeated the space.

"Tapovan?" Ajit sputtered. "You're going to Tapovan?"

"It's a day hike from Gaumukh. People tell me the most beautiful meadow of wild flowers is there."

"You are going on a vacation in the midst of our final action?"

"I'm taking a short break." Chetti observed the monitor; it showed the corridor inside the temple. "I also came here to see how you are doing."

"I've put two cameras inside the temple to record the comings and goings of people."

"So what is your assessment?" Chetti sat down on the only chair inside the van.

"I'm ready and waiting for Swami Rangaraj's signal." He paused for a few seconds. "We met once, but he can't decide when to go to the secret place. He has not contacted me again. He might be having second thoughts."

"Could we see him tonight?"

"We can talk with him while Swami Narayan meets with his disciples."

"How are your arrangements?" Chetti asked. "Do you need more money?"

"Everything is fine." Ajit's lips curled in a satisfied smile. "I've hired two young men to help me. While they dig for rocks and divert people's attention, I'll make several trips and take some gold out." He paused to gauge Chetti's reaction. Chetti was listening calmly. "I have figured out the best time to enter the temple," Ajit told him.

"That's good but have you figured out any clues from the set of numbers?" Chetti asked.

"No. I've been too busy setting this up." He looked at Chetti. "I think the priests are very smart. They must have alternate means of access. Swami Rangaraj must lead us there."

"You're right." Chetti nodded. "The monks have guarded the treasure for centuries. They surely have more than one way to get there."

"I plan to make a copy of the key to the secret room."

"Good idea." Chetti looked out through the window at the market. "It'll come in handy in the future."

"I've trained my assistants to help me."

"The critical part is Swami Rangaraj. Who are your assistants?"

"Don't worry about them. They know nothing. They think we are digging for thorium in the hills around here."

"The plan seems good to me." Chetti glanced around at Ajit's meager living conditions with only one shirt hanging on a hook. He stood up. "I'll come back around 7 pm."

"Swami Rangaraj is, after all, a monk. You must persuade him to act. People will soon get suspicious of my activities."

"I'll do my best."

"I hope my work is completed by the time you return from Tapovan. Why don't you spend a few more days up there, relaxing, then I'll certainly be done." Ajit opened the door for Chetti.

◆ ◆ ◆

Chetti and Ajit arrived at the temple a little after 7:30 to avoid Swami Narayan. Swami Rangaraj greeted Chetti warmly, almost obsequiously. "It is a great honor to have you in our temple. Please come to my room. I wish I had known you were coming."

"I'm going on a hike tomorrow morning, but I knew it would be a shame not to stop by and say hello to you." Chetti stepped into the monk's room. The light was dim. A table, a chair, and a bookshelf were placed at one corner. One book was open on the table with a writing pad next to it. Two ocher color shirts hung on a line strung between two nails on the wall. A brass kamandalu (monk's water pot) and a small metal tumbler were lined up on the floor near the bookcase.

"Do you meditate in this room?" Chetti asked, looking at the colorful rug on the floor. It was the only noteworthy item in the room.

"This room is not conducive to meditation," Swami Rangaraj said in an apologetic tone. "I study here."

"You need better lighting." Chetti said.

"We have good light in the puja area, but low-power bulbs in the three rooms back here. No electric lights in other parts of the temple. We use oil lamps and large candles."

"I guess a monk's life is not easy," Chetti said. "I have good news for you. I've received two replies from my contacts in America—one from New York and another from San Francisco. They are very interested in having you come for a lecture tour."

"That's great news." Swami Rangaraj's eyes sparkled. "I can go this winter."

"They offered to cover your travel expenses. Now I will work with the executive committee to finalize the details and ask someone to prepare your passport and visa applications. I think we should send a second person with you."

"Wouldn't that add to the expenses?" Swami Rangaraj stroked his beard and glanced at Chetti. "I can handle myself in America. Swami Vivekananda did it a hundred years ago."

"Money is the main problem, yes. But times have changed." Chetti studied Swami Rangaraj. "We need the second man to publicize your visits. Otherwise your lectures in America will amount to little. We need to engage in a vigorous campaign to build you up in America. That will also help the SMS." Chetti paused for a moment. "About money. Have you found out how much gold is in the treasure?" Chetti arched his eyebrows questioningly and held Swami Rangaraj's gaze.

"Well, no. I know where the key is, but I haven't yet seen the gold."

"You know how important it is for the SMS," Chetti said in a commanding voice. "We are depending on you and Ajit." He added softly, "Millions are oppressed in India. I know you want to help them."

Swami Rangaraj's face dropped and darkened. He had dreaded this encounter for several weeks. Now he found himself tongue-tied and hung his head.

Ajit spoke up. "Swamiji, I'll be at your doorstep any time you tell me."

"Yes, I know, and I have promised you my help. I've been remiss in this matter."

Chetti chimed in quickly. "It'll only take a few minutes of your time to go to the vault with Ajit."

"I know that," Swami Rangaraj said, looking at the floor, "Still it is hard for a monk to do something stealthily."

"I understand your quandary," Chetti nodded. "You can trust Ajit. Remember, we are all in this together. You will be helping millions of Indians. Aren't their lives worth some effort on your part? You are our guide. If you don't have the courage, where will we go?"

"You are right. I must exhibit courage when the cause is so great." Swami Rangaraj turned to Ajit. "Let's go to the chamber three days from now, right after the morning Aarti."

"You mean Thursday?" Ajit asked him to make sure.

"Yes. That's good."

"I shall be in this room, waiting for you."

"Excellent," Chetti said, then added conversationally, "I enjoyed the few hours I've spent in this town. I could see why people become sadhus so they can stay here."

"It is a wonderful place," Swami Rangaraj said, warming to the change of subject. "You will discover more if you extend your visit. The Vedic truth is embedded in this place."

Chetti, not wishing to continue a discussion on Vedic truths, moved toward the door. "How big is the inside of the temple?"

"We have a long corridor, but only three small rooms."

'Only three rooms?' Chetti wondered. "By the way," he told Swami Rangaraj, "you should prepare notes for your lectures in America. I'm making big plans. We plan to publish your lectures, to draw in expatriate Indians. They are an important resource. We must bring them in."

"I'm also thinking along those lines," Swami Rangaraj said. His voice became cheerful. "I shall prepare my notes in the coming few months."

"Please write in a way that Westerners will also understand, not just the Indians."

"Certainly. That's what made Mahesh Yogi succeed in America."

The three men walked out of the temple and through the courtyard; the moonlight cast a bluish glow over the scene. They stopped on the steps to the river and watched the ripples reflect the moonlight.

"Have you been to Tapovan?" Chetti asked Swami Rangaraj.

"Yes, I have spent several months there. It is a wonderful place for meditation. You will like it." After a few moments, Swami Rangaraj took his leave. "Namaste."

"You know you are our Swami Vivekananda; we depend on you for our progress. Arise and be bold," Chetti said.

"I needed your encouragement. Thank you for visiting me." Swami Rangaraj went back to the temple.

Chetti turned to Ajit. "I shall return Thursday afternoon."

22.2

Ajit opened his eyes as soon as he heard the first twitter of birds before dawn on Thursday. He lay in his sleeping bag, thinking over the items he must accomplish. He then reassured himself he would accept no more 'sticky' jobs like this one. He fondly remembered his afternoon tea with Lajjorani. He would keep his promise to his wife and go with her on a real vacation.

The chorus of birds rose to a crescendo. Ajit got up and pushed the curtains from the window. The white light of dawn lifted her wings over the landscape. He stepped outside the van, spread a small mat, and did his sit-ups and yoga exercises before going for a stroll along the river.

Ajit had timed the morning worship service and found it always ended around ten. The cameras he installed inside the temple revealed that no monks remained after the morning puja. No one entered the temple again for some time. This would be the ideal time for a trip to the secret chamber. Swami Rangaraj had also arrived at the same conclusion independently. A silent smile spread over Ajit's face; everything would work out just right.

The night before Ajit had given specific instructions to his assistants, Gujral and Sanju. "I've found trace amounts of thorium in a sample from the hill above the temple," he told them. He spoke excitedly as if eager to verify his assessment. "If this turns out to be correct, we've succeeded in finding what we are looking for."

His assistants were very happy with the news. "So I want to confirm the observation with new samples as soon as possible," he concluded. "You must start work tomorrow by 9 a.m." He instructed Gujral to go up the hill early and get new samples from more than a foot below the surface, so they would be pristine, untainted by centuries of accumulated debris. "I want to hear your machine going by 9:30," Ajit told him sternly.

Looking at Sanju, he said, "And you'll be on top of the temple, ready to receive the sample bags and place them on the other cable to the van."

"No problem," Sanju said.

"Are you used to the crampons now?" Ajit asked him.

"I'm still not very good at it, but I'm getting there."

"Make sure you don't fall—we don't want an accident! Your safety is of utmost importance to me. I won't be able to see you from the van and will not be able to help you. The project will be ruined if you fall. So be extra careful."

"I will," Sanju said.

"I'm so excited," Ajit told them, "I can't wait till the morning to verify what I've seen. So put your hearts into the work. Okay?"

His enthusiasm excited the two young men. They went away exhilarated—they were making progress and a positive contribution to India.

After breakfast, Ajit went to Subodh's dharmashala, intending to bring the ingredients for the feast to the courtyard as early as possible. Cooking must start by 8:30 so the feast would be in full swing by 9:30. The day before he had spread a rumor in the marketplace that excellent food would be served, but only a limited amount of laddus had been brought from Delhi. Anyone wishing to have the delicious sweet must line up early.

Ajit helped Subodh transport rice, lentils, eggplants, and large, cooking utensils to the courtyard. Truly pleased with Ajit's high spirits, Subodh said, "You don't talk about God, but I know you are a good man. God will reward you for your deeds."

Ajit stared at him for a few long seconds. "I hope God will understand what I'm doing."

"Sure he will."

After another trip to the courtyard, Subodh told Ajit that he could handle the rest. "The cooks and their helpers will arrive at 8 a.m. You can rest now."

"I shall meet you at nine then," Ajit said and left him.

At the van, he collected several items. Locksmith's wax was one. He had no idea what kind of locking mechanism he would encounter—whether it would be a wooden Egyptian pin tumbler lock, a Roman bolt, or simply an old Indian key. Or they might have updated the lock on the treasure in the last few decades. Whatever it might be, he was prepared to take a mold. He also picked up a miniature camera.

He was about to close the door when he stopped and looked back at the filing cabinet. "You never know," he whispered and went back. He opened a drawer and pulled out a small, plastic bag from the file of miscellaneous items. He found a mini-injector there, about two and a half inches long, and examined the two compartments inside the small syringe: one had a powdery substance and the other a liquid. He shook it gently; the powder was loose.

Ajit put it back in the bag and took it with him.

22.3

Golden, morning light streaked through the window when Sovik opened his eyes. He had not slept so well since he left the States. It took him a few moments to realize he was sleeping in the Guesthouse in Gangotri. Then he noticed the clothes hooks on the bare wall, and the haphazard luggage, shoes and backpacks on the floor.

Exhausted they had returned to Gangotri in the dark. Breathing comfortably for the first time in five days, Sovik and Pinky ate quickly at the hotel cafeteria and headed to bed, passing by Be'ziil dawdling over his alu-paratha.

"Staying up to meet your old buddies?" Sovik asked him with a glint in his eyes.

Be'ziil considered. "No. I don't trust myself. I'll stay here or sit outside, then go to bed."

"Good." Sovik left him there.

Sovik felt relaxed; his mission was now complete—the fears and worries that overwhelmed him were in the past. The scene at dawn in Gaumukh came to his mind, and a wonderful, happy feeling came over him. The trip gave him what he craved. Life is a journey and each moment gives one a fresh start. He stayed in bed, enjoying this blissful mood.

They had only this day left in Gangotri. That thought made Sovik spring from bed. Suddenly he longed to be in the temple courtyard and visit with the monks.

Pinky was curled up in her sleeping bag, with a blanket pulled over the bag for extra warmth. She slept soundly.

Sovik took a shower, put on clean clothes, and went to the cafeteria for tea and paratha. He observed the few people in the cafeteria talking animatedly, hurriedly drinking their tea, so they could start the hike to Gaumukh. He had done the same thing just five days earlier. He knew a wonderful experience was in store for them. He ordered another cup of tea and sat on the porch, watching the morning sun on the temple dome and breathing in the familiar scene of the river.

As he ambled across the bridge, a sense of belonging to this world and its timeless order came over him. Everybody is important in this world; each makes a contribution, however small, and all are connected and related in some way. He was not alone and all his deeds, however small, meant something. A cool, gentle breeze rose from the river. He looked across the narrow channel and saw the Geological Survey van.

He had forgotten Ajit during the last few days. The two antennae dishes on top of the van were like two big eyes staring at him, a weird looking thing in this place. He saw that Ajit and his assistants had added some new gadgets—rather unsightly in these surroundings; a cable ran down the hill to the top of the temple, and another went from the temple toward the van. Ajit must be getting his samples down by pulley and cable, Sovik thought. He would chat with him about his progress before he left town.

In the temple courtyard several men labored near the smaller building where a makeshift kitchen had been set up. Two fires were going, one with a large aluminum pot and the other a large iron wok filled with oil for frying. Someone had arranged a food offering for the pilgrims. Sovik knew people often did this to thank God for something good that had happened to them, or wishing for something good to happen. Bundles of round, dry-leaf plates and cone-shaped, red earthen pots for drinking water, the 'paper cups' of India, lay piled up against the wall. He noticed that Ajit was helping the cooks. Then he heard the temple bells and went to the foyer for the morning ceremony.

Swami Narayan and Swami Rangaraj performed the puja. Sovik stood at the back of the small crowd and participated in the service without drawing the monks' attention. He would talk with them later and say goodbye. This was not the time to distract them.

23

Tunnels and Caves

23.1

As devotees tossed flowers to the deities near the end of the worship service, Ajit slipped past them and went to Swami Rangaraj's room. He stood behind a clothesline where two saffron robes hung, felt the tiny camera and the injector in his pocket, and heard the chorus of the Aarti song:

> Aum jaya Jagadisha hare
> Swami jaya Jagadisha hare
> Bhakta jano ke sankata
> Kshana me dur kare
> Aum jaya Jagdisha hare.

> Om, glory to the Lord of the world
> Glory to the Lord of the world
> You remove instantly
> The difficulties of devotees
> Om, glory to the Lord of the world

The song ended, and he heard the footsteps of people leaving the temple.

Swami Rangaraj came to his room sometime later. "Good, you're already here," he said in a hushed voice. "We only have an hour."

"Do you have the key?"

"Yes."

"Then let's go." Ajit took out a small flashlight from his pocket and beamed a dim circle on the floor.

Swami Rangaraj paused, his face pensive. "Wait a minute," he said and ran back to the foyer.

Ajit went to the corridor. He had searched the area before, but had not found anything there. It ended at a rock wall.

Swami Rangaraj returned with a double wick kerosene lamp. He had clearly used the antique-looking brass lamp often and comfortably held the stem between the base and the globe. The glass chimney was open. Ajit smelled the strong odor of kerosene burning. The light cast Ajit's long shadow on the corridor. Ajit turned to walk toward the end of the corridor, but Swami Rangaraj said, "Not that way."

"The entrance to the chamber is not in this corridor?"

"No. It is in Swami Narayan's room." Swami Rangaraj led the way.

Ajit had visited Swami Narayan's room several times before, but today, in the light of the kerosene lamp, it was barren and dingy. The plaster on the walls had clearly not been painted for years and its surface was rough. The bed was neatly done, with the woolen comforter folded on top of the pillow. An old book lay next to it.

"I do not see an opening," Swami Rangaraj said under his breath, "but Swami Narayan told me it's here." He kept on looking around the room.

Ajit stood at the center of Swami Narayan's room and examined the walls while Swami Rangaraj stood forlornly near the bed. An idea struck him. "Look," he told Swami Rangaraj, "a large Om is painted in red sindur inside that closet. Why is the sacred symbol there?" He walked toward the Om. In the dark closet, he could not see anything special. Could there be a button on the wall? His hand went over the symbol carefully. Nothing. With his back to the symbol, Ajit scanned the room once more. He noticed a dark patch below the clothesline where Swami Narayan's ocher shirt hung. He pushed the shirt to one side and saw an opening in the wall. "There it is!"

Swami Rangaraj stooped down and peered through the opening. "Swami Narayan was correct! He told me it is here, but no one notices it." He held the lamp in front of him and entered the passage. Ajit followed. Both men kept their heads bent; the ceiling was low and uneven.

The passage immediately turned to the left and down. The walls looked like a tunnel dug through earth toward the mountain—lots of lateral debris, many rocks of different sizes and shapes, jammed together. No rocks on the floor, though; someone must have removed the debris from the passage. It was cool and there was no unpleasant smell. Ajit soon felt they were entering inside the mountain, as large rocks of granite were embedded in the walls.

"Swami Narayan said the gold chamber is under the Shaligram Shila," Swami Rangaraj muttered, "but the path is going in the opposite direction."

"I'm sure it will turn around," Ajit told him. He was beginning to feel breathless and inhaled the cool, scentless air deeply.

Soon the passage opened into a round chamber, no more than six or seven feet wide. Swami Rangaraj stopped. Here the ceiling was high enough for them to stand with ease. The surface of the granite wall was rough, but the floor was flat and clean. "Swami Narayan meditates here in the afternoons. It is so silent, so peaceful." He lifted up the hurricane lamp to find a c

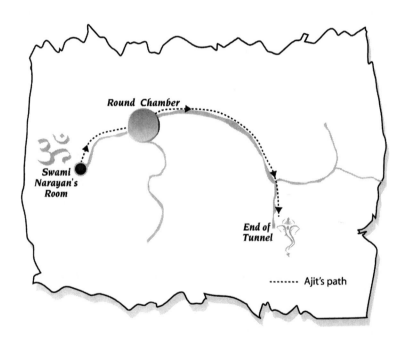

Ajit and Swami Rangaraj's path under the temple

hiseled female figure. "An old image of Goddess Ganga," he mumbled. "That's why I could never find him in the afternoon," Ajit whispered.

The smoke from the lamp started to fill the room. Across from where they stood they saw a wide path, a tunnel of lower height and another narrower tunnel on the right. Swami Rangaraj walked into the larger tunnel with Ajit on his heels.

The passage curved to the right. It sloped downward, and grew narrower. They walked bent-backed through the cool dark tunnel. The floor was uneven with rocks that, over time, had fallen from the ceiling. The granite walls sparkled when Ajit shown his flashlight on them. There was no moss or any plants. Dry and odorless, it had a crisp, clean feeling.

Swami Rangaraj stubbed his foot on a rock on the floor and cried out. The echoing sound of 'oof' startled them. They paused near a small opening on their left. Swami Rangaraj peeked in; it was too small to enter. Then they came to a cave-like opening on the right. Ajit shone his flashlight inside. It was merely a depression in the wall and was full of large protruding rocks—impossible to have a door for a secret chamber in there.

They continued down the passage and came across two more arch-shaped, hollow spaces in the walls, one on the left, and one further down the passageway on their right, which was shallow, but taller. They inspected them and moved on.

The tunnel was not long and came to a fork. Swami Rangaraj stopped for a moment. "The tunnel to the right goes toward the Shaligram Shila. Let's go that way."

Ajit saw that the tunnel on the left had many rocks protruding from the walls, many loose rocks on the floor, and was narrow. The path they were following was wider and the ceiling was higher. He silently followed Swami Rangaraj.

Now the air felt stale and stagnant. It was becoming harder to breathe. He shivered a little. They could not stay in this tunnel too long. Soon they saw the end of the passage completely blocked by a rough granite wall; but in the light of the kerosene lamp no further cracks or caves came into view.

23.2

Larry and Amrita heard the sounds of temple bells. They increased their pace down the trail without saying a word, but they could not reach the temple before the morning service ended. Just as the devotees were coming out of the temple, the couple hurried down the steps to the temple courtyard. Larry stopped at the entrance and looked around. Nothing had changed. The river tumbled to the bottom of the courtyard and Bhagirath Mountain stood majestically in the distance. Sunshine shimmered in the air.

No one could plan anything evil in this sacred place, he thought, ashamed of his suspicions.

The courtyard was unusually crowded with people happily milling around. 'I'll have my chat with Swami Narayan and that will be the end of my inquiry,' Larry told himself. Then he noticed the little bags coming down by cable from the hill.

"What's going on up there?"

"Before we left," Amrita said, "I heard government workers planned to collect rocks for testing."

"Hmm. A good way to bring their samples down the mountain." Then he looked at the young man standing atop the temple with crampons on his feet. "Wow! They could also transport material out of the temple that way!"

Amrita looked up at the young man on the temple roof. Probably doing repair work, she thought.

"Have you read a story called 'The Red-headed League'?" Larry asked her.

"The Sherlock Holmes story?" She shaded her eyes with one hand to look more closely at what was happening on the roof.

"I think more is going on here than meets the eye," Larry said.

Amrita didn't say anything and turned her attention to the cooks busily frying eggplant slices dipped in gram-flour batter.

They meandered through the crowd and went up the stairs of the temple. Larry looked back at the courtyard for a second. So many had jammed the place—all eating, chatting and enjoying the morning! What was going on? He threw a questioning glance at Amrita, but she shrugged her shoulders. Then he saw Sovik. "Look, who's here," he told Amrita and went to him.

Sovik was pleased to see them again, but before he could say anything,

Larry pulled him to a corner away from the crowd. "We've figured out the meaning of the code numbers in the manuscript," he told Sovik, his face flushed with excitement.

"What?" Sovik leaned forward. He had not been thinking about the riddle of the numbers, but it all came back in a rush. "Tell me."

"It means the Gita. I think the Swastika symbol also has something to do with it," Larry said.

"It refers to the Gita? Wow! So we don't have to be concerned with a secret revealed in the manuscript."

"But Sovik, why would they go through all this trouble to describe the most common, sacred word and symbol in India?"

Amrita chimed in. "Larry has been so wrapped up in this, we had to return to the temple in a big hurry."

"I think it holds the secret of a treasure in the temple," Larry said. "Just a hunch. I want to talk with Swami Narayan. I'm sure he can explain this to me."

"But Swastika symbols are all over the temple," Sovik told him. "I doubt they'll have Swastika symbols leading to the temple treasure."

"There've been too many coincidences," Larry said, ignoring Sovik's comment. He glanced at the temple. "I'm pretty much sure I've seen the man who was with Chetti at the Connaught Place café—right here in Gangotri."

"What did he look like?" Sovik asked, with some interest.

"I saw him only once. He is tall, thin, fairer than most Indians. He looks like an egg-head—more smart than handsome."

"You think they may be planning something here?"

"I've no idea. But coincidences bother me. The numbers in the manuscript fit so well with what they were talking about in the cafe."

"I must confess," Sovik said, "I don't know why the SMS has treated me so well. I don't really know them."

"You know the SMS is desperate for money," Larry said, "otherwise such a patriotic organization would not be willing to sell a valuable manuscript." He paused, then continued. "Even good people do bad things when desperate. Anyway, you haven't seen anything unusual happening around here, have you?"

"No. I find the place quite the same." Sovik looked thoughtfully at Larry for a moment. "You know we'll be leaving tomorrow."

"Have you heard of a special edition of the Gita in this temple?" Larry asked Sovik.

"I'm sure you will find an old copy of the Gita in every temple."

"I ask," Larry said, "because Laal Baba was singing about the Gita in Gangotri."

"Why sing about it unless it has some special relevance?" Amrita chimed in. "Perhaps this edition of the Gita has an explanation for the code numbers. Perhaps there's some notation on this book?"

"I don't know anything about that," Sovik said.

"Let's go and find Swami Narayan," Larry urged Amrita.

"You'll find him inside," Sovik said and immediately corrected himself. "The Aarti has just finished. I don't know where he is now."

"Let's check the temple first," Amrita said.

"You wanted to find spiritual India," Sovik said, putting his hand on Larry's shoulder, "I think you're finding it through your search for the sacred symbol." Sovik smiled. Strange, how things work out.

When Larry and Amrita entered the temple, it was quiet. Fresh flower garlands draped the deities and flower petals were strewn on the floor. There were no priests at the altar. The fragrance of sandalwood incense hung in the air. Amrita folded her hands in prayer.

Larry's eyes deliberately shifted to the bright red Swastika sign above the altar. Yes, the four dots formed a perfect circle. His heart started to beat hard. Larry concentrated on the sign. It appeared freshly painted. He visualized the numbers in a circle around the Swastika. The bottom numbers 135 and 225 stared back at him. His jaw muscles tightened.

"There are many swastika signs in the temple," Amrita murmured from behind him, gently pulling his shirt. "What are you looking for?"

Larry went closer, not saying anything. He had hurried back from Bhojbasa over a set of silly numbers. Now what?

The bottom odd numbers are most relevant, but how? Larry connected the bottom two numbers and extended the line on both sides. One went inside toward Swami Narayan's room, the other toward the wall on the mountain side. He narrowed his eyes, focusing intently on the wall; his eyes followed the line and saw a faint marking—another swastika symbol. He walked to the end of the worship room— a wall of solid rock.

"I don't know what I'm looking for," he muttered, then saw three small holes on the Swastika sign, one at the center and the other two on the bottom red dots. The holes blended in nicely with the surroundings, but they had to be man-made. Certainly the holes had been there for a very long time and repeated paintings of the Swastika sign had made them look ancient. He put his hands on the Swastika sign to get a feel for the wall.

"If a priest sees you," Amrita whispered, "he'll be furious. You are touching sacred things in the temple."

Larry ignored her words, put his fingers through the three holes, and gave a strong pull. A good size rock came out in his hand, startling him and revealing a small compartment like a small shelf. He steadied himself and, flabbergasted, he put his hand into the compartment and pulled out something covered with dust.

"A palm-leaf document," Amrita whispered. "This must be a secret book for the priests."

Larry dusted the cover. The size felt peculiar, about 14 inches long and 6 inches wide, but it was quite thick, almost 4 inches. The letters on the cover were indistinct. He gave it to Amrita. "Can you read anything?"

"Sanskrit," she said, and looked over the cover for a few moments. "Very old script. I can vaguely figure out the letters." After a few moments she said, "The cover reads Gita."

"The Gita from Laal Baba's song?"

A sudden burst of happy sound floated in from the courtyard.

"Please put it back," Amrita said, agitated. "We shouldn't be touching auspicious things in the temple."

Larry opened the book, anyway. The leaves were thick. As he turned over the pages, he found a small space carved out in the book. The pages were deliberately cut to make a hole, about 3 inches by an inch and half, the cuts going through some of the words. "Look!" he uttered excitedly, "something was kept hidden here."

But the hole was empty.

Larry turned the pages carefully. He looked again at the rectangular hole carved inside the book. He could only see faint, rusted marks. Disappointed, he placed the book back in the hole. However, something on the inside of the hole caught his fingers. A rod-like piece of metal sticking out on the side. He pulled the thing and it seemed to move a little. But a voice from behind startled him.

"What are you two doing here?"

Larry turned and saw the saffron robe of a monk, approaching them. They had been caught. He put his back against the hole on the wall.

Amrita took a step toward the monk, saying, "We came here to talk with Swami Narayan."

Swami Anand observed them quietly.

"We came to Gangotri with Sovik," Larry told him.

"Oh! I thought you all had gone to Gaumukh."

"We've just returned from the hike," Larry said. "Sovik spoke very highly of Swami Narayan. I want to ask him a question."

"You know that Swamiji doesn't speak English?"

Larry took a second to think of a reply. "Amrita will act as an interpreter."

"Amrita? Haven't we met before?"

"Yes, Swami Anand. I've been here before. Sovik has also introduced me to you."

Suddenly something clicked with Larry. "Are you the monk who invited Sovik to the SMS meeting?"

"Yes. How did you know?"

"Sovik has told us about the SMS and how much you are helping the organization."

"We hope people like Sovik will support us from abroad." The tone of Swami Anand's voice changed from that of an interrogator to that of a friend. "I don't know where Swami Narayan is now. There are too many people outside. You two stay here. I'll try to locate Swami Narayan for you." Swami Anand studied Larry for a moment. "Visitors normally do not enter this area. Please be respectful of the sacredness of the temple."

"We will. Thank you."

Swami Anand went back outside to the courtyard.

Amrita was shaken. "Close that secret compartment right now."

Larry ignored her words and pulled on the metal rod inside the compartment again. The rod felt stuck and he struggled with it. A creaking noise accompanied the opening of a section of the rock wall next to the compartment. "A passage!" Larry exclaimed. He peeked into the narrow slit to see a downward sloping path. The opening was barely wide enough for a man to squeeze through. "This could be a path to something hidden," he told Amrita, "perhaps to a secret treasure." But he couldn't see anything through the opening—only darkness. He put the slab of rock back into the secret compartment, closing the opening. "You stay here. If I don't return in half an hour, get help."

"I'm not letting you go alone."

"We don't have time to argue." Larry squeezed through the opening.

Amrita dropped her bag and followed Larry. It was easier for her to get in through the narrow opening. "So glad I didn't wear a sari."

The opening closed just after she went in.

23.3

Swami Rangaraj stopped near the end of the tunnel and looked around. Ajit could not see a door or any unusual rock that might be moved. Swami Rangaraj turned the flame of the lamp higher for more light, examined the end wall for a minute or two, and then asked Ajit to hold the lamp. He felt the side walls with both hands, searching for something. "I knew the keyhole would be hard to locate," he said. "That's why I brought the big lamp. Could you please focus the light here? I feel an opening."

Ajit did as he was told. "What kind of opening?"

"A small hole between the rocks . . . no, no. There is another hole below it . . . It is less than a hole, it's a slit."

Ajit couldn't see the holes.

"My key has only one shaft. It fits in the top opening, not the bottom one. I wonder why there are two holes. I heard the man who created this chamber was a foreigner," Swami Rangaraj continued. "No one knows anything about him because he came through Afghanistan and is said to have died in this tunnel."

"The king who commissioned him also buried him here?"

"That's one way to keep a secret." Swami Rangaraj said. Suddenly he recalled Swami Narayan's words: no one with evil motive has ever entered the secret chamber. We're here only to have a look, he told himself, and nervously put the key in through the top hole. He found it hard to turn; he struggled. The key fell to the ground.

Ajit picked up the key and examined it in the light of the lamp. He had never seen such a key. Its teeth were rectangular.

Dark smoke gathered near the ceiling above them.

Ajit heard a voice in the tunnel. It could be Swami Narayan going to his meditation place. Or someone else? Ajit decided to investigate. If it was Swami Narayan, they might have to postpone their exploration. But if it was another intruder, he would have to divert the person's attention by some means.

He thrust the key and the lamp into Swami Rangaraj's hands, whispering, "I'll be back in a moment." He went in the direction of the sound, counting his footsteps so he could return to the same spot.

23.4

Sovik stood in the crowded courtyard after Larry and Amrita left. People had come for the free food. Happy sounds of the feasting crowd and their small conversations filled the area. It was a gorgeous morning—pleasantly warm, a clear, azure sky. A festive atmosphere prevailed. Only the monotonous, mechanical noise of the hillside drilling disturbed the atmosphere. He looked toward Bhagirath Mountain. Now that Sovik had been so close to its base, the mountain was more beautiful to him than before.

He saw Jagdish staring at the roof of the temple. What could be happening there? He went to Jagdish.

"Very strange!" Jagdish told him and pointed toward a man on the main dome of the temple.

Sovik saw a young man, crampons on his feet, walking on the dome. He had a cable in his hand. He recognized the man: one of Ajit's assistants.

"Why are you worried?" he asked Jagdish.

Jagdish's face creased into a scowl. "Don't you see he was on top of the temple during the Aarti ceremony?"

Sovik looked at Jagdish, perplexed.

"How could a Hindu fellow put his foot on top of God's head during puja?" Jagdish was quite disturbed. He shouted at the man, but the noise of the drilling from the hill and the feasting crowd drowned his voice. "This fellow must be a badmaash—up to no good," he told Sovik. "I must tell this to Swami Narayan."

Jagdish rushed up the temple steps. In a few minutes, he came out alone. Where could Swami Narayan be? He looked around and saw that Swami Narayan was standing near the Shaligram Shila. He knew Swami Narayan loved to be there. He went to him hurriedly. "Look, Maharaj," Jagdish told him, quite agitatedly, pointing toward the man on the roof, who was speaking into a walkie talkie.

Lines appeared on Swami Narayan's forehead. He shaded his eyes with his hand and looked around. He noticed the young man on the north hill. He was operating a piece of heavy equipment, and its noise flooded the area. Swami Narayan noticed that everyone was busily enjoying the feast. "Where is Swami Rangaraj?" he asked Jagdish in a weary voice.

Jagdish took a few steps toward the foyer and peeked through the door. "Swami Rangaraj is not in the puja room," he shouted over the noise and waved his hand negatively to Swami Narayan.

Sovik looked at the temple roof again. The young man held a small bag and attached it to a different cable near the pulley. "Ingenious," he thought, "they could easily transport many small bags of rocks to his van that way." He appreciated Ajit's clever contraption. Then suddenly an unusual thought came to his mind, and he stared at the people milling in the courtyard, some eating, some waiting in line for food, all busily absorbed.

"Have you seen Mr. Boka recently?" he asked Jagdish, as he passed by him.

"The man from the big van?"

"Yes."

"He was working with the cooks," Jagdish said. "He's the one who has organized the food offering. I'll go and get him."

"Yes, please. Mr. Boka should know about the cable. He could tell us what's going on."

Jagdish went away. Sovik walked to Swami Narayan who was looking at the cable. Together, they watched intently as a small brown bag came down the cable from the mountain. The little wheels and pulleys of the cable worked smoothly like the movement of a ski lift. It was beautiful to watch.

Jagdish pushed through the crowd and hurried toward them. "Mr. Boka is nowhere," he told Sovik. "He was there just a while back, but no one knows where he has gone."

Swami Narayan walked to the temple meditatively as if each step meant something. His composure prompted Sovik to follow him, but only to the foyer. Swami Narayan went in, then returned, baffled. "Swami Rangaraj is usually here at this time. But he is not in his room. Could you search the ghat?" he asked Sovik. The monk took a few steps out to the courtyard and looked back at the man on top of the temple.

Jagdish stayed with Sovik. "Swami Narayan would not have allowed the man on top of the temple during puja," Jagdish told Sovik confidently. "He is upset."

It was hard to have a conversation in the midst of the surrounding noise. Sovik thought of what Larry had told him a few minutes before. He stopped abruptly and told Jagdish, "You look for Swami Rangaraj. I want to ask Swami Narayan something." He caught up with Swami Narayan near the steps of the temple.

"Could I ask you a question?"

Swami Narayan glanced at him and nodded.

"Probably an absurd question, but I am puzzled at some things going on here. Is there anything valuable in the temple that someone might be tempted to steal?"

Swami Narayan's eyes narrowed and he looked at Sovik with a startling intensity. "The temple is old; it has some items that many would like to have."

"Something is not making sense to me," Sovik said. "The other day, I talked to the men collecting rocks from the hills for geological studies. They know nothing about geology. This puzzles me. Could they have another motive?"

"A disquieting thought," Swami Narayan said and gazed off into the distance for a few moments. Then, without saying anything, he hurried in to the temple, closing the collapsible steel gate behind him.

When Jagdish returned without Swami Rangaraj, Sovik saw (through the collapsible gate) Swami Narayan sitting in front of the deities in the lotus position. He cleared his throat to catch Swami Narayan's attention and shook his head and his hands to indicate that they hadn't found Swami Rangaraj.

Swami Narayan fixed his eyes on the goddess. Then, as if in a trance, he lifted the idol and put his hand under the statue. There was nothing there; the key was gone. He put the image back into place, and quickly got up. "Jagdish, Jagdish!"

"What, Maharaj?" Jagdish asked and came forward.

"Come with me."

As Jagdish slipped through the steel gate, Swami Narayan turned to Sovik and asked, "Can you get in touch with the police in Uttarkashi?"

"I have a mobile telephone for emergencies."

"Something is wrong here. Very abnormal! Could you please talk with Mr. Bahuguna, the district police officer? Mention my name. They will respond immediately."

Swami Narayan turned and rushed into the temple corridor with Jagdish.

23.5

Larry found the tunnel smooth and examined it with his flashlight. "It's man-made . . . we are on the right track," he told Amrita. But soon large rocks appeared and the floor became uneven. They had to walk carefully to avoid the rocks. Their flashlights lit only a small area, which slowed them down further. "We are now under the mountain," Larry told Amrita, seeing granite. The passage was arched and fortunately high for Larry's head. One side of the passageway was smooth granite and the other side had big blocky chunks of randomly oriented rocks. Some of these rocks had fallen over time and made the floor rough. It had a dry and musty smell. They felt cold. The tunnel went downward and the floor became less rocky. After following a winding path, they came to a round room with a flat floor. Two openings came into view: one on their right and another on the left.

"Look, there is an image of a goddess on the wall," said Amrita.

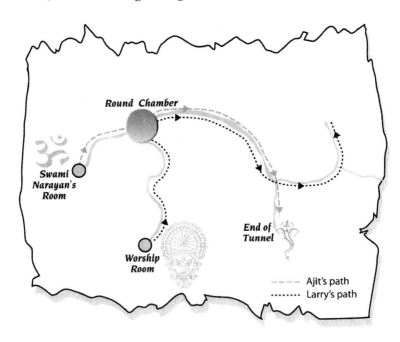

Larry and Amrita's path under the temple

Larry noted the image but kept his attention to the tunnel on the left. It sloped upward; the tunnel on their right went downward. He did not want to linger in the room and moved forward through the passageway on the right.

The passage turned slowly to the right and sloped downward. Like Ajit and Swami Rangaraj before them, they passed by four caves, peeked into them, and found nothing of interest. They felt oxygen was low as in Bhojbasa and took quick, short breaths. They came to the fork where Ajit and Swami Rangaraj had taken the right-hand tunnel.

Larry paused, not knowing which way to go and what to do next. The tunnel was dark and soundless. The left fork was rougher, with rocks of various sizes protruding from the floor and walls. Larry followed the left fork, thinking that if there was a secret cave, it should be located in the difficult part of the tunnel. He immediately banged his knee against a rock. The floor was uneven with big outcrops and they had to walk slowly and carefully. The tunnel became narrower and rougher. In some places big rocks butted out from the walls.

"There could be animals hiding here," Amrita whispered, stopping suddenly.

Larry picked up a large piece of rock and threw it forward as far as he could. The sound of the rock hitting the wall reverberated in the tunnel. They could not hear any sounds of animal movement. Larry touched the walls. Even if there was a hidden door on these walls, there was no way he could find it. And these natural fractures could go on in different directions with more forks. Their search was futile. They should return.

Just then, they heard a man's voice. "Who's there?"

Amrita grabbed Larry's shirt and shivered in fear.

Larry put his forefinger to Amrita's lips. He turned off the flashlight. They heard footsteps going away from them, toward the round chamber. He threw another stone.

"Why did you do that?" Amrita whispered in a scared voice. "The man may come back."

"We can hide in the dark. A thief does not steal from a house if he knows someone is awake."

"Are you crazy? He may have a gun."

"I want him to feel there are others here. He may go away."

The footsteps returned. Larry pulled Amrita and moved on, flashing the light occasionally to look for obstacles. They came to a second fork in the tunnel and stopped. The footsteps came closer. Larry moved to the right fork, made some shrill sound, and moved quickly back into the left fork, pulling Amrita with him. The man in the tunnel would think they were on the other side. The two stood silently, breathing as quietly as possible. The footsteps came closer and stopped in front of the fork. Larry and Amrita held their bodies tightly against the wall.

Ajit beamed a flashlight toward the center of the tunnel, but didn't see them. He moved to the right fork, where the noise came from.

Larry and Amrita were relieved. After a moment, Larry whispered to Amrita, "Now we run."

"He'll hear us," she whispered back, breathlessly.

"That's the idea."

Larry threw a large rock at the wall of the fork they just left and ran away with Amrita as fast as they could. They went back the way they came, their footsteps echoing in the tunnel, and stood panting for a few seconds. Then they started walking. "We need to hide separately, so one is around to get help if needed," Larry told Amrita.

No sound of footsteps came from any part of the tunnels.

"I'm scared," Amrita spoke softly to Larry.

"We can't do any more," Larry said. "We have no weapons. But I hope he knows by now that he is not alone. He can't just take the gold out."

They arrived at the place where they had taken the left fork. Out of breath, physically and mentally drained, they stood there for a few moments to collect themselves. "We need to hide. We had seen two recesses in the walls that, I think, are close. You go to the right one," Larry told Amrita. "I will hide in the first one on the left. Stay there hidden."

Larry came to the cave on the left first and handed his flashlight to Amrita. "You keep this. Use it only when absolutely needed." He entered the cave and stood quietly against the wall.

Amrita had never been so afraid in her life, but there was no choice. She crept forward.

Larry felt weary and light-headed. It was quiet and eerie.

After some time, he felt a strong hand on his shoulder. Before he could turn, a hand covered his mouth and held him against the wall. He felt a prick on his neck. His energy drained away. Everything went black. He slumped to the floor.

24

The Treasure

24.1

It seemed like a long time to Swami Rangaraj, but it was probably no more than a few minutes before Ajit returned.

"Just a little thing I had to take care of," Ajit said.

"I fiddled with the key in the top hole, and something came out partly through the bottom slit." Swami Rangaraj said. "It's a metal plate, but it didn't come out all the way and I couldn't take it out. I could move the rock a little, but am having trouble opening the door. Where did you go?" he gave the lamp to Ajit.

"I heard some noise and went to investigate."

Swami Rangaraj pulled the large rock with his left hand while turning the key with his right hand. "Pull the rock," Swami Rangaraj cried out. He was out of breath and at the end of his strength.

Ajit shifted the lamp to his left hand, shoved his right hand through the crack and pushed. With two people pulling and pushing the rock rotated, revealing a small, cave-like chamber. They quickly entered the room and saw a red Swastika sign on the opposite wall in the lamplight. The room was empty.

"The gold must be in a cave behind this chamber," Swami Rangaraj said.

24.2

Jagdish nervously followed Swami Narayan to his room, then to the passage under the mountain. Swami Narayan held a large candle and walked fast. They crossed the round chamber where he meditated in the afternoons and followed the tunnel in front of them. They came to a fork and took the right fork, quickly arriving at the end of the tunnel. It took them only a few minutes, but Jagdish started to feel the lack of oxygen; his breathing became shallow and fast.

Swami Narayan pulled out a pouch hanging from his neck and took out a small metal object. Jagdish glanced at it and stood obediently, waiting for instructions. The object looked like a thin brass plate, almost three inches long, with a sharp right angle bend at the end. There were no teeth. The bent part was about ¾ of an inch in height, an inch in width. Swami Narayan held it firmly, making sure that the bent part was pointed up. He pushed it through an opening in the rock wall with a little force, using it like a key. When it was completely in the opening, he drew out a small piece of flat metal from a slit on the rock wall; then he pulled a large rock on the left side of the key hole. It moved easily, revealing a cave-like room. He took out a block of wood from his pocket and used it to keep the door ajar. Clearly he had done this before.

Swami Narayan stepped in and immediately pulled the hem of his shirt up to his nose. The room was filled with smoke and smelled of kerosene fumes. His foot bumped something on the floor.

"Oh! Bhagavan!"

The bodies of Swami Rangaraj and Ajit Boka lay on the floor of the tiny space, a key chain dangling from Swami Rangaraj's fingers. The candlelight cast a ghostly glow on the two bodies.

"What fools," Swami Narayan whispered. He picked up the key from Swami Rangaraj's hand and called Jagdish to come in.

Jagdish entered and immediately started to cough. The smoke was awful. In the light of the candle he saw Swami Narayan bent over Swami Rangaraj, measuring his pulse.

"Take him outside as fast as you can," Swami Narayan told Jagdish. "He must breathe fresh air. The other man is dead."

The Treasure

Jagdish lifted Swami Rangaraj up and hurried out through the tunnel.

Swami Narayan came out of the secret room. "How stupid they were!" he murmured. "Swami Rangaraj didn't know the key is a test. If a monk takes it, he cannot be a true monk, and if a thief takes it, he cannot succeed."

He entered the room again and stepped over Ajit's body on the floor. "For centuries we have protected this gold!" he murmured. He put his key through the center of the Swastika sign on the wall and opened another rock-like door. He peered inside.

An enormous pile of gold and jewelry sparkled in the candlelight.

He closed the door immediately. So many Munis and Rishis had fallen. But how could Swami Rangaraj fall into this trap? He didn't know the false key could open the door to the first room but it doesn't open the door to the treasure. And the first door closes by itself if it is not propped open. Swami Narayan gasped for breath and stepped out.

After a few seconds, he returned to pull Ajit from the room. He took out the kerosene lamp and closed the door, which quickly and smoothly blended with the surrounding rocks; no one would know there was a room behind the wall.

This man must have died quickly. Swami Rangaraj survived because of his yogic power. He could slow down his breathing and survive with low oxygen for a longer time, but the smoke from the kerosene lamp must have poisoned him—he had to be taken to a hospital immediately. Swami Narayan dragged Ajit's body a short distance away from the secret cave. "Poor fellow!" he said under his breath, and stared at the body.

24.3

When no sound came for some time, Amrita went to the cave where Larry was and beamed the flashlight around. Larry was lying on the floor; she rushed to him. He was breathing. "Wake up, wake up," she whispered, massaging his face and shoulder. Larry stirred and started to wake up.

"What happened to you?"

"I don't know. I suddenly felt very weak. . . . I don't know."

"I haven't heard anything since I left you," Amrita told him.

Larry stood with Amrita's assistance and leaned unsteadily against the wall. "I feel a little pain in my neck, otherwise I'm okay. Let's get out."

They started to walk, but didn't know where they were going. They took the fork that led to the secret cave.

Swami Narayan heard footsteps in the tunnel. He went back to the keyhole, put the key in again, pushed the key hard and replaced the piece of metal he took out earlier. He then examined the wall; the door blended perfectly with the surrounding, exactly as it was before—rough, natural rocks. He put the key back in the pouch on his neck and walked toward the footsteps. "Did they all come as a group to rob the temple?" he wondered. In the light of his candle he saw Larry and Amrita walking cautiously. "What are you two doing here?" he demanded.

"Swami Narayan ...," Larry said and looked at Amrita to talk with the monk.

"We're looking for you, Swamiji," Amrita said in a relieved voice.

"For me?" Swami Narayan asked in an incredulous tone. "That's why you are in this tunnel?"

"Swamiji. We have a long story to tell you." Amrita translated Larry's reply.

"How did you find the entrance to the tunnel?" Swami Narayan looked Larry over from head to foot.

"I found this path from the corridor where the deities are."

"Are you also after gold?"

"No, no. We are not thieves," Amrita said quickly. "Larry felt there was some mischief going on here, but he wasn't sure what. We came to the temple to tell you."

"Is there a plan to rob this temple?" Swami Narayan asked him.

"I thought someone was planning to steal gold from the temple," Larry said and Amrita translated.

"People make that mistake all the time." Swami Narayan said slowly to Amrita, while watching Larry's face as she translated.

"Swamiji, please understand I'm not after gold." Larry said. "I don't even know if gold is here. Peculiar events have led us to this place."

"Swamiji," Amrita spoke out after translating Larry's words, "there was a man in the tunnel a little while back. He chased us. We thought he might be a thief. Larry threw rocks to make noise and let him know he was not alone down here."

"I thought that would deter him," Larry added.

"You are courageous—perhaps foolishly. If they were robbers of temple gold, they might do anything to achieve their goal." Swami Narayan continued his penetrating gaze for a few moments. These two were sincere, not robbers. "Come with me," he told them, and walked back to where Ajit's body was. "Here is a dead man. I do not know how he came here and what he was doing."

Larry shone a flashlight on Ajit's face and exclaimed, "I've seen him before in New Delhi." He bit his lip as he examined the body.

"This is not the first time someone has died in this tunnel." Swami Narayan said. "People think we have hidden gold under the temple. Over the centuries many have tried to find it. Some have gone mad in these tunnels. They don't listen to us." He paused for a moment. "Let's get out. I don't want you two to die in this tunnel too—not enough air here . . . Can you help drag this body out?" he asked Larry. "Very foolish man! These people do not understand the meaning of gold. They do not see the gold in their own hearts."

"How did he come here?" Amrita asked. "Is there another entrance to this place?"

"There are several ways to enter. But the tunnel is treacherous and there is little oxygen. No one can survive long, and, if one carries a kerosene lamp, as he did, the carbon monoxide in the fumes kills you. That must have happened to this fellow." He lifted up the kerosene lamp in his hand for them to see.

Swami Narayan's firm voice echoed in the tunnel. It echoed in Larry's mind, as well. He picked up Ajit's body.

Swami Narayan led the way back to his room.

24.4

Jagdish brought Swami Rangaraj to Sovik in the courtyard. "He is unconscious," he told Sovik and laid him on the ground. "He needs fresh air. Please see what can be done." Jagdish stared at Swami Rangaraj for a second. "A man died just like this during the flood in my village."

Sovik examined Swami Rangaraj for obstructions in his air passage and immediately started CPR. There was no response. Sweat formed on Sovik's back. He breathed into Swami Rangaraj's mouth again and pressed on his chest repeatedly. He looked up and wished there was a medical doctor in the courtyard. He saw Jagdish watching him silently from the huge crowd that formed around them. There was no chance of any help from this crowd, no alternative. He continued the CPR.

Larry brought Ajit's body to the other side of the courtyard, and everyone's attention turned toward that direction. The presence of a dead body created an unspoken fear in the courtyard. Many stared at the temple gate. Would more be brought out? What an unusual phenomenon in the history of the temple. No one was able to grasp what was happening. People approached the corpse.

Subodh recognized Ajit's clothes and edged closer, exclaiming, "Oh, Bhagavan! He organized the feast for today!"

As soon as Swami Narayan came out of the temple, he rushed to Swami Rangaraj. The crowd parted and made a path for him. "How is he? Any hope?"

"He needs a doctor immediately," Sovik said, gasping for breath.

Swami Narayan saw Swami Anand approaching and told him, "There is a dead body with the American fellow. Please see what needs to be done."

Sovik called out, "His lips are moving. Maybe he wants to say something."

Swami Narayan waved his hands for people to move away. He bent down and put his ear close to Swami Rangaraj's mouth. Swami Narayan could hardly hear but felt a whisper of words, ". . . not in Brahma's plan."

"What's not in Brahma's plan?" he put his ears closer to Swami Rangaraj's mouth. Swami Rangaraj's lips moved involuntarily, but no audible sound came out. Then Swami Rangaraj's head dropped to one side; his bright eyes became dull.

"Sovik, Sovik," Swami Narayan called out.

The Treasure

Sovik lifted Swami Rangaraj's head, but he was already dead.

Swami Narayan bowed his head in contemplation. "One lifetime is not enough," he murmured. This happens throughout the ages. Many fail for many different reasons. He then stood erect and looked at Jagdish. This illiterate farmer had more spiritual power than many monks he had known. "Please bring a little Ganges water, Jagdish."

Frustrated, exhausted, and depressed, Sovik retreated to a less crowded corner of the courtyard. 'Death' that everyone is so worried about had just happened in his hands. No anger or sadness overwhelmed him. He did not wonder, what happens after death.

Instead, the scene at the source of the river came to him. We are all part of nature and death is a natural part of life. The real question is: what is a person supposed to do while he is alive? Sovik didn't care to know how Ajit died. The idea that went through his mind was that both these men were driven to achieve something; but that meant nothing now. Their drive didn't lead them anywhere and didn't matter anymore.

The crowd waited for Jagdish. When he brought water from the river in a pot, Swami Narayan put a few drops of the sacred water in Swami Rangaraj's mouth. He gazed at him, murmuring some mantras. Then he went around the body, sprinkling Ganges water, praying

"Na jaayate mriyate vaa kadaacit
Naayam bhutvaa bhavitaa vaa na bhuyah
Ajo nityah saasvato ayam puraano
Na hanyate hanyamaane sarire."
– Bhagavad Gita 2.20

"There is no birth or death (for the soul) at any time
Having come into being, it does not or will not
come into being again
It is birthless, eternal, permanent, the oldest
It is never killed even when the body is dead."

Jagdish could hold his emotions no longer and wailed loudly, "Hai Raam!"

Swami Narayan then went to Ajit's body. From the pot in his hand he put a little Ganges water in Ajit's mouth, and walked around the body, performing the same ritual he had for Swami Rangaraj, quoting the same lines from the Gita.

Swami Narayan looked at Sovik's stoic face, as he walked back to the temple. "A tragedy like Abhimanyu's," he spoke softly to Sovik. "They only knew half: how to get in, but not how to get out."

Part VIII

Temple Legacy

25

Sagacious Priest

25.1

Chetti knocked at Ajit's van. He had just arrived from Topovan and was eager to know the result of Ajit's visit to the secret treasure. No one opened the door. The curtains were down and he couldn't see anything inside. The area was so quiet. Chetti stood there for a few minutes, wondering where he could find Ajit. Stores nearby were closed and small groups of people in the street, vendors and visitors, spoke in hushed tones. He approached a man and asked what was going on.

The man looked at him as if Chetti came from a different planet. "You don't know?"

Chetti only raised his eyebrows in surprise.

"For the first time in the history of the temple, a monk has been killed."

"A monk?" Chetti was baffled. "Who?"

"Swami Rangaraj."

Chetti's face turned dark, reddening the old scar on his cheekbone. He was certain Ajit had no weapon. There was no plan to use one. Swami Rangaraj was very valuable to the SMS. Did a quarrel develop between the two? "How did that happen?" he asked the man anxiously.

"No one knows. Some think he was poisoned."

"Do you know where I can find the man from the van?"

"He's also dead."

"What?"

"The police have taken away his body."

"Oh, God." Chetti walked toward the temple. He must find out the truth quickly.

Several police officers stood in a group in the courtyard while four men brought logs to the bank of the river. He stopped for a second and watched them. A man carried several garlands to the temple. Chetti walked across the courtyard. He couldn't imagine how anything could have gone this wrong.

Swami Anand stood in the archway of the temple with all the cares of the mortal world etched on his sad face. He saw Chetti from a distance and hurried to him. "I'm glad you're here. What sad news, Mr. Chetti! What a tragedy for the SMS organization."

"I just returned from my hike. Please tell me what has happened."

"Swami Rangaraj went into an underground meditation room, which is rarely used, and died of carbon monoxide inhalation."

"Was he alone?"

"There was another man with him, the man from the geological survey. He has also died."

"How is Swami Narayan taking all this?"

"He is the one who discovered them in a tunnel. He is in his room."

"Could I talk with him?"

"Certainly. Please come with me."

They passed a police guard as they went inside the temple. Chetti saw the body of Swami Rangaraj on a cot in the corridor. His body was dusty, his ocher robes rumpled, his face contorted and shrunken as if in disgust.

"Those are the clothes he died in," Swami Anand told Chetti. "We'll dress him up properly before the funeral."

Passing the body, they continued to Swami Narayan's room. He sat on his bed in the lotus position with closed eyes.

"Maharaj," Swami Anand spoke softly, "This is Mr. Chetti from the SMS organization."

Swami Narayan opened his eyes and gestured Chetti to sit on the only chair in the room. He waved Swami Anand out of the room and looked at Chetti impassively.

"I've heard about you from Swami Rangaraj," Swami Narayan said softly. "He has told me good things about your selfless work for the SMS."

"Thank you Maharaj. But please tell me what has happened. This is such a shock."

"How intimately involved was Swami Rangaraj with your organization?" Swami Narayan studied Chetti with the eyes of an examiner.

"He was the spiritual guide of the SMS. I am very saddened. How did this happen?"

"And did you know Ajit Boka?" Swami Narayan asked Chetti, disregarding Chetti's question.

"Yes. He worked for me for many years when I was with Advanced Defense Systems."

"He's also dead."

"I do not understand it."

"Was Mr. Boka working for the SMS also?"

Chetti did not want to admit it; he glanced away and then back at Swami Narayan, but the monk's penetrating gaze overpowered him. "Ajit expressed an interest in helping us."

"A very intelligent man, but more of a doer, wasn't he?"

"Your assessment is correct."

"And these two knew each other?" Swami Narayan said, while watching Chetti closely.

Chetti shivered a little. Had he figured out their plan? Anything Chetti said would reveal more of their scheme. Swami Narayan kept his gaze on him. It was hypnotic. A spontaneous answer came out of Chetti's mouth, "They met here."

Silence lingered between them for a few moments. "I've known Swami Rangaraj for many years," Swami Narayan finally said. "He was a learned man. I supported his involvement with the SMS, particularly to spread the knowledge of our religion. He told me you encouraged him to speak in several cities, even planned to send him abroad."

Chetti nodded.

Swami Narayan stared into Chetti's eyes for a few seconds, but it felt like a long time to Chetti. Then he said in a firm but measured voice, "But you were short of money."

"Yes. That is our major problem. I was working to send Swami Rangaraj to America, but it's too late now."

"You convinced Swami Rangaraj to help you with the money also," Swami Narayan stated in a matter of fact tone.

"His talks were very useful. We thought his trip to America would bring us new funds."

"I mean more directly than that."

Chetti sat in silence, his hands gripping his knees. He knew Swami Narayan had discovered the bodies inside the tunnel. Had the monk figured out their plan?

"Mr. Boka and his assistants were collecting samples from the hills for geological analysis," Swami Narayan said, "but they had no knowledge, no training in geology."

Chetti's face felt warm.

Swami Narayan got up and walked to his table. He picked up two small items. "I found these two gadgets on the walls when I examined the inside of the temple this afternoon."

Chetti recognized the objects, two miniature cameras.

"Would you please give these to someone for their proper use?"

Chetti accepted them mechanically and put them in his pocket. His face was ashen now, but he couldn't move or say anything.

"You cannot achieve a good goal if your path is not good." Swami Narayan said in a calm, even hypnotic tone. He paused for a moment and looked sternly at Chetti. "You know the same thing has happened through the ages—many great rishis have fallen because of ego and craving. We must pay for our bad karma even if we didn't personally do anything bad. We must pay for sinful plans and encouraging others in malevolent acts."

"I'm sincerely sorry," Chetti said, looking at the floor, feeling shame and humiliation.

Chetti had not killed anyone but he was the cause of the deaths of two men and there was nothing he could do to change that.

Swami Narayan broke into his chain of thoughts. "There is no short cut to spiritual progress."

"Thank you, Maharaj." Chetti got up and bent down to touch Swami Narayan's feet, seeking blessings from the monk.

"Brahma has a plan for everyone. For you also."

Chetti left Swami Narayan with a heavy heart.

25.2

When Sovik returned to the Guesthouse, Pinky was packing. "Sharmaji told me about the accident at the temple," she said, looking at her husband's stricken face. "He said Swami Rangaraj died in your lap." She held him in an embrace. "How terrible!"

"Horrible. And very sad." Sovik sat down on the bed. He had no energy left. "Swami Rangaraj was the most renowned monk in India. I don't understand how he could make such a mistake."

"What are you talking about?"

"He must have been mentally distracted. He didn't realize smoke from a lamp could kill him. Carbon monoxide is extremely dangerous; you don't realize it until it's too late. I think he was stuck in a small chamber."

"How could he be so engaged in what he was doing, not to notice a headache, or weakness, or dizziness?"

"Have you heard that the man from the van is also dead?" Sovik asked.

"The geologist?"

"Yes." Sovik stared blankly at his wife. "I knew there was something strange about the man," he murmured and looked out the window.

Pinky understood his preoccupation and sorrow. She sat quietly, her arms wrapped around her husband.

"I don't completely understand a remark Swami Narayan made," Sovik said after a while.

"The monk whose lectures you attended at night?"

"Yes. He said, 'like Abhimanyu's situation. He knew how to get in, but didn't know how to get out.'"

"Who is Abhimanyu?"

"Swami Narayan referred to a character in the Mahabharata. On the thirteenth day of the Great War between the Pandavas and the Kauravas, Drona, the commander of the Kaurava army, devised an ingenious wheel formation for their army. It had seven circular fronts, in the shape of wheels, which were constantly moving, very hard to penetrate. If the Pandava army could not get inside, they would have to fight on seven fronts from the outside—a very disadvantageous position. Arjun knew how to break the formation, but he was away, fighting in another part of the battlefield. So the Pandava commanders were in trouble. Arjun's teenage son, Abhimanyu, remembered his father describing the wheel formation to his mother. Arjun explained how to get in; but he left before explaining to his wife how to get out of such a formation.

"The teenager told the generals he could lead them inside, but he didn't know how to get out. The Pandava army promised to follow him and defend him. So he got through the formation, but the Kauravas were able to close the opening quickly and the Pandava army could not follow him. Abhimanyu was helpless, being alone in the middle of a large army; he fought heroically, but was killed."

"A sad story," Pinky said. "Perhaps Swami Narayan meant they were not thinking through the consequences of their actions."

"Swami Narayan discovered them in a tunnel under the temple. I think he meant it literally. The two must have been trapped in the tunnel."

"Like Abhimanyu?"

"Yes, like him; they went inside, not knowing how to get out."

"We'll remember them and the Abhimanyu story for a long time."

Sovik nodded.

"I've packed our stuff," Pinky said, changing the subject. "Are we going in the morning?"

"Yes, Swami Narayan has advised me to move on. It's not worth staying here any longer. People would only gossip and spread rumors about the deaths."

25.3

M r. Bahuguna, the chief of the district police, arrived in Gangotri in the afternoon. The detectives and other police experts had already come earlier and examined the dead bodies; they had taken many samples and photographs. They had done nothing with the body of Swami Rangaraj, but had taken away Ajit's body. After receiving a report from his subordinates, Bahuguna went to Swami Narayan.

He took his hat off and touched the monk's feet. "What a sad time to visit the temple, Maharaj. I wish I was here under different circumstances."

The monk sighed. "Don't worry about it. When the time comes people die. Nothing we can do about it."

"My men are investigating the cause of their deaths. Do you wish to tell me anything?"

Swami Narayan looked directly into Bahuguna's eyes and said, "This is a holy place."

Bahuguna pondered Swami Narayan's words and looked at the monk's calm face; peace emanated from him even at this time. The police chief finally said, "I understand. We cannot bring them back, but we should preserve the holiness of the temple."

Swami Narayan nodded. "Life and death are equal here. We're insignificant in the big scheme."

"You think it was an accident?"

"Yes. You know, accidents come in many forms. There are accidents of action and of inaction. These two men were in a small, closed space with a hurricane lamp—there was little oxygen."

"They were there for a long time?"

"I don't know, but that is irrelevant. Something went wrong. They died for lack of knowledge; kerosene lamps produce a lot of carbon monoxide. Inhalation of carbon monoxide has killed them."

"Strange. Isn't it?" Bahuguna scratched his head.

"I'm thinking of this temple," Swami Narayan said without delving further into the cause of their deaths. "People come here for rejuvenation, to strengthen their lives. A monk's death, even an accidental death, raises many questions and could destroy that heritage."

"Maharaj, I see your point," Bahuguna said after a moment's reflection.

"Swami Rangaraj was a great sanyasi."

"The other man?"

Swami Narayan looked at the police officer's face for a moment. "Mr. Chetti of the Sarva Mangal Society is here. He knew the man. You may have a chat with him."

"Thank you for your advice. I shall preserve the holiness of this place." Bahuguna touched Swami Narayan's feet again. "The temple will remain sacred," he repeated as he left.

The police Chief stopped at the top of the temple steps and looked around. The courtyard was deserted; no one wanted to be involved with police matters.

The sky was bright and blue and seemed immense from where he stood. The Bhagirath Mountain stood majestically in the distance, and the sound of the river floated in. What a beautiful, quiet place! If there was a place to be considered divine, this must be it. He wished he could come up here more often. Finally, he noticed two of his officers standing below him. He asked them if they had received the medical report.

"The report is straightforward, Sir," one of the officers replied. "The doctor's report pinpointed the cause of death as carbon monoxide poisoning. There is no evidence of a struggle or any injury."

"It was an accident then?" he asked.

Both the officers nodded in agreement.

"We have no charge against anyone," Bahuguna told them. "Release the bodies as soon as the next of kin can be identified."

"We don't know where the man is from," one officer replied.

"I'll be meeting with Mr. Chetti, who knew him."

"Should we stop any further investigation?"

"Yes. And remove the guards from the temple compound."

"Thank you, sir."

"One more item," Bahuguna told them in an official tone. "Issue a press release immediately that it was an unfortunate accident. There was no foul play. It will stop any gossip from spreading. We must maintain the sanctity of this temple."

25.4

Bahuguna went to the Traveler's Lodge, the best hotel in town. He had a hunch he would find Chetti there.

Chetti sat in the lounge, preparing himself to call Ajit's wife. Bahuguna introduced himself and said, "I understand you knew the man who died along with Swami Rangaraj. I'd like to ask you a few questions. I have to do this as part of my duty."

"Certainly."

"You are a well known man," Bahuguna said. "That helps greatly in this case. Please tell me what you know."

"I feel so bad. Ajit worked for me for many years when I was at Advanced Defense Systems. A very intelligent and patriotic man. He resigned from the company recently and was interested in developing a private research and development company. I believe he came here exploring for uranium and thorium. He was a staunch supporter of nuclear energy for India. He told me India does not have enough uranium, so they must use thorium. He was developing this idea privately. He didn't want to publicize it. He was that kind of a man. First he wanted to be sure of his idea. So he was here on his own. Then this happened. What fate brings!" He sincerely lamented Ajit's death.

"One thing I don't understand though," Mr. Bahuguna said. "Why did he use the Government of India Geological Survey sign? When we called the Geological Survey of India, they said they had no project in Gangotri, and they were very surprised."

"I don't know. I could guess he didn't want anyone disturbing his work and used that as a ploy. We used such tactics often at Advanced Defense Systems."

"The instruments inside the van also do not quite fit with the mineral exploration." Bahuguna said, with some disbelief in his tone.

"I see."

"Was he investing his own money into this project?"

"Yes, his own money, and I gave him a small loan myself. If he succeeded, I'd have gladly invested in his company."

"Thank you. That's all I needed. We will declare this an accident and close the case. Would you please identify the body?"

"Surely."

"And could you please call his family to inform them of the accident? We will contact the family as part of our official duty, but it will be better if you talk with them first as a friend."

"That's what I was just about to do. It's my duty."

After the police chief left, Chetti sat in his room, staring out the window. He glanced at the telephone a few times, but could not pick it up to call Ajit's wife. Instead, he got up and walked out of the room without closing the door.

A strange force led him to the river. He walked a distance and stood, watching the water. The sound of the flowing water quieted his mind. He observed intently a leaf being carried away by the water. How forcefully the water was moving it. He looked up at the dome of the temple. What a beautiful day this could have been!

Soon restlessness and anxiety ran through his mind. He never thought that Ajit and Swami Rangaraj could die during the execution of their plan. How could they be so stupid as to go inside the tunnel without proper precautions?

He became angry with himself for giving Ajit complete freedom with the project. He should have supervised the operation. He thought Ajit was smart and could outwit any individual, but this small temple had ruined everything. Was there any hope for the SMS now? What about him?

And then, a profound sadness came over him for their deaths. Two good men would not have died if he had not directed them in this effort. He was the cause of their deaths.

Then his thoughts drifted to the idea that even if they had succeeded in discovering the gold, it would not have solved India's problems. The problems were too big. And probably other, yet unknown, issues would have popped up from the secret gold, perhaps in ways more insidious than he had ever thought through.

Why did he think up this scheme? The whole idea was wrong.

The area was unusually deserted, and he walked back and forth in the little clearing on the bank. A crow cawed loudly from a tree, drawing his attention to the green leaves where the bird was hiding. Beyond the tree, the distant white peaks of Bhagirath Mountain glistened. What a wonderful view! But quickly his thoughts returned to the events of the day. It had spoiled his hopes for the SMS. How silly of him to think of stealing gold from the temple! A sarcastic smile spread on his face. He started to walk upstream along the bank.

There was no way he could raise enough money for the needs of the SMS.

Should he report immediately to Mr. Thappa? What would be his reaction? Better not face him at all. Simply vanish from the earth! Better than seeing his reputation die. He thought of the Japanese tradition of hari-kari; then he remembered the legend of the Bhairav Temple in nearby Kedarnath; there many devotees had jumped to their deaths from a cliff as a sacrifice to Lord Shiva.

However, he couldn't bring himself to die: failure had no place anywhere, even in death, he thought.

He stopped where a stream joined the Bhagirathi River and watched how violently the two streams mixed together and made the sacred river wider and more forceful. Then a story from high school days came to him. He had read it in his Sanskrit class. It was the story of practical advice, summarized in one phrase: "For the sake of the family, one can be sacrificed, and for the betterment of a village, a family can be sacrificed." Ajit and Swami Rangaraj's deaths were sacrifices to save the village.

He was a devotee of karma-yogi and must not simply vanish from the world. He must rise again. He was not a coward. He would find other ways to support the SMS movement. He surmised that stealing gold from temples couldn't be done the way he had envisioned. As he pondered his options, Swami Narayan's penetrating eyes came to him.

"I removed these from his pockets," Swami Narayan had told him just before he left the monk, "No one needs to analyze what he was up to with these items," he said, as he handed over the locksmith's wax and the injector.

Swami Narayan must have figured out what Ajit was there for. The priests are smart beyond imagination; that is how they have protected the gold. It would be a formidable task to get the temple gold—much more difficult than he had originally thought.

'I must plan better next time.'

Chetti hurried back to his room.

25.5

When Bahuguna went to the market area, an officer came to him. "Sir, we have found out where the van came from."

"Anything nasty?"

"No sir. Mr. Boka rented it from an outfit in New Delhi. He had already paid them in cash. They will come to get the van."

"Fine. Anything else, before I head home?"

"We have the two young fellows—Mr. Boka's assistants. They are here if you want to interrogate them."

Bahuguna perked up. "Yes. I want to talk to them."

Sanju and Gujral were standing nearby and came to him nervously.

"What can you tell me about Mr. Boka?" Bahuguna asked them.

"Sir, we met him this summer," Gujral told him. "He was a great man. He employed us only for a short time. We liked what he told us about the project and we were really hoping this would lead to new mineral discoveries for the country."

Bahuguna didn't say anything, but his eyes shifted from Gujral to Sanju.

"Mr. Boka told us if this project succeeded, he'd form a company," Sanju added. "We feel very sorry. I believe his death is a loss for India."

"So, you didn't know of anything he might have been doing with Swami Rangaraj."

"No, sir," Gujral said. "We have never talked about religion or the temple."

"That's enough. You are free to go. One thing. Could you help Mr. Chetti take all the equipment from the van? He could perhaps find some use for them somewhere."

"Surely."

"You will find him at the Traveler's Lodge."

Bahuguna climbed into his Jeep and asked the driver to take him back to Uttarkashi.

Part IX

Final Journey

26

The Ocher Cloth

Sovik, Pinky, and Be'ziil went to the temple in the late afternoon. When they reached the bus stand, Sovik looked at the van. Someone had taken down the two TV dish antennas. The Geological Survey signs were gone. The large van stood there naked, rejected by the holy place.

The three walked through the desolate market; no one was in a mood to talk. The old, corrugated tin doors of the stores were padlocked shut. The life of the small town seemed to have drained away. Only the crows had become bold; one or two even walked in the middle of the road.

As the three approached the courtyard, the sound of chanting floated on the air. They saw four monks seated on the floor of a small concrete building at the far end of the courtyard, reciting Sanskrit texts. Their combined baritone voices sounded well-rehearsed, solemn, and lofty. The loud chanting made the place feel auspicious.

A white cloth had been stretched out from the temple steps to the middle of the courtyard, where Swami Rangaraj's body lay on a cot. One could only see his head and feet; the rest of the cot was wrapped in flowers. Garlands hung from the middle of the cot to the ground—white tuberoses, yellow marigolds, and red roses covered his body. Large bouquets of red roses were also placed on both sides of his head. Sovik was amazed such a profusion of flowers could be brought so quickly to this place, 10,000 feet up in the Himalayas. The delicate smell of incense, the kind of fragrance one finds inside temples, pervaded the courtyard. Four monks, dressed in their usual saffron robes, stood at the four corners of the cot, holding brass vessels of flowers. One of them was Swami Anand.

The Ocher Cloth

The white cloth reminded Sovik of his meeting with Swami Rangaraj in the courtyard; Swami Rangaraj was walking slowly, holding in his hands a small, brass pot containing Ganges water for the evening worship service. He was walking toward the entrance of the temple in slow and steady steps, as if in meditation. Sovik imagined Swami Rangaraj's last journey out of the temple— several monks carrying his body on their shoulders and walking on the white cloth. His final journey could not have proceeded on the bare ground.

People and monks quietly filed in to the courtyard, surrounding the chanting monks and Swami Rangaraj's bier. Saffron and ocher-robed monks mingled with the crowd. It seemed to Sovik that all the monks and sadhus from the surrounding mountains and temples, and people from the nearby towns had come to pay their last respects to Swami Rangaraj. A somber atmosphere replaced the usual carefree spirit of the courtyard; except for the sound of the chanting, they were folded in an all-pervading, hushed quietness. Several men and women wiped tears from their eyes.

Visitors approached the cot to pay their last homage to Swami Rangaraj; the monks handed each mourner a flower. After placing the flower on Swami Rangaraj's body, some put their palms together and prayed silently, some touched his feet and then touched their head. Some simply stood there, wiping their eyes.

Bhagirath Mountain stood tall in the distance as a witness; the setting sun spread pink and violet shadows over its white peak, as if the mountain was also mourning for the occasion. Chanting reverberated through the valley:

Asabdam asparsam arupam avyayam
Tatha arasam nityam agandhavac ca yat
Anaady anantam mahatah paramang
Dhruvam nicayya tam mrityu-mukhaat pramucyate
– Katha Upanishad 1.3.15

Realizing the Atman, which is without sound
Which can't be touched or felt, and is
Un-decaying, tasteless, odorless, and eternal
Without beginning and without end
Beyond the great and unchangeable
One frees oneself from the face of death.

Pinky pulled Sovik's hand in the direction of the cot, and they proceeded to pay their last respects. Pinky received a flower from a monk and put it near Swami Rangaraj's feet. Sovik placed his flower near the senior priest's heart, looking at his face. To Sovik it seemed Swami Rangaraj's half-closed eyes gazed fixedly toward the sacred river. Compared to his last impression, when Swami Rangaraj breathed his last, Sovik felt the monk now appeared calm. He had achieved peace. Be'ziil laid flowers in the middle of the cot and put his palms together in salutation. The three of them went round the cot and then toward the northern corner of the temple. They stood there silently.

Sovik scanned the mourners and found Chetti near the river, and Ajit Boka's two assistants, Sanju and Gujral, in the crowd. Sovik could not see Swami Narayan and wondered where he was.

As all waited for the next step, sunlight dimmed; still more people poured into the courtyard. Sovik heard the faint sound of bells from the temple and went to the foyer. He saw Swami Narayan sitting in a lotus position in front of the deities. He had created a small fire and was performing the yagnya ceremony. Then he noticed Jagdish on his knees next to Swami Narayan. He was handing Swami Narayan flowers. No other monks were present. Swami Narayan uttered mantras softly and offered flowers to the fire. He had made the simple villager from Sitamarhi his assistant even though so many senior priests and monks had arrived from nearby towns. Sovik was confounded, but remained there for some time meditating on how this illiterate man had earned the confidence of Swami Narayan, the head priest.

Soon electric lights flooded the courtyard. The surrounding mountains disappeared in the gathering darkness. One set of lights focused on Swami Rangaraj's body; the flowers made the bed look wonderfully colorful and beautiful.

The spotlight was on a man who was highly regarded in India but who kept to himself in Gangotri. Perhaps Swami Rangaraj never realized he was loved so much in this community. Sovik felt Swami Rangaraj would not dream of going to America if he knew how much he was adored right here in his own adopted town.

When Swami Narayan came out of the temple, the chanting stopped. Suddenly the whole crowd froze; there was pin-drop silence. Only the sound of mother Ganga could be heard. Swami Narayan walked alone on the white cloth. He held a small brass pot and a few flowers in his hands.

He put the flowers on Swami Rangaraj's forehead. Then he sprinkled Ganges water from the pot systematically in all directions, saying, "Om Shanti! Om Shanti! Om Shanti!" Peace, peace, peace.

The crowd received a few drops of peace water on their heads. Then Swami Narayan stepped back, and eight monks lifted the cot up.

The crowd burst out, "Swami Rangaraj Maharaj ki jai! Swami Rangaraj Maharaj ki jai! Swami Rangaraj Maharaj ki jai!" The air vibrated with the sound: Hail to Swami Rangaraj.

The eight monks slowly proceeded toward the river. Swami Narayan walked behind the funeral bed. As they moved, a path opened spontaneously through the crowd of mourners. People threw flower petals on Swami Rangaraj's body as it passed by. The crowd, wailing, followed the procession.

Swami Anand was the lead pallbearer. He led them to the spot where the Kedar Ganga met the Bhagirathi River, where a pyre had been prepared. The monks placed the whole cot on the pyre.

Swami Narayan poured ghee on several parts of the cot while repeating some mantras from the Gita:

> "Vaasaamnshi jirnaani yathaa vihaaya
> Navaani grihnaati naro aparaani
> Tathaa sariraani vihaaya jirnaani
> Anyanaani samyaati navaani dehi."
> – Bhagavad Gita 2.22

> As a person takes new garments
> When his clothes are worn out
> The same way the soul takes a new body
> When the old one is worn out.

He stepped back. A narrow passage opened through the crowd and Jagdish came into view, walking slowly but steadily and carrying a vessel filled with fire from the yagnya ceremony.

The eight monks took the vessel together from him and shouted, "Om Shanti! Om Shanti! Om Shanti!" They placed the flame on the pyre.

People bellowed, "Swami Rangaraj Maharaj ki jai! Swami Rangaraj Maharaj ki jai! Swami Rangaraj Maharaj ki jai!" The sound of the crowd burst through the air and rose to heaven.

The fire became larger and larger. Smoke from the pyre rose high. People stopped shouting in praise of Swami Rangaraj and gazed at the fire. The yellow-orange fire glowed in the dark. Behind, the waves of the Bhagirathi River shone in the firelight. The sound of the flowing river continued unceasing in the background, but the crackling of the fire dominated the air. Shadows of people stood as silent sentinels. The orange-colored robes of the monks attending the fire added to the surreal atmosphere.

Sovik, Pinky, and Be'ziil stood close by, watching the ceremony. Fire wood burst, sparks rose, and a few sparks and pieces of ash occasionally flew up on the flames from the pyre. People left the place one by one, but the three stayed—watching the cremation.

Swami Anand stood on the bank of the river and held a lamp that had five ghee-soaked wicks burning with small flames. As people left, they passed their hands over the lamp and then over their own heads, a way of taking blessings from the fire. Another monk, a few steps down from Swami Anand, sprinkled sacred Ganges water on their heads and uttered, "Om Shanti, Om Shanti, Om Shanti." Peace be with you.

After a long time, when the crowd had thinned, Pinky pulled Sovik's hand, and, hesitantly, they left the ceremony.

Sovik placed his hands over the fire of the brass lamp and looked at Swami Anand.

"We will push the ashes into the sacred River, when the cremation is complete," Swami Anand told Sovik.

Sovik nodded; he was well familiar with the custom.

"Have a safe trip home."

"Thank you."

Sovik could say nothing more and moved on. Pinky and Be'ziil walked ahead. Sovik lingered, gazing at the river. This was why he had come back to India; he had seen the source of the river, and had learned so much about her.

He looked back toward the burning pyre for the last time. As he stared at the final journey of Swami Rangaraj, a bright little thing floated in the breeze and he caught it, a piece of ocher cloth. There was a small Om printed in the unburned middle, just like his mother's cloth. It was warm and he put it in his pocket.

Epilogue

E1

In spite of the death that had overwhelmed the town, people bounced back quickly, showing their resilience. Local residents knew the realities of life: stores opened, buses and cars resumed their regular runs, new pilgrims arrived, and temple worship continued, as if nothing extraordinary had happened just two days earlier.

Larry and Amrita did not attend Swami Rangaraj's cremation ceremony. They were physically and emotionally exhausted. They slept through the evening and the next day. Finally, in the afternoon, Larry found the energy to venture out to the market. He was happy to see the town vibrant. There was no trace of Ajit Boka's van. He strolled through the market and bought Indian clothes—a kurta-pyjama—because all his clothes were dirty. He returned to the hotel, took a shower, and put on the new clothes.

"Let's visit the temple," he said to Amrita. "The town has moved on past death. Shouldn't we?"

"Glad to see you in fresh clothes." Her eyes cast an admiring glance his way. "I've made an Indian out of you," she smiled.

"And I'm failing to make you into an American."

Amrita liked that Larry was his old self again. The riddle haunting him was finally resolved. "Give me a little time to change." She went back to her room and put on a silk sari. She powdered her face and then, as an afterthought, placed a bindi on her forehead, using the green that Larry had admired in Dehra Dun.

The shop owners stared at the handsome couple as they walked to the temple by the river. The last pink rays of the sun streaked the sky above Bhagirath Mountain.

The stores started to hang large kerosene lamps from metal rods on the frames of the doors and pilgrims crowded the path buying puja material—flowers and sweets. Larry stopped at a flower store and bought one fragrant garland of jasmine and tuberoses.

"Did you buy the mala for the puja at the temple?" Amrita asked him.

"No, I got it for you," Larry said.

"Could you buy another?"

Larry bought a second garland and gave her one. When they reached the temple, people were just gathering at the courtyard for the evening Aarti. Larry and Amrita stood in front of the steps of the temple and peeked in. Swami Narayan and Swami Anand were making arrangements for the evening ceremony. Swami Narayan saw Larry and gave him an approving nod.

"Do you know the man helping Swami Narayan?" Larry asked Amrita.

"Jagdish," Amrita told Larry. "Remember the man singing off-key in the courtyard when we first arrived? That's him."

"Sovik told me he was the man who alerted Swami Narayan something was wrong at the temple. That started the hunt for Swami Rangaraj and sent them to the tunnels."

Amrita glanced outside at the impending dusk and whispered to Larry, "This time of day is called Godhuli Lagna."

"Godhuli Lagna?"

"The time in the evening when cows return home and dust from their hooves rises in the air," she told him. "It's a special time in India."

Larry looked intently at her face, waiting for her to explain more.

"An auspicious hour when, in ancient times, people got married without a priest."

"How?" A genuine query came through Larry's voice.

"One simply puts a flower garland on a willing partner."

Larry raised the garland in his hands, put it over her head and around her neck.

"Do you really mean it?" She looked intently into his eyes.

"I do with all my heart."

She put the second garland around his neck.

Just then Swami Narayan rang the bells and the sweet sound filled the air.

E2

Jagdish collected his things in the morning and placed them on a cloth spread on the floor, the same way he had in Sitamarhi the day he began his pilgrimage. This time Sukhi was not there to advise. Only Subodh, the dharmashala owner, watched him silently.

"I have purchased a reserved seat for you," Subodh told him. "Ask the train conductor in Haridwar for the seat for Jagdish Lohar."

Jagdish nodded and put the locket for his wife in a pouch tied to his body. "I have been away from Sitamarhi, from my family for so long!" he lamented. "I hope everything is fine there." How flat and how beautifully green Sitamarhi was, miles of subtly different greens, only one or two trees standing here and there. The boys must be taking out the cattle for grazing now, he thought. And Sukhi was probably feeding their cow. Her young face came to him from the day when he first brought her to his house. How long he had not seen her skewed eyes!

He tied the cloth into a bundle and said, "I am ready now."

The two walked to the temple, Jagdish with his bundle on his head. The sound of the river reverberated in the morning air.

Swami Narayan asked Jagdish to sit on the floor near the deities. The fragrance of sandalwood incense rose and soon the temple bells sounded for the worship ceremony.

After the service, Swami Narayan gave a small packet to Jagdish, saying, "Please give this to Gopal and tell him to visit me some day."

Jagdish touched Swami Narayan's feet for his blessings.

"Continue living the way you have," Swami Narayan told him, and gave him some flowers from Goddess Ganga. Jagdish accepted those reverently to take home.

Jagdish wanted to pick up the bundle and put it on his head, but Subodh picked it up, saying, "I'll carry it for you to the bus stop."

Swami Anand and other monks came out on the steps to see him off.

"Bahut shukriya, bahut shukriya," Jagdish said to them several times with folded hands. Tear came to his eyes and he couldn't look at them any more. Subodh pulled his arm and led him toward the path.

"Have a safe journey home," they said in a chorus.

Epilogue

The store owners stopped business when he passed by their stores and said, "Aapki yatra suraksit ho—we wish you a safe journey."

"Dhanyabaad," Jagdish told them with folded hands. "Thanks."

Some local people followed the two to the bus stop, where his bus to Haridwar waited. Subodh embraced him, saying, "I am fortunate to have known you."

The bus started. Those present shouted, "Jagdish-ji ki samman—honor to Jagdish." They stood there until the bus could not be seen any more.

Glossary of Indian words

Aarti	Hindu worship service using oil lamps
Acharya	A learned man, especially in religious matters
Ahamkar	Pride, ego
Alpana	Designs made of rice flour paste on the floor for auspicious occasions
Aloo paratha	A flat bread of unleavened dough stuffed with a mixture of spices and mashed potato (aloo), fried on a griddle
Annaprashan	Ceremony to celebrate a child's first solid food (usually rice pudding)
Baba	A common and casual way of saying father
Babu	Honorific term for a gentleman. It is also used as suffix to a person's name to show respect
Badmaash	A person who is mischievous or indulges in anti-social activities
Bahenchod	Hindi obscenity implying incest with a person's sister
Banyan tree	Common Indian tree, which sends roots down from its branches to the ground. Ramakrishna, a famous Indian mystic, meditated under such a tree in Dakshineswar, near Calcutta.
Barfi sandesh	An Indian sweet—firm, but not hard, and flat made with milk, sugar, ghee, and often ground nuts in the shape of rectangle, diamond, or square
Batasha	Almost flat and circular sweet made with sugar
Bauji	Father in Hindi
Besan	Chickpea (Gram) flour
Bhagavan	A name for God; often used as a non-personified God
Bahu	A daughter-in-law who lives with her husband's family
Bahut Shukriyaa	Many thanks
Beta	Affectionate Hindi word for son

366

Bhaisahib	An affectionate term for brother
Bhakti	Devotion
Bhajan	Devotional song
Bharat	India
Bindi	A colorful, decorative mark worn in the middle of a woman's forehead
Biri	Cheap tobacco cigarette wrapped in dry leaves
BJP	Political Party in India, Bharatiya Janata (Indian People's) Party
Brahma	God, the Creator—among the three supreme Gods in Hindu religion along with Vishnu, the preserver and protector, and Shiva, the auspicious one who is also the destroyer
Brahmin	A person of the highest caste in India
Chador	A large shawl or cloth wrapped around the upper body for warmth
Chalo Delhi	March on to Delhi
Chamar	One who works with leather; also the name of the caste that does this work
Chapati	Unleavened flat bread, cooked on a dry grill. Also called roti or rooti.
Cha-Walla	One who sells tea (cha) from a cart or stall by the side of the road
Chulha	Small Indian "bucket" oven that sits on the ground; cow dung patties, firewood and coal are used for fuel
Dadaji	Grandfather
Dahl	Soup or stew made with lentils and spices
Dalit	People of the lowest caste, the untouchables (self-chosen political name)
Dhanyabaad	Thanks
Dharma	Signifies the order that includes duties, rights, laws, conduct, virtues and right way of living that makes life good and worthy
Dharmashala	Place where pilgrims can stay, often at no cost
Dhoti	Plain length of white cloth used by men in place of pants; also called dhuti

Diksha	Initiation by a guru in Hinduism, Buddhism, and Jainism.
Diwali	Hindu festival of lights to celebrate the winning of good over evil
Dholaks	Indian folk drums
Durga	Mother-goddess of the world, wife of Shiva.
Engraaji	Hindi word for the English language, people, customs, and styles
Ganga	Ganges in English; The Ganges River is known as Ganga in India
Ganja	A preparation of marijuana used for smoking
Garuda	A bird-like magical being that appears in Hindu mythology—designated as the Carrier of Lord Vishnu
Gaumukh	Cow's mouth—name given for an ice cave in the Himalayas from which the main tributary of the Ganges River originates
Ghat	Series of steps leading down to a body of water, especially a holy river
Ghee	Clarified butter
Godhuli Lagna	The time when cows return home from fields—dusk
Gur	Unrefined sugar, usually yellow in color
Gurudev	One's own religious instructor/teacher
Guru-ma	Female guru, from whom one has received Diksha
Hai Bhagavan	Oh God. Bhagoban is a non-personified God
Hai Raam	Oh God
Hanumanji	God in the form of a monkey. Hanuman helped Rama in the ancient Hindu epic, Ramayana
Hare Raam	Greetings to Raam
Haramjada	Bastard
Haat Jao	Move
Hanumanji ka Jhanda	The flag of Hanuman
Hindi	Language in northern India

Glossary

Hindu	Main religion in India
Hookah	A flexible smoking pipe where the smoke is filtered through water in a pot
Jai	Glory, Win
Jai Ho	Be victorious
Jaya Jagadisha Hare	Glory to the Lord of the world; a Hindu religious song for Vishnu composed in 1870; ften sung during Aarti as a prayer
Ji	Polite word added for respect as a suffix, e.g., Sharmaji for Mr. Sharma
Kali	A Goddess
Kamandalu	Water jug, used by monks
Karma	Sum of one's actions in this and past lives, which determines one's fate in current and future existences
Karma Yogi	One who devotes his life in selfless service to others
Katha	Words, discourse
Kesava	Name of Lord Vishnu in Hinduism; often used for the name of Krishna
Khichuri	A dish made chiefly with rice and lentils; also known as kichdi or Kichri
Kofta	Meatballs of ground meat mixed with spices and onions
Krishna	Name of Hindu God, an incarnation of Lord Vishnu
Kukri knife	Nepalese knife with an inwardly curved blade
Kurmi	A Hindu agricultural caste in India
Kurta	Shirt
Kurta-pyjama	Loose upper garment like a shirt with lightweight trousers
Laddu	Round sweet made with chickpea flower, sugar, and ghee
Lal	Red

Lassi	Yogurt drink
Lingam	A phallus object worshipped as a representation of Lord Shiva
Ma	Mother
Maha	Great
Mahabharata	An ancient Indian epic (the longest in the world), describing a war of succession between the Kaurava and Pandava cousins; this is the source of the Bhagavad Gita
Mahadev	The great God; refers to Shiva
Maharaj	Great King, but the word is used to address reverent monks as they are kings of the spiritual world
Mala	Flower lei or necklace
Mali	Gardener
Mandir	Temple
Mangal	Wellbeing
Mani	Jewel
Marg	Road, street or path
Maruti	Name of a car made in India
Mantra	Chant or specific words used in religious ceremonies
Mata	Mother
Maya	Illusion
Mung beans	A legume; also known as Moong bean; used in savory and sweet dishes
Muni	An ascetic and sage; one who is silent because of deep thoughts
Murti	A statue or idol of a deity
Naan	Leavened, oven-baked flatbread
Namaste	Greetings; meaning I salute you (the god within you)
Nabagraha	Nine planets
Nimitta	An instrument or reason, cause
Nirmaan	Construction
Nirmama	Without claiming any personal proprietorship or nepotism
Nirahamkara	Egoless, without pride

Om	Sacred sound, an incantation used at the beginning of every Hindu prayer
Paan	A preparation of betel leaf with nuts, hydrated lime, fragrant spices, and sometimes tobaco. It is chewed and the juice spat out.
Paani Puri	Street snack; a small, round deep fried bread (puri) stuffed with spicy potatoes or chickpeas and filled with tamarind flavored water
Paduka	Wooden shoe, which is simply a sole with a post and a knob for the toes to hold
Pakora	A deep fried snack; usually vegetables coated with batter of chickpea flour and spices and fried in oil
Palki	Palanquin
Panchayet	A panchayat is a village level administrative body
Panditji	Pandit is a scholar and a teacher; ji is added as assign of respect
Panchaas	Fifty
Papad	Thin, crisp, fried dough made of urad beans, lentils, chickpeas, or potato flour
Paratha	A lightly fried, often many layered, unleavened flatbread
Peepal tree	Same as Bodhi tree under which the Buddha attained enlightenment
Praan	Life, breath of life, vitality
Pranam	Pay respect; often seeking blessing of an elder by touching his or her feet
Prasad	A gracious gift; typically, an edible food, that is first offered to a deity—a form of Hindu communion
Puja	A Hindu prayer ritual or worship service done with reverence, homage, and adoration of a deity
Puri	Puffy, deep fried, round bread made usually from whole wheat flour
Raam, Raam	Uttering the names of Rama twice, wishing blessings from God
Rama	Rama is the seventh Avatar of Lord Vishnu

	and the central figure and hero of the epic Ramayana. He is worshipped as God all over India
Ramayana	One of the two epics of ancient India the other being the Mahabharata); it is considered the older epic since it is included within the Mahabharata.
Radha	Consort of Krishna
Rishi	A seer who realized truths and eternal knowledge; composer of hymns
Roti	Unleavened round, flat whole wheat bread, cooked on a dry griddle; also called rooti and chapati
Sabji	Vegetable curry
Sadhu	Holy man; Hindu holy men usually wear ocher colored, loose clothes
Sahib	Originally used to address a white man in India, now used for any man of higher standing
Salwar Kameez	North Indian tunics with loose pants for women
Samman	Honor, respect, homage
Samosa	A triangular shaped, savory, fried pastry snack with a spicy filling
Sanyasi	Hindu ascetic who has renunciated material interest and devoted himself to spiritual life
Sardarji	A title used to address a man of the Sikh religion
Sari	A long length of woven cloth wrapped around the body and worn as a dress by Indian women
Sarva	All people, Everybody
Sataranchi	Woven cotton mat
Saub thick hai	Everything is all right; OK
Savitri	Savitri, through her intense devotion, love and wits, persuaded the God of Death to restore her husband's life; a famous story from the Mahabharata
Shakti	It is the concept, or personification, of divine feminine creative power; the primordial cosmic energy that moves everything
Shala	Brother-in-law, but often used as a derogatory term of address
Shaligram stone	It is a sacred, black stone, found in river-beds such as the Gandaki river in Nepal, and is an iconic

	symbol of the Hindu god Vishnu.
Shanti	Peace
Shiva	One of the three major deities in Hinduism along with Brahma and Vishnu
Shivaji	Founder of the Maratha kingdom in India
Sindur	Red vermillion powder—used on the forehead and parting of the hair of married women in India
Sita	The central female character in the Ramayana; wife of Rama
Sudra	The lowest caste in the four caste system in Hindu religion (Brahmin, Khatriya, Vaisya, and Sudra)
Surya	The Sun
Swami	Honorific title for monks
Swamiji	Honorific way to address a monk
Swastika	Sacred symbol in Hinduism; the word means 'it is well.' It represents God
Tabla	A hand drum (played similarly to bongos), often used in Indian music, especially in Hindustani classical songs
Tandoori	Pertaining to a tandoor, a cylindrical clay oven used in cooking and baking; food is cooked very quickly as its temperatures are very high; Tandoori chicken is chicken prepared with yogurt and spices and roasted in a Tandoori oven.
Teji	High spirited, sharp, bright
Tiffin	A light midday meal
Tiki	A lock of hair at the back of one's head
Trishul	Lord Shiva's trident
Upma	Savory dish made with cream of wheat with vegetables
Upanishads	Ancient texts that describe Hindu philosophical thoughts and traditions
Vanaprastha	The third of four stages of life for Hindus: "retiring into a forest"
Vedas	Ancient religious text—the essence of Hindu

	religion is contained in the Vedas
Vegetable chop	Spicy cutlet of mashed potato and other cooked vegetables, fried crisp on the outside
VHS	Political Party in India, Vishva Hindustani Sangathan (World Hindu Association)
Vishnu	The supreme God, preserving and protecting the world
Viswanath	Lord of the world
Yagnya	Hindu fire ceremony where offerings are made to God through a sacred fire
Yogi	Person proficient in yoga
Zari	Gold or silver threads used to create intricate patters on silk garments

Acknowledgements

I wrote this multi-cultural, multi-character novel on and off over twenty years. Sacred River started in Idaho Falls, Idaho, after I returned from a hike to the source of the Ganges River in India. I continued developing it in Vienna, Austria, where I worked for three years; the storyline kept on evolving and changing, and finally it came into being during a one-year stint in London, UK. It has been a long journey. I read a few sections at several meetings of writers' groups in these three cities. The enthusiasm of the members of these groups has energized me and kept me going. These aspiring writers deserve my sincere thanks.

I mention a few names of those who have read the manuscript in the last few years and helped me with edits and suggestions. The novel would not have materialized without their encouragement. My gratitude goes to Leon Torossian, Jade Gibson, Karen Finnigan, Lorraine Fico-White, Jerry Brady, Barbara Brown, Dianne Scott, and Julianne Eberl who deserves special thanks for her help with the final edit.

I am grateful to our Navajo friend, Barbara Dejolie, for providing me with the Navajo chant and its translation.

My wife, Catherine, has not only given me the time to pursue this effort by carrying out all the day-to-day chores of family life and providing the comforts needed for living, but she has read all my drafts using the insights of experience gained during her many travels in India. I am grateful that she came into my life and cannot thank her enough.

Born in India, Debu Majumdar received a doctorate degree in physics from SUNY at Stony Brook. His first book, *From the Ganges to the Snake River*, a creative non-fiction, interweaves Indian culture with north-west American reality. His four children's books (*Viku and the Elephant* series), set in village India, explore universal themes such as friendship, perseverance, and preservation. *Sacred River* is his first novel, written from a background of India's ancient heritage. He and his wife live in Idaho Falls, ID and Bellingham, WA. For further information, please go to Debubooks.com.

CPSIA information can be obtained
at www.ICGtesting.com
Printed in the USA
LVOW10s1538140217
524243LV00002B/551/P

9 780996 851633